Blood Hunter
C.M. Kennedy

Copyright © 2024 by C.M. Kennedy

All rights reserved.

No part of this publication may be reproduced, distributed, or transmitted in any form or by any means, including photocopying, recording, or other electronic or mechanical methods, without the prior written permission of the publisher, except as permitted by U.S. copyright law. For permission requests, contact cmkennedyauthor@gmail.com.

The story, all names, characters, and incidents portrayed in this production are fictitious. No identification with actual persons (living or deceased), places, buildings, and products is intended or should be inferred.

Book Cover by Novel & Navy Designs

Edited by Hope Hughes and C.M. Kennedy

First Edition 2024

blood hunter

C.M. KENNEDY

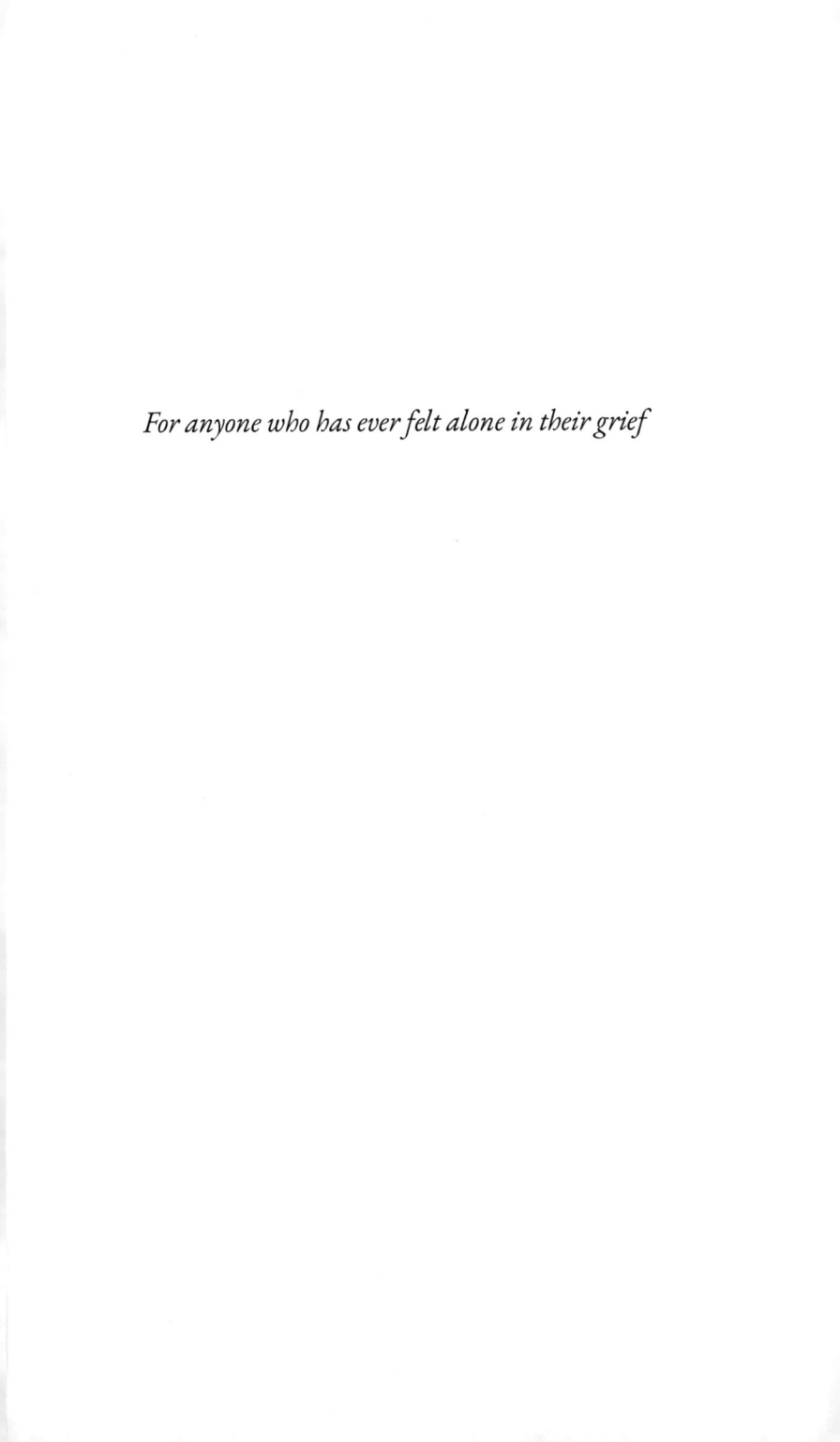

For anyone who has ever felt alone in their grief

Content Warnings

Murder & Violence
Profanity
Depictions of grief, anxiety, PTSD, and depression
Mentions of suicide/suicidal thoughts
Depictions and mentions of motor vehicle accident
Loss of parents (off page)
Death (off page)
Nonconsensual & dubious consent of blood drinking
Brief mention of sexual assault
Brief gun violence
Mentions of human trafficking
Mentions of emotional abuse & manipulation
Smoking
Stalking (not between MCs)

Prologue

Fear is a funny thing.

Sometimes it waves hello and is on its way before you even really know it's there. Other times it sticks around and intimately familiarizes itself with you. Some people know fear as just that—an acquaintance. Something they experience every so often before logic takes over. But some people know fear far more personally.

Fear and I are on our way to becoming fast friends as I stand rooted to the spot in my living room, watching my best friend get the blood sucked out of her from what I can only assume is a vampire.

Time moves like the last dregs of sand in an hourglass. Too slow and too fast. My bag falls from my hand, making a sound I can't hear, its contents scattering across the floor. My limbs, as I attempt to move them, try to do something to stop what is happening. And my mind... my mind can't seem to catch up to the situation in front of me. Surely I'm hallucinating and there can't be a *vam-*

pire in my house. But as my voice finally starts to work and I let out a scream, the *creature* whips their head up at the sound.

It's too dark to get a good look at them, but the figure is unmistakably male. Gleaming white fangs protrude from his mouth, blood dripping down them, leaving a trail of crimson from his chin to his neck. The sight of it is absolutely sickening.

So. Much. Blood.

All over him as he kneels over his victim. On the floor. On the wall. And on Serena.

Serena. Oh, god.

Serena—the girl I grew up with. The girl I share everything with. The girl I consider a sister. My best friend is lying prone and bleeding out on the floor. The silk party dress she wore out is dark enough that you can't quite see the blood on it, but its dishevelment tells me something is utterly wrong.

Another scream escapes me as I take in the sight of her bloody, limp form. I once again try to move my legs, too caught up in seeing Serena like that to care what the vampire might do to me if I get too close. But my feet are concrete blocks, and my arms jelly—too stiff yet also too loose to properly control my own body.

Even in the dark, I catch the sight of him licking Serena's blood off his lips. The action finally has my mind catching up to speed. I take a step towards my best friend, but the vampire is faster.

He crosses the space between us in mere moments, his face just inches from mine. I can smell the coppery tang of blood still on his face and neck. I can feel his warm breath as he leans into me. The sheer proximity forces a whimper from my mouth, then another when he grips my shoulders hard enough for his nails to cut me, skin splitting beneath my shirt.

His mouth attaches itself to my neck as he starts to sink his fangs into my flesh. The cold, sharp bite wipes away any thoughts and leaves me with only one sensation: pain.

The darkness presses in around us, or maybe it's just my vision going black. Either way, it's useless trying to make out any discernable features on him. I know he's large—definitely taller than me—and I have the vague impression that his hair is dark. Even now, facing inevitable death at this man's hands, I want to at least try and fight back in some way. If by some miracle I make it out of this alive, I want to identify him, make him pay for his actions. I kick and flail my limbs as best I can in his iron grip, but it's no use.

A car revs its engine from down the street, speeding off. The abrupt noise startles my attacker into releasing his fanged mouth from my neck. Carelessly, he tosses me against the wall. My head cracks against the plaster, ears ringing with the force of it, and I slump to the floor. Pain begins to spread from the base of my skull and up, but it's dulled by the sting of the open wound at my neck.

When I muster the strength to stand, I just catch sight of the vampire disappearing outside with Serena in his arms. "No," I moan weakly, staggering towards the kitchen door. When I finally get outside, there's nothing and no one out here. No sound save for the back door swinging on its hinges, and a distant dog barking. It echoes against the corners of my mind, making my blooming headache worse. The tree line at the back of our house is silent and undisturbed.

The frigid air whips at my face, painting streaks of red on my cheeks to match the blood dripping down my neck and shoulders. Even in late August, the weather never warms much in Pine Falls. My whole body shakes. Whether it's from the cold or adrenaline or blood loss, I'm not sure. Probably a combination of all three.

I grip my hair at my scalp, frustrated, and wince at the searing pain. Despite the agony in my skull, I'm beginning to wonder if I imagined it all. That I'll go back inside to find Serena in her room blaring music or getting ready to head out. That eventually Meg and Josie, my other roommates, will come back from whatever party they were at and laugh about the wild hallucination I must have had.

But seeing the giant blood stain taking over a portion of the living room floor sobers my wishful thinking. So does the blinding pain now jarring my head with each step, and the blood on my palm from where I gripped my skull.

Staring numbly at the stain, I fumble for my phone in my jacket pocket. Even through my progressive disorientation and shock, I'm still lucid enough to know I should call for help.

I manage to dial 911, but my voice has begun to slur as I speak to the operator. Just as she tells me help is on the way, I collapse into the puddle of Serena's blood.

Too late for help, I think before the darkness pulls me into its sweet embrace of nothingness.

THE PINE FALLS PRESS

ATTACK NEAR CAMPUS LEAVES ONE INJURED, ONE DEAD

On the evening of August 21st, the shared home of four Pine Falls University students was broken into. Two of the residents were home at the time, Miss Juliette Jennings and Miss Serena Mitchell. Miss Mitchell's body was missing from the scene when police and paramedics arrived but was found a half mile away an hour later. Miss Mitchell sustained stab wounds to the neck and shoulders. Official cause of death is blood loss due to the severing of her carotid artery. She was found by police after search parties were assembled. Miss Mitchell is survived by her father, philanthropist and entrepreneur, Laurence Mitchell.

Miss Jennings is the sole survivor and witness of this brutal attack. She also sustained knife injuries to the neck and shoulders, as well as head trauma. Miss Jennings did not respond to our request for an interview, and her family asks that they be given space during this difficult time. Police have shared that Miss Jennings was unable to provide a sufficient description of her attacker.

If anyone has any information that could assist police in their investigation, please contact the Pine Falls Police Department.

1

Juliette
Two Months Later

I'm seeing things.

There's a man, and he's staring at me.

Or is he?

He's wearing a hood that conceals his features, but I swear I can *feel* his gaze on mine. It burns into my soul like a brand, making it seem so real.

I squeeze my eyes shut and rub my temples. When I open them again, he's gone. The space on the sidewalk he occupied is empty, the steady drizzle of rain in his place. Still, I stare at the spot across the street for a little while longer, just in case.

It's been sort of a game for me—albeit a depressing one—these past few months. Trying to prove myself right. After my head injury, I no longer trust my memories or even the things I see right in front of me. No one knows about the vampire because I can't be sure if he was real or if my mind created an outlandish scenario to cope with the brutal attack I endured. The doctors told me I got lucky, that my neck wound was an inch away from my artery. That it could have been fatal. I hate thinking of it like that—as something I survived. It makes my heart clench painfully because, while I made it out, Serena didn't.

They found her in a field of flowers near our house. One of our roommates, Meg, informed me of this when I woke in the hospital days later. Apparently I had lost a lot of blood, and that combined with my head injury caused me to fall into a mini coma. Just thinking about it has guilt crawling up my spine, sinking its claws into me... not unlike my attacker's nails. According to the police and my team of doctors, however, those wounds were caused by a "knife." I touch the faint scar left behind by the "knife" and wince. I was lucky to get off with just a scar and some mild disorientation. Serena didn't even have a chance. I didn't know one person could have so much blood until I saw hers pooling on the living room floor.

I know it's unreasonable for me to feel guilty over what happened to her. I know it, my family knows it. Everyone has told me over and over again that I couldn't have done anything. That I just came home at the wrong time. Still, I can't help thinking, what if that was supposed to be the *right* time and I was too scared to take advantage of my unexpected appearance? What if I was meant to save Serena, and that's why I arrived home at that time? I wasn't even supposed to be home that early. I usually help my family close up the restaurant, but that night I needed to get some studying done. I thought I would catch Serena on her way out the door to some party or club, but I caught the tail end of her murder instead.

Mom watches me carefully from the entrance to the kitchen of our family's restaurant. I'm seated at one of our most well-lit booths, the one next to the front window with a large pendant light above it. Even though the brightness of the fluorescents hurts my head, it's better than being in the dark. Mom knew I'd sit here—it's why she put the bin of napkins and silverware here.

Ever since I got out of the hospital and wanted to return to work at our family's restaurant, she's given me menial and mindless tasks to do. Supposedly it will help me not get confused if I'm doing something repetitive. Little does she know that the boring jobs she gives me actually cause my mind to wander to unpleasant memories. I tried to tell her that if I could keep up with my schoolwork, I could man the host stand—which used to be my usual job. She gave in one night and let me take up my old position, but after several panic attacks due to the many strangers approaching me, we both decided it would be best if I helped out behind the scenes for now. *However long that will be.*

The bitter part of me doesn't even know why we bother anymore. The restaurant isn't as busy as it used to be. The attack on me and Serena was just the beginning. There are new reports weekly of bodies being found with sizable lacerations in their necks. The news has dubbed the killer "The Pine Falls Knife Man." Zero points for creativity, negative points for accuracy—not that anyone knows it's actually fangs causing all the wounds. Nor do they know that the reason for the alarming lack of blood on and around the victims isn't because the killer dumped their bodies somewhere different from where they were murdered. Serena's murder was unique in that way... There was almost *too* much blood instead of a lack of it.

Subsequently, the community is terrified. Pine Falls isn't known for being the safest city in the world, but at least there's never been a murderer on the loose. People barely leave their homes for fear of being the Knife Man's next victim. And if they do, it's not to come to an expensive restaurant in the heart of downtown.

I hate to see my parents struggle. Besides me and my cousin, Hayden, this restaurant is their life. They built it from the ground up, starting as a hole in the wall eatery to one of the highest-rated fine dining experiences in the city. Now our only customers are the few rich and powerful who don't fear leaving their homes because they believe they are somehow untouchable.

Mom gives me one last lingering glance before returning to the kitchen. Her eyes are tired, and her shoulders slump as she turns away. I know I mirror her exhaustion. None of us sleep much anymore, for different reasons. Whether it's financial stress or nightmares of blood and fangs, sleep deprivation has come for us all.

A flash of movement outside pulls my attention away from the napkin I'm folding and to the window where my stalker has reclaimed his post on the sidewalk. He stands outside the pastry shop across the street, its pastel pink sign and brightly decorated cakes on display shining through the dreary October afternoon. It almost makes me want to laugh—the shadow shaped human in front of the vivid storefront is quite the image. This would make an excellent study in contrast, if I felt up to sketching again.

I've seen him before, this man in the hood—outside my bedroom window shortly after the attack. My parents made me move back into their house, and they insisted my other roommates, Meg and Josie, move in as well. The two of them aren't from around here originally—Meg being from California and Josie from

Ohio—and couldn't find another place to rent in time after we moved out of our old house.

I've seen my shadow on campus, too. And here outside the restaurant. He's been a constant presence in my life these past two months, and I still don't know if he's real or not. If the man who killed Serena was actually a vampire or not.

This man in the hood always disappears when I try to get someone else to notice him. He hasn't approached me and doesn't seem too concerned with communicating with me in any way. He just stands at a distance. Always watching.

Again, he's here now, standing on the sidewalk in front of that pastry shop. I hear footsteps behind me, but I don't turn around, intent on holding the persistent gaze of my shadowed stalker.

The smell of marijuana and cheap cologne invades my senses as my cousin, Hayden, appears in my peripheral. He sneaks into the alley adjacent to the restaurant to get high sometimes. My younger cousin thinks my parents don't notice, but there's no escaping the telltale smell of weed. I don't mind it. Sometimes, I still smell the phantom scent of Serena's blood, so really, anything is preferable to that.

"Are you ready to go?" Hayden asks, bending down to look at me. I'm still staring at the hooded man and I wonder what I must look like to my cousin, completely frozen and potentially staring at someone who isn't even there. "What are you looking at?" He waves his hand in front of my face. "Hello? Jules?" When he moves his hand away the hooded man has vanished.

Frustrated, I sigh, "Nothing."

I finish preparing the last of the silverware and get up to leave it near the host stand. Hayden and I bid my parents goodbye before heading out the back. We anticipate another slow dinner service, so they don't need our extra help tonight. Not that I'm much help anymore, anyway.

Hayden leads the way to his car parked in the lot, completely uncaring of the rain pelting us. I scowl at his back and pull my hood up a bit more aggressively than necessary.

He spreads his arms wide, turning around and giving me his signature grin. "Nothing like a good rain to wash all your worries away, right Jules?"

My scowl deepens at the cheesy platitude. Hayden is endlessly optimistic, always trying to cheer me up and take care of me. It's times like these where his caring attitude only makes me feel guiltier than I normally do. I'm older—only by eighteen months, but still—so it should be my responsibility to take care of him. Unfortunately, my current mental and emotional states beg to differ.

When I don't respond, he just shrugs it off. None of his attempts to cheer me up have worked these past couple of months, but he keeps trying nonetheless. I appreciate his attempts, even if I've forgotten how to tell him that. Even though I only feel the pangs of anger and guilt through the numb haze I've been living in, there are still slivers of love for my family that shine through the darkness.

"Ten bucks we hit zero traffic on the way home," Hayden announces, practically skipping to his car—my old one since I'm not cleared to drive and haven't bothered to renew my license.

Not only is Hayden my chauffeur for the time being, he's also my pseudo-bodyguard. My parents insisted that I needed someone with me at all times. Meg and Josie were all too happy to volunteer, needing the companionship after the trauma of their two friends being viciously attacked, but my parents politely refused their offers and demanded I take my close male relative everywhere I go.

Apparently, my stoner cousin is a much better fit to play bodyguard than Meg—who has done martial arts her whole life and is super fit from being a figure skater—just because he's a guy. My parents don't know that I already have an unwanted set of eyes on me, courtesy of my hooded man.

You'd think the attack was bad enough that I would have been placed in witness protection or something, but the cops are pretty sure the killer won't come after me. "Pretty sure" isn't the reassurance they think it is, and I definitely don't trust it. My mind definitely doesn't if I'm possibly imagining the killer following me around.

The cops' lack of worry for my safety could also be due to the fact that I'm a suspect. While I'm not high up on their list, the list is very small, and I'm still on it.

Hayden holds the passenger door open for me, and I slide in, relieved to be out of the rain. Droplets pelt the car from all angles as it steadily picks up. Hayden shakes himself off like a dog after a bath before he settles into the driver's seat.

We head home, back to the house I grew up in. My parents wanted me to stay with them after the attack, not that I had any other options. The morbid part of me didn't want to leave our house near campus, even when the school locked it up for the year due to the horrors that happened inside. I wanted to be reminded of what occurred there and my failure to stop it. However, the giant blood stain soaking the living room floor had the more rational half of me interceding.

In truth, it felt like leaving the house would be like leaving Serena behind. My parents and roommates said a fresh start would be healing. That I would always remember Serena, and living in that house would only cause me to relive the worst night of both of our lives. While they may be correct, staying there would have been a visceral way of remembering Serena and what happened to her. It would further fuel my need to figure out who killed her—and attacked me. To find whoever is *still* attacking people, ruining lives left and right.

What my friends and family don't know is that it doesn't matter if I don't live in that house with the reminders of That Night. I replay those horrific moments over in my mind every second of every day. I think about it constantly.

When I see girls with dark hair and pale skin, I think of Serena as her body drained of life.

When Hayden pours obscene amounts of ketchup on his fries at lunch, I'm reminded of the pool of blood I collapsed in. Reminded of the blood that was drained from both me and Serena.

When I'm faced with darkness, I see the vampire and his shadowed face—fangs flashing.

As if on cue, we pass the large news stand on the corner a block away from the restaurant. *The Pine Falls Press* was the first to publish about the attack, and the words used in the article echo in a constant loop in my mind:

Was unable to provide a sufficient description of her attacker.

Was unable to provide.

Was unable...

Useless, the words whisper to me. The words that appear between the lines. The ones only I'm able to read. My heart rate picks up, my brain pounding a steady rhythm against my skull.

I'm fine, I think to myself, hoping it will ease the panic creeping up on me.

I'm fine.

I'm fine.

I'm fine.

Hayden and I ride in companionable silence home. He doesn't mind my silence and thankfully doesn't try to force conversation out of me like my parents and their many futile attempts at it. My cousin just taps his fingers on the steering wheel to the beat of the music drifting from the radio, singing off-key under his breath. His voice only broken up by the rain hitting the windshield.

A few miles later, we pass the intersection that would have led to my old house on campus. Instead, we head straight—towards home, where I live with my parents, Hayden, Meg, and Josie. Hayden has lived with us ever since he lost his parents in a car accident ten years ago.

And just like with my cousin, my parents happily agreed to let Meg and Josie stay with us.

Hayden parks in the driveway, dangerously close to hitting the garage door, and I pop my door open before the engine has even turned off. I owe him ten bucks; we didn't hit any traffic.

The fir trees surrounding the house sway in the gentle wind, the branches about to be battered by the downpour. The Halloween decorations my mom set out are getting completely soaked.

"I'm melting!" Hayden wails from behind the witch inflatable. Another attempt to lighten my mood. The me from two months ago would have chuckled at the lame joke, but now, I just adjust my hood and continue towards the front door. I try not to notice the slight frown on his face at his latest failed attempt at cheering me up, just like I try not to notice how something inside me shrivels up at his disappointment. He quickly shakes it off and bounds after me.

Once inside, Hayden heads off to his room in the basement to do god knows what. He has a penchant for experimenting with illicit activities. After learning how to make elephant toothpaste in ninth grade, his curiosity knows no bounds. My parents let him get away with almost everything, and it's a miracle he has grown up to be a somewhat polite and decent member of society.

I hear giggling and music as I trudge up the stairs to my childhood bedroom. The room next to mine that Josie and Meg share is cracked open, and I can see them getting ready to head out for the night. It amazes me how quickly they began their ascent back into normality. How they can go out to frat parties and clubs like our roommate wasn't murdered and I wasn't attacked mere months ago. Not that I was a big partier before, but enjoying myself isn't high up on my list of priorities, especially on a Monday night.

No, trying to solve Serena's murder has been my focus for the past few months. And yes, solving a murder with zero experience and a brain injury is about as difficult as you'd think it is.

I shut my bedroom door and open up my closet to reveal my murder board. There's really no other name for it—it's the definition of a creepy murder board complete with red string, gruesome photos, and hastily written notes pinned on the surface. Keeping it hidden is imperative. If my family and friends knew what I was up to, I would be in for the lecture of the century. I don't want to hear about how my obsession with Serena's murder is "unhealthy"—thank you, therapist I was forced to see when I woke up from my coma. I don't want to see the horror in their eyes as they look at photos of Serena's dead body, knowing my own would reflect none of the same emotion.

I've stared at the large photo in the center of the board more times than I can count. It's the photo the police took when they found her body dumped in that field of flowers. They showed it to me to scare me, I think. I almost laughed at the macabre nature of the shot when I saw it. A beautiful dead girl surrounded by equally beautiful life. Another lesson in contrast I wish I was up to sketching. I snuck it into my pocket when they left the room and now it's here, in a place of honor on the board.

As a senior in college, I *should* be working on assignments that are due. I *should* be researching jobs and internships relevant to the marketing degree I'll receive in less than a year. I *should* be trying to move on from what happened to me two months ago. Instead, I'm sitting on the floor mulling over whether or not vampires exist outside of fiction.

Most of my investigation so far has consisted of extensive research on vampire lore. I delved into any ancient vampire stories and theories I could get my hands on. There's a surprising amount of people who claim to have been in the presence of a vampire, but it's hard to sort out the true accounts from the wishful thinkers.

Romanticizing a mythical creature is exciting until one murders your best friend and almost kills you, too.

No one in Pine Falls has suspected a vampire as being the Knife Man. Not surprising—who would even consider that? I wouldn't, had I not gotten a front row seat to the killer's fangs.

Other than that, I don't have much to go off. The only potential lead I have is whoever Serena was always on the phone with at night. It wasn't me, or Meg, or Josie, so it had to have been some other friend she had... maybe even a boyfriend. I have no idea who the killer could be. Or why they would be killing a bunch of random people after Serena. Or how Serena knew a vampire. Or *if* she knew that they were a vampire. Or if the killer really is a vampire. So many questions with no answers in sight.

Is our attacker even connected to Serena? Or is he someone completely random? All the other attacks would suggest the latter. That we just had the unlucky honor of being this guy's first victims.

Serena also kept a diary. She wrote in one daily for years, but never let me see it. If I could find the diary she used for the last year—green leather with gold embossing on the front—it might do wonders for my investigation. There could be all sorts of clues and insights into Serena's personal life. Sure, it's a little invasive but she's dead. She would want me to do whatever it took to find her killer.

A knock has me shoving the murder board back in the closet just as my bedroom door opens a few inches. Meg pops her head in, and I try to calm my suddenly racing heart at her intrusion.

"We're going out, want to come?" she asks hesitantly.

She already knows what my answer will be, but every time she asks me anyway, hoping I'll change my mind and lose myself in alcohol and sweaty bodies for one night.

She arches a manicured brow in question, her make-up done to perfection as always, and her gold dress complimenting her dark skin. She looks like a literal goddess waiting for my response. I try to ignore the fact that I'm in an oversized jacket and jeans I've worn the past three days, my hair a rat's nest. Old insecurities about never measuring up come to the forefront as Meg crosses her arms over her body.

I've always felt like the odd man out with my friends. Even when we were young, Serena attracted attention from friends, boys, or teachers. It was work to keep up with her, and exhausting to be labeled as "that girl Serena hung out with." My insecurities only intensified when we met Meg and Josie freshman year of college. It became even harder to find my place among my friends.

Not as pretty as Serena. Not as confident as Meg. Not as kind as Josie. I was too tall and lanky. Too shy. Too awkward. It's not their fault, but the harsh bite of my insecurities is there all the same.

"No. You guys have fun though." I shift away from my closet and shed my jacket on the floor, waiting for her to leave.

"C'mon, Jules," Hayden, appearing behind Meg, pleads. Based on the spicy scent wafting into my room, I can only assume he has doused himself in more cologne.

I hate drunk college students more than anything, but what would be the harm in going out? I'd be safe and with my friends. But the murder board waiting in my closet is too tempting, so I shake my head. Their grumbling fills my ears until they meet Josie at the front door and head out, the lingering scent of cologne the only sign they were here.

I shut my door again and get the board out, settling in on the floor in front of it. I stare at the photos of the other victims. People of all ages stare up at me, and my heart clenches. I trace my finger over a sketch I did of Serena a couple of years ago that I also pinned on the board. I like to remember her like this instead of how I last saw her.

Does she know, wherever she is, that I'm going to do whatever I can to find the person responsible? I hope she does. Most days my need for answers is the only thing that keeps me going. I fear sometimes that when I do find the person who did this—and I *will* find them—I won't know who I am anymore. And I'm scared to discover what might be left of me.

2

ALEX

DESPITE THE HEAVY RAIN pounding the awning, I can still hear the man's slurred mumbles of confusion.

"We good here Osman?" Jeffers asks, nudging the drunk guy with the toe of his boot. The drunk is sprawled on his back in the middle of the alley. Neon signs from the nearby buildings surrounding this secluded area reflect off the damp concrete, casting the man's face in a cacophony of colors.

I take one last drag of my cigarette and crush it under my boot.

"Yeah, we're good. Thanks for coming," I reply.

Jeffers hoists the drunk guy up and drags him to the mouth of the alley where his car is waiting.

He'll take him back to our boss, Silas, to receive a verbal reprimand and maybe a few days in isolation to dry out and wise up. What the guy revealed, even in his inebriated state, would usually warrant a harsher punishment. He's lucky everyone else in the bar was just as wasted, so they probably won't remember what he said or take it seriously.

Silas takes our secrecy *very* seriously. Now more than ever with all that's happening in the city.

Jeffers throws me one last wave before loading up the drunk and driving off in his SUV. He's the only one of Silas' men that doesn't look at or treat me differently.

Usually I would be hauling people like the drunk guy back to Silas' place, but tonight, I have somewhere else to be. My boss has assigned me the impossible task of tracking down the Pine Falls Knife Man. My first task is to speak to the only person to have survived the Knife Man's attack so far—Juliette Jennings.

I step out of the covered doorway and follow the path Jeffers and the drunk guy took leading out of the alley. The streets are empty, as expected for a Tuesday night, but even more so than usual with the storms—both the rain falling in sheets and the paranoia brewing in people's minds.

A shop displaying TV's shows only the news. Reports of the latest murder blast across the screens, painting the sidewalk with their grim reflections.

Juliette Jennings works at her family's restaurant a few blocks away. When I stop in front of the huge, rain splattered glass windows, I'm surprised to find that the place is even open, considering there are no customers dining inside. Fear travels fast; the deserted restaurant in front of me can attest to that.

I catch a bit of my reflection, black hoodie pulled up against the rain, and startle at the other reflection I find staring back at me. A young woman sits in a booth next to the window, brow furrowed. She stares at me, and I awkwardly stare back—finding myself caught in an unintentional staring contest. I think she might be winning until her eyes shut and her fingers press into her temples. A hand drifts to her neck and absentmindedly rubs where a wound might have once been. I do the same to some of my scars sometimes.

This must be Juliette Jennings. I recognize her from the news coverage back when her attack and friend's murder were the only incidents. The press shuffled her out of their stories once more bodies started popping up, but I remember her vividly. I remember the photo they used for her whenever they would mention the young college student attacked in her own home—the only survivor of the Knife Man and an eyewitness to her friend's murder. I remember thinking she looked so bright, a shy smile on her face, but her eyes lit up, not deserving of what happened to her. The girl inside is unrecognizable to that girl from the photo I saw months ago.

She's still rubbing her neck and forehead when I enter the restaurant. Light classical music plays over the speakers at a low volume, the only sound filling the space. No chatter, no clinking glasses or cutlery, no scraping chairs. This is the quietest restaurant I have ever stepped foot in. The only occupied table is the booth Juliette has commandeered, papers and books strewn across its surface. Curious, I take a peek at one of the open textbooks and see it's about marketing and consumer behavior.

Her eyes fly open and snap up to mine as I move towards her. I intentionally made my steps loud so it wouldn't seem like I was sneaking up on her and startle her, but she appears nervous anyway.

"You," she says in a whisper. I halt my steps.

"Me?" I answer, stupidly looking around as if I'm not the only one standing right in front of her.

"You've been stalking me." The accusation carries an air of resolve, and a hint of relief.

I push my hood back so she can see my face and determine for herself that I am not a threat. But all that does is bring attention to the tattoos on my hands. She studies them, avoiding my face.

"I haven't been stalking anyone," I tell her in a firm tone, one I hope conveys the assurance I want to provide.

Someone's been stalking her?

Her gaze wanders the length of my body before meeting my own. Whatever she finds seems to appease her. For now.

"Sorry, I was mistaken," her reply comes quietly before she looks away.

I study her for a moment, the way she seems to shrink into the booth she's in. Her eyes are shadowed, wary.

"Are you Juliette Jennings?"

"Why?"

"Are you her?"

"Why?" She repeats, crossing her arms over her chest and straightening in her seat.

I sigh, wondering what I've gotten myself into.

"I'm a private investigator." I stuff my hands in my pockets then add quietly, "Of sorts." If the restaurant were louder she might not have heard that. I feel bad lying about what I do, even if I am bound not to reveal it without proper authorization.

"*'Of sorts?'*" Unfortunately for me, we're the only ones in here so she heard my small confession.

"You're either a private investigator or you're not. Which is it?" She stares me down, expression turning shrewd, though she looks tired more than anything. There's bruising under her eyes from lack of sleep. They're stark against her pale skin.

I wish I were physically incapable of lying, but I'm not. Grinding out a simple, "I am," I try to justify what I said as being a half-truth. It's not like powerful figures who need to keep themselves and their entire community a secret hand out licenses.

"Okay..." she draws out skeptically. I don't think she buys it, but she answers my question anyway. "Yes, I'm Juliette. What do you want?" There's a small bite to her tone. Even though the light has left her eyes, I sense a spark still exists somewhere deep inside her.

"I wanted to ask you some questions about the attack." Might as well get right to the point with this one. I don't specify "the attack" because there's little doubt in my mind she knows what I'm referring to. Her expression visibly shutters, and I'm proven right.

"There's nothing to tell." Juliette casts a glance towards the doors at the back of the dining room that must lead to the kitchen.

"I already told the cops everything." She's fixated on the door, and even though she's physically here, I have a feeling her mind is somewhere else.

Slowly, I slide into the booth across from her.

"Yeah, but I'm not a cop."

Her gaze returns to me, my words breaking her from her stupor.

"No, you're just *sort of* a private investigator," Juliette retorts.

I open my mouth to say...something. Reassure her again? I don't know, and I don't get the chance to because she orders me to leave.

"Read the police reports. I'm sure as a *'private investigator'* you can get ahold of them somehow. There's nothing more to tell. Please leave."

My jaw clenches at her words. I really need to see what she knows so I can find some momentum in this case.

I was only recently assigned—after Silas got the proper confirmation he needed and also realized none of his regular "investigators" were cut out for this case—but I need it solved quickly. Not just to stop whoever the bastard is that's terrorizing the city, but also to uphold my end of the deal with Silas. Hopefully this case is big enough to warrant me leaving Pine Falls for good once it's solved.

Accepting that I can't force someone to talk who doesn't want to, I pull out the first card I find with my name and number from my pocket.

"Just in case," I tell her softly.

Juliette takes the card, and I feel the slightest spark as our fingers brush and she pulls it from my grasp. Her gaze lingers on the ink on my hands for longer than necessary as if she's studying one of her textbooks.

I'm used to the judgement in people's eyes when they look at my tattoos, so I'm surprised to find none in her hazel ones. There's only mild curiosity written on her face as her head tilts to examine the small snake tattoo on my middle finger. I start to feel... exposed, cut open by her gaze, so I step out of the booth and shove my hands in my hoodie pocket.

I don't bother with goodbye, and neither does she. This entire visit lasted all of five minutes. Silas will be disappointed when I meet with him next and have little to update him on. I'm just glad she took the card at all. Maybe, for whatever reason, she'll decide to talk to me instead of just redirecting me to the police reports I've already read a dozen times over.

The rain has let up for now, so I pull my lighter and another cigarette from my pocket. It's a bad habit I picked up years ago to deal with the stress of my life. Now when I breathe in the smoke, I relish the burn filling my lungs as the tobacco scrapes against them. I make myself focus on the slight pain of it. It's merely a drop in the bucket of penance I've yet to fill.

As I walk, my mind drifts back to Juliette Jennings. I've been in the presence of victims before, either asking them questions... or me being the reason they're a "victim" in the first place. I'm not proud of it. It's all part of my penance.

Seeing Juliette tonight with that gaze that seemed half in the present and half stuck in the past has me feeling doubly ashamed. Ashamed that I am the reason for that look on so many other faces.

I could have driven, but I don't mind the rain. As my mom used to say, *"Let the rain wash away all your pain from yesterday."* There's not enough water in the world to rid of me all the pain I've inflicted and retained, but I'll try anyway.

My boots splash in the puddles gathered on the sidewalk, and when I see the clouds gathering again, I toss my cigarette and pick up the pace.

Empty shops and restaurants line the streets, a once bustling downtown reduced to silence. There's a palpable tension in the air, not unlike the one before lightning strikes. My steps quicken for reasons other than the rain, like I can almost feel the Knife Man watching me. Waiting in the shadows for the perfect time to strike. I'm not usually this jumpy, especially since I am more than capable of defending myself, so I'm glad when the tension I feel slowly dissipates as I put more distance between myself and the heart of the city.

To get back to my apartment building, I have to cut through some side streets I would usually avoid. A certain tattoo on my forearm practically vibrates on my skin at the awareness of where I am. I shudder at the reminder.

A clanging sound has me throwing a look over my shoulder. A distant motorcycle backfiring has me backing into the alley wall. The tension I thought had left me returns. It adds to the layers of paranoia and fear clinging to the city. This can't go on forever. Someone has to stop this killer, and with any luck, it will be me.

3

Juliette

The darkness is impenetrable, but white gleaming fangs pierce their way through. They invade my field of vision and get closer. I try to scream, but the sound is lodged in my throat. I try to shut my eyes, but they are forced open. I try to run, but my legs stay rooted to the floor. The fangs meet my flesh.

I wake up suddenly and sweating, my heart racing. My room is pitch black, clouds obscuring the moon. I struggle to catch my breath as I scramble to turn on the lamp on my nightstand. My heart rate slows a little at the soft light illuminating all the dark corners of my room. My mom must have come in here and turned it off because I sure as hell didn't. I *wouldn't*. It's times like these—panic attacks following a nightmare—where I wonder if I should've kept seeing that therapist. The one I was basically forced to talk to.

I sigh and rub my hand down my face and reach for the glass of water my mom must have left on the nightstand when she turned off the light. The cool liquid eases some of the remaining tension from my nightmare.

Next to the lamp is a business card. *His* card. I wonder what Mom thought of that, if she saw it.

Alex Osman, it reads. The name on his card has burned itself into my mind. When I got home from that strange and short encounter, all I did was lie in my bed and stare at it. I must've fallen asleep like that. I'm not sure why I kept it. There's nothing for me to say to him... *Right?*

In all honesty, I did consider talking to him for a good five seconds before I decided to just keep my information to myself. It's not like he would have believed me, anyway.

Alex Osman. I trace over his name and chew on my lip, thinking. I thought he was my stalker, and maybe he still is. But I can't just go accusing every guy in a black hoodie of stalking me. If he is my stalker, it would be a shame because he was pretty attractive. Objectively.

I flip the card over but the only text there is his phone number. His card doesn't even say he's a private investigator.

Why even have a business card then?

His claim of being a "sort of" private investigator isn't even backed up by this sorry excuse for a business card. It's bothering the marketing major part of me. If there's one thing I've learned in my almost four years of college, it's that a good business card should tell you everything you need to know about a person and the services they offer. Even the material of it is strange. It's too thin. If his plain card is any indicator, Alex Osman is boring and secretive.

Rolling onto my stomach, I drag my laptop towards me. I had set it on my bed earlier when I was researching different ways to kill a vampire. The internet can't decide between a stake through the heart or decapitation. I personally think fire could be an effective option, too. The unfinished draft for my capstone project glares at me from the bottom of the screen, but I ignore it and click over to the web browser.

Opening up a new search page, I type in the two words that have been teasing my curiosity all night:

Alex Osman.

I'm immediately met with a great big heap of nothing. At least nothing relevant to the Alex I'm looking for. A lawyer's website from Minnesota is one of the first results, but he's got about thirty years on my Alex and about sixty percent less hair.

My Alex? Get a grip, Juliette. You just met him.

There's an Instagram profile for an @alexozman, but the Alex I met doesn't strike me as a big musical theater fan judging from these photos. There's also a severe lack of finger tattoos.

Is it odd that I had never met anyone with tattoos on their hands before tonight? I have certainly seen them on tv or on the occasional patron at the restaurant, but never up close. Don't finger tattoos hurt? He must have a high pain tolerance or some sort of masochistic tendency to have endured the process of getting so many.

I'm about to give up on my search when a news article from the third page of results catches my eye. The headline reads: *Orphaned Boy Finds New Home*. It's a short article, barely even a paragraph, from almost ten years ago.

Fourteen-year-old Alex Osman has finally been released from the hospital after the fatal accident that occurred nearly two weeks ago on the night of October fifteenth. He is the sole survivor. The other two victims, his parents, have yet to be found, but they are presumed dead by police. A distant relative has reportedly been granted custody of young Mr. Osman.

That's it. That's all the article says. That can't be all of it, right? It looks like someone went in and took out the rest of it. Or they were just super lazy with their reporting.

The words *sole survivor* tug at my chest, a strange feeling of connection with this Alex. Whoever he is, I feel a surge of empathy for him. Especially since the ten-year anniversary of this accident was just over a week ago.

What will I be like in ten years? Still wracked with grief and guilt or will I move on? Do I want to move on?

There's a link to another article, probably one about whatever accident sent him to the hospital for two weeks, but the link is broken. *Page not found*, my screen blinks at me.

I return to the previous article and study the site itself. *The Bellevue Reporter* is pasted at the top of the page, along with a "not secure" pop-up next to the URL. None of their stories are that exciting, and a quick search tells me the paper is headquartered in the small town of Bellevue, Vermont.

Is that where the Alex I met is originally from? The town name sounds familiar for some reason. I bookmark the article to print out and add to my murder board later.

I know Serena and her dad moved here from the East Coast, but I'm pretty sure they hailed from Massachusetts. Hayden and his parents—my mom's sister and her husband—lived on the East Coast, too, before they died and my cousin came to live with us. I make a mental note to ask my mom about it and to make sure Hayden is out of the house when I do.

He hates talking about that day. Although I empathized with his trauma, I never really understood it until recently. It's probably why he's been so patient with me the last few months. What happened to the Levitt's was tragic and I realize as I'm searching the short article for any hidden clues that Hayden would relate to this Alex as well: *Sole survivor* of the deadly car crash that took his parents lives.

A couple searches of *Alex Osman + Bellevue, Vermont* and *Alex Osman + Pine Falls, Washington* drag up nothing else. His internet presence correlates with his business card—boring and secretive.

Groaning, I shut my laptop and slide out of bed. My back cracks as I stretch out. It's almost two in the morning. I never used to have nightmares, but after That Night, I'm constantly plagued by visions of blood and fangs and dead girls. As if I don't already think about those things during the day.

I try to force the images out of my mind for the moment then toss Alex's card on my nightstand. It lands haphazardly next to the water glass my mom brought up with the side with his phone number showing. Maybe I should call him. What's the harm in telling him what I know? The cops aren't making any progress, and there have been so many murders since Serena's. Another set of eyes on the case—a "private investigator's," especially—could be helpful.

Finally deciding that yes it wouldn't hurt to just send him a quick text, I snatch the card back up.

"Shit," I swear under my breath, quickly fanning the card, but it's soaking wet.

The condensation from the ice water Mom brought me formed a puddle on my nightstand, and I unknowingly threw his card right into it. Now the phone number is nothing more than smudges, made worse by my fingers.

I hurry into the bathroom and blot the card with a towel, but it only spreads the ink. Josie's hairdryer sits on the counter, and I quickly plug it in, hoping that the heat will salvage the number. As evidenced by my failed web searches, Alex seems to be a hard man to come by, so this could be my only way to contact him again.

The dryer comes to life, and I switch it to the lowest setting, carefully fanning it over the small, flimsy card. *This is why they invented glossy cardstock, Alex*! I curse him and his unfortunate choice of paper.

The card starts to dry, and I let out a sigh of relief, ignoring the fact that all I'm doing is setting the smudges of the numbers further. Except... what is *that?*

Above his horrendously off centered phone number, something starts to appear on the paper. The design of the card starts to make sense as letters, one by one, become visible.

When Hayden was thirteen, he went through a spy phase. My parents bought him all kinds of fake spy equipment so he could pretend he was on missions for the CIA. He would slip notes under my door—labeled as *top-secret correspondence*. They were seemingly blank pieces of paper that I would have to wet and heat to reveal hidden messages.

Alex's business cards must have used a similar ink... but why? As the letters become clearer, I find my answer.

The card reads:

Alex Osman
Vampiric Investigations

4

ALEX

THE CITY FADES AWAY. Buildings and streetlights are replaced with trees and fog the further north I drive to meet my boss, Silas, who requested I meet him as soon as possible. He lives on the outskirts of Pine Falls on a massive piece of property large enough to house all his "responsibilities." The guards recognize my car as I pull up to the gate and wave me through, eyeing me from their booth when I drive past.

I've been coming here for three years. Three years of heeding Silas' wishes, his every beck and call. Three years, and they still look at me like I'm *other*. One of *them*. That look is one of the many reasons I want to get the fuck out of this town. As soon as my debt is paid, of course.

Silas' house is a monolith of concrete and glass, a square structure rising three stories high and twice as long. The countless windows and sharp corners loom over the surrounding woods. There are other houses on the property, just as lifeless, that sit beyond the main house. Close enough for Silas to maintain a measure of control while giving the illusion of privacy from his looming mansion. And, of course, the prison sits far below all of it. Every Head of Council presides over one.

Out of sight of the main buildings and only accessible through a hidden entrance deep inside Silas' property, is a containment facility. I've never seen it and hope I never have to, but I have heard many chilling and disturbing stories about what happens down there. Vampires locked away for their misdeeds, never to see the sky or smell the pines again. Forever isolated in an eight-by-eight cell.

My old Mustang looks out of place amongst the modern architecture. Yet another reminder—albeit inconsequential—that I don't quite fit in. The doorbell emits a melodic chime when I ring it, reverberating through the front door until it's swung open by Jeffers.

"Hey Alex," the vampire grins. It's strange to have someone in this place look happy to see me. I wouldn't consider him a friend, necessarily, but he doesn't look down on me which is close enough.

"Hey." I step inside and follow him through the house, glass windows stretching along the walls. The sun barely peeks through its cover of clouds and is further blocked by the many trees encompassing the property, casting the interior in a dim light that makes the space feel even less inhabited.

We arrive before Silas' study, and Jeffers raps once on the wooden door before allowing me to pass through. His assistance was hardly necessary—I've been here enough times in the past few years to know my way around. I've also had enough appointments with Silas for him to expect me on certain days. Still, Jeffers opens the door and nods once at Silas.

"Catch you later," he winks at me before going to stand guard at the end of the hall.

Silas waits before a tall window looking out into the woods, next to a concrete desk that was apparently featured in *Architectural Digest*. I can't for the life of me see why. But it does fit the modern totalitarian aesthetic he has going. His hands are clasped behind his back, posture impeccable as always, looking very much like the type of man who would purchase a desk made out of concrete. He's taller than my six-foot-three frame and an imposing male authority figure I could have used when I was growing up, after I lost my dad. My mind automatically wants to remind me that the ten-year anniversary of losing my parents recently passed but I bury it deep, ignoring the reminder.

Silas waits a beat before turning to face me, a slight smile on his angular, pale face as if he's greeting an old friend, instead of someone he's essentially forced into his employ. It takes effort not to roll my eyes at his behavior.

I survey his office while he surveys me. Like the rest of the house, it is completely devoid of personality. Tall windows, a fireplace, and concrete floors and ceiling. The only pop of color exists in the form of a painting hanging above the mantel. It depicts two abstract figures with what I can only assume is blood coating their bodies.

"Alex," Silas greets me, a hint of his fangs peeking through when he speaks.

He resides over the West Coast Vampiric Council as well as the Vampire and Human Assimilation Society. Although he promotes secrecy of our kind, he doesn't hide who he is in his own home. Because of that, the recently displaced or turned vampires under his care are put completely at ease with who they are.

His compound houses stray and newly turned vampires, as well as half vampires. I was offered housing here once, back when Silas and I struck our deal, but I declined. I much prefer the ambient sounds and bustling activity of the city over the stillness of the country. And no way was I going to risk seeing Silas more than I was already forced to. Nowadays, however, the streets are just as quiet as it is here. And the terms I agreed to with Silas keep me in his presence more than I would like.

The vampires who don't pass through here at one point or another are usually off Silas' radar and, more pressing, out of his control. Vampires turned by one of the many groups who disregard the Council and their rules are the biggest offenders to Silas' rule. They wreak havoc on both the human and vampire communities. I can't count how many I've collected and deposited to Silas for "rehabilitation," or the numerous messes I've cleaned up at his bidding because of these rogue groups.

Then again, my experience with these groups is the reason he agreed to our deal in the first place and why I had to be faced with said deal at all. If I hadn't been caught, I'd be on the other side of those messes. Part of me thinks I wouldn't—that I would have acted on the whims I once had of doing better, *being* better. But the influence of my former boss, Slade, was too great. The only reason I agreed to switch sides was because I had no desire to discover the true horrors of the prison beneath our feet.

Lowering himself into the chair behind the concrete slab he calls a desk, my current boss gestures for me to take the seat opposite. I once again feel out of place in the presence of his easy grace, coupled with his immaculate three-piece suit that my hoodie and jeans seem to affront.

"Do you have an update for me on this supposed serial killer case?" Silas steeples his fingers together, a casual smile still on his face.

I don't know what is "supposed" about this case. If you murder more than three people in multiple locations over the course of one month or longer, you're technically a serial killer. A quick Google search will tell you that. Not sure what else Silas needs to call this killer one.

I guess in his mind, he can't fathom a vampire being termed something as human as *serial killer*. To Silas, it's just a rogue who needs to be brought to swift justice with a reminder of who's in charge.

I shift in my seat and recite the answer I prepared.

"The police don't suspect it's anything other than a person with a knife."

"Whoever it is obviously has complete disregard for our rules, we're lucky the neck wounds are so jagged. If they weren't, the police might start questioning what made them." Silas tilts his head thoughtfully and adds, "The size of the neck wounds suggests a frenzy, wouldn't you agree?"

I nod, he is most likely correct on that account. Normal wounds from fangs are small, barely visible to the eye, if a vampire is in control of their feeding. One who isn't in control, so overwhelmed by the smell of their victim's blood, won't pay any mind to the size of wound their fangs will make.

"Anything else to add?" Silas tilts his head to the other side, not a single strand of his smoothly combed light hair falling out of place.

I flex my fingers and focus my gaze just past his shoulder, out the window into the foggy day. I've got nothing else, which doesn't bode well for me in a meeting with Silas Chamberlain.

"What did the witness I told you to speak to say? Juliette something."

Her face pops into my mind, pale and wary, eyes lit with an inner fire when they weren't shadowed and dull.

"She seemed skittish, sir. Didn't say much."

His eyes narrow, a reprimand surely brewing on his tongue, and I rush to add, "But I'll approach her again. I'll get her to talk."

My assurance that I can, in fact, do my job seems to appease him for now.

"Good. I'm counting on it." I simply jerk another nod in return.

I'm counting on getting this job done, too. And he knows it. He holds all the power here—I don't solve these crimes for the fun of it. The main foundation for our deal is my freedom. Freedom that he doesn't believe I have a right to until he deems it so. Until I've sufficiently made up for the sins committed in my past. If he thinks like me, then no amount of hunting rogues will be enough to absolve me.

"What are your thoughts on the Blood Ring?" Silas muses, the sudden mention of the traffickers coming out of nowhere.

I keep my composure and fiddle with the drawstrings of my hoodie as I consider his question. The Blood Ring has been around for ages, vampires who deal in flesh and, as the name would suggest, blood. Silas and the different Councils across the country have been trying to take it down since its inception.

"You think they have something to do with this?"

Silas hums. "Just a thought."

His eyes meet mine, clearly waiting for me to expand on his thought, or rebuke it.

"The blood drained could be going to them, but usually they like their victims... alive."

It's unsettling, but true. Humans are sold as concubines, essentially, but instead of using them for sex or bearing children, their blood is taken. Their lives are reduced to being nothing more than a source of food. While no two stories about the Blood Ring are alike, it's said that warehouses and compounds, much like Silas', exist for the sole purpose of housing the humans they take. Their victims are confined to cots and dark corners and only brought out for feeding.

I may have a past I'm ashamed of, but at least I'm not that kind of fucked up.

Most vampires take blood consensually from those they trust enough to share their heritage with or just drink from animals. Of course, there are a number of vampires who take it by force; I am unfortunate enough to have seen plenty of the latter. There's also the option to purchase bagged blood, which my father and uncle used to do. Though I'm not sure where it's sourced from.

There's also a misconception among humans that vampires need blood regularly to survive. I've heard full vampires feel as though something is missing until they get their fill of blood—a gnawing ache they can't satisfy with human food. When they do drink, their senses sharpen and their enhanced abilities heighten.

"As I said, just something to consider," Silas adds, rising from his seat swiftly, buttoning his suit jacket as he does so. "I'd also like you to look into Slade. His people seem like the type to do something like this." He barks a rough laugh, "God knows they've done it before!"

A vicious gleam enters his eyes, waiting for me to disagree with him, or disavow my former leader.

I make a noncommittal noise instead, and stand. "I'll look into it." Absently I rub my left forearm, just above one of my tattoos.

He won't listen to any arguments against the matter, so that's the best I can do to appease him for now.

A buzzing fills my chest and spreads down my arms. I haven't been able to avoid Slade and his group as easily as I thought I could these past few years, and I should've known Silas would suspect him on this case. But mixed with my nerves is an urge to defend him because even though he's done some bad shit over the years, he would never do something as demented as this... *Would he?*

No. Getting into turf wars with the other rogue group, Crimson, and orchestrating robberies and petty crimes is not the same as going on a frenzied killing spree across the city.

"Look into Crimson, as well, if we're thinking the Blood Ring could be involved."

If by *we* he means himself and his unfounded theories, then sure. I don't actually think Crimson or the Blood Ring are involved, but I'm not about to argue with him. I also avoid pointing out that, just because a rogue group goes by the color that blood happens to be, doesn't mean they're connected to blood traffickers. But in Silas' mind, if you're not with him, then you're against him. And if two groups are against him, they might as well be working together. No matter that feuds run as rampant in these groups as their despisal of Silas does.

"Yes, sir," is all I say instead.

"Well, if that's all."

Silas looks at me expectantly from under lowered brows as he inspects the cuffs of his sleeves.

"Get that witness to talk or I'll be forced to step in. This case is important, Alex, in a number of ways. We don't need the humans getting suspicious."

It's a reminder I don't need, but he gives it anyway. He smiles but it's all teeth and fangs.

"This case is important to you, too. I trust you'll solve it in time."

With that he sweeps out of the room, leaving me alone with my rising anger.

It is important. Could his assertion possibly mean that this case is my final one? The one that could wipe away my debt if I solve it?

Something in me wonders if Silas doesn't believe I can and I'll be stuck performing measly jobs for him for the rest of my days.

But I *will* solve this case, and I'm counting the days until I'm free of him.

5

JULIETTE

I still haven't contacted Alex Osman even though the invisible ink on his business card should have been enough motivation to do so. Conflict wages a war in my mind just like my headaches do. What if the card is some big practical joke? What if Alex Osman is a lunatic who only *thinks* he investigates vampires? Is he even an investigator? What if he's the killer and is just trying to trick me?

My thumb and forefinger have rubbed my temple raw just thinking through all the possibilities. His strange card also poses the question: if it is all some elaborate prank, how did he know I would see the invisible ink? Which leads to my next question: are the people he usually gives his card to supposed to know the ink is there?

More questions and even less answers. I wish it were easy. I wish a note would show up on my doorstep one day saying *Hey Juliette! The killer who's been terrorizing the city for months is, in fact, a vampire. Here is his name, address, and place of work. Happy hunting!*

If only it were that simple.

It takes effort to ignore these questions and to try behaving like a normal college student for one day. It's not lost on me that some of these could be answered if I talked to Alex Osman, Vampiric Investigations.

My mind is pulled from thoughts of murder and mysterious "sort of" investigators by Hayden's voice, deep and questioning.

"Jules," he singsongs my name. "Where's that pretty little mind of yours floating off to? You've got that look in your eye."

"What look?" I ask, defensive.

"The one that says your body is here, but your thoughts are somewhere else," Meg replies.

I stifle the urge to roll my eyes. Sorry if my thoughts are currently more interesting than the latest Pine Falls U gossip. Which, last time I tuned in, was centered around some girl in Josie's sociology class who may or may not be sleeping with the professor. I put my sunglasses on because apparently I need to guard my eyes from nosy friends as well as the sun, which is making a rare appearance today.

My attempts to behave like an average college student are why I'm here sitting at our unofficial meeting spot on campus. A few months ago, I would have eaten up the gossip like my mom's famous beef stew on a rainy day. I would have laughed and looked around at my friends at the table, the sun making their features luminous and open. I would have taken out my sketch book and drawn Hayden's sturdy profile or Josie's kind smile. I would have even shared my own gossip in between strokes of my pencil.

What could I share now? That a guy covered in tattoos and claiming to be an investigator showed up at the restaurant last night?

"Hey, hey. Check this out." Hayden juts his chin towards the administration building, where a few figures are emerging.

Meg turns her nose up in disgust. "What is *he* doing here?"

"Maybe it has something to do with this?" Josie retrieves a crumpled piece of paper from her bag, passing it around. "I found it yesterday. Forgot to show it to you guys."

We take turns peering at it.

Pine Falls University is not a highly esteemed temple for academics in any way, but it was the best my family could afford. They may own one of the most upscale restaurants in the city, but their take-home pay certainly isn't enough to send me to some Ivy League school.

The way things are going now, I don't know how much longer they'll even be able to afford my and Hayden's tuition here.

Pine Falls U is nothing special, so why is Laurence Mitchell doing a guest lecture here?

Meg echoes my thoughts exactly as Hayden passes her the flier, Mitchell's name in bold at the top.

"In all the years Serena was here he never stepped foot on campus, and now he suddenly cares enough to teach its students about *smart business investments*?" Meg vocalizes my exact thoughts, down to the tone edged in ice.

"Are any of us surprised? The man is a Grade-A Asshole," Hayden chimes in.

Serena didn't like her father, so none of us—her friends—did either. Normally I would add my own bitter opinions about Serena's father, but I'm currently being sucked into the black void of my memory.

Instead of my friends chatter, I start to hear the beeping of monitors. I feel the scratchy hospital sheets. I see the light creeping in from the hallway through the cracked door. The cracked door that let in all of Laurence Mitchell's tirade.

"What do you mean she's not a suspect at this time?" His voice boomed off the walls, or maybe my pounding head made it seem louder than it was. A warning from

a nurse to keep his voice down confirmed his volume level, though.

"Explain," he continued in a harsh whisper, still loud enough for me to hear in my quiet hospital room. Where were my parents? My friends? Serena—

I choked back a sob as memories assaulted me, instead focusing on the man outside my door. Who was he talking to?

"Given her injuries, it would be impossible for her to have transported your daughter's body. It also seems highly unlikely she inflicted the injuries on herself," a voice responded.

"She could be working with someone! Why else is she still alive, when my daughter isn't?" Laurence Mitchell hissed. There was an edge of pain in his tone—one that speared me right through the heart. Because he was right, why was I still here when Serena wasn't?

"Sir—" The other man, who I suspected might be a police officer, was cut off by Laurence Mitchell's firm accusations.

"There was no forced entry. Nothing was stolen. Someone went there to kill Serena, and she either let them in herself or they had their own way in."

I closed my eyes after that and tried to drown out the rest of what he said. Tried to go back to that blissful sleep where I was none the wiser to Serena being dead. It didn't work, and I was forced to lie there and listen to this man accuse me of something so horrific.

I don't know if his yelling in the hallway of the hospital will ever fade from my mind. If more bodies hadn't started showing up, I'm not sure how long it would have been until the cops started to believe Laurence Mitchell's accusations. His little visit to the hospital that day only intensified the hatred my friends and I had for him.

I'm fine.
I'm fine.
I'm fine.

A sharp shushing noise startles me back into the present. Hayden is waving his hands around to get Josie and Meg to stop talking, frantically gesturing with his head to the people across the quad.

Laurence Mitchell strides along with Dean Warton as the dean's assistant stays right on their heels. Mitchell's gait is smooth and confident compared to the dean's awkward shuffling. Another man trails behind the group of three, obscured in the shadows of the other figures.

Meg makes a sound that resembles a cat hissing at another cat invading its territory. "Look at him, strolling across campus like he owns the place."

"He probably does," Hayden mutters under his breath.

Meg and Josie huff in amused laughter, but I'm too focused on the man making his way towards us to listen to them.

"He's coming this way. Why is he coming this way?" Hayden slumps down on his side of the bench, covering his face with his upside-down textbook. He glares at us over the top.

"Don't keep staring at him! Act natural," he hisses and resumes his reading of the upside-down book.

Yes, you would have made a great spy, Hayden. The words sit on the tip of my tongue, but I can't get myself to say them out loud. It's weird, not being able to joke with him like I used to. It's like I've been stuck in this emotionless void for so long that I'm compelled to force any sense of normalcy away on instinct.

"What a studious young group we have here," Laurence Mitchell drawls, sidling up to our table.

The bench is damp from the morning dew, and our loose papers have stuck to it. None of us care, it's not like we were actually studying. It's been our tradition the past three years—two in Hayden's case—to take out our notepads and textbooks so we don't feel so bad while we just gossip the whole time.

The dean, ruddy faced and shooting nervous glances at the imposing man next to him, says, "We pride ourselves on our students' academic ambitions."

We're one of the worst performing colleges in the state, but okay. His assistant quietly backs away, sensing the discomfort from all parties.

Laurence glances at the crumpled, damp flier with his name on it that we were passing around. His nose twitches in what I can only assume is disgust, like he's unnerved to discover we didn't immediately laminate the paper and put it on a shrine. It would go right next to framed covers of business magazines he's been featured in, of course.

Laurence snaps his fingers, and it's then I remember someone else is with him. The man from the shadows jumps and fumbles with the clasp of the messenger bag slung across his body. He looks like he's auditioning for the role of a young Laurence Mitchell in the movie that will inevitably be made about him. I'm not the only one who notices the similarities in their appearances. Hayden catches my eye and tries to hide his smile with his hand. My own lips twitch in response, but I tamp down the reaction.

The younger man—his assistant, I presume—pulls a freshly printed stack of fliers from the bag. He begins handing them out to the four of us and we accept them reluctantly. Whatever it takes to make them leave. Our fingers graze when he holds one out to me, and I try not to flinch at the icy contact. I don't hide how I pull away from him, though. Let them see how much I object to their presence.

The guy moves back into the shadows once the fliers are passed out, eyes darting from the ground and to Laurence's back.

"I do hope you consider attending," Laurence says. "Young people today lack the motivation and ambition needed to become the next business leaders of America."

The dean bristles at his words. Laurence taps Josie's flier—who sits closest to where he stands—and meets our gazes, unaware or uncaring of her stiffening body.

"I cover all the basics needed to start your own business and start making smart investments." His stare lingers on mine with those last words, like he knows my parents' restaurant is floundering.

It's not their fault a murderer is on the loose, scaring away the customers. He probably thinks it's my fault, actually.

Hayden raises his hand and looks Laurence dead in the eye. "I'm currently taking a ceramics class and have mastered the art of bong making. Would you consider bong production a smart business investment?"

Josie covers her snort of laughter with her hand and Meg rolls her eyes, but a slight smile pulls at her mouth. Hayden continues staring at Laurence, feigning seriousness. I have to hand it to my cousin, he knows exactly how to drive someone to speechlessness. I didn't think it could be done to the suave man in front of us, but here we are.

Laurence blinks at Hayden, trying to determine if he's being serious or not. With Hayden, you never know.

Then he gives us all a cold smile and simply says, "Hope to see you there."

The two men walk off, leaving their assistants to trail behind. We catch the dean hastily apologizing for Hayden's remark, shooting glares at my cousin.

"Don't count on it," Hayden says to their retreating backs.

As soon as they're a safe distance away, my friends burst into laughter.

"Bong production?" Josie gives Hayden a questioning look in between laughs.

His grin broadens and he throws an arm around her shoulders, kissing her hair. My brows furrow at the two of them. Are they a thing now? I feel like I blinked, and the past two months have zoomed by, leaving me to wonder what's going on in their lives.

"It's gonna be the next big thing, just you wait."

I let out my own soft huff that could be perceived as laughter or an exhalation.

"That was fucking weird," I say once the giggles fizzle out completely.

"Yeah, it's like he didn't even recognize us," Hayden replies.

Meg shakes her head. "No. He knew. Why do you think he made such a show of handing us the fliers? And what about that jab about smart business investments? Not everyone wants to make their money illegally like him."

"You think he's got dirty money?" Hayden asks.

"Obviously. I mean, do any of you even know what he does for a living? Serena didn't even know." The table falls quiet at the mention of Serena, and Hayden jumps to switch topics with an anxious glance at me.

"What about that assistant, though? Do you guys think Mitchell Enterprises figured out cloning?"

They erupt into more laughter, pondering the possibilities of Laurence Mitchell clones locked in a lab somewhere.

I have to wonder how the man got his job. He didn't seem particularly relaxed in his role as Laurence Mitchell's assistant. But I guess a job where someone has to report to Laurence Mitchell could hardly be defined as relaxing.

I'm contemplating bringing the topic up, and attempting to assimilate back into our old dynamic, when movement catches my eye from an upper classroom window.

A hooded man stares down at me.

Meg, Josie, and Hayden start a new conversation—one that's free of Laurence Mitchell, his strange lookalike assistant, and guest lectures no one plans on attending. I tune them out like I've done so often lately and stare at my stalker. He doesn't move, not even to shift on his feet. He's still as a statue, always watching.

I think I'll contact Alex Osman.

6

ALEX

The sunshine from earlier gives way to a drizzly evening. I'm perfectly fine staying in my lonely little apartment, with only instant noodles and thoughts of killers for company, when I get a text.

> **Unknown:** it's juliette from the restaurant last night. meet me at sal's diner. 8pm.

Silas' warning still echoes in my mind from our earlier meeting about him getting involved if I couldn't get answers from Juliette. It's enough for me to trash my noodles and hurry down to the diner.

I take my car this time, not needing to feel the cleansing wash of the rain tonight. The diner comes into view on the corner, and I park across the street, hurrying to get inside as the rain picks up. A discordant bell announces my arrival.

Sal's Diner is a dated place, the tile floor chipping in some places and layers of grime climbing up to meet the windows. Halloween decorations that look about fifty years old are sparsely placed around the interior, completing the all-around *uncomfortable* vibe. There's no hostess stand like at the Jennings family restaurant, just a waitress bustling around who vaguely points towards an empty booth in the back.

I sink into the cracked leather seat just as the waitress comes by with a single menu and place setting. Waving her off, I ask for a coffee and two waters instead. When she returns, I barely sip the bitter coffee in the steaming cup, instead fidgeting under the table while I wait. The clock on the opposite wall reads eight-oh-three. I take another sip of coffee.

The off-key bell chimes again and I look up to see her. Juliette Jennings. She pulls the hood of her jacket down as she searches the tables, finding me in the corner. She's taller than I expected her to be and for some reason I find my gaze lingering on her long legs as she strides towards me.

Juliette sits down across from me, and it's unsurprisingly awkward, given our last interaction. She makes no move to remove her coat or crossbody bag, sitting rigidly while fiddling her fingers on the laminate tabletop. She's looking anywhere but at me, which is when I realize I've just been staring at her for about a minute straight.

"So why this diner?" I finally ask. "Do you come here a lot?"

Juliette slowly turns her head and blinks at me, looking like an owl. "No." She seems about as into small talk as I am.

"You didn't want to meet at the other restaurant?"

"I don't need my family wondering who you are." *Ouch?* Juliette flags the waitress down as she speaks, barely looking at me. When she arrives at our table, looking more harried than before, Juliette orders a hot chocolate for herself with extra whipped cream. I fight the slight upturn of my lips at her order, but she notices anyway.

"What?" I can't decide if her tone is more offended or daring. Daring me to question her order.

"Nothing." I hold my hands up in a show of placation, and she narrows her eyes at me slightly.

Neither of us makes a move to broach why we're at this cheap diner on a Wednesday night. It isn't until the waitress deposits the hot chocolate in front of Juliette that I realize I'll have to initiate the conversation. She pokes at the mountain of whipped cream on her mug with a spoon, content to ignore me even though she's the one who requested we meet.

"I take it you agreed to meet with me because you're ready to talk...?" I trail off but am met with silence. I clear my throat and take another sip of my now lukewarm coffee. "I wanted to ask you some questions about the attack."

She scoops some whipped cream up and eats it, arching one brow. I track her swallow, the way her throat bobs, and realize I am once again quite obviously staring at her.

"So you said last night," she replies flatly.

"Right." I shake my head as if to clear all thoughts of her pale, slender neck. "Well, I just want to hear your version of events."

She abandons the spoon and her drink and sits up even straighter in her seat, clasping her hands.

"You're a private investigator." It's more statement than question.

"Yes," I reply. The half-truth, like last time. I don't feel like opening this can of worms with her again. Her gaze darts to my tattooed hands and I self-consciously tuck them into my lap, out of her piercing gaze.

"Of sorts," she repeats, narrowing her eyes. Again, not really a question. I meet her stare across the table. She's waiting for me to expand on her comment—my own comment from the night before. Her eyes hold questions, like emeralds buried in dirt, waiting to be unearthed. There's curiosity layered with desperation, and wariness too, which is understandable.

She leans across the table, the pleasant smell of lilac and vanilla drifting towards me. For a moment I'm transported home, sitting on the porch steps while my mom tends to her flower beds. Lilac was always her favorite to grow in the spring.

Juliette lowers her voice as she says, "A vampire investigator."

My whole body freezes. In all my life, I've never met someone who figured out what I am on their own. It's damn near impossible. Unless…

Shit. The card I gave her. I wasn't even thinking when I pulled it out. That one's meant for vampires—their heightened senses allow them to see the hidden ink without having to wet and heat it. Silas hands them out at events, and he makes me carry some too. I have other ones to give to humans. My sight isn't that powerful, and I was a bit flustered by her the night we met, so I just handed her the first card I touched—a card meant for vampires. She must've figured out the ink, somehow.

Her lips lift as she studies me curiously. She must sense I'm trying to piece it together because she explains in a bored voice, "I spilled water on it. I didn't want to lose your number, so I used my blow dryer." She shrugs. "The words appeared when it dried."

"You're not freaking out…" I lean back into my seat and cock my head to study her.

"Part of me still wonders if what you're saying is even real."

"It is real. I mean, I am real." I trip over my words, utterly failing at trying to convince her I am, at least, capable of coherent speech.

I've never really been in this situation before. Most of my life, I have only been surrounded by vampires. Or by humans who knew about the vampire community and accepted it—like my mom. I'm not sure what the protocol is for telling this human girl we exist. Silas would penalize me greatly if he knew.

Juliette shifts uncomfortably, and I arch a brow at her. "I'm not the first vampire you've encountered, am I?" I need to hear her confirm it. That she knows the "Knife Man" is really a vampire. If she already knows about vampires, then I can't really be punished for telling her about myself... right? Loopholes.

She meets my gaze and slowly shakes her head. "That night..." Her throat works, and she's back to looking anywhere but at me. "It... *he* was a vampire. He had his fangs in her neck, and her blood was everywhere." Juliette's voice is hard, her eyes distant. Her fingers absently trace a spot on her neck. I can tell that she's disappeared into the memory of her attack and her friends murder, and I feel the sudden, desperate urge to bring her back.

I reach out and place my scarred, tattooed hand over her small, trembling fist on the table. She jolts at the contact, and I almost pull away, embarrassed. But then I feel her trembling ease, and the tension in her face dissipates.

Hesitantly, she tells me the rest of what happened that night. How she came home to a quiet, dark house. The fanged man she saw over her best friend. How, with impossible strength, she was slammed into a wall after he bit her. The empty night he disappeared into. And the pool of blood she stared at as she lost consciousness.

Neither of us moves, my hand still resting on top of hers, my thumb moving in subconsciously slow circles over her wrist. She recites her story monotonously, like she's done it a dozen times before. The only time a hint of emotion creeps into her voice is when she recounts the vampire sinking his fangs into her neck.

When she trails off, her story complete, I clear my throat and abruptly remove my hand from hers. "Thank you." I don't know what else to say besides that. The whole ordeal was clearly traumatizing for her, and she was just made to relive it again in some sketchy diner with a guy she doesn't even know.

"You really think you'll be able to do what the cops can't?"

"Yes," I reply without hesitation. It's not arrogance, just simple fact. "I know what I'm dealing with. They don't." And I've done it countless times in the past. Maybe I haven't solved any serial killer cases before and maybe I'm not a *licensed* private investigator, but I know how to deal with morally ambiguous bad vampires. And straight up bad ones. I've been doing it almost half my life. I look away from her, hoping to field any further questions about my *occupation*.

I pull my wallet out of my pocket and fumble for the cash to pay for our mostly full drinks. Her mountain of whipped cream has melted, turning the hot chocolate a sickly tan color.

"Thanks again for speaking with me. If you remember anything else just call."

"Wait," she says, and I still. "So, you're... a vampire?" The last part is a questioning whisper instead of the accusation I expected.

"Well, obviously you are. I already kind of asked this... You are one, right?"

Now she's the one stumbling over her words. It's kind of cute.

Juliette's done me a favor sharing the truths she hasn't shared with anyone else. For some reason, I trust that she won't share my secrets. "Sort of."

"'Sort of?'" She scoffs. "Is that your answer to everything? Either you are one, or you're not, right?" A coy smile plays on her lips, but her eyes are full of disbelief once again.

I grimace involuntarily—years of not fitting into the right boxes haunting me. "My mother was human, and my father was a vampire."

Her widening eyes are enough for me to know the hundreds of questions running through her brain. Stories and myths don't do our kind justice, and the consequence is humans with a skewed perspective on how things really are. She's practically vibrating with the questions brimming inside, but right now I don't feel like answering them. Especially since I'll likely never see her again.

The money I toss on the table makes no sound, but she flinches at the movement anyway. "I have to go." Outside, thunder cracks against the sky. Silas will be content with what I've learned, at least for a short time.

Juliette visibly deflates, her curiosity quickly replaced by a blank look. "Yeah. Although, you can't just tell someone you're sort of a vampire and then leave without expecting questions." One brow lifts and I bite back irritation that's mixed with some amusement. I'm beginning to realize that the words "determined" and "Juliette Jennings" are interchangeable.

I don't know what prompts me to do it, maybe the weather or the fact that she just shared a traumatic event with me, but I offer, "Do you need a ride home?"

"Can I ask more questions about how you're *sort of* a vampire?" Those eyes—those emeralds in dirt imbued with questions, holding back so many emotions I want to uncover—have softened slightly. They seem brighter than they were just a few minutes ago. Not like that photo I saw of her on the news, but a sliver of that light appears to have returned. I'm determined to keep them lit, if only because I know now how much darkness they've seen.

So I sigh, only partially reluctant at this point, and say yes.

7

Juliette

I should be wary of all vampires I cross paths with.

I should question when someone says they are one.

I should be worried that I'll end up like Serena.

And yet, I'm climbing into one's car.

Seriously, what the hell *am I doing?*

Hayden was confused, and blatantly curious, when I texted him and said I was getting a ride elsewhere. I had to sneak out of my parents' restaurant to meet Alex. Thankfully, Hayden was busy getting stoned in the alley when I left. He's been doing that more often than he used to. Maybe he's not coping with the events of the past two months as well as he'd like everyone to think he is.

My cousin has texted me at least twenty times asking if I have a "secret paramour." No, just a "sort of" investigator who solves vampire related crimes, made me share one of the worst nights of my life, paid for my hot chocolate, and offered me a ride home.

We reach an old muscle car parked across the street from the diner, and he pops open the passenger side door for me. I take one last look at the street around me, and at him, before sliding in with a mumbled thanks. Accepting his offer of a ride home feels dangerously close to a life-or-death decision. But he seems nice.

Was this what happened to Serena? Did she invite one into our house because he *seemed* nice? He's certainly kind, I mean he's paid for our drinks, and held the diner door *and* his car door open for me. *Wow, the bar of standards is horrendously low.*

Alex rounds the hood of the car and takes his seat behind the wheel, the leather shifting with his weight. I can't tell from his bulky black hoodie, but he might be hiding some serious muscle under there, definitely enough to overpower me if it came down to it.

I watch Alex closely and notice that he looks about the same height and build as the vampire I saw That Night, but it was so dark in the house, I couldn't make out any other features. Alex has dark hair. The killer vampire *might* have dark hair. There's only one thing I know for sure about that vampire...

"If you're a vampire, where are your fangs?" I aim for a casual tone, but my voice comes out a bit sharper than intended. He's an investigator, so he's probably used to getting the answers he wants. He could figure out where I'm going with this.

"I have fangs, I just don't have them on display." He turns the key in the ignition, the engine rumbling to life. His response just ignites more questions within me. He doesn't have them *on display*? As if they're the latest phone model at a store.

Alex pulls away from the curb, and I direct him to the freeway. He nods and keeps his focus out the windshield.

"You can keep your fangs hidden?"

"Yep." *Okay, then.* Alex may be more anti-conversation than I am. A small voice in my head tells me to keep going anyway, even though I know from experience how annoying it is when someone tries to force conversation. Serena used to be my buffer for that. She could always tell when I wasn't in the mood for socialization. She jokingly called it my "hermit mode."

Don't bother, she would tell whoever was trying to get ahold of me. *Juliette's in hermit mode.*

My lips twitch faintly at the memory, then abruptly stop when I realize Serena's voice isn't as clear as it used to be. I'm forgetting what she sounded like. No one warns you about that part of losing someone you love. Maybe time heals all wounds, but it also erases the little details that made up the person you lost. I'll have to rewatch some old videos of her, if I ever feel up to it. If I will ever be able to look at footage of Serena and not picture her corpse.

I'm fine. I'm fine. I'm fine, I repeat to myself. Three times seems to be the trick, at least enough to push those haunting memories away before they consume me.

I inhale deeply in an attempt to organize my thoughts, and get back to the task at hand—interrogating "sort of" vampire and investigator Alex. The faint smell of smoke and spice distracts me, though.

"I didn't know vampires could control their fangs like that," I say, ignoring the pleasant masculine scent drifting around. It must be ingrained in the leather of the car's interior because now that I've noticed it, I can't seem to escape it.

"You didn't even know vampires actually existed until half an hour ago," Alex points out. That's not fair. I was about eighty percent sure they were real, he just confirmed it for me.

My eyes roll automatically before I can get a handle on them. I watch as his profile lights up with a smirk before quickly returning to the stoic expression he seems to always keep. "How long have you been a vampire investigator?"

He shrugs, his focus solely on the near empty road ahead of us. "A few years."

I stifle a groan of frustration. Is he trying to dissuade me from asking him about being a vampire? If so, his aloofness is fooling the wrong girl.

"A few years," I mimic his flat tone. "How old does that make you, then?"

"Twenty-four." He answers simply and I take a moment to study him. He looks about that age, and why would he lie about it? He catches me staring and chuckles lightly. "What were you expecting, one hundred and twenty-four?"

Heat rushes to my cheeks and I dart my gaze back to the window, watching the dark trees rush past.

"No." *Yes? Maybe?* If I've learned anything tonight, it's that expectations are hardly reality. Although, sometimes they are and it's scary as hell.

"You're not really a private investigator, are you? You hunt vampires," I say in an attempt to change the subject.

He glances over at me again. "Yes. That's what I do but 'vampire hunter' doesn't sound as diplomatic as 'vampiric investigations.'"

"I'm trying really hard not to make any *Buffy the Vampire Slayer* references right now." Then my eyes widen with a sudden thought, "Wait, you're half human, half vampire, right?"

Before I can say anything more, he cuts me off. "Please refrain from any *Buffy* or *Blade* references or I might just have to drop you off in the middle of the road." His tone is flat, but I can see a hint of a smile on his face. I'm surprised to feel my own lips twitching upwards. Again. That's twice in the span of five minutes, which is twice more than the last two months.

"Besides," he mutters, "Buffy hunted more than just vampires. She's way more badass than me."

Soon enough he's taking the exit towards my parents' neighborhood and my opportunity to question *an actual vampire*, dwindles. Seriously, what is my life currently?

I don't know if I can trust Alex, or if I'll ever see him again. That thought makes me uncomfortable for some reason. We just met, but I want to know more about him.

Any person would, I reason. It's not often you interact with an actual vampire. Well, one that isn't trying to kill you, at least.

"How many vampire investigations have you done?" I rush out as he turns onto my street.

"Enough."

Really, we're back to this? I'm hopelessly underqualified to solve Serena's murder. It's been months and I've gotten nowhere. But maybe if I had help from someone who knew what they were doing, who has done this sort of thing before, I might be able to get somewhere. And if he is the vampire I saw That Night...

It's like they all say—keep your friends close and enemies closer and all that.

But no. As ideal as an experienced partner sounds, I don't even know if I can trust this guy. I mean, he's not exactly the most forthcoming person. I hear Hayden's amused voice in my head, *Oh, and you are?*

He asks me which house is mine and I direct him further down the street. We pass my house and I tell him to keep going, that it's at the end. No way am I showing him exactly where I live.

Alex pulls up to the curb in front of a house I've passed a million times but never been to before and parks. Staring at his profile in the dim light cast by the streetlamps, I start to flashback to That Night.

What was I thinking, accepting a ride home from a stranger? My self-preservation instincts are apparently delayed. Is this the part where he puts his fangs on display and drains me of blood? My heart races at the thought and my palms grow sweaty. No amount of thinking *I'm fine* will halt the anxiety spiral I've now found myself in.

"Thanks for the ride," I say in a rush, the words condensing into one on their way out of my mouth.

Scurrying out of the car, I slam the door shut before he has a chance to reveal his fangs. A confused Alex stares at me as I rush past the window.

Oh well. If I have act strange to stay alive, then I really don't care about the impression I leave on people.

I slip into the shadows and wait until I hear the distinct sound of his car driving away before racing down the street toward home.

The house is silent when I creep in through the front door. No one else must be home. Thank god, too. I really did not want to be given the third degree by Hayden on who drove me home.

I go through my nighttime routine almost mechanically, my mind elsewhere. *What if Alex is the killer and I just showed him where I live?* Well, down the street from where I live, but I'm sure he could find my actual house if he put his mind to it.

Frustrated, and a little scared at my stupidity in trusting a stranger, I drag my school bag off the desk with a little more force than necessary. Laurence Mitchell's stupid flier falls out, fluttering to the carpet. As I kick it away from me in disgust, I notice the date for the lecture is tomorrow night. Maybe I will go. With some tomatoes.

You have better things to do than heckle the man who thinks you're capable of murder, I remind myself. Although, if I told Hayden about it, he'd be down to go. I pick it up and shove it back in my bag. Just in case.

I pull my laptop out, intent on resuming my search for information on Alex "sort of a vampire, sort of an investigator" Osman. This time, I narrow my search to Alex Osman + Pine Falls + Vampire.

Of course, there's not much. Not like I was really expecting there to be, but is a Facebook profile with everything I want to know about him too much to ask for? I would even settle for an abandoned Twitter account.

Scrolling through the results—Alex's located in Pine Falls, a book titled *The Fall of Vampires*, an Osman Repair located in Eureka Falls—my eyes catch on a link near the end of the first page.

It's a Reddit post with the title: *vampire in pine falls???* The post has been cross posted in both the *City of Pine Falls* subreddit and *vampires* subreddit.

Eagerly, I scan the post.

u/razyrmannn: 1 day ago

Yoooo I heard some crazy shit at the bar off Lakim Ave just now. They were playing the news in there, talking about the knife man. Anyway this guy was going on and on about how we need to be careful, that the killer is a vampire or some shit. He even said he *was a vampire. I don't know if I believe him, but it was pretty funny. Especially when, after like an hour of this, these two guys came in and dragged him off into the alley. So what do you guys think? Vampires in Pine Falls?*

I stare at the post when I'm done, mouth slightly agape. There are a few comments, so I check those to see if the original poster provided some more information.

TheMonkeysUncle: The bar off Lakim? The one near that club Sinner? Don't believe a word out of anyone's mouths down there. Everyone is either high or drunk all the time.

The few other comments agree with the first one; that neighborhood is known for drug deals and sketchy characters. I can't help but wonder, though, who the two men were who dragged the drunk guy away. It seems to me like they wanted to shut him up, and why do that if he wasn't speaking some truth?

There's another comment replying to *TheMonkeysUncle*, disagreeing with him.

user93750143356: I don't know, I've seen some weird shit at Sinner. If there's no proof saying otherwise, we shouldn't count out the possibilities of vampires existing.

It's not like I'm in disbelief about vampires anymore, and even if I still had some niggling doubts, this post helps me believe that others have similar suspicions that I do. Even if they are most likely alcohol and drug induced delusions.

Deciding I'm done for the night, I shut my laptop and place it on the floor. My search for information on Alex was once again fruitless, but at least I found a semi-informative Reddit post. *Never thought I would think that.*

Alex's card is still on my nightstand from after I dried it and discovered the hidden words. I give it one last lingering glance before turning my back to it.

In the morning I'll throw it away.

Maybe.

8

ALEX

VAMPIRE GANGS ARE MORE common than you might think. In fact, I'm headed to meet with the leader of one right now.

Per Silas' request, I am looking into Crimson and the Blood Ring as potential suspects. I personally don't think they're involved, but he doesn't care to listen to my opinions when his mind is set on something. He tells me to jump, I better ask how high. Hopefully now that I've spoken to Juliette and relayed our conversation to him, he'll be appesed for a little while.

After listening to Juliette's story and hearing her describe how she was thrown, it's obvious the vampire was at full strength. The blood he drank from her and her friend definitely added to his strength. He's also likely in a frenzy, something Silas and I agreed early on, to have killed so many people so messily. Usually vampires don't go into frenzies unless they've been recently turned or are unable to control their thirst. I wasn't sure if I should explain all that to Juliette. I didn't want to freak her out, and I also wasn't clear on the protocol of revealing such things to a human, even though I'd already revealed far more than Silas would be comfortable with.

Given I let her play twenty questions with me last night, though, I'm long past worrying about her knowledge of vampires. I did my best to evade or answer vaguely, but she is persistent as hell. She better be careful if she decides to share her newfound knowledge. She could attract the attention of Silas, or someone worse.

The Blood Ring has been around for years, and Silas will do anything to try and catch them. To start, Silas wants me to meet with Crimson, a local gang of vampires. They're harmless, really. Nothing compared to the other rogue group in this city. Their biggest offense is not listening to Silas. Of course, because they do their own thing, Crimson is thought to be associated with the Blood Ring.

The Crimson vampires run a few popular gyms and bars in the city. I've had run ins with them in the past before I worked for Silas. They aren't on the best of terms with who I used to run with, being as my former employer was accused of monopolizing the nightlife industry, forcing Crimson to close some of their clubs. Mostly their altercations involve some stupid dispute over territory, or one group trying to blame the other for something.

Kai Nakamura, Crimson's leader, has backed off since then—deciding it wasn't worth the trouble to deal with my old boss and his territorialism—and now spends most of his time focusing on the gyms. That's who I'm going to meet, at their downtown location.

I'd be lying if I said I didn't hold some resentment for Crimson. It was during an altercation with some of their members a few years ago that put me on Silas' radar in the first place. The human cops were called, and because Silas has eyes and ears everywhere, he sent his men to take care of it instead. Then he found me and learned of my history of misdeeds which led to our current arrangement.

He doesn't directly attack or arrest members of the two main rogue groups without provocation, mostly due to fear that it will lead to something bigger. Something that would attract the humans' attention. Better to arrest one member and force them to do your bidding, or throw them in prison and let them serve as a warning and reminder to those who step out of line, than try to take down the entire group.

Crimson gyms are known for housing state of the art equipment, mixed martial arts lessons, and the occasional underground fight. Before tension between the two groups reached a boiling point, I used to fight at these gyms for money.

The downtown location is sleek, a row of treadmills lining the floor to ceiling windows. Looking inside, I see that only one is occupied. A sharp contrast to their usual full house.

The receptionist glances up from her phone when I walk in, but before I can ask about Kai, another voice penetrates the quiet space.

"Oh shit. Guys, look who's here." Internally I groan and look to my left to see Tyler. He's standing with a few others, loitering by the weightlifting machines. "This dude beat my ass a few years back. You here for round two?" He asks me, a daring glint in his eye. I roll my eyes and turn away, ignoring him. Unfortunately, I did not fight Tyler for money, I only wish I had.

Tyler is a human who—for reasons unknown to me—has been a part of Crimson since he was in high school. He graduated from Pine Falls U a couple of years ago but still insists on keeping the company of current members of the fraternity he was in. A few years prior, he interfered with some business of my old boss, and I was sent to "teach him a lesson." I guess it worked since this is the first I've seen him since that day. Probably because I was arrested and then given the option of either working for Silas or checking myself in for a permanent stay at his underground prison.

Even though Tyler is annoying as hell, I don't blame him for my misfortune entirely. I can own up to the fact that I shouldn't have instigated the fight, but I can also admit that manipulation ran deep in my veins. Still does, to an extent.

"I'm here to see Kai," I tell the receptionist. She gives me a blank stare before returning to her phone.

"Marissa, don't worry about it. I'll take him to Kai." Tyler appears beside me, a strange smile on his face. Marissa doesn't respond, just swivels around in her chair until her back is to us. "Don't mind her. She's the boss's cousin. Easy on the eyes but prickly." He laughs and I can't help but roll my eyes again. I've interacted with this guy like three times, but that's enough to establish a hatred towards someone.

I follow Tyler through the gym and up a set of stairs, treated to the unpleasant view of his too-tight gym shorts and loose tank top. His large, sweaty muscles bulge with every movement.

He stops halfway up the stairs and turns to me, sweat and a cloyingly spicy body spray assaulting my senses. Placing a hand on my chest, in what I'm sure he thinks is an intimidating way, he warns, "You're on our turf. You better watch yourself."

His "threat" brings me some amusement on this hassle of a visit. Enjoying myself, I pry his hand off my chest finger by finger. I grip his wrist and bend it back, reminding him exactly how our last meeting went. How I broke a couple of these fingers. How his high-pitched yelps echoed around the empty alley we were in.

For some reason, out of everything I've done, beating him up isn't something I'm sick over. Maybe because a week before that, there was a story in the paper about him sexually assaulting a girl at a party and how he walked away clean because his rich daddy knew the right person.

His throat works as he gulps, staring at my hand encasing his wrist. "Don't touch me," I say in a low voice with ten times the warning his measly threat had. Letting go of his wrist, he wisely listens and turns back around. He doesn't say anything else, not until we enter an office and Kai tells him to bring us some drinks.

"Yeah, sure thing." Tyler scurries out of the room.

"What's up, Alex? You just here to intimidate my men or what?" Kai gives me a warm smile and leans back in his chair. I take the seat opposite him. Kai is fine. He'd be better if he cut guys like Tyler loose.

"I wish it were just that. I'm here on Silas' behalf."

Kai groans. "That fucker still has you working for him?" I nod.

"Is this about 'The Stabber' or whatever the news is calling him?" Something dark enters his eyes at the mention of the killer, and he practically spits the wrong name out, like he knows what the real moniker is but refuses to say it. *Interesting.* I give him a grunt this time.

"Shit, man, I don't know anything about that."

"I know. But you know how Silas is. He thinks the Blood Ring is involved."

"So naturally, Crimson is involved too." Kai sits up straight in his chair, his geniality gone.

"If it's worth anything, I don't think you're involved."

"I don't doubt that," he says. "Just get me off that bastard's radar. We've already lost most of our business thanks to the killer—we don't need Silas taking the rest. Not when Slade is already doing that," he adds in a mutter.

Kai has always been congenial to me, even when I was running with his rivals. I got involved in this world when I was just a kid, and Kai always seemed to understand that.

"I'll get him off your back."

"Thanks Alex. You know, there was always a place for you with Crimson if you didn't want to stay with the DBC. You didn't need to go to *him.*"

I stifle a sigh at the fact he thinks I had any choice in the matter and at the mention of my old group. Sometimes I wish I had taken Kai up on the offer he gave me years ago, but even though he hides it better, I would have been doing the same shit I used to. Maybe to a lesser degree, but I'd still be playing the intimidation game. Not like I'm *not* doing that for Silas, but again, I don't have much choice. All this conversation is doing is making me want to leave this city even more than usual.

"I appreciate that," I tell him, rising from my seat. He follows and reaches out to clasp my hand.

"I got two coffees and two waters, wasn't sure what you guys were in the mood for." Tyler bustles back into the office, two disposable coffee cups in his hands and water bottles tucked under his arms.

"Alex was just leaving," Kai informs him. Tyler's lips purse in frustration, and I can't help but smirk a little.

"Later, Kai." I push past Tyler, causing him to drop the water bottles with a curse.

Once outside, I message Silas and tell him—for what seems like the hundredth time—that I don't believe Crimson and the Blood Ring are involved in these murders. I receive a response from him almost immediately.

> **Silas Chamberlain:** Meet me at The Grand Hotel ballroom. ASAP.

Sighing, I put my phone back in my pocket and head south a few blocks to the hotel. Why he wants to see me in person, I have no idea. It could be that he wants to pester me more about the Blood Ring or Slade and the DBC or pull some other random suspect out of his ass for me to look into. At least he's here in the city and I don't have to drive to his concrete compound up in the woods.

The Grand Hotel lives up to its name, and I can feel the staff's eyes on me as I pass through the gleaming lobby to the ballroom. I'm surprised they don't ask me to leave. I'm certainly not the type who usually passes through the front doors.

Silas is chatting with an older guy inside the empty ballroom. He catches my eye and motions for me to hang back. The human manager appears completely at ease with Silas' faux human façade. His fangs are hidden, his eyes holding less of a gleam. He looks the part of a wealthy businessman looking to host an event that will boost his considerable status even further.

Waiting for them to finish, I stroll around the space, taking in the details. A few tables are set up along one wall, empty although I don't think they'll be bare for long. There's also a sign next to a large flower arrangement. It reads: *Chamberlain Foundation Annual Char-*

ity Fundraiser for Underprivileged Youths. I suppress a scoff but can't help rolling my eyes.

I know all about these "fundraisers" Silas puts on. He invites the richest people he can find—humans and vampires alike—and they donate hefty sums to what they *think* will go to some important cause. In truth, Silas just reinvests the money into the Council. Last year he held an auction for "cancer research," which paid for five new buildings on his property.

"Alex." The manager retreats back to the lobby, papers in hand, and Silas motions with his head for me to join him. We walk side by side in silence, me waiting for him to say something, him taking in the features of the expensive venue.

"My son is returning from Bellevue tomorrow. He's gotten it into his head to host this year's fundraiser." He casts a sidelong glance at me. "He thinks it will make him a more desirable candidate when he starts applying for jobs on the Council next year."

I stifle the urge to make a rude comment. Oliver Chamberlain is a little shit. Mostly because, in the few years I've known him, he's tried and failed to imitate his father. Where Silas is cool and commanding, Oliver is gangly and too overconfident for a high school senior. Once, when his father was out of the room, Oliver tried ordering me around. I ignored him—because I'm not a dog Silas brought home for him to play with—and all that imitated composure melted like ice on hot concrete. I didn't think anyone over the age of ten stomped their feet in fits of anger, but Silas' son proved me wrong.

Of course, he wants to follow in his father's footsteps and join one of the Councils. "Good for him," I respond in my best attempt at politeness.

"I expect you to be in attendance," Silas says, surprising me. The past few years, I've been explicitly told to stay far away from the event. Something about "marring Silas' pristine reputation by having a criminal such as myself hang around."

"I'll be there," I assure him, even though it's the last place I want to be. I want to question why he's even going through with this year's event with all that's going on in the city, but I know the answer. Silas has always been detached from situations such as this.

Sure, a vampire is wreaking havoc, and it's his job as Head of Council to take care of it. But he's not the one directly affected by the violence. The only thing affecting him is the possibility of the vampire community's secret being revealed. Why cancel a chance to receive money from "generous donors" when he and his guests are completely safe?

After issuing orders to pick up a suit from one of his tailors, and sternly reminding me to not be late next week, Silas dismisses me. Maybe I'll solve this thing before then and have this city in my rearview mirror—all thoughts of vampire gangs and charity events left in the dust.

9

Juliette

Scrolling through a dead girl's social media profile is about as chilling as you'd think. I've avoided Serena's accounts like the plague, but in an attempt to learn more about the victims—and possibly find a motive to the killings by connecting them—I decided to look through some of their accounts. The knowledge that my own accounts were close to becoming graveyards never fails to send a shiver down my spine.

Serena is not the focus of my sleuthing tonight. The second victim, Milly Johnson, is.

Besides Serena, Milly is the victim that sticks out to me the most. Her murder happened about a week after Serena died, while I was still in the hospital. It proved to the cops that I wasn't involved and proved to me that the killer didn't just target me and Serena. Or he just targeted Serena and I happened to be there. Laurence Mitchell didn't care, though. He's deluded himself into thinking

I had help killing Milly since I was physically incapable of being at the crime scene.

To anyone who passes through the restaurant, it looks like I'm just doing schoolwork on my laptop in my favorite booth near the window. In reality, I've gone through every social media platform I can think of to get a sense of who Milly Johnson was.

According to her LinkedIn, she graduated last year and just started interning at a law firm downtown—*Law Offices of Thomas and Smelter*. According to her Instagram profile, however, she liked to party.

There's one photo that catches my eye as I scroll through her very public feed. The photo shows her standing in front of a large, red, neon sign that says *Sinner*. The name stands out to me for some reason, and I rack my brain trying to remember where I've heard it before.

I click on the location tag and find hundreds of similar photos as well as shots of people dancing and drinking. It's obvious that Sinner is some type of club. I screenshot Milly's photo for later reference. Maybe Serena went to this club too, which could be why it sounds familiar. It was hard for me to keep track of the places she liked to go since it was never really my scene. And it still isn't—no matter how hard Hayden, Josie, and Meg try to drag me into it.

The Reddit tab I still have open from last night is what reminds me. More specifically, user *TheMonkeysUncle* and their comment.

TheMonkeysUncle: The bar off Lakim? The one near that club Sinner? Don't believe a word out of anyone's mouths down there. Everyone is either high or drunk all the time.

And this other comment:

user93750143356: I don't know, I've seen some weird shit at Sinner. If there's no proof saying otherwise, we shouldn't count out the possibilities of vampires existing.

It could be nothing but the ramblings of people who spend too much time on Reddit, but this is twice in just twelve hours I've seen this club, Sinner, mentioned somewhere.

I could ask Meg or Josie if they know about it. They've certainly visited their fair share of nightclubs since starting college and have been to plenty with Serena. But I've been avoiding all mentions of her around my roommates lately. If I randomly ask about what nightclubs she liked to frequent, that could lead to other questions I'm not up to answering right now.

There is one person who might have more information on this club, and luckily, I still have his number saved.

> **Me:** do u know anything about this club?

I attach the screenshot of Milly's post and, only hesitating for a second, send the message. Impatiently, I wait for a response and exit out of Milly's profiles.

Done with my searching, I go to close out of Facebook, but Serena's profile icon stares up at me from the side where all my friends are listed. I stare at the photo that she hadn't updated since last Halloween—her dressed up in a glittery angel costume, making her appear innocent and demure. She really only had Facebook to keep in touch with some relatives on the East Coast. The photo is one that was hung up at her funeral, tucked between red roses so dark they looked almost black. Serena would've howled with laughter if she knew that was one of the photos they decided to use of her.

Really? The angel costume? I wore that ironically. A pang of overwhelming grief hits me as I imagine her speaking through laughter.

Nope. Not right now. I shut my laptop and emotions down choosing to instead focus on my phone. Maybe if I stare at it long enough, Alex will respond faster.

My eyes drift to the sketchbook peeking out of my bag. I haven't sketched anything for months—my own art account is as active as any of Serena's accounts these days. Years ago, she convinced me to make one, and I gained a bit of a following. But I haven't posted since That Night, and I doubt I ever will again. Art requires passion and inspiration to transfer the life we see around us onto paper. And right now, all I see is death.

Sketching was one of the bright spots in my life, next to Serena and my family. It gave me respite from the taunts of my classmates, the stress of getting good grades, and every other gloomy part of my life. I need it now more than ever, but I can't bring myself to pick up a pad and pencil. As much as I want to sketch, I'm finding that it's just another thing for me to grieve now.

Finally, my phone buzzes with an incoming text, pulling me out of my somber mood.

> **Alex Osman:** I'll look into it.

That's good, someone else to help out with research. I'm a bit relieved, until his next message comes through.

> **Alex Osman:** Thanks for the heads up.

> **Alex Osman:** Stay safe.

Stay safe? We just met, bro.

I drop my phone back on the table, not bothering to respond. Maybe I should just come out and ask him if he wants to partner up? Help each other out? Who am I kidding, I have no experience in hunting vampires. I'm just a victim he wanted details from to pursue his own investigation. Still, his opinion about the club would have been helpful.

"Who are you texting? Your secret lover?" Hayden wiggles his eyebrows and sidles up to the table, already dressed in his busboy uniform even though I'm currently the only one in the restaurant and we don't open for half an hour.

"I don't have a 'secret lover,'" I glare at him.

"So I'm just supposed to believe you took an Uber home last night?" He waves vaguely out the window. "In these uncertain times? Do your parents know?"

No. There's a lot they don't know, and I hope they never find out.

"Did you need something?" I ask with a bit of an edge creeping into my tired tone.

Hayden does a poor impression of a cat meowing angrily, adding claw hands and all. "Someone's in a mood. I came to invite you to a party, but now I don't think I will."

"You're always inviting me to parties."

"A pointless task," he sighs dramatically. "But I'm determined to make you go at least once. This one is different from all those lame ass ones, anyway." He props his hip against the table, enthusiasm clearly written on his face.

I stare out at the darkening sky, wondering if we'll have any customers when the doors open. Earlier I overheard my mom on the phone with the building's leasing company, inquiring about an extension for the rent this month. It pained me to hear her so dejected and desperate.

"Why is this party different?" I ask to push the thoughts of the restaurant's financial struggles out of my head.

"Well..." he draws out the word.

"Hayden." I don't know how much longer I can keep playing this game. The urge to look up Sinner's address and go right now is overwhelming.

"It's the Alpha Pi Gamma annual Halloween bash," he says, with an attitude I'm sure he thinks will convince me it's worth going to.

Serena went to this party every year. She and the rest of our friends always sang its praises, but I've never been interested. I've only been to a few parties since I started college. There was no enjoyment for me at any of them, and I only went because Serena wanted me to have the "full college experience." *Is witnessing a murder and being attacked part of that full college experience, I wonder?*

Before now, I haven't looked at attending these parties in any other way than it being a waste of my time. But now I'm wondering that if Serena frequented these parties, particularly this Halloween bash, someone there might have information on her. Yes, she was my best friend, but she had lots of other friends too. Friends who may know something I don't. Friends who were active in that part of her life.

"Alright. I'll go," I cede.

"Wait, really?" I'm enjoying the stunned look on his face way too much. I should have agreed to go to one of these parties weeks ago just to get him to shut up. I briefly close my eyes, reigning in my temper. My good-natured cousin doesn't deserve it.

"Yes," I groan, opening my eyes.

"Well, you need a costume."

"No I don't," I say with a hint of assuredness, as if Halloween isn't a holiday you're supposed to dress up for.

"*Yes*. Josie, Meg, and I are going as the sun, stars, and moon."

"What the hell am I supposed to be then? The earth?"

"We'll figure something out for you," he waves his hand dismissively. He slaps the table before bounding away. "This is going to be so much fun!"

It's hard to keep my smile in check at his excitement.

10

Juliette

I can't remember the last time I dressed up for Halloween. Maybe my junior year of high school? Not that I'm super dressed up now. Hayden decided I was to be "the night sky" to compliment the moon, sun, and stars costumes my friends are wearing. All my costume requires is that I wear black, so I'm not complaining.

Looking in the mirror, I realize that I kind of look like Alex. And—with a shudder—my stalker. Black hoodie, black pants, black shoes. Josie and Meg wanted me to wear a dress, but it's freezing cold out with a chance of rain. Even if the house party is warm, my current ensemble is infinitely more comfortable than what the other girls will be wearing. I can understand why this is my stalkers and Alex's preferred form of dress.

I finally threw his card away—shredded it, more accurately. I also sent him one final text before deleting his number.

> **Me:** looking into sinner myself. good luck on ur investigation.

He hasn't responded yet. I wonder what he's discovered so far. If he's anywhere close to finding the killer.

A knock sounds at my door, and I open it to find Hayden on the other side. He's wearing a white suit—his moon costume, I guess—and a shit eating grin, holding a large bouquet of roses. The petals are such a deep red they look almost black. A chill goes up my spine when I recognize them as the flowers from Serena's funeral.

What the hell?

"Flower delivery," Hayden says. Snatching the vase from his hands, I notice a folded note sticking out from between the petals. "Could these be from whoever gave you that ride home?"

My eyes shoot to his, gleaming with curiosity and mirth. "Would you let that go," I groan. "It was one time."

He ignores me, practically bouncing on his feet. "So, are these from him? Or her? Or them?"

I roll my eyes. "I don't know. Now go away. I'll be down in a second."

Hayden nods sagely, amused at my expense. He's mistaking my annoyance for embarrassment. I don't think Alex sent me these flowers. Why would he? I need Hayden gone so I can see who really did.

I set the vase on my desk and pluck the card up, unfolding it. I almost drop it when I read what it says.

These looked so beautiful at Serena's funeral. Maybe they'll be used at yours.

For a few long moments, I clutch the paper in my hand and just stare at it, not really seeing the words. Processing them takes a few more. It's not signed, and there's no logo on anything so I wouldn't even be able to track down what shop they came from. It's clear to me what this is, though.

A warning.

The stench of stale beer is even worse when it's seeped into floorboards. This house is disgusting—any relatively clean person's nightmare. It truly is a miracle that any of its inhabitants manage to graduate with passing grades each year. Mismatched Halloween decorations are haphazardly placed around the house, and purple and orange lights drape the walls and ceiling. I genuinely cannot figure out why everyone I know raves about this party.

Despite the decorations and the costumed party goers, I'm not in the Halloween spirit at all. Coupled with the fact that there was another murder last night, my mood to party is no higher than it usually is.

The news of the dean's assistant being killed in her office is buzzing around the house the minute we step through the door.

"Josie!" A girl—who I think is in a study group with my friend—calls across the living room. She rushes over, the expression of someone who has a good piece of gossip to share etched all over her face.

"Hey Laurel!" Josie beams at the girl, apparently oblivious to the fact that Laurel wants to cut right to the tea. "How are y—"

"Did you hear?"

Josie's delicate brow crinkles. "Hear what?"

"The dean's assistant," Laurel says in a rushed whisper, like this piece of gossip is meant to be kept on the downlow. As if everyone at the party isn't already talking about it. She addresses Josie, content to pretend the rest of us aren't here, I guess. Meg and Hayden quickly extract themselves from the conversation, abandoning me.

"What about her?" Josie asks.

Laurel leans in, her petite frame wobbling on the stiletto heels she's wearing. I think she's supposed to be a sexy version of some superhero. "She was *murdered*! In the dean's office!" Laurel can barely keep her morbid interest contained.

Rolling my eyes, I step away from the conversation. Josie must sense my discomfort—and quite frankly my offense—at Laurel bringing up a murder so casually and excitingly, because she excuses herself.

"God she can be so fucking annoying." I almost snort at my bubbly friend's rare show of bitchiness. "I'm sorry, Jules. She must not have noticed you." Josie means well with her placation, but it doesn't do much to soothe me. *That's me, easily unnoticed Juliette.*

Standing on my tiptoes I try to search the crowd for where Hayden and Meg disappeared to. Even with my taller than average height all of the bodies packed into this tight space make it hard to see much beyond cheap costumes and noxious vape clouds. "It's fine."

"You sure?" Josie wrings her hands together, looking around at the crowd. Probably looking for our friends as well, though I'm sure it's more so they can rescue her from this exchange.

"I'm sure," I lie. This seems to soothe her worry as she smiles and declares she's going to go get us some drinks.

Apparently, no one is as bothered as me about an innocent woman—who we just saw alive and well the other day—being murdered in the same building we meet our advisors in.

Sure, I didn't know her that well, but to think she died the same way I watched Serena die—and the way I almost died—makes my stomach hollow out. Add that she was murdered on campus, and my stomach and mind are warring for most unsettled.

Due to two murders now occurring on or near the campus, Pine Falls U might be shutting down—at least until the killer is caught. As if I care that much. My class attendance has steadily declined since That Night and my injured brain makes it hard to focus—or become invested—in topics like brand management. But I am worried for Meg. Pine Falls U may offer subpar education, but it has a great figure skating team. Meg is on track to go to the Olympics in a couple of years but that dream will be dashed if the school ends up shutting down.

Josie never returns, and I don't have any luck locating Hayden or Meg, either. I decide to make the most of the night and start my search for information.

It goes surprisingly well. However, I really do not need to know how many frat guys "almost slept with

Serena" aka Serena probably once said hello to them or accepted a drink from the keg and their fingers grazed.

"Serena Mitchell? Yeah, I knew her!" One guy dressed as a pirate, probably named Chad or Kyle or Josh, shouts to me at the "bar"—really just a kitchen island crammed full of beer and tequila. "She was hot, like *really* hot. I would've slept with her, but she said she had a boyfriend. I didn't want to be disrespectful." He gives me what he probably thinks is a charming smile as he looks me up and down, and I inch further away. There are some useful tidbits in his rambling. Most importantly, Serena openly told people she had a boyfriend.

Was it true? Or did she just say that to get this guy to leave her alone? The latter seems likely since he was two more sleazy smiles away from me pulling the same card. But if she did have a boyfriend, why not tell me, her best friend? I'm trying not to let that sting too much.

"Did she say anything else about this boyfriend?" I raise my voice, the sudden crescendo of the pounding music rattling my head.

"Nah. Just said she had one. We partied a lot together after we first met, but I never saw any guy with her. Anyway, what do you want to drink?" I decline his offer of the frats special "witch's brew punch" and speed walk my way out of the kitchen, away from the nameless frat bro.

Having new information about Serena, even if it isn't true, makes me feel slightly better about coming to this party. It's also making me a bit irritated that Serena's party friends may have known her better than I did.

Taking up a post by the back door I once again wonder where my friends disappeared to. Hayden was quick to inform them that I received flowers from a "secret admirer." An admirer who's truly secret from everyone—including me. I don't think they're admiring me so much as plotting my murder, but semantics. What my friends don't know is I snuck outside and disposed of the *lovely* bouquet in the yard waste when they were piling into the car. I saved the note, though, just in case.

I think I'm most unsettled by the fact that the flowers were delivered to the house. The person who sent me the note—who could also be my maybe stalker—knows where I live. I should check the doorbell camera footage on my dad's phone when I get the chance. Hopefully he hasn't looked at it yet. I don't need my parents worrying about anything else right now.

Is it bad that, if I die, at least I know Alex will be there to find my killer? I wish Serena had that reassurance when she was killed.

Real nice, Juliette. Thinking about death while at a party. Although, to be fair, everyone else brought up the topic first when news of the dean's assistant started circulating.

My phone buzzes. It's a text, from an unsaved number but one that I almost have memorized.

Unknown: Don't go to Sinner.

That's it. That's all the text says.

Don't go to Sinner. Well now I really want to go.

I write back:

Me: who is this?

Sure, it's a little petty and stupid, but I don't care. In fact, I find the corners of my mouth tilting up when I hit send.

"Who are you texting with that smile on your face?" Hayden comes up to me and slings an arm around my shoulders. He's smiling lazily, swaying slightly on his feet and his breath reeks of the witch's brew concoction. "Actually, I think I know who," he sing songs.

"Why are you drunk? I thought you were supposed to be the DD tonight," I demand, exasperated. Mostly with myself for not anticipating this. If I wanted to ensure Hayden didn't drink free booze at a party, then I should have followed him around all night.

He frowns at me. "I thought you were. I don't see a drink in your hand, haven't all night." He waves his own plastic cup in front of my face. Some of it sloshes out the top and splatters on my sneakers.

"Hayden," I say with forced calmness. "I have a brain injury and no license. I can't drive us home."

Said brain injury decided it was a good time to remind me of its presence as soon as we walked in the door—the pounding in my head rivaling that of the music shaking the floorboards. Even though I'm still concussed, I could probably drive us the ten minutes home, but what can I say? I'm a stubborn bitch sometimes, and I don't want to on principle. This is me trying to prove a point, even if it ends up with all of us crashing on the dingy sofas in the frats living room.

My friends do things like this all the time, expecting me to be the boring, responsible one. What if I decided to get drunk tonight as well? Then we'd all be screwed.

Heaving a dramatic sigh, Hayden removes his arm from my shoulders and saunters away, throwing a few "whatevers" and "you're no funs" over his shoulder at me. I try not to let his drunken words affect me, but they leave a bite nonetheless. It's why I never liked partying with Serena. I always felt like I couldn't keep up with her since I wasn't as "fun" as she was. I was always worried she'd realize that and drop me.

My phone buzzes again.

Unknown: Ha ha. It's Alex.

Me: i know a lot of alex's, can u be more specific?

He sends a rolling eye emoji and then:

Unknown: Osman. Stop acting like you don't know who I am. I'm just trying to help you

Uknown: Also, I think its "Alexes."

Me: trying to help me by telling me not to investigate what i want to investigate?

Me: you're joking about the "alexes" right?

Unknown: I hadn't realized you were investigating.

Unknown: But, I'm serious, Juliette. Don't go there.

Unknown: Please.

Unknown: Not joking. The internet says its "Alexes."

He attaches a screenshot of a search page explaining the correct plural form of "Alex."

I can almost hear his deep voice rumbling with the warning, I remember what my name sounded like flowing past his lips...

What the hell? I'm not seriously thinking about him that way, am I? *Get a grip, Juliette.*

I've met him all of two times, and the first time, I was convinced he was my stalker. Well, the second time I was still partially convinced and was also worried that he might kill me. Not to mention that getting close to someone new isn't the best idea for me right now. I can barely manage my current relationships; I don't need to add a new person into the mix. Especially if I'm attracted to said new person. What I need to do is end this conversation and delete his number again.

> **Me:** i can't deal with this right now. goodbye alex.

Once his number is deleted for the second time in as many hours, I turn my phone off. I need to find Meg and Josie and assess their drunkenness. But before I can do that, my phone vibrates in my pocket. I groan inwardly. Was a clean break so hard for him?

> **Unknown:** What do you mean? Is everything okay?

Oh my *god* why does he have to do things like that? The worst part is, I'm sure he actually cares whether or not I'm okay. My concerns on whether he was my stalker and possibly the killer have dissipated greatly.

Fine. If he really wants to know...

> **Me:** no, everything is not okay. i made the mistake of accompanying my friends to a frat party and now they're all drunk.

> **Unknown:** Are you drunk?

I frown at the screen and send back:

> **Me:** that would be unwise given my semi-permanent concussion. also, i don't have my license, so unless i want to drive without one we're stuck here.

And then, to justify my own reasoning I add:

> **Me:** i'm making a point. don't judge me.

The three dots indicating that he's typing appear, then disappear, then appear once more before his messages come through.

> **Unknown:** Never.

> **Unknown:** Where's the party? I'll come pick you up.

I don't want to analyze why my heart flutters at his response and offer.

> **Me:** it's fine, i'll get an uber. it's not fair to make u be my taxi service. again.

> **Unknown:** Lol

> **Unknown:** Send me the location.

I stare at his messages, trying to decide what's stranger: the stoic, non-conversational man who drove me home the other night using "lol" or the way my pulse has skyrocketed at the prospect of him coming here, essentially to my rescue. At getting the chance to see him again...

Without giving myself any more time to hesitate, I drop my location to him. He replies with a thumbs up, because of course he does, and says he'll be here in twenty minutes.

Leaving my vigil by the back door, I head deeper into the party to gather my friends and get them ready to leave.

Twenty minutes pass in a blur of sexy versions of regular costumes, frat guys shouting and jeering, and the occasional person mistaking me for someone else. Luckily my resting bitch face is enough to deter most people from my path, including the aforementioned jeering frat guys. Unluckily, I can't find my friends anywhere. They must've all gone off to who knows where to do god knows what.

I'm standing on my tip toes, searching the crowd in the living room again when the Chad/Kyle/Josh from before approaches me. "Having fun?" he asks. I barely give him a cursory glance. He's at that in-between stage of inebriation—not drunk, but not quite sober either. His eyes are partially glazed, but he's steady on his feet. I don't like the vibes he's putting out at all; I especially don't like them when he places his hand at the small of my back uninvited.

"What are you looking for? Maybe I can help you find it."

His breath is stale and hot from the alcohol, and it takes everything in me not to physically cringe away from him. *I'm fine. I'm fine. I'm fine.*

Before I can tell him to back off, another large hand pries frat guy's hand away and protectively wraps itself around my waist.

"Hey, man, she's with me."

Alex towers over the frat guy like some dark avenging angel. He looks different tonight, but I can't place why. Or maybe it's just my perception of him that's changing.

Getting close to someone new is not what I signed up for when I agreed to speak with Alex the other night. So far, he's proven hard to avoid. The way I'm starting to think and feel about him worries me. Like how my skin tingles where he touches it, and the way my heart races at his words and the sound of his voice.

She's with me. That phrase alone sends a shiver down my spine. I've never really been in a relationship before. Never belonged to someone and had someone belong to me. He's just saying it to get the guy to back off, but a small part of me wonders what it would be like if it were true.

I quickly squash the thought. *Nope, not doing that.*

Chad/Kyle/Josh holds up both hands. "Shit, Alex. Sorry. Didn't realize she was taken."

They know each other? He looks up at Alex, and his usual all-black ensemble and tattoos, with a bit of fear in his eyes.

"She didn't mention a boyfriend earlier, my bad," he stammers, practically groveling at Alex's feet for forgiveness.

Alex waves him off. "Whatever, Tyler." The frat guy, Tyler, dips his head to Alex and scurries off without another look at me. Alex squeezes my waist before dropping his hand hastily, as if catching himself.

"Geez. What did you do to him?" I stare in the direction Tyler ran off to.

Alex isn't paying attention, looking around like he'd rather be anywhere else. I can't fault him for that.

"What?" he asks, distracted and looking anywhere but at me.

"That guy? Tyler? Never mind." I shake my head when I notice he's still glancing around the party distractedly.

"You ready to go?"

It takes me a moment to come back to the present, still occupied with thoughts of Alex's hand and how he knows the grabby frat bro. "Yeah. I need to find my friends first, then we can leave."

I suggest we split up and try to find them, but Alex refuses. I'm sure it has something to do with drunk guys not knowing how to take no for an answer. I don't bother to remind him that I spent two hours here dodging guys all night without his help.

We find Meg in the bathroom, throwing up the witch's brew drink. What originally started as a cute yet sexy stars costume—silver dress, glitter dusting her brown cheeks, and a tiara made of stars—now looks like a complete mess. The glitter is smeared down her face, her dress has stains from her drink, and the tiara is long gone.

We drag her along until we finally locate Josie and Hayden in the backyard. They're making out on a bench, and I almost want to go back to that bathroom and throw up myself. Alex and I have to physically pry them away from each other. Josie's sun costume is at least in better shape than Meg's, but Hayden lost his suit jacket sometime between when I last saw him and now.

"Thanks," I say to Alex once we have all three of them buckled into the backseat of his Mustang.

"Didn't want to leave you stranded and at the mercy of the Sigma Pi Whatever bros," he says flippantly. I know he means it, though.

Through their drunkenness, Hayden, Josie, and Meg still manage to interrogate Alex. But slurred questions of "who are you," "how'd you meet," and "are you dating" don't phase him in the slightest. He gives vague responses to each question, probably figuring they won't remember his answers in the morning anyway. He could confess to being the Pine Falls Knife Man and they'd be none the wiser come sunrise.

When we pull up in front of my parents' house—thankfully Alex refrained from mentioning it was a different house than the false one he dropped me off at last time—I look at the time on my phone. It's close to one in the morning, but I'm wide awake with thoughts of Serena and her supposed boyfriend. The three drunks in the backseat stumble out of the door and up the front path, leaving me alone with Alex.

The air in the car thickens, the music from the party still echoing in my bones. It buzzes through my ears and drowns out my rapid heartbeat. My pulse is beating overtime due to once again being in this car with Alex, but this time I don't think it's from fear.

"What are you supposed to be?" He looks me up and down, a curious frown marring his face.

"Huh?" I'm lost to the way he's staring at me.

"Your costume," he elaborates.

"Oh. Can't you tell? I'm you," I deadpan. He surprises me with a low chuckle. The sound fills the space between us, and I'm enthralled by it, finding myself wanting to hear it again. My own lips twitch in response, another surprise.

"I'm supposed to be the night sky," I clarify. He nods like it makes sense, even though my best effort was to dress in a black hoodie and jeans.

We sit in silence for a few awkward beats. Despite his kindness in the last hour, my earlier frustration at his lack of wanting to help me investigate resurfaces. What would he do if I asked to partner up? Would he go for it if I proposed it? I guess there's no harm in asking.

"Do you need a partner?" I blurt out before I can doubt myself further.

Alex turns in his seat to fully face me, and levels me with a strange look. "No," he says simply, slowly. Like he's confused, and rightfully so. Embarrassed, I fumble with the door handle.

Of course he doesn't need a partner! Maybe if I had more experience he'd be open to it, but he's a literal vampire hunter. He doesn't need the help of a witness slash victim who is only useful for providing a first-hand account of That Night. It's obvious, based on his lack of answers to my questions the other night and giving me nothing on Sinner, that he has no interest in sharing anything with me—let alone having me drag him down on this investigation.

"Okay, thanks for the ride," I repeat my mumbled thanks from the last time he dropped me off and rush out of his car for a different reason. This time it has nothing to do with fear he might kill me but rather dying of embarrassment.

11

ALEX

A COLD BREEZE SWEEPS through the campus scattering dry leaves and loose papers. There was another attack two nights ago, in the exact spot I'm standing, and I was tasked with breaking into the administration office to get a good look. Even though the police already gathered everything they needed yesterday, the place was still locked up tight.

Margie Wilson was the dean's personal assistant, and she was found by the dean yesterday morning. Police believe the Knife Man is responsible for her death due to the gash found in her neck. There's no body on the floor here anymore, and hardly any blood—which confirms my theory about the killer draining his victims.

Margie's body was found near her desk with the estimated time of death being late Thursday night. There was a lecture going on that night, held by none other than Laurence Mitchell—the first victim, Serena Mitchell's, father. It was likely that Margie was working late, or had attended the lecture herself, when she was attacked. But why? Why her? What is this vampire's endgame?

I sigh and snap a few photos for later reference. When I'm done, my thumb hovers over the messaging app, my mind wandering back to Juliette and what she asked last night. If I needed a partner.

The truth is, a partner would be great. But I could never partner with a human. It's not that I don't think Juliette is capable. Rather, Silas would be furious if he knew a human had knowledge of what was really going on. Although, it's not as if she doesn't already know and is using that information to work on her own investigation...

No. Absolutely not. Juliette has been through enough already. There are also strict ramifications for a human finding out about our world without permission from the Council. Most aren't believed if they tell someone they saw or were attacked by a vampire and keep it to themselves after a while—the community doesn't bother with those cases. But I confirmed to Juliette that the Knife Man is really a vampire.

After years of people not believing me, I wasn't just going to sit there and convince her that what she saw wasn't real. I know firsthand how frustrating that can be.

Your parents are dead, Alex.
They died in the accident, Alex.

Staring at my phone and thinking of my texts with Juliette has me remembering the photo she sent the other night—the one of the second victim at Sinner. I was casual with my reply, thanking her for the info. In reality, I couldn't look away from the photo. That stupid neon red sign is burned into my brain at this point.

Two days ago, I wasn't swayed by Silas' adamancy that Slade and the DBC are involved, but after seeing that picture, I'm not so sure. It's not like they're the pinnacle of innocence. They've been involved in kidnappings, robberies, fights, and even more bad shit. The urge to deny their involvement dwindles with each new piece of evidence I find. But part of that denial remains because they've never done anything this out of control. This... *sick*. Slade's chaos is a controlled one.

I haven't shown the photo to my boss yet because I know as soon as I do he'll be marching down to the club with me to arrest Slade. There'd be nothing I could do to stop him either. Once Silas is convinced he's right about something, he'll stop at nothing to compile evidence that backs up his claims—even falsify some if he has to.

And he *would* have to. This case provides the perfect context for him to finally pin something on Slade. If he were to try and arrest the rogue vampire without concrete evidence of his misdeeds, Silas would have a war on his hands. He's tried to get me to turn on Slade but my loyalty isn't so easily swayed. Especially by the man who dangles my freedom over my head so I can do his bidding. No, it's better if I just stay quiet and do as I'm told so I can get out of this city.

This photo might end up proving nothing, or it could prove everything. To my boss, they are one and the same. As long as he gets what he wants in the end.

12

JULIETTE

My own embarrassment haunts me. What was I thinking, asking Alex to partner up? He's a professional... *I think*. Maybe I'm more naïve than I thought, just taking his word for it that he's a vampire hunter. Investigator. *Whatever*.

This case is getting away from me. If I have any hope of solving this on my own, I need to return to the source of my motivation: Serena. The more answers I find surrounding her death, the closer I am to solving the whole thing. She was the first victim—that has to mean something, right? Or maybe it doesn't mean anything at all. The vampire attacked me as well, so he clearly wasn't being selective with his food.

The nightclub, Sinner, is at the top of my list to investigate, but right now I'm headed to Laurence Mitchell's house—Serena's childhood home. After Serena's funeral, I went back to the house we shared to... I don't even know what. Say goodbye? Look for her phone or diary?

Whatever my reasoning, when I got there, all of her things were already gone. It seemed that Serena's father had already sent his people to pack up her stuff. Probably to cart it all off to a landfill. What use would he have for all her worldly possessions?

However, since Serena wrote in a diary religiously, there's a chance Laurence kept some of her most personal belongings, and I need to at least *try* to convince him to let me take a look. Anything of hers that could point me in the direction of her potential boyfriend, or any other secrets she might have kept, could get me one step closer to finding her killer.

Laurence Mitchell lives in a gated neighborhood twenty minutes outside of Pine Falls. The houses are grand and no doubt five times the price of my parents' modest suburban home. There are no bus stops nearby, so to get in, I had to walk five miles in the rain. Then I had to climb over the fence half a mile down from the gate. It's the only spot without cameras. Serena told me about it in high school when I asked how she was always able to sneak out. I could've asked Hayden to just take me through the gate pretending we were delivering food or something, but the last thing I need is for him to start bombarding me with more questions.

If only I had a partner with a car who could do this with me, I think bitterly. Attending the lecture I skipped this afternoon might have been the wiser option to avoid the rain.

A motion-activated witch pops up as I pass a house, cackling through the rain and grey afternoon. Hayden would definitely get a kick out of it, but for me, the assault of its high-pitched laughter and cartoonishly gnarled face nearly cause me to jump out of my skin.

I've only been to the Mitchell house twice before. The first time was when Serena and I were eight, just after she and her father moved here from the East Coast. She invited me over for a playdate—supervised by her nanny at the time—and I thought it went well, until she told me the next day that I wasn't allowed over anymore. Serena only ever came to my house or we went to the park after that. It confused me greatly, and I would have thought Serena didn't like me if we hadn't continued to hang out together.

It wasn't until much later when Serena confessed that her father was the one who didn't want me around. She felt bad about it, but there wasn't much she could do since he never provided a solid reasoning for banning me from the house.

The second time I went to her house was our sophomore year of high school. It was the night of the homecoming dance, and Serena was supposed to come over to my house to get ready. When she never showed up and didn't answer any of my calls or texts, my mom and I drove over to her house to check on her. She was on the front lawn when we arrived, in a shouting match with her father. Laurence composed himself as we pulled up and marched back into the house, slamming the front door with finality. Even though the argument always gnawed at my curiosity, I never pressed Serena about it. She stayed with us for a few weeks after that.

In our thirteen years of friendship, she always veered away from the topic of her father. She didn't love him, and it seemed to me that he didn't love her. Serena claimed it was because she resembled her mother so much, that her father was wracked with grief over his dead wife anytime he looked at his daughter. Whether she was trying to convince me or herself with that explanation, I don't know.

If I wasn't ninety percent sure that a vampire was responsible for the murders, my first suspect would be Laurence Mitchell. Then again, maybe he is a vampire. Now that I know they actually exist, I can't help but suspect every person who crosses my path, even the people I'd least suspect.

I climb up the driveway of the Mitchell house, stopping once to admire the silver Maserati parked there. He has a six-car garage, yet this beauty has to sit out in the rain? Shaking my head at the display of wealth,

I wonder what could be inside taking up space inside the massive garage. The worth of that car alone could probably save my family's restaurant, and we'd still have enough left over that we wouldn't have to worry about it for months.

The house itself is beautiful yet extravagant. Rain-slicked vines snake up the pillars lining the path to the front door standing twice my height and just as wide, with an ominous brass lion doorknocker nailed to the wood. Ignoring the lion's intense metal stare, I ring the doorbell. The melodic tune chimes for all of two seconds before the door is pulled open.

"Can I help you?" An older woman with bright red hair and wearing an honest to god, old fashioned maid uniform frowns down at me. Taking a quick glance at myself I see what she's so sour over. My sneakers and the hem of my jeans are streaked with mud, and my oversized Pine Falls U sweatshirt is soaking wet. If the drops of water coating my forehead are any indicator, my hair is probably a stringy, sopping mess.

I haven't been focused on myself for months, and it's never been more apparent to me than right now. Why would I bother with better fitting clothes and an umbrella when I have more important shit to be doing?

Sorry, lady, you're just going to have to mop up after me when I leave. If I'm even allowed inside, that is.

"I need to speak to Laurence Mitchell," I say in my most authoritative voice. When she doesn't budge I add, "I was a friend of his daughter's."

She gives me a sympathetic look. "So sad what happened to her." I lower my gaze, putting on my best distraught expression, the one I'm sure I wore the night Serena was killed and haven't used since. "Yes. She was my best friend."

"Oh, I do recognize you! Juliette, right?" I meet her eyes and find them full of pity. The maid sighs—either resigning herself to the mess she'll have to clean up by letting me past the threshold, or sadness at Serena's death—and holds the door open wide.

"He's in his office. Down the hall, second door to the left."

Muttering a quick "thanks," I scurry in the direction she indicated. I try to keep the dripping to a minimum, but unfortunately, short of stripping in the middle of this ostentatious mansion, there's nothing I can do about it.

Normally, I would want to take in this architectural dream of a house and take some mental images to sketch later, but I'm too nervous thinking about what Laurence Mitchell will say to me. At best, he'll kick me out. At worst… I don't even want to know what he might do. Especially if he really is the Knife Man. That fear I felt in

Alex's car the first time is magnified by a hundred. I'm alone in this man's house.

What am I doing?

Well, I'm here now. I didn't walk five miles in the rain to back out due to a little anxiety. I'm intent on seeing this errand through.

The door to Laurence Mitchell's office looms in front of me. It's just a normal, wooden door, but it holds a sense of foreboding behind it. Like it's warning me away.

I'm fine.
I'm fine.
I'm fine.

My mantra calms my racing heart. Taking a deep breath, I push away the fear creeping up me like the vines outside and knock twice.

"What." His deep voice rumbles through the wood, irritation prevalent in his tone. I twist the knob and walk in. "You better have a good reason for interrupting me, Joann," he grumbles. That must be the housekeeper's name. Laurence is hunched over his sleek mahogany desk, flipping through papers furiously.

"Where's Serena's stuff, Laurence?" I cut right to the chase, matching my tone to his. His head snaps up at the sound of my voice, not Joann's, filling the room.

Laurence Mitchell somehow manages to look down at me from his seated position, giving my soaked state a disgusted once-over. He already dislikes me for some reason, so who cares if I give him another reason to.

Laurence presses a button on his desk phone and barks into it, "Caleb. Get in here. Now." I wait near the doorway, dripping all over the hardwood floor, staring him down. Now that I don't feel so bad about my soaked state I try to let loose some intentional drips.

This man thought I was responsible for Serena's murder, even when I was in a coma in the hospital. The least he could do is allow me access to wherever he stashed her things.

"Where. Is. Her. Stuff." I repeat, firmer this time. He regards me silently. "Is Caleb going to get it?" I add when his stare becomes too much. Why else would he call whoever Caleb is in here?

Laurence's thin lips twist into a smile, slow and cold. "Perhaps. He's the one who takes out the trash." He doesn't elaborate, and I'm not sure what else to say. The barb stings, but I try not to let it burrow any deeper. There's nothing I want from this man besides his daughter's stuff. What he thinks of me shouldn't matter.

I take the silence as opportunity to look around his office. It's not as big as you might think the all-important Laurence Mitchell's office would be. Especially given the size of his house. All it contains is a desk and office chair, two chairs for guests, and lots of bookshelves. It's also suffocatingly masculine, with dark wood paneling covering the walls and matching hardwood on the floor. Photos hang behind the desk. One shows a group of young men in black and white. I'm too far away to make out all the details, but there's an insignia at the bottom. It looks like a 'B' with some sort of coat of arms around it.

As I let my gaze wander, Laurence keeps his own fixed firmly on the papers at his desk, acting as though I'm invisible. His posture is stiff, his fingers flicking through pages like he's annoyed at their very existence. There's a cigar stub cooling off in a tray to his right, the lingering scent of spice and smoke causing a prickle in my brain—the start of a new headache. I rub my temple in a meek effort to combat it.

A few moments later the door flings open. The lookalike assistant who was trailing Laurence around campus the other day steps into the room. "Yes, Mr. Mitchell?" The man who must be Caleb rushes into the room, a bit on edge. His eyes dart from me and then back to his boss, just as twitchy as the last time I saw him.

"Please escort this young woman out of the house and send Joann in here." He gives me another contemptuous look. "Apparently we need to have a discussion about who my housekeeper allows inside." Of course he didn't call Caleb in to help me.

For a moment, I feel bad that I got Joann in trouble, but that's soon wiped away by anger at his blatant refusal to give me this one simple thing. After witnessing his daughter's murder, you'd think this is the least he could do. And I didn't walk five miles in the freezing rain to be denied so quickly.

"Where is her stuff?" I demand again.

Laurence ignores me, looking back down at his papers and muttering, "Caleb, take care of this." His assistant grips my arm and forcibly drags me away from his boss.

I struggle in his grip, trying to shake him off, but the jerking of my body only makes the pain in my head flare to a fiery intensity. It doesn't even do any good—his hand is like a band of steel around my arm. How the hell is he this *strong*? He definitely doesn't look it with his string bean figure outlined by his perfect suit. I dig in my heels, but that only makes me slip on the puddle I left on the floor.

Caleb easily pulls me to my feet with both hands under my arms, picks me up without much effort, and carries me out of Laurence's office back to the entrance of the house.

"Put me down!" I shout, huffing and kicking my feet in a meager attempt to delay the inevitable—and salvage my pride. I figured Laurence would make me leave, but not in such a humiliating way.

For a moment, I'm not in his mansion but my old campus housing. I shut my eyes, but even in the darkness behind my lids, I'm being gripped by the vampire who killed Serena instead of Laurence's assistant. My heart starts to race. Any moment now, he's going to slam me against the wall. He's going to put his teeth to my neck and drain me of blood. He's—

"Caleb! What in God's name..." Joann's voice interrupts my panic and my eyes fly open to see her standing in the foyer, her hand on her hip and a mop in the other.

"Open the door so this girl can go home. Then the boss wants to see you in his office." Even after carrying my struggling body, Caleb doesn't sound the least bit breathless. But his voice has a nasally quality, which undermines his attempt at imitating his boss. His nails dig into my skin beneath my sweatshirt, and I hate that right now I'm too paralyzed by memories to fight back any harder. I don't know what I was thinking coming here. I humiliated myself and didn't even get Serena's diary.

Joann hurries to the front door, opening it wide and avoiding my narrowed gaze. Caleb swiftly exits the house and plops me on my feet at the bottom of the front steps.

Right in front of Alex.

13

Juliette

"Juliette?" Alex has his hood up but pushes it down to get a better look at me. Wide eyed, I stare at him, completely embarrassed that he bore witness to my forced removal from Laurence Mitchell's house.

So, I do what anyone would do in my situation.

I run away.

I almost slip on my sprint down the driveway, using the Maserati as leverage to regain my balance. "Juliette!" Alex calls after me through the rain, his voice rising above the water pounding the pavement. It's hard to ignore him, but I sure make a good effort. I pass his old Mustang parked by the curb, briefly wondering what story he must've spun to get through the security gate, and book it for the fence.

"Juliette! Wait!" He calls again. I slow down enough to glance over my shoulder at him. I'm overreacting. There's no reason I couldn't have just stood there and had a normal conversation with him, but embarrassment is a mysterious force, especially for those of us who try so hard not to care what other people think. And for me, embarrassment usually leads to anger, which is hitting me in full force right now.

Alex rejected my offer to work together—without any hesitation, doing wonders for my self-esteem—and now... now he's seen me literally thrown out of someone's house. If he didn't want to work together before, he most certainly doesn't want to after witnessing that shit show.

The whole situation is just a giant reminder that I'm in over my head. I don't hold any sway or have a single shred of authority in the *human* world. That was proven when Laurence Mitchell refused to answer a simple question about his daughter's belongings and then threw me out of his damn mansion. What will I do when I need to deal with vampires?

Alex probably never doubts himself in situations like this. Intimidation radiates off him like the fear radiating from the community. Those sharp grey eyes make someone want to tell him everything—even people like Laurence Mitchell... Probably.

A hand wraps around my elbow and jerks me to a stop halfway down the street. "Stop," Alex says, not sounding the least bit out of breath for someone who just sprinted a quarter mile after me. I'll add *do half vampires have enhanced speed?* to my list of ongoing questions about the vampire community.

"Let me give you a ride home. It's pouring rain."

"Oh is it? I hadn't noticed," I spit out, sarcasm dripping on every word. As if on cue, my entire body shivers. Though that might have something to do with Alex's hand warming my skin through my sweatshirt rather than the icy downpour. Maybe a bit of both.

He rolls his eyes at my remark. My sarcasm would have come across stronger had I not just participated in some involuntary exercise. "I'm serious. You'll catch a cold in this weather."

I cross my arms together, trying to hide the shivers now wracking my body. Finally, he drops his hand and steps back. Droplets of rain cling to his dark hair, making it look like spilled ink across his brow. I try again to push down my growing attraction towards him. He's annoyingly hard to resist, in a bad boy tortured soul kind of way. Maybe it's a good thing we aren't working together. He would be an unwanted distraction.

"That's just a thing people say; I don't think it's actually true," I lie through my chattering teeth. He rubs at his jaw, the tattoos shifting with every move of his fingers. I catch myself staring and quickly look away. Freezing my ass off in the rain is definitely not the time to develop a fascination with Alex's body.

He takes my hand in his and tugs me back down the street. It's warm and rough and feels nice against my own cold and wrinkled one. "Let's go, Juliette." His tone leaves no room for argument and though I do consider myself a stubborn individual, my pride isn't so fragile as to deny a ride home in the rain. The temperature has dropped significantly with the sun, and standing here for barely a few minutes has me reminiscing on times I was warm and dry.

Once we're inside the car, Alex cranks the heat up all the way, and we sit for a few minutes to let everything thaw. The Mitchell house looms outside us, mocking me.

I alternate between blowing on my hands, rubbing them together, and sticking them in front of the vents, feeling like I just jumped into a frozen lake fully clothed. Alex leans back in his seat, watching me and completely uncaring that he also just got soaked by the rain.

"Aren't you cold?" I speak through chattering teeth and look him up and down, trying to spot any of the same dampness on his clothes that's sticking mine to my skin, but the black fabric hides any trace of rain.

He just shrugs, making me scoff in disbelief. Again, I think maybe it's for the best that we aren't working together. I don't think we'd get much done in between our collective annoyance and non-answers.

I pull off my sweatshirt, realizing a moment too late that the only thing I have on underneath is a white top. My bra is clearly visible through the wet fabric and I hastily cross my arms in an attempt to cover my chest. Alex, who was closely watching my movements, shifts his gaze, clears his throat, and fumbles with the gear shift before putting it in drive to take us away from Laurence Mitchell's fancy neighborhood.

"So, what were you doing at Laurence Mitchell's place?" Alex asks after a few minutes of silence.

"Wasting my time." The response is vague, and I feel a small amount of satisfaction at the irritation prevalent in his clenched jaw. I've asked him questions too, and I always get ambiguous answers from him. Why should I need to explain myself?

He unclenches his jaw and asks, "How was it a waste of time?"

"It just was, okay?" I snap, immediately regretting my harsh tone. Especially when a new tension forms around Alex's mouth, keeping his gaze firmly on the road. Here he is, giving me *another* ride home, and I'm snapping at him.

Clearly getting the hint that I'd rather not answer his questions, Alex is silent for the remainder of the drive. I debate asking him about Sinner again, this time in person, but I'll probably get the same information he told me before. *Thanks for the info. Don't go there.* I imagine his flat, deep voice warning me away in person this time.

At this point, a clean break is probably best. He'll drop me off, I'll delete his number again, and hopefully we'll part ways for good. No questions asked. No favors owed. No exchange of information that could prompt further curiosity. Even if I am itching to know what *he* was doing at Laurence Mitchell's house. Why he always seems to know where I am and why he bothers to help me, whether I ask for it or not.

The car rolls to a stop outside my own home, my mom's inflatable Halloween decorations lying deflated and soaked in the yard. I used to love decorating with her and making our house the most festive on the block. Now Halloween is a week away, and I couldn't care less.

Alex hangs an arm over the steering wheel and peers over at me. Avoiding his gaze, I push the door open in my usual routine of scurrying away from his car. "Thanks for the ride, again." I hop out without looking back, slamming the door shut right as he calls my name.

It's only when I race up to the front door that I realize I left my sweatshirt in the car. How I could've forgotten when it's pouring rain and I'm in a thin short sleeved shirt, I have no clue. That's the *Alex effect* I suppose. His car still idles on the curb, but there's no way I'm going back for it. I didn't like that sweatshirt, anyway. I'm due for a new one.

I rush inside and try to sneak up the stairs when I hear Hayden call out, "Woah, not so fast!" I reluctantly slow down to hear what he has to say. "You've got *another* flower delivery, Miss Popular," he grins. Then, holding up a finger, he disappears into the kitchen. He returns a moment later holding the same deep red roses from the other night. I take an involuntary step back at the sight of them, grappling for the wall to keep me steady.

I am not emotionally or mentally sound enough for yet another threatening note tucked into Serena's funeral flowers.

"Don't just stand there—take them!" Hayden encourages with a wide smile. My sweet, ignorant cousin. He has no idea what the last flower delivery held or what this one likely holds as well.

Hesitantly, I take the vase from him like a snake is coiled inside ready to strike if I move too fast. As predicted, there's a note neatly folded and tucked between the petals. "Who delivered these?" I ask.

"Don't know. They were on the porch when I got home. I tried to check the doorbell camera, from today and the other night, but the battery was dead," he shrugs. I know for a fact that my dad changed the batteries in the doorbell last week. He, like everyone in this city, is paranoid about the Knife Man.

"Thanks for bringing them in," I mumble and try to act as normal as possible while heading up to my room. *Nothing amiss here, no amateur detective being sent threatening notes via flowers used at her best friend's funeral.*

I can't believe Hayden doesn't recognize them. Or maybe I'm just *that* messed up that all the details from my friend's funeral are permanently etched in my mind, right down to the floral arrangements.

Footsteps follow me up the stairs, and Hayden asks in a goading tone, "So? Who are they from? That guy from last night?"

"I'm surprised you even remember that," I deflect.

"Please. I wasn't *that* drunk."

"Drunk enough to make out with Josie."

"That? That was nothing."

"I'm sure she feels the same," I mutter.

"She does!" Hayden says defensively. "I swear. It's just something we do for fun sometimes." Not wanting to think more about the two of them together, I quit adding to this line of conversation.

When I reach my room, my cousins' presence still heavy at my back, I turn around and block the entrance, pointedly repeating, "Thanks for bringing the flowers in." He backs off, thankfully taking the hint, and ambles down to his room.

After switching the light in my room on, I shakily shut the door and place the vase on my desk. I really don't want to see what this one says, but morbid curiosity is killing me. I pull out the note and it takes me three tries to unfold it. It reads:

I wonder what happens to girls who stick their noses where they don't belong.

Similar to the last note, it takes me a second to process the words. Definitely a threat. I shove the paper into the top drawer of my desk where the other one lives, slamming it shut. Is the killer sending these notes? Or is it my stalker? Are they one and the same? Are they even *real*?

I sink down into my desk chair and rub my temples, the headache from before now waging a full-on war inside my skull. My heart won't stop its thrashing against my chest, and for the first time in a long time, I want to cry. Waves of helplessness and fear crash over me, similar to That Night. Seeing these notes transports me back to my old house—watching Serena die and feeling fangs pierce my skin.

With a heavy sigh, I decide that this particular episode of the *Juliette is not naked but afraid* show is over. I roughly grab the vase and throw my door open, marching back down the stairs and outside. Icy rain lashes at me, but my anger keeps me from noticing, or caring.

Glass shatters into dozens of pieces as I toss the vase in the garbage bin. The aggression is cathartic, even if it might have been a bit unnecessary. Maybe whoever sent the flowers is watching me right now. Good. Let them see what I think of their little *gifts*. I hope they see that they can't shake me... at least not outside the confines of my bedroom.

As soon as I have the thought, I feel eyes on me. *Shit*. My brazenness leaves as soon as it arrived. But when I turn around, I'm met with familiar grey eyes and a stoic expression.

"Alex?" I question the man who has now appeared unexpectedly in front of me twice in the same day. I thought he would've left by now.

He holds up my sweatshirt, the light grey color now three shades darker due to the rain. The Pine Falls U logo blends into the now dark fabric. "You left this in my car," he mutters distractedly, too busy trying to look at what I threw into the trash bin behind me. I strain to hear him over the pounding of water against the metal bins. "You should go inside," he adds sympathetically, his attention returning to me. I really should remember that I'm wearing a flimsy white top by now. A very see-through top. I was so on edge from the flowers that what I was wearing and the chill in my bones disappeared for a bit. Now, all that discomfort comes back with a vengeance.

I don't argue with him this time, motioning him to come with me into the house. Why should he be left in the rain when we have dry towels and central heating?

Alex follows close behind, and I lead him to the laundry room, going as fast as I can to minimize the drippage since we aren't lucky enough to have a maid like Laurence Mitchell. I grab two towels from a cabinet and hand one to Alex, using the other to dry myself off and wrap around my top.

"Thanks," he says, setting my wet sweatshirt on the dryer. I try not to look too creepy as I watch him towel off his face and hair before raking his fingers through the strands.

"Thanks for bringing my sweatshirt back," I say at the same time he asks, "Why were you throwing flowers away?"

"You first," we say at the same time, again.

"Jinx," we echo, and then, "Jinx again." The beginnings of a smile form on my face. Alex mirrors my expression.

"Damn," he shakes his head, that small smile growing. "So who owes who a soda?"

"I think we both do? I was never too sure of the rules." I clear my throat, the hint of a smile disappearing. "What were you saying?"

"Right." His own smile fades as mine does. "What was with the flowers in the garbage can?"

"Oh. That." I bite my lip, wondering what to tell him. So much for our clean break.

"Someone's been sending them to me. It's a little weird because they're the same type of flowers used at Serena's funeral." Shrugging, I try to downplay it, but Alex isn't convinced.

"What the fuck?" The intensity in his tone makes my heart skip a beat. "Juliette, that's a more than a *little weird*."

"It's nothing..."

"But it's happened before." He levels me with a look. "Were there notes with the flowers?"

My hesitation is answer enough. He purses his lips. "What did the notes say?"

Again, I hesitate.

Why is he even here? Why couldn't he just throw my jacket away? Why did he have to come back and be nice and worry about me?

But he's here now, and it'd be a relief not to have to keep these notes to myself. Plus, I could gauge his reaction as he reads them. I'm pretty sure he's not the killer or my stalker, but if he acts like he's never seen the notes before that will be proof enough for me. Or maybe he's just a *really* good actor. Whatever. He hasn't killed me yet, right?

"They're in my room if you want to look at them." I sigh, then trudge back upstairs, thankful that the door to the basement is shut and Hayden is blasting music. It only takes a few moments of rifling through my drawer before I pull out the two notes and their not-so-thinly-veiled threats against my life. Alex looks them over with a furrow in his brow, eyes hard like granite. Maybe he isn't responsible. I really want to believe he isn't.

"I changed my mind," he finally says.

"About what?" I go to take the notes back from him but he holds them out of my reach.

"I could use some help..." He trails off, almost sounding... nervous. "If you're still down?" His fingers rub at the notes absently, his eyes intent on mine.

For a second, I don't even know what to say. I'm in over my head, I know that. Especially with the notes and school and my family's restaurant. Add vampires to the mix and I really have no clue how to go about solving this case. But this feels grossly like pity, and I don't want that to be his reasoning for wanting to work with me.

He must sense my train of thought because he adds, "I didn't initially turn down your offer because you're incapable. There are rules in my world that prevented me from accepting." He sighs and tosses the notes onto my desk. "But fuck it. You already know what's really going on in this city. And I don't think you should be doing this alone anymore."

My ability to form words has apparently stopped working, so I just nod. Does he want to protect me? Is that what this is? Whatever it is, I'll take it.

"You want to be partners?" I ask, just to confirm it once more, and also make sure that he didn't hit his head sometime between the last time I saw him and today.

"Two people working together for mutual benefit," he clarifies, holding up a tattooed finger.

I stifle my smirk and hold my hand out. "Partners?"

Sighing, he rolls his eyes up at the ceiling, the familiar movement not irritation but feigned exasperation. He sticks his own hand out and I grip it in mine, feeling his warm palm against my own chilled one, and give it a firm shake.

"When we first met, you said something about a stalker," Alex says when we pull our hands apart.

"Yeah..." I trail off, embarrassed.

His stare pins me in place. "So, what's that about?"

I shrug. "I don't know. I've been seeing a person; their face is always hidden."

"Juliette—" he starts, worry creasing his brow.

"I have a brain injury. Who knows if what I see can even be trusted? How do I know that you're even real?" I joke to try and ease the tension, but he doesn't laugh. Not even a pity chuckle.

"I'm real. Trust me." He sighs and runs his hand through his hair again. "Next time you see this maybe stalker, point him out to me, alright?" I open my mouth and then close it again, like a gaping idiot. Alex wants to help me with this case, or rather wants *me* to help *him*. And I think he wants to protect me, even though he didn't outright say it. Now he believes me about maybe having a stalker. My pulse thumps erratically at his words and the intense way he's looking at me.

"Yeah, sure," I finally say, distracted by a lock of dark hair that hangs over his eyes. My fingers itch to push it back from his face.

"Good," he replies.

I snap my attention back to him, and I realize almost immediately what a mistake that is. He's staring at me with such an open, concerned look it makes my once lively heart swell. I'm not doing this alone anymore, and that's enough to make me feel a bit of hope.

14

JULIETTE

ALEX IS COMING OVER today. Being partners—sorry, *two people working together for mutual benefit*—unfortunately did not magically solve the case immediately. We're going to "discuss the investigation" (his words) and then figure out the best way to put our combined skills and knowledge to use. Whether Alex changed his mind about working together because he feels protective of me after seeing the notes or because he genuinely wants a partner, I don't know nor do I care. It's a relief knowing I won't be doing this alone anymore.

As previously established, solving a murder is hard. Well, *trying* to solve a murder is hard. My murder board has looked the same for a while now. There's nothing I can see that connects the victims, and I'm being warned against one of my only leads by Alex.

It's times like these I wish I could talk to Serena. One, so she could just tell me who killed her. And two, because she always gave the best advice and encouragement.

What would she say to me now? *There's nothing you can't do once you set your mind to it, Juliette. You're the most determined person I know.* It's her voice I'm imagining—although the memory of it fades with each passing day—but the words don't feel right. She was the determined one. The brazen one. The fearless one. I'm just... Juliette. Serena's friend. The brunette one. The quiet one. The forgettable one.

The chime of the doorbell pulls me from my morose thoughts.

Alex is here.

I haven't really come up with a good excuse for how I know him or why he's at our house. Luckily, my friends were too drunk the other night to fully wonder where he came from, even if Hayden was curious the day after. The best I have is "study" partner. It's not entirely untrue, and as long as the other occupants of the house don't linger around my room or find the murder board, I think we'll be fine.

I fly down the stairs, but Mom beats me to it, giving me a strange look over her shoulder as she opens the front door. My parents decided to close the restaurant for the day. Even before a killer was on the loose, Sundays were never busy.

"Hello. Can I help you?" Her tone is polite enough, but it's understandably laced with suspicion due to the stranger at our doorstep.

"Yeah, I'm here to see Juliette," Alex responds from across the threshold. I'm practically vibrating as I push past my mom and hold the door open wider for him.

"I'm here. Let's go." I motion for him to follow me in, and he does after a moment's hesitation and an apologetic look to my mom.

She doesn't let us get far. "Hold on just a minute," she says. "Jules, aren't you going to introduce us to your friend?" I can see it in her eyes—hope. Hope that I've maybe, *finally*, started to move on from Serena's death and my attack. This would be the first time in forever that I've invited a friend over who didn't already live with us. Probably the first time I've ever invited a guy over, actually.

"It would be rude not to." My dad saunters in from the living room, Hayden right on his heels. My cousin is positively giddy at the awkwardness now radiating throughout the foyer.

"Right. Sorry. This is Alex. We are working on a project together." I flash him a close-mouthed smile and hope he understands my discretion at our working together.

"Yeah," he says slowly, catching on.

"That's so strange—I've literally never seen you before... Until the other night," Hayden adds, tilting his head in mock contemplation.

Meanwhile, my dad is eyeing Alex like he's his next meal—the irony of Alex being the vampire in the room is not lost on me. I ignore his scrutiny. I know it's just an act because my dad is the furthest thing from judgmental. When Hayden came out as bi a few years ago, my dad insisted we all start attending the annual Pride parade as a family to support my cousin.

My mom shifts her attention from Alex to me. "What's this project? I haven't heard you mention it before now." Before I can fabricate another lie, she turns to Alex. "Are you a marketing major, too, Alex?"

"You don't strike me as one." Hayden says, rubbing his chin in a show of guessing Alex's nonexistent major. His eyes dip to my "partner's" tattooed hands, curious. "I think the real question is, what class is this *project* for?" He wiggles his brows, smirking. "Some kind of... sexual studies class, maybe?"

"Oh my god!" I exclaim, cheeks reddening.

"Hayden Levitt-Jennings!" My mom halfheartedly admonishes, but I notice she's holding back a laugh, my dad too. They're probably secretly grateful for his goading comments since they're way too polite to make Alex uncomfortable.

"C'mon, Alex. Let's go." His warm hand is almost an expected comfort at this point, and I use it to tug him up the stairs. When the warmth from his hand transfers to me—traveling up my arms to my face and down my chest—I quickly let go, mortified. With the way my cheeks are surely flushed, I'm thankful my back is to him.

Once we're safely in the confines of my room I sink into my desk chair, exhaling loudly. "Sorry," I say sheepishly, feeling the color in my cheeks. "Hayden's just annoying. I'm sure you put that together the other night."

Alex peers around my room, and I'm struck with an image of him doing the same thing at a crime scene, searching for evidence. "Is he your brother?"

"My cousin, but he's basically like a brother to me. My parents adopted him after his own passed away." Alex's whole body goes tense for a moment, and I probably wouldn't have noticed if I wasn't observing him so carefully.

Snapping back to himself, he stops his assessment of a shelf of trinkets on the opposite wall, gingerly placing one back where he had lifted it. It's so strange having him in my room. Last night he wasn't in here very long, and not all the lights were on. Plus, there was the more pressing matter of the threatening notes. There's an obvious juxtaposition between him in his all-black attire and the pastel decorations of my cluttered room.

"That's cool that you guys are so close." The words feel strained, the air tenser than it was a moment before. "So." He straightens, and his face automatically shifts, like a slate being wiped clean. "I brought you something." Reaching into his hoodie pocket, Alex produces a small soda can and tosses it to me.

My brows furrow in confusion after catching the can and inspecting the label. "What's this for?"

"I owe you a soda, remember?" he replies, giving a nonchalant shrug. The corners of my mouth twitch as I stare at the can. Unknowingly, he brought my favorite—*Dr. Pepper*. "I thought I owed you one?" I ask, forcing the smile off my face.

"Get it to me later." He winks, swiping a hand through his dark hair, and my flush returns full force. Seriously, does he not know how attractive he is sometimes? I'm close to developing heart palpations against my will based on his presence alone.

While I'm preoccupied with the strands of hair that have fallen over his brow, his eyes zero in on the murder board laying on my floor. A look crosses his face when he spots it, a look I can only describe as amused intrigue. "Crafty," he smirks. "Normally I just write everything down and hope for the best, but this is certainly another method."

Is he teasing me?

"Don't make fun of my murder board," I huff.

His lips twitch. "I wasn't. I was admiring it."

"*Sure.*" I roll my eyes.

He leans against my dresser, looking like a Rodin sculpture come to life. He's got on that same black hoodie I've only ever seen him in. Is it his only one, or does he have a closet full of them? My fingers flex on their own accord, itching to grab my pad and pencil to sketch him—hoodie and all. Since Serena died, I haven't sketched anything for fun, and it bothers me that my urge to do so now would just be a waste of time since it won't further the case.

Alex's own fingers flex, the ink stretching across his knuckles. From what I've seen, there's no coherent design. Just random images, like someone used his body as a canvas to practice on. I'm still wondering if his tattoos extend past his hands since I've never seen him without that damn black hoodie.

Tattoos can tell you a lot about a person. And, as I currently know very little about the man across from me, I would love to see what he deemed important enough to permanently ink onto his skin.

"It's a bit morbid, what with all the dead body photos, but it gets the job done." Alex steps closer and lifts the board up so it's leaning against the bed. "Oh look, I made the cut." My gaze drifts to his face then to the board where Alex is studying the news article I printed out. I guess the boy orphaned from that accident in Vermont ten years ago *was* him.

Something passes over his expression as he reads through the short article, but I can't decipher it. Guilt has me shifting uncomfortably as he stares at the printout. Guilt that he's most likely reliving whatever the accident was, and guilt that I included him on the board in the first place. I hope he doesn't think I think he's a suspect.

A few tense moments of silence pass until he seems to shake himself out of his stupor and taps on a sketch by Serena's photo; the one of the killer leaning over her body. What I remember of it, anyway. "Did you draw this?" At my nod he raises his eyebrows and says, "It's good."

Heat rises to my cheeks once more with the praise, and I look away in an attempt to counteract the butterflies in my stomach.

It's a hobby I've kept mostly to myself, besides the art account I made, but no one knew who I really was with that. I would have loved to go to art school, but my parents have high expectations of me. There's a certain pressure that comes with being an only child—even if they treat Hayden as their own.

"I wouldn't have pegged you as a marketing major." He tilts his head at me, studying me like he did my room.

Avoiding his gaze I ask, "Did you go to college?"

He snorts and replies with a simple, "No."

"I wonder what you were like in high school," I muse. Probably one of those quiet kids who sat in the back of the class. The ones who doodled in the margins of every assignment and secretly loved anime. And even though no one knew their name, they were one of the top students in the school. Not like I'd know that from my own experience or anything...

"Didn't go there, either," Alex doesn't meet my eyes as he responds quietly, back to focusing on the murder board. I decide not to bring up anything else about his educational history. God knows I don't like to dwell on my high school years. It seems a bit of a shock to me, though, that a vampire hunter doesn't have a formal education. But I guess the vampire community must not care about credentials if someone is good at catching killers.

It makes me wonder what his other cases were like. How many crimes involved vampires that we humans were none the wiser to?

After a few more seconds of terse silence and perusing my murder board, Alex asks where I am in my investigation.

"I feel stuck. I don't have a lot of resources at my disposal, and there's only so many times I can replay That Night in my head in search of new clues."

Alex hums in agreement. "I get that. I haven't had much luck either, but I think our first step is figuring out how the victims are connected."

I agree completely, but... "That's the thing. I don't think they're connected."

"Exactly."

"What do you mean?"

"There appears to be no rhyme or reason to victim selection or where the bodies were found, which says a lot about the killer."

"So, a vampire serial killer is no different than a human one?" I ask, and he shrugs.

"I don't know, I haven't had much experience with either."

"Wait, *what*?" I ask, maybe a tad too sharply. "I thought you were a pro at these things!"

He perches on the edge of my bed and raises a finger in correction. "All I said was that I was a private investigator—"

"You said you were a private investigator *of sorts*," I cut in.

"Will you ever let that go?" he grumbles. "I couldn't really say I was an investigator for a secret community of vampires, could I?" He arches a brow at me, daring me to say anything more about it. "I mostly just investigate one off kills or attacks, or vampires making public scenes. Serial killers are as new to me as they are to you. It doesn't make me any less motivated to catch the bastard, though."

"Fine. I get it." I wave my hands around to reassure him I understand. "What now?"

"We start with timelines and locations." He looks down again. "Something your board is severely lacking."

I follow his line of sight and frown. Throwing my hand in the direction of the board I protest, "What are you talking about? I have plenty of information there."

"I don't know if I'd count 'Serena possibly at a club' as viable information." He settles himself further on the bed. If Alex simply existing in my room was a strange sight, Alex seated on my light green duvet is even stranger.

"She was at a club—I'm sure of it. I just don't know which one. Well, I have a guess given that another victim was at a certain club."

Alex sighs heavily. "You mean Sinner."

"Yep," I reply tartly.

"One victim went there. It's not a trend. And Milly Johnson was killed near her apartment before she left for work."

"You really don't want to go there, do you?" I question. What is with his aversion to that club?

"Until we have more concrete evidence, I don't see why we need to look into it," Alex says with finality.

I decide to leave the topic alone—*for now*—and we move on. I won't give up so easily in the future, though. Maybe I'm not as brazen as Serena was, but I do have a stubborn streak.

"The other night at the frat house I met one of Serena's party friends, that guy you scared off." Alex smirks a little at the mention. "He said Serena had a boyfriend."

He tilts his head, considering. "She probably just said that to get him to back off. He was probably *flirting* with her," Alex says as a look full of disdain crosses his face. The way he said "flirting" implies what he really thinks Tyler was doing. Pestering. Bothering. Annoying. Any other adjective to describe his poor attempts at speaking to a woman.

"That's what I thought, but when it comes to her party side, I didn't know that Serena well since I never went out with her. Maybe we could talk to the guy again? It seemed like you knew him," I suggest. Alex snorts, looking both annoyed and amused and I find I like this expression a lot more than his usual stoic one.

"Yeah, I know him. I'll set something up." Satisfied that talking to this guy might lead somewhere, I settle back in my chair and we begin our first meeting as "partners."

15
ALEX

BEING AROUND JULIETTE AND her family is... strange. Nice, I guess? I'm still not sure how I feel about it. I don't have much experience with a normal, loving family. After my parents disappeared ten years ago, all sense of normalcy disappeared along with them.

Juliette's mom popped her head in soon after I arrived—Juliette hastily threw a blanket over her murder board—and offered to bring up drinks and snacks. Juliette was embarrassed, claiming she was over twenty years old and could get her own snacks. After her mom left she then questioned me about my own snack habits.

"Can you even have something to eat and drink, that isn't, you know... *blood*." She lowered her voice on the last word as if the mere mention of it would prompt me to take hers.

"I don't need blood to survive," I assured her. "Being half human allows me to eat human foods and drink human drinks. Don't worry." Her questions didn't bother me. It had just been a while since I interacted with a human who knew what I was.

"I wasn't worried you were going to drink my blood or anything," she hastily said. "I just didn't want to make you uncomfortable if you couldn't eat something." There was a weird tug in my chest at her words, the care in them, but with that we both returned to our work in silence.

Her roommates, who I met the other night—though I doubt they remember much—came in after I'd been there an hour. Josie was excited to meet me, going so far as to give me a hug and thank me for driving them home from the party before Juliette shooed her out of the room. Meg just arched a dark brow at me and left.

"So, when did you start on this case?" Juliette asks me once we've settled back into our work—her looking through some of the victims social media accounts and me trying to learn more about the locations they were found in.

"Recently. Shortly before I first came to speak to you." Silas and some of his men tried to hunt the killer down before he eventually gave up and told me to do it.

"Wow. Not long at all, then." Juliette blows out a frustrated breath. "I've been trying to figure this out for weeks." She flings a hand at her blanket shrouded murder board. "And apparently I don't have anything substantial."

I don't respond, but that doesn't deter her. A few moments later she shoves her phone in my face, and I blink rapidly from the sudden bright phone screen glaring right into my eyes. The same photo she sent me a few days ago is opened up: Milly Johnson in front of the bright red neon sign, proclaiming she's at Sinner. "I can't explain it, but I just have this gut feeling that we'll find *something* here." She gazes imploringly at me and I almost give in.

If she's wondering why I changed my mind about partnering with her, this is part of the reason. My world is a dangerous one, and she's ready to walk into it blind. Those notes she's been receiving are proof enough. Whether they're from the killer or someone else, the threat in them is clear. I can't have whatever will happen to her on my conscious on top of every other dangerous thing I've played a part in. If she insists on involving herself, then I won't let her do it alone. Of course, I would never tell her that. For some reason I don't think she'd appreciate me wanting to protect her like that.

"What else have you found?" I change the subject and gently push her hand holding the phone and that damn photo away.

It takes Juliette a second to collect herself. She's irritated. I can see it in the way she clenches her jaw and avoids my gaze. This is not the first time I've ignored her curiosity about Sinner. Sooner or later, she's going to figure something's up.

"I've noticed something about some of the victims. They kind of look like Serena." She taps around on her phone before showing me the screen again. Scrolling through the photos, she shows me at least five other victims besides her friend who are conventionally attractive with dark hair and pale skin.

"The connection *could* be their appearance. But not all the victims look like that. Most are random. Serena was the first victim, so it's likely the killer..." I trail off, unsure of how to continue.

"Go on, the killer likely what? I've watched enough *Criminal Minds* to come up with some theories. I want to hear yours." Juliette straightens in her chair, eyes hard on mine, her tone flat.

"It's likely the killer wants to relive her murder. The others are probably impulse kills."

"So he finds other victims who look like her to do that?" she asks and I nod. Like our conversation at the diner, she doesn't appear phased by the gruesome nature of her friend's death. It should concern me, but I get it.

Unfortunately she's already desensitized, if the contents of her murder board are any indication.

Juliette stands and begins to pace her small room, lilac and vanilla wafting up my nose as she passes me. "What about suspects? Do you have any yet? Any idea what type of person—*vampire*—could do this?"

I haven't shared my newfound suspicions about Slade and the DBC. I can't be sure of their involvement, and a part of me foolishly hopes that my former friends wouldn't be so cruel with their kills. But Slade has always been unpredictable in a very predictable manner. Not to mention the twins.

There's also the very real possibility that the vampire responsible is in a frenzy, which means they are *completely* unpredictable. Vampires in a frenzy can't control their thirst and will do anything for that next taste of blood. Even kill. However, frenzied vampires tend to kill way more than this killer so maybe something else is going on.

My response sits on the tip of my tongue. It's more of a question, for her. She told me she didn't see much of the vampire when she was attacked, but I feel the need to ask again. "You don't remember what the vampire looked like, from that night?"

She pauses her pacing to stare into space before answering, clearly pulled back into the memory of her attack. The indifference she has shown so far on the matter is replaced by the quiet unease I glimpsed at the diner for our first meeting. A deep inhale has her shoulders shaking, and I subconsciously fist my hand on Juliette's comforter to keep from reaching for her. To give her some semblance of comfort. To let her know she's not alone.

"No," she says in a small voice. "I didn't get a good look... it was dark. He had fangs, obviously," she shivers. "And pale skin... I think." Her description matches most vampires, including Slade and Silas.

Before I can reply or ask any follow-up questions she spins around, a determined look on her face, the shakiness gone. "What if Serena really did have a boyfriend, and he was a vampire? If she was dating a vampire, she would keep him secret, right? At least from me." Bitterness laces her tone, and she picks up her pacing again, her hands running through her hair. Her deep brown tresses fall haphazardly down her back from her tugging. I hadn't noticed before how *interesting* the color is.

I've never been interested *in a girl's hair color before... the fuck?*

"We'll talk to Tyler," I tell her, shaking away the strange turn of my thoughts. Even sudden interest in her hair can't take away my annoyance at having to speak to that imbecile again.

Juliette slumps back into her chair. "I'm learning that Serena was very secretive." She twists her mouth to the side, thinking, and then says, "She did keep a diary, though. It might be at her dad's house. That's what I was trying to get before he threw me out. Maybe she wrote about the guy in there." Her mouth twists into a scowl.

The mention of Serena's father brings me back to yesterday when Juliette was thrown out of his house. I never got around to speaking to him after that. Being too occupied with Juliette, I abandoned the reason I visited him in the first place. "We'll pay him a visit too," I respond.

She scoffs, "I bet I'll be welcomed with open arms. I'm sure being physically forced out of there was just for fun."

"What'd you do anyway? To get kicked out, I mean."

"I just asked for her stuff. He wouldn't even answer me."

"And then his lap dog threw you out."

She gives me a bitter smile, "Yeah. Who knew his assistant was jacked under those suits."

My lips twitch unbiddenly at the memory of her, soaked from the rain, putting up a fight while being carried out the front door by Laurence Mitchell's little clone. The fury on her face. I wish I could have been present to see what transpired to cause her being thrown out.

"Don't laugh at me," she says indignantly, crossing her arms across her chest with a small frown.

I bite my lips to keep the smile from widening. *What is happening to me?* "I'm not, I promise." I'm smiling at the fact that Laurence Mitchell will have a hard time deterring this girl, and I hope to witness every second of her determination.

"Why were *you* there?" She asks me.

"Well, it's routine to speak to the victims' families."

"And they're willing to talk to someone who claims to be an investigator?"

It's my turn to frown. "I have a business card." I keep the information that no, they usually don't want to talk to me, to myself.

Juliette mutters something under her breath about the quality of my business card, but before I can take offense, her mom knocks on the door announcing that dinner is ready. Juliette kicks the murder board under her bed just as her mom opens the door.

"Do you want to stay, Alex?" Juliette's mom, who told me to call her Christy, asks.

I look to Juliette, who just stares at me and shrugs, seemingly indifferent as to whether I stay or go.

"I should head home, but thanks for the offer." Closing Juliette's laptop, I hand it back to her before sliding off the bed.

"Are you sure? We have more than enough." Her mom looks a little disappointed, and it's enough to make me hesitate. When was the last time Juliette had a friend over who didn't already live with her? Are *we* friends?

"That's very kind, but I wouldn't want to intrude."

Juliette rolls her eyes in what is quite possibly the hardest eyeroll I have seen from her yet. "Don't overthink it, Alex. It's just dinner. My mom is the best cook in all of Pine Falls—you won't regret it."

"Juliette," Christy chides. "Don't be rude to your friend. But... thank you for the compliment." She gives us a warm smile before retreating downstairs. "I made chicken alfredo. Be down in five. And wash your hands!"

Unexpected warmth fills me at her motherly admonishment and caring attitude. It's been so long since I've been anywhere near a motherly figure. An ache accompanies the warmth in my chest. An ache that feels an awful lot like longing, mixed with grief and loneliness.

Yet it's hard to feel alone in the Jennings household, even if I do feel like I'm on the outside looking in. The seat I've been instructed to sit in is to the right of Juliette's father at the head of the table and across from her cousin, Hayden. Juliette sits to my right, and her mom is situated at the other head. Meg and Josie are crammed in next to Hayden, and I get the sense that I've displaced someone with my presence. Christy is quick to assure me that no one minds. The table hasn't seen an extra person in months, so they're all excited. I can only assume that missing seventh person is Serena.

The table is decorated with an assortment of fall and Halloween paraphernalia. A candle burns somewhere making the entire house smell like cinnamon and cloves. It reminds me of home. Of cloudy days and snowy nights curled up by the fireplace with my parents. Of scary movies and gorging on candy with my older cousin. I hate that a *smell* is making my chest ache so fiercely with nostalgia.

Juliette's quiet through the passing of plates and light conversation, preferring to focus her attention on the Caesar salad than on everyone else. The one time she gave me her complete attention was when she handed me a soda can as I took my seat. "Clearing my debt," was all she said.

"You can't smoke this grass, kid," Juliette's dad says to Hayden as he fills his nephews plate up with salad, tossing him a wink.

Hayden stabs his fork into the lettuce. "Ha ha. Very funny, old man." He gives his uncle an eyeroll, and for a moment, he and Juliette look so similar. Another wave of longing hits me, but this time it's not for what I've lost in the past, but what that past cost me. How things could have been.

Juliette and Hayden have the same hazel eyes. Except where Hayden's light up with mischief at any given moment, Juliette's remain closed off.

"You catch me smoking one time in the alley..." Hayden groans.

"And in your room," Christy adds.

"In your car," Josie pipes up, much to Hayden's annoyance.

"That was one time and you were supposed to keep it to yourself!" He exclaims with fake indignation. They continue pestering Hayden, to everyone's enjoyment except his and Juliette's, who's barely paying attention.

From what I've gathered, they don't actually care that he smokes, but he admits he partakes more than he used to. I'm guilty of relying on a bad habit during times of stress, and I wonder if Hayden knows that he's doing the same. The more I observe him, the more I recognize the same shadows that swirl in Juliette's eyes. The same ones I find so often when I look in the mirror. It doesn't seem like anyone else notices, though.

"So, Alex." Juliette's dad, Samuel, says, and the weight of five stares settle on me. I brace myself for whatever questions they might throw my way. "How long have you known Juliette?"

My pulse kicks up a notch, and I rub my palms on my jeans at the subject of my relationship with Juliette, if you can even call it a relationship. Rationally, I know that I shouldn't explain precisely how and why I know their daughter, but that doesn't mean I don't feel bad lying to these people.

"Not long." I glance at Juliette from the corner of my eye where she's observing me carefully, watching my mouth like she's marking every word that comes out of it. "We probably would have never met if not for the project we're working on."

"What is the project, exactly?" Christy repeats her earlier question. We should have expected that I would be mildly interrogated by Juliette's parents when I was asked to stay for dinner. Maybe if I thought it through a bit more, I could have been prepared for the uneasiness in my stomach that accompanies me whenever I try to lie.

Lucky for me, Juliette tackles her mom's question. "It's on project management. We have to come up with a marketing strategy for a business of our choice and determine how much it would cost to start up and how profitable it might be. And of course, we have to present it in front of the class." Should I be worried how effortlessly Juliette came up with that fake project?

"Sounds... exciting," her mom replies, sounding anything but. "What sort of strategy have you come up with? Maybe we should have you manage the marketing for the restaurant to bring in some more customers." She smiles, but it's strained. Her husband offers her an obligatory chuckle but a cloud of tension settles over the table. Juliette ignores her mother's comment.

"We found a private investigation firm," she answers and I almost choke on a sip of water. "How profitable are they really? We can only go up from here." What were once empty hazel eyes now brighten with amusement. It only lasts a second as she offers me a small smirk, but in that moment, she resembled her mischievous cousin even more.

Dinner flies by after that with only a few more questions directed at myself or Juliette. Everyone acts as if Juliette's standoffish behavior is normal. As if they don't want to push her away from the table by speaking too much to her.

"Text me if you find anything," Juliette says as she walks me out of the house, everyone else cleaning up dinner or retreating to their rooms. I offered to stay and help wash dishes, but Christy shoved a container of left-over pasta in my hands and told me not to worry about it.

"Same goes for you." I bid her goodnight. The door clicks softly, Juliette and the warm domesticity I was able to experience for a couple of hours closing behind it.

The drive home is quiet and mercifully short. Too many thoughts are running through my head for me to make sense of, and I don't want to sit with them for too long. Instead, I drown out the buzzing with whatever is playing on the radio. I immediately change the station when I recognize the song—"Present Tense" by Radiohead. It was one of my father's favorites, and what was playing in the car during the worst moment of my life ten years ago.

The parking lot of my apartment building is full of cars and crumbling pavement. I'm thankful that Silas at least offered to bankroll an apartment for me after I refused his offer to stay at the compound, even if it is sort of a dump. The poor state of the complex was intentional on his part, I'm sure.

A month's old "out of order" sign hangs limply on the elevator doors. At this point, I don't think the landlord even cares anymore. Not that I mind—I prefer the stairs anyway.

My apartment is small but not cozy. I complain about Silas' empty house, but my place is not much better.

Barren would be the best word for it. There are just the essentials with some of my favorite books scattered around. Even when I lived with Slade, I didn't have much, and it's not like he ever went out of his way to cram my room with personal belongings.

I'm suddenly struck with just how *empty* my apartment is. And not just in terms of furniture but energy and life as well. Juliette's house was so warm. It reminded me of a house from some sitcom with a perfectly functioning family. How it used to be for me. Her friends and family brought the house to life, even her room allowed me to see a glimpse of who she is under the carefully neutral mask she wears around me.

What would she see if she came here?

Nothing. And maybe that's the point.

I head into the bathroom, ready to wash away this melancholy that's been consistently shrouding me. The shower sputters before the pressure adjusts, and I test the water to make sure it's hot enough before peeling off my hoodie and the rest of my clothes. Steam floats around the cramped bathroom, but I stand there for a moment, staring at myself in the slowly fogging mirror.

I trace a particularly long scar that curves around from my back to my navel. If I close my eyes, I can still feel the glass from the windshield cut my skin as I dragged myself out of that overturned car. I can still smell the spilled gas and loam from the damp forest road. I can still hear the empty *click click click* of the engine and the distant owls hooting and that damn Radiohead song. But when I open my eyes, my breaths coming quicker than before, the humidity inside the bathroom sets my mind right. A barbed wire design overlaps with the scar, and I trace that instead—reminding myself that I am not on that road all alone anymore, my parents' bodies missing from the front seat. Even if, after all these years, a part of me still feels stuck there.

My tattoos mean nothing and everything. It's been the only way for me to carve out my own identity. Literally. Most have been to hide my scars, but the rest have been my attempt at figuring out who I am.

The first tattoo I got when I was only sixteen—the skull on my left forearm. It's more of a brand, really; although I didn't realize it at the time. For some reason, I still can't find the drive to cover it up.

My mother's name on my ribcage, *Nadia*, came after that. Over the years I've filled in almost every space on my arms and torso, testing out different designs until I find one that reveals some part of who I am.

The truth is, I'm still unsure. I could fill every inch of skin and not come anywhere close to discovering who I really am.

There's a lilac inked onto my left wrist, under the skull tattoo, that reminds me of Juliette. It was my mom's favorite flower, and it covers the worst of my scars. The one I gave myself years ago when life became too bleak. *As if it's much better now.*

But looking at that tattoo, thinking of Juliette... Maybe a purpose is what I've really been missing. Or someone to mourn me if I left this world. Not that Juliette and I are that close, but I can tell she harbors intense loyalty to those she grants permission into her life.

What would Juliette think if she knew of my sordid past? Would she still want to work together? The unease that question fills me with is enough for me to drop the topic altogether and enough for me to vow to keep my past to myself lest I scare her away.

It's been years since I had a friend. I don't know if Juliette and I will ever be *friends*, per say, but the potential is there. Hopefully I don't screw it up. This case will be solved and then I'll be out of the city like I've planned; away from Juliette and these confusing thoughts of relationships and attraction. Away from my past and all those who have played a role in shaping me into the unidentifiable monster I see in the mirror.

16

JULIETTE

My hooded stalker likes the willow tree on the campus quad. Serena and I used to love lounging there after long lectures in the spring on those rare days when the sun would shine. But my stalker doesn't lounge—he just stands there under the weeping branches and watches me from under his hood. If only Alex were here so I could point him out and confirm whether or not my mind is trustworthy.

October usually brings chilly days and colder nights, with rain that won't stop until next summer. However, today the sun is out, reminding me of those lazy days with Serena.

Hayden, Meg, Josie, and I are taking advantage of the break in storms by sprawling out at our usual table in the quad. My hooded man had the same idea, apparently. The burst of much-needed Vitamin D has me feeling inspired to sketch yet again, even if it is just of the buildings surrounding us.

"What about tomorrow?" Josie says, her voice not unlike the chirping birds that are also taking advantage of the weather today.

I look around our table and notice they're all staring at me, waiting for my reply. "What's tomorrow?"

Meg rolls her eyes, giving me a pointed look. "I knew she wasn't paying attention."

"Sorry," I mumble. In truth, I couldn't care less what they're talking about. Probably another party they want to drag me to just for them to get drunk and leave me.

"Give her a break, Meg. Besides, it's not like she'll wanna go anyway. I'm sure she has a hot date with *Alex*." Hayden throws his arm over my shoulder, and I shove him away, scowling. If only they knew the truth of what we're doing. Then again, I don't really want them to know. It's better that they're shielded from the truth of just how horrific the murders are.

"Ok but for real, who is Alex, and where did you meet him?" Meg arches a brow at me.

Hayden pretends to fan himself, smirking at the blush creeping up my neck. "He's hot," he adds bluntly.

"He seems nice, too," Josie pipes in, smiling and giving me a look of approval.

Hayden sighs dramatically and props his head on a fist. "I can't believe you didn't introduce me to this *study* partner sooner."

"What were you *studying* again?" Meg asks with mock curiosity.

"Each other, I think." Hayden winks at me and I groan, covering my face with my hands.

"Please stop," I moan. "We are working on a project together. Nothing more." Despite my annoyance—and, okay my embarrassment—at having them discuss Alex like that in front of me, it feels nice to participate in their teasing again. I've been avoiding any "normal" interactions like this because it didn't feel right to laugh or smile without Serena here. It feels too much like moving on, or forgetting her.

Luckily, they move on to other topics of conversation, and I'm saved from confronting my growing attraction to my new partner and the embarrassment that my friends can tease me so easily about it. It's... nice to sit and listen to my friends talk about their lives. I'm glad to hear that talk of the campus shutting down seems to have halted for now since Meg was so worried about her spot on the figure skating team.

"Excuse me?" A voice interrupts Meg's complaints about her overbearing coach. Judging from the questioning looks we're all wearing, it's safe to assume none of us knows the girl shifting on her feet next to our table. Her short brown hair floats gently in the breeze, her makeup reminiscent of something Serena used to pull off. The girl twiddles her thumbs together, glancing around like she isn't sure if she should be here.

"What's up?" Hayden asks, giving her a smile and putting her a little more at ease.

The girl bites her lip, looking down at her hands. "Sorry to interrupt, but I didn't know who else to go to."

Meg holds up a hand and all but demands, "Do we know you?" Causing Josie to lightly swat Meg's arm before giving the girl an apologetic smile.

The girl stumbles over her words, pink staining her cheeks. "No, you don't know me. I knew your friend, though. Serena. I'm Marissa." We all stiffen at the mention of Serena but don't say anything.

"Sorry," she repeats. "We used to party together, at this club called Sinner."

Whatever she says after that fades away, my heart stalling in my chest at the mention of the club. *Sinner*. The club Milly Johnson frequented. Well, okay, for all I know she went there once, so *maybe* she frequented it.

The girl's voice comes back into focus, adrenaline coursing through me at the information she's shared. I'm more alert now, keen to hear what this girl has to say while simultaneously wishing she would hurry up so I can tell Alex.

I knew it was worth looking into!

"I'm really sorry about what happened, by the way. Anyway, we were at Sinner together before she... that night—"

"The night she was murdered," I finish for her. Everyone looks at me cautiously. Josie and Hayden shift in their seats.

"Yes," the girl confirms. "I got super drunk and left before her, so I don't remember much about what happened that night. But I was randomly looking through my camera roll this morning and found this."

Marissa pulls her phone out of her back pocket and swipes around on the screen, her nails tapping out a nervous rhythm. Once she finds what she's looking for, she slides her phone towards us and we crowd around it, watching as the girl in front of us appears on the screen.

The video shows her singing incoherently, loud music drowning out most of the words. The date at the top confirms that it was taken the night Serena died, just a couple of hours before her murder. Then a face I know all too well comes into view.

I almost don't recognize her at first. She's so *alive*. The memory of her limp, dying form and then her corpse in a field of flowers has been ingrained in my mind. It's strange and comforting and cruel to see her singing along to the music and dancing around, no idea that her light will be snuffed out in a matter of hours.

Watching on this tiny screen what are Serena's last moments on this earth, and being unable to do anything to prevent the inevitable, has a familiar tightness forming in my chest.

The wave of emotion intensifies when a man's hand appears on screen and grabs Serena's arm. She tries to shove him away, laughing, before disappearing from view.

"Who was that guy?" I ask, a little too forcefully but at this point I'm past caring. Whoever this Marissa is, she's just given me a much needed lead. A lead that's caused new questions to sprout in my mind.

That man in the video could very well be the vampire who killed Serena and attacked me. He could be out there right now looking for his next victim—if he hasn't found one already.

Or he could be Serena's boyfriend.

The girl gives a tiny shrug and answers in a small voice, "I don't know. Like I said, I was drunk and left right after I filmed the video." She shifts on her feet some more. "I tried calling the police, but they said it wasn't important."

Wasn't important? Heat rolls through me, anger forming at the utter incompetency of those supposed to help us. This is why I'm willing to put myself in danger if it means getting answers. Someone has to.

I need to get out of here. I need to talk to Alex and go to that club. There's a good chance the killer frequents the place if two of the victims liked to party there.

Just as I'm about to pack up my things and leave, I throw one last question at the girl. "Could the guy in the video be her boyfriend?"

Marissa's eyes go round. "I don't think so," she replies in that same unsure tone. My head snaps up at that. "I mean, I never met her boyfriend so I can't be sure. She was on the phone with him once, though. Called him 'K.'"

K? My body freezes while my mind speeds up—everything she's told us running through my mind on a loop so I don't forget it. I need to get out of here.

"Thank you for showing us this," I say, throwing my stuff into my bag and jumping off the bench, not sparing another glance at the table or my friends before walking off.

Serena was at Sinner. Some guy grabbed Serena. The boyfriend might actually be real.

"Jules!" Meg's voice carries on the wind, but I ignore her. "Jules, wait." A hand grabs my arm, and I shove it off. "Stop!" Against my will, I do.

Meg is huffing beside me, arms crossed and hair mussed by the wind. I look back and notice that I made it all the way across the quad already. The empty space under the willow tree tells me my stalker moved on.

"What is going *on* with you?"

I scoff. *That's a great question, Meg. What* isn't *going on with me?*

Suddenly, all the anger and guilt I've tried to keep to myself these past couple of months comes bubbling to the surface, dying to escape at her simple question.

"What's going on with me?" My hand goes to my chin in mock contemplation, my words spilling out in harsh waves. "Well, let's see. My best friend was murdered right in front of my eyes. The person who killed her is now on a rampage, not to mention the fact that he attacked me and put me in a coma." Short, angry breaths pour out of me. "The restaurant might go under, I have no desire to keep up with my classes, and I'm having trouble feeling anything that isn't guilt, grief, fear, or anger. Serena had the blood sucked out of her and I just stood there and watched while that—" I stop myself, but it's too late.

Meg studies me carefully. "What did you say? The 'blood sucked out of her'...?" Her voice is firm, the tone she uses when she demands an answer with no argument.

"No," I say, too quickly.

"Jules." Meg's tone is softer now, and she takes my hand in hers, enveloping it in her warmth. "You can tell me anything," she says with compassion in her eyes.

I yank my hand out of her grasp and snap, "Sometimes it feels like I'm the only one who cares that she died. There, you happy?"

Meg's eyes harden as she opens her mouth to respond, but I don't stick around to hear what she has to say.

Me: i'm going to sinner.

Alex Osman: I told you it's not important.

Me: yes, it is.

Me: serena was there the night she died.

Me: two of the victims went there.

Me: i'm going.

Alex Osman: Fine. 9pm. I'll pick you up.

17

JULIETTE

I STARE AT MY reflection in the mirror for the umpteenth time, smoothing the cool silk of the green dress I have on. I stole it out of Josie's closet. She won't care anyway. I didn't want to ask Meg; I'm still avoiding her after our conversation earlier. And if I took one of her dresses without asking, she would know and then that would open a whole new line of questioning. Alex had texted me earlier and told me to wear a dress, that girls aren't allowed in to the club if they're not "dressed up."

Sexist bullshit, I had messaged back. To which he replied, *Yup,* with a rolling eye emoji. I wonder how often he uses it.

Our plan is to ask for the security tapes to see if there's a good shot of the man who grabbed Serena on the dance floor the night she was there. Alex said going at night is our best bet to *avoid confrontation*, whatever that means.

I briefly filled Alex in over text about the girl who showed us the video of Serena. It was enough for him to finally drop some of his determination to avoid the club. Even he had to admit it was probably more than a coincidental connection between Serena and Milly Johnson.

The killer could have very likely found them both there. It's possible, given the way that man grabbed Serena in the video, she knew her killer and invited him back to the house. Could he have gone back to the club and targeted Milly Johnson because of Serena?

"What the fuck?" Meg appears behind me in the mirror's reflection. *Shit.* My parents are at the restaurant, and Josie, Meg, and Hayden were all supposed to be at some frat party tonight. I had left my door open thinking I was alone. Apparently not.

I whirl around, breaking eye contact with my reflection, and ready myself to spew whatever excuse I can find. Meg's arms are crossed over her chest, and she's looking me up and down like she can't quite believe I'm voluntarily leaving the house—in a dress no less.

"You going somewhere?" She accuses in an icy tone.

I swallow despite the sudden dryness in my throat. What would she think if I told her the truth? The truth about Alex and what happened to Serena?

"Yes, actually. You remember Alex?" I say in what I hope is a casual and innocent tone. She narrows her eyes at me, annoyed. That was a stupid way to start. We just had a whole conversation about him this afternoon.

"Well, we're going out," I blurt. It's not *technically* a lie.

She unfolds her arms and steps slowly into the room. Her outfit is the same one she had on an hour ago when they all left.

"What are you doing back, anyway?" I ask, casting a surreptitious glance towards my murder board to make sure it's covered up.

Meg holds up one hand and waves her phone at me. "Forgot my phone. Party's not too far away so I walked back."

My body tenses, worry for my friend replacing the panic that she might see my murder board or somehow figure out that I'm headed to a club to investigate Serena's murder.

"You walked back alone?"

Snorting softly she responds, annoyed, "Josie and Hayden are all over each other tonight, so I didn't mind getting away for a bit." I'd rather they take advantage of each other than some stranger taking advantage of them. After walking in on them on top of her bed a couple weeks ago, Meg would rather they keep what they do with each other behind a locked door.

A knock on the front door has both of us jumping and I check the clock by my bed. *Eight fifty-nine.* Thank god Alex is prompt. I don't think I have it in me to come up with more floundering excuses. It seems all I've been doing for weeks is lie to those closest to me.

"He's here," I state the obvious, snatching the clutch I dug out of my closet for tonight. Ushering Meg towards the door, I stuff my phone inside the compact bejeweled bag.

"Do you think he'll mind giving me a ride back to the party?" Meg stares at me with a small smile. She walked here just fine by herself, but she knows I won't say no. I don't *want* to say no, I want her to be safe. She's banking on that to interrogate Alex, I just know it.

"Yeah, no problem," I tell her and hurry down the stairs to meet Alex as Meg trails behind me.

"Hey—" Alex cuts himself off when he sees me, staring down at my dress, then back up to my face. My cheeks flame at his slack jaw and hooded gaze before he gets his expression under control. I try not to be too disappointed—because why should I be?—when he jerks his gaze away, clearing his throat. "You look nice," he says, and I mumble a thanks, locking the door when Meg and I are clear of it.

"Hello again. Jules said you would give me a ride back to a party." Meg tilts her head up at Alex and when he echoes my agreement she saunters over to his car, pulling open the back passenger seat and sliding in.

"She doesn't know about anything," I say in a low voice to him, trudging down the path at a slower pace than Meg. The chilly air nips at my exposed skin, making me feel more vulnerable than I'd like. "If she asks you any questions just pretend we're going on a date." Alex nods and holds the passenger door open for me. A few seconds of tense silence pass while we wait for him to round the car and get in.

It's ridiculous to be afraid of what my friend might say. Meg has always been the most self-assured of our group, even more so than Serena. But on top of that, she's fulfilled the stern mother hen role that no one asked her to take on. She cares about all of us, which is why I know she'd tell me to drop the investigating if she knew. She would call me ten kinds of stupid if she found out what Alex and I were *really* up to.

The short drive to the party is filled with questions for Alex, which he does a great job answering. Meg grills him about his age, the pretend degree he's working on, and what his plans for the future are, firing off questions before he can even finish answering the previous ones. They're a lot more aggressive than the drunken questions from the other night. Luckily Alex is a good liar. Although I can tell it's making him uncomfortable based on the tension around his eyes, like he's internally wincing at each word that leaves his mouth.

When we finally arrive at the frat house—a different one from the Halloween Party—it's teeming with people, loud music, and discarded drink cups. So, not *that* different from the last one.

Meg hops out of the car but holds the door open. "Jules," she says in a sweet tone I've only heard her use when she wants something. "Can I talk to you for a sec? Alone?"

I get out, Alex casting me a concerned look, and follow her up the sidewalk. She pastes on a smile and waves at Alex before hooking her elbow with mine and steering me towards the house.

"Something's up. Are you really dating him? I wanted to give you space on this, but I'm not so sure anymore."

Automatically I open my mouth to respond but shut it just as fast when I can't think of a single thing to say. As much as lying has seemed to come easy for me these past months, it doesn't mean I want to do it all the time.

She must sense my inner turmoil because she holds up a hand, a look of grim resignation on her face. "You don't have to tell me anything right now." She squeezes my arm. "Just be safe, okay?"

Before I can reply, she releases my arm and starts up the path. I don't even know what I would have said if she'd stayed.

Sorry I've been a shitty friend?

Sorry for being more involved in solving my best friends impossible murder than being present with the friends that are still alive?

Nothing feels right. We've been friends for years, but never has the disconnect between us felt so... tangible. We're in different places—mentally and emotionally—and maybe we always were, but now is the first time I've truly felt separate. My friends have always been my safe space from the world that I could never quite fit into. I have no sense of self without Serena's murder and my attack defining me, guiding my every thought and action. I can barely remember who I was before them.

How can I be present for someone else if I don't even know who I am?

I hang my head back and let out a long breath, staring up at the misty night sky, hoping the cool air will put a stop to the twisting in my gut and chest.

I'm fine.

I'm fine.

I'm fine.

I need to find answers tonight. I need this solved. I need battles to stop waging in my mind.

"Everything okay?" Alex asks when I get back in the car, the smell of leather and spice wrapping around me like a familiar, comforting shroud. He shifts the car out of park and steers us away from the house full of drunk college students and towards a club full of them instead.

"Yeah, everything's fine." *Lie.* As established, I've gotten pretty good at them. Alex begins tapping his fingers against the steering wheel and his left leg bounces up and down. It takes everything in me not to reach over and still him. "Are *you* okay?"

He spares me a glance before turning his attention back to the road. The tension in the car seems thicker now than when Meg was grilling him. "I'm fine." *Lie?*

I look pointedly at his tapping fingers and shaking knee. "Are you?"

"Some dangerous people own Sinner," he blurts out. *Dangerous people?* Did Serena know that?

"So that's why you didn't want to go? If the club has shady owners, that seems like even more evidence that Serena and Milly were targeted there."

Alex sighs, stopping his finger tapping to run his hand through his hair. I'm drawn to the slide of his fingers, and the silky strands they touch, wondering what they feel like. Cheeks flushing, I force my gaze out the window before he can catch me staring.

"The owner and I... we don't get along," he explains, the words heavy.

Understanding dawns on me, about why he was worried about a confrontation. "Oh." Silence envelops us for long moments, neither of us speaking. It isn't until Alex pulls off the freeway to head downtown that I ask, "Who owns the club?"

For a while I think he won't answer me, but then he finally says, "A bunch of criminals known as the Dead Boys Club and their leader, Slade."

"The *Dead Boys Club*?"

He nods, "They think it's cute, despite the fact that they aren't actually dead."

"So, they're vampires too?" We pull onto a street, and he takes off across town, the Mustang's engine rumbling beneath my legs.

Gripping the steering wheel, grey eyes hard, he replies, "Yeah, but not the good kind."

"Good kind?" I ask incredulously.

He gives me a look. "I haven't tried to suck your blood, have I?"

"You told me you didn't need blood to survive," I point out.

Alex rolls his eyes. "Whatever. What I mean is they don't go out of their way to hide the fact that they're vampires. Slade encourages that kind of behavior. I think he mostly does it to irritate my boss." He sighs again. "Which means, people like me have to constantly clean up their messes." I'm sensing more of a story there, but I avoid adding on to what is clearly an uncomfortable topic for him.

"Do you think whoever killed Serena could be a part of this Dead Boys Club?" I ask, goosebumps rising on my arms. This nightclub might *really* not be safe, at least not any safer than I was already expecting it to be given that I'm a young woman headed to a club.

Alex shrugs, "I don't know. My... employer," he fumbles over the word, "certainly thinks it's a possibility."

"But you don't?"

"I don't know." He repeats, sounding exasperated, with my questions or the situation I'm not sure. Probably both.

A shiver skates down my spine at his words, my resolve about going quickly dissipating. "Well now I'm not so sure if we should go. Especially if you already have beef with them." I try to muster some of Meg or Serena's brazenness but fail miserably.

His expression softens just slightly as he looks over at me, one hand coming down to squeeze my thigh through the silk of my dress. My entire body jolts at the contact, but luckily he doesn't seem to notice. "They won't hurt you, not if you're with me. I shouldn't have said anything." He purses his lips and looks back to the road ahead, removing his hand. I shouldn't feel less safe, now that he's not touching me, but I do. Discreetly, I rub my palm over the place he grasped my thigh, hoping to capture some of the warmth left behind.

His fidgety attitude makes more sense with the added details. Not just dangerous people that own the club but vampires he's had run ins with before.

"I don't want to cause an issue," he continues, oblivious to the way I'm practically massaging my leg. "We manage to stay out of each other's way for the most part. I hoped to keep it like that. Besides, it's not so much Slade I'm worried about but the Russo twins."

"Who are they?"

"You'll see," he mutters.

I don't have a chance to respond to his ominous reply before we're pulling into a small parking lot behind a nondescript building. It's quiet out here, but as soon as we get out of the car and round the building, chatter and a thumping bass grow increasingly louder.

Sinner is a large brick building that looks like it might have been a warehouse at some point. A long line of people stretch along the side of the aged brick. Not even a killer roaming the streets will deter these people from having a night out, apparently. Women dressed in skin tight cocktail dresses huddle together against the chill while men leer at them from all sides. I cross my arms, glad for the tall man with the permanent frown walking next to me.

He leads the way to the entrance, the guard letting us through at the mention of Slade's name and a flash of a tattoo on Alex's forearm. The space is packed, the music deafening, pounding through my body as we walk in. It's certainly not helping my ever-present headache. The infamous bright neon sign with the club's name hangs on the wall to the left, the ghost of Milly Johnson filling the space in front of it. The red of the sign reminds me of blood even more so now that I know who owns the club.

There are two levels, the lower one housing the dance floor, DJ, and bar. On the upper level, people linger by the railings, watching the revelers down below. On this floor the bartender pours shots for a group of rowdy young men, dodging their advances with ease. One touches her arm and she pins him with a glare so fierce I almost laugh. But I'm also creeped out because she kind of looks like Serena, especially with that glower on her face. Or maybe I'm just seeing what I want to see given that this club was one of the last places Serena visited.

"Stick close to me," Alex murmurs in my ear, his hot breath tickling my skin. My body warms when his hand hovers over the small of my back. It's such a small gesture, but I'm thankful for his presence beside me especially now that we're inside the club.

All the people, combined with the music and scent of the place—sweat, perfume, and liquor—are not only making my brain feel like it's about to combust, but also causing my breaths to come quicker, focus waning.

This is my first time at any nightclub, and it's simultaneously just how I expected it to be and so much worse. The loud music, the sweaty bodies grinding against each other on the dance floor... all of it. I'd be lying if I said I didn't want to plop myself at the bar and just take it all in. Not only to catch my breath but also to observe the patrons and live vicariously through them for a while, carefree and acting without consequence.

What would it be like to feel the music's vibrations without being bothered by a headache? To feel another's body sliding against mine as we move around the room? Tattooed hands gripping my waist while we sway to a song with a sensuous beat?

Jesus, get it together Juliette.

I force myself to think of something else, like the fact that Serena's killer could be here right this very second. Besides my attacker, Alex is the only other vampire I've been around—*that I know of*. Now, I can't help but dart my eyes around the room, wondering which of the clubbers could secretly be hiding fangs behind their painted lips and colorful cocktails.

Just as we push past the initial crowd by the entrance, two figures with white blond hair make their way towards us. A man and woman approach, both with the same near black eyes and lithe bodies. These must be the Russo twins. They don't look much older than me or Alex, but I'm still unclear on the lifespan of a vampire.

The woman speaks first in a slight accent, "Well, well, well. If it isn't the blood hunter himself." The all-black ensemble she wears looks molded to her body, the leather of her pants not creasing even an inch as she prowls closer to us. Those pants combined with her black turtleneck have me sweating just looking at her, but not a bead of it dares to moisten her beautiful face.

"Hello, Alex. What are you doing here?"

Her brother circles behind us and I can feel Alex tense as he shifts his body slightly closer to mine.

"Who's she?" The man inquires seductively, leaning closer to me.

While the two are definitely twins in features, the similarities end there. It's interesting how there's barely a trace of whatever accent the woman has when her brother speaks. Dark roots show through the white of the guy's hair, like he's a few months due for a touch up, unlike the woman's pristine fair ponytail. Like his sister, he wears all black, but his outfit looks more haphazard than intentionally intimidating. Silver glints in his nose, lip, and ears, the piercings reflecting the low lights of the club, while the woman's face remains unmarred. His chipped black nails run down my arm, and I pull away, uncomfortable.

"Someone in search of answers, like me," Alex replies cryptically.

A small, knowing smile spreads across the woman's face. "Oh, Alex. I heard you were doing some kind of investigative freelance work." She waves her hand around, somehow looking down on him from inches below his tall stature. "I had hoped our paths might cross again someday." Her smile turns sultry and a twinge of jealousy creeps up, surprising me; although Alex gives her no reaction besides a glare. Her words confuse me, though. I was under the impression that Alex ran into them often. I don't know what he did before he was an investigator, but whatever it was, it's clear she knew him from before.

Taking a deep breath, I look her right in those bottomless black pits you could call eyes. "We need to look at the club's security footage." Her expression transforms into something stern, and I squeak out, all confidence leaving as soon as it arrived, "If that's okay?"

The woman's face goes back to the small smile she seems to permanently don, amusement now lighting her eyes. Her brother lifts a strand of my hair and sniffs it between two fingers, inhaling deeply while his eyes drift shut "You smell like flowers."

Alex eyes him closely but doesn't step in. "Thanks..." I say, slowly pulling my hair away from his grasp.

"Anthony, take the girl to the security room," the woman says to her brother, who is still trying to sniff my hair even though I keep pulling away from him.

The man, Anthony, flicks his eyes to her. "Sure thing." He then takes my hand in his and tugs me away from Alex and the woman, his grip icy.

Before we even make it two steps, Alex snatches my hand out of Anthony's. His skin a warm contrast to the other vampires. "We go together," Alex growls. The way he says it, so matter of fact, has the warmth from his skin spreading through to my chest.

The woman lets out an exasperated, overly dramatic sigh. "Fine. I was planning on taking you up to Slade. If you go where she goes as you say, then you can both have an audience with him when you're done. I'm sure he will find this situation, and her, very intriguing."

"Alina—" Alex warns, but she cuts him off with a raise of her perfectly manicured hand.

"Uh-uh. You barge into *our* club making demands and think I'm not going to tell Slade about it?" She huffs a laugh and turns on her heel, weaving her way through the crowd expertly. She makes a stop at the bar, shoving aside the men still pestering the bartender. Whatever she says or does makes them skulk away. The bartender gives Alina a grateful look and the two exchange a few words before sharing a quick kiss. I look away.

Alex seems to contemplate something for a moment before facing me and Anthony. He gestures for Anthony to continue.

"Lead the way."

Anthony grabs my hand again, this time holding it tightly, looking at me like I'm his next meal—which, based off the way he was sniffing me a few minutes ago, I might be.

We head down a hallway lined with people waiting for the bathroom then turn a corner where a single door sits at the end. Anthony grabs a keyring from a chain on the side of his black jeans and pulls a key out, releasing my hand. I have to flex my fingers to loosen them from his death grip.

Alex looms closer behind me than he has since we arrived, gently touching my shoulder as if to reassure me nothing bad will happen with him right beside me. My skin tingles where his fingers linger, but he pulls them away when Anthony unlocks the door and shoves it open.

The room is cramped with monitors lining a desk and the wall above it. Each one shows a different angle of the club, all feeds timestamped. Anthony plops down in the single chair in front of the desk and scoots it closer, clicking out of the current screen. "What's the date you're looking for?"

Alex and I answer at the same time, giving him the day of Serena's murder. Anthony smirks as he looks between us and turns back to the computer. He opens a folder on the desktop and scrolls through a bunch of files before double clicking on the one he's looking for. All the monitors instantly change, showing different people on a different day and time.

He fast forwards the footage until my gaze snags on a tall white woman with long black hair wearing a silk black dress. "Wait, stop!" Serena is standing in the middle of the dance floor behind the girl who showed me and my friends that video. It's the same moment, just a different angle.

Anthony follows my gaze and tilts his head, "I know her. She used to come around a lot."

I don't break my study of the screen, taking in this moment of Serena. One of her last moments alive. Warm fingers graze my arm, and I break out of my trance to find Alex watching me carefully.

"You good?" He mouths, and I nod. *I'm fine.* I have to be.

Anthony plays the video again, and the mystery guy walks up to Serena and her dance partner. Just like the other video I saw, his face is shielded, this time from the shadows of the dim club lights. He grabs her arm and drags her away. I track them through the cameras on the different monitors, but she disappears from view when they exit the club.

"Where did she go? Who was she with?" I turn to Anthony but he just shrugs.

"Sorry, there's not many cameras outside. As for the guy? You could ask Slade. There's been a lot of new people in the past few months, I can't keep up with all of them." He waves his hand and turns back to the computer.

Alex tosses a thumb drive onto the desk. "Here. Download that footage for us, would you?"

"So pushy," Anthony murmurs, grabbing the drive and sticking it into the computer. Once he downloads it, he tosses it back to Alex, walking past us out of the room.

"Let's go, I'm sure Slade can't *wait* to see you," he snickers.

This time, Alex doesn't give Anthony the chance to grab my hand and drag me along. He places his hand on my upper back and gently leads me forward towards the stairs that will take us up to the second level.

People laugh and dance and sip their drinks around us, but I focus my gaze on Anthony's boots, my vision pulsing with the pounding in my head. I feel stares on us as we pass, people looking at me or Alex or both. Either way, it makes me uncomfortable.

The second floor is a bit quieter—the heavy bass of the music not quite reaching all the way up here. Most of the area is roped off with people lounging in comfortable-looking velvet couches and chairs as they view the club from above. Past that is another hallway like the one below with bathrooms and a door at the end. This door is wider and has a red and black mosaic of a skull with blood leaking from its eyes.

Anthony knocks right on the glass blood, and a voice from within tells us to enter. He turns and winks at me before twisting the handle and going inside. Unease fills my gut—from Anthony and whatever lies beyond the door.

The room we enter is decently sized, spacious enough to house a small bar on the wall to the right, and a massive oak desk with bookshelves behind it on the left. Alina sits in a chair before the desk, legs sprawled over the arms with her smirk back in place. A man who looks startling like Alex sits behind the desk. They have the same dark hair and defined jaw, and while their eyes are both piercing in their intensity, this man's are amber instead of Alex's familiar grey.

I glance at Alex, confused as to whose office we just stepped into, but he's not looking at me. His eyes are on the man behind the desk. The one who must be Slade.

When I first saw Alex in the restaurant, I thought he was hot; even when I did mistake him for being my possible stalker. He just has one of those faces that everyone can agree is conventionally attractive yet rugged enough to be pleasing to look at.

Objectively, of course.

Slade, however, is *hot*. Devastatingly debonair. Chiseled jawline, sharp cheekbones, perfectly styled hair, and a fitted suit. Those amber eyes flick towards us, a flash of something passing through them as we step into the room. Surprise, perhaps? Surprise that Alex has dared step foot in his club? Before I can contemplate it any further, a blank, mildly curious look slips into place across his features. The action reminds me so much of Alex.

He rises from the desk, buttoning his jacket as he does. "Hello, cousin. I would say it's good to see you again, but Alina tells me you aren't here for me." Alex winces, casting me a sidelong look. *Cousin*? I guess that explains the similarities. Did he not want me to know that he was related to one of the "dangerous vampires" he mentioned before?

Alina's smirk widens into a twisted grin, as if she anticipates a fight between the two and is content to lounge in her chair and watch it unfold.

"Sorry, duty calls," Alex says coldly as he crosses his arms and straightens to his full height, his eyes hardening. He's not the most energetic person I've ever encountered, but he wasn't this sullen at the beginning of the night.

Slade nods and tucks his hands in his suit pockets, rolling back on his heels. "I see." He turns his amber eyes on me. "And who is this?"

Before Alex can answer for me I also hold myself up a little taller and say with more confidence than I feel, "I'm Juliette. We were just here to look at some security tapes. My friend is..." I hesitate, "...*was* hurt by someone, so we came here in hopes of finding a lead." Glancing at Alex, I add, "I made him come here, so don't blame him."

I turn back to Slade, his expression still carefully blank as he looks me over. Not creepily like Anthony, but assessing. Everywhere his eyes go, chills follow in their wake.

"Your friend was hurt here?" He asks, his voice casual and smooth.

"No, not here."

He hums like he doesn't believe me, or like we're wasting his time. "Your friend, do they have a name?"

"Serena. She's white with long black hair. Anthony said she used to come here a lot. On the tape we watched, some guy showed up and dragged her outside."

"Probably to the alley for a quickie," Anthony mutters.

I shoot him a glare, but that only causes him and his twin to snicker.

"I usually keep to my office during business hours, so I'm not sure I would recognize your friend or anyone who might have hurt her. Did Anthony give you the tapes to look over in more detail?"

I nod.

"Good. I hope you find what you're looking for, Juliette." The way he says my name sends shivers down my spine.

His assessing gaze lands on Alex, and he waves a hand in our direction. "You may leave now. I'll review the tapes myself when I get a chance."

"Thank you," I say, relieved that we can get out of this club and that he is willing to help, even without us explicitly asking. I should be glad that Slade is letting us leave without causing a fuss since I seem to be forgetting that all the people in this room, apart from myself, are vampires.

Something I'm soon reminded of when Anthony steps closer to me again.

"Can I have a taste, Slade?"

My entire body immediately stiffens in warning at his words, and I become acutely aware of the sudden pounding of my pulse. Anthony's eyes track every movement I make, and he reaches for my hair again.

Alex shoves him away from me before Slade can say or do anything.

"Don't touch her," he all but growls. "No one is tasting anyone." He grabs my shoulder and pulls me into him, angling us out of the room. My heart rate picks up even more as sweat begins to coat my palms.

Slade holds up a hand. "Wait. We gave you information to help your friend, you don't expect us to receive nothing in return, do you?"

There it is. There's the reason Alex was so wary to come to this club. To bring *me* to this club.

Alex's grip on my shaking limbs tightens and it seems to be the only thing keeping me from falling down. My headache reaches a point of pain that makes my eyes flutter closed, memories of That Night leaving room for nothing else. When my eyes open again, that sharp ache in my brain a constant companion, I spare a glance at

Alex. Fury is visible on all the lines of his handsome face as Alina watches the scene unfold with a gleam in her dark eyes and Slade waits patiently by his desk.

My body jolts when Anthony traces my neck with a finger, leaning down next to my face. "Your scent alone makes me want to taste you. I won't be able to get you out of my head until I do." His voice is a lover's caress, and it only adds to the shivers now racking my body.

I look to Alex again, who is still glaring at his cousin. "Call him off," he orders his cousin through gritted teeth.

"C'mon, Alex. It won't hurt her. Just a little pinch and she'll feel lightheaded for a while. It'll make her feel good, too," Slade says, giving him a knowing grin. When Alex's response is still a glower, Slade sighs heavily, a new bite of impatience to his tone.

"Do you want our help or not?"

He waves a hand and Alina rises from her chair, sauntering over to us. She runs a hand up Alex's chest, only adding to the storm of emotions running through me, and reaches behind him to grab the drive from his pocket. Alex grabs her wrist—his other hand still firmly locked around my own—as she pulls our evidence away, but Slade is there in a flash, taking it from her.

I swallow down my panic. *That's our only good lead so far!* I won't let them just take it away like that. If it means allowing Anthony a taste of my blood, then right now, it looks like I have no other options. There could be more worthwhile footage on that tape. I won't let Serena's killer go unpunished because I was too scared or too lost in the past. Not again.

Turning to meet Anthony's gaze, still zeroed in on my pulse, I relent. "Fine."

Alex protests, his grip on me getting impossibly tighter, but it's no use. Right before my eyes I see fangs replace Anthony's normal, human canines. It's a gruesome—yet fascinating—sight, how they push their way out of his gums, the other teeth retracting up into his mouth as the fangs take their place. Suddenly his mouth is on my neck, those fangs piercing my skin. I cry out at the sudden wave of pain and unwanted memories. I'm no longer in Slade's office but my old house.

But before my body is completely overtaken by That Night, a rush of warmth surges through my veins. My senses cloud and I couldn't muster up the energy to think about That Night even if I wanted to. For a moment all I feel is Alex beside me murmuring words I can't understand, and Anthony's warm mouth on my neck.

Anthony drinks deeply, lapping up anything that escapes the holes in my neck with his tongue, the sharp sting dissipating with every pass. My skin feels like it's on fire in the best way, and Alex's grip on me only adds to the burning sensation. He rubs slow, soothing circles around my wrists pulse point and my eyes flutter closed on a sigh of pleasure. That's when Alex shoves Anthony away.

"That's enough," he barks.

I'm ashamed to admit I almost protest, wanting to return to the painful pleasure that clouded everything else for a brief period of time. It was so different from the last time I was bitten, yet frightening all the same because of how much I enjoyed it.

I look at Anthony, watching with disgust as he licks his lips and groans in satisfaction. Touching my neck where he bit me, I notice the wound has miraculously already scabbed over, something that did *not* happen the last time.

Now that the mind-numbing pleasure is gone, I can feel the effects of the bite. My legs are shaking, head throbbing anew, and a slight sheen of sweat sticks to my forehead.

"You taste as good as you smell," Anthony says before taking up a place next to his sister, not bothering to hide his satisfactory grin. His teeth are stained red with my blood, and the sight alone makes me want to vomit.

Slade walks over and gives the drive back to Alex, barely sparing me a glance. He brushes a thumb over my clammy skin, landing on the bite mark. "Get her some juice or something, she's looking pale." I feel more violated by his touch and shrewd eyes than I did by Anthony's teeth in my flesh.

Alex turns us to the door to leave but Slade stops us again. "You're welcome," he says airily, yet with authority. Alina laughs almost maniacally.

"Thank you, cousin," Alex says through gritted teeth. Then we're gone, Alina's cackle following us through the hall, down the stairs and out of the club.

We don't speak during the walk back to the car. Alex still has his hand on my shoulder, and I'm glad for it. I'd probably collapse without his steady touch guiding me. My mind is reeling from what just went on inside the club.

A vampire sucked my blood. Again.

The cold air helps with the flush I feel on my skin, and it sharpens my senses slightly, bringing me back to the present. We have the footage from the night Serena was attacked, even if it cost a small part of my dignity to get.

"I'm sorry," Alex finally says as we reach his car. He opens the door for me and goes around to the driver's side to get in. Once inside he turns the car on but doesn't drive away just yet, instead turning to face me.

"I should've known they would…want something like that." He sighs and runs his fingers through his hair.

I look away, trying not to touch my neck where Anthony bit me. "Why did he ask Slade for permission to bite me?"

"Anthony and Alina feel like they owe my cousin a lot. They look up to him and Slade keeps a pretty tight leash on them because of it. Which is why Anthony had to ask permission. Slade really only lets them feed when he needs to... *take care* of someone, if you catch my drift."

I nod although I'm not sure I fully understand. I thought I had experienced all the horrors the vampire world had to offer already, but apparently there is much more to discover.

"I should've known they would ask for something like that in exchange for the footage. I'm sorry," he apologizes again. His face has gone back to the blank look he had on earlier. The hardness in his grey eyes is gone, but the tension around his jaw remains.

My blood chills at the memory of Anthony running his fingers down my arm and smelling me. Of the way his bite brought me pleasure even as he was taking my blood. I should be glad it was nothing sexual, that he was probably just hungry and I smelled like a tasty snack to him. But somehow the knowledge of him being desperate for a taste of my blood doesn't ease the knot in my stomach.

"It didn't feel like last time," I shudder thinking back. "It felt... *good*." I think a part of me just died admitting that.

"He used his venom," Alex replies grimly. "It used to be seen as a mercy for a vampire to use it while feeding. Now it's just common practice so whoever they're drinking from won't feel pain."

"Some vampires don't use it?" Obviously I know this. The vampire killing most of the city's population sure as hell isn't bothering to use this pleasure venom.

"No. Especially if they're in a frenzy."

"You don't go into frenzies?" I ask, tilting my head and studying his face. Something akin to irritation flashes in his eyes before he finally backs out of the parking space.

Alex shakes his head. "I'm not like them." His voice is low, and I'm not sure if he's trying to convince me, or himself.

I shake off his sudden annoyance. I know it's not directed at me but at the vampires we just left behind.

I want to ask him more about his parents and his life as a half vampire. About Slade—the dangerous leader of a literal *vampire gang*—being his *cousin* and why he didn't tell me. But I know now is not the time.

I hope there is time later for more questions and glimpses past Alex's careful mask because I want to know him. And I hope I get the chance to. For now I say, "Thank you for coming with me." Despite myself I let a small smile spread across my face. He glances at me before offering a tight smile back.

This world is a lot scarier than I originally thought. The Dead Boys Club might have nothing to do with this case—other than owning a club Serena frequented—or they could have everything to do with this case. Whatever it may be, I don't think this will be our last encounter with them.

18

ALEX

GLANCING AT JULIETTE IN the passenger seat, I know she's feeling the aftereffects of Anthony's bite. The shaking and light headedness from the blood loss along with the tingling as your body tries to come down from the pleasure high. Her eyes are tired, and her skin is paler than usual. I don't like lying, so I won't say she doesn't still look beautiful.

When she opened the door at her house earlier, I had to fight not to stare. It's completely inappropriate to be thinking of her in that way, and a waste of time. We're supposed to be working together to solve a murder case, not to mention that my life is completely unsuitable for relationships.

But that green dress... It brings out the flecks of emerald in her hazel eyes, creating a vision that is pure Juliette—like moss on a tree branch just after it snows. Out of place yet you can't help but admire the beauty it holds.

She hasn't spoken since we left, and I feel bad for not telling her Slade was my cousin. It's not the only thing I withheld; there's still so much more she doesn't know about me. But she hasn't asked, and I don't know how to broach the topic of my past any other way—not that I really want to. Besides, after we solve this case, we probably won't see each other ever again. For some reason, a pang goes through my chest just thinking about that inevitability.

Seeing Slade and the twins rattled me, but having Juliette there helped to keep me focused and grounded. And it wasn't all for nothing like I feared. We got the security footage from Serena Mitchell's final night, which is enough for now. I doubt that Slade has any intention of "looking into" the footage himself like he claimed he would, though.

It's even more clear now that Slade and the rest of the Dead Boys Club should be at the top of my suspect list. He might keep Anthony and Alina on a short leash, but he lets the others wreak havoc on the city—whether that's by stealing cars, trashing Crimson gyms, or participating in underground fights. And most of the cases I take on almost always connect to them in some way, even though Slade does his best to keep his own hands clean. I hate to admit when Silas is right, but he might be in this particular case.

There are other rogue groups of course, like Crimson, but none of them are as influential as the DBC. To get information on them, I would have to talk to someone from the Dead Boys Club, and after tonight, I would rather not interact with any of them for a long, long time.

I've known the twins for ten years, since they were twelve years old. At the time they were orphaned and scared, just like me. Though Alina has always been fierce, something we relied upon in those early days of our fledgling family.

The twins' mother had died in a plane crash and their father drained himself of blood in a fit of despair soon after. Alina was very tight-lipped about their past and made Anthony keep quiet as well. All I know is that their human grandmother—their mother's mother in Poland and only surviving relative—gave the twins a one-way ticket each to America from Italy, where the twins grew up.

There was a camaraderie between the four of us—Slade, the twins, and myself. All orphans with pasts' filled with tragedy. The twins became family to me and Slade and there was a time when I couldn't imagine my life without them. Now, I've lost them too. Sometimes I recognize them as much as I do myself—which is to say barely.

For the first time, I imagine Slade in Silas' underground prison. I would have been fine never seeing from or hearing about him again. Working for Silas makes that impossible considering the man's boulder-sized grudge against my cousin. Even after everything he made me do over the years—all the manipulation—I don't truly wish him harm. But after tonight, what he did to Juliette... I picture him in a cell so far underground no one will be able to hear his demands and manipulations ever again.

I spare another look at Juliette, quiet in the passenger seat, ready to ask if she wants to check out the footage at her house, but her sunken eyes and shaky hands stop me. Slade—the bastard—was right. She needs something to eat.

She gives me a confused look as I pull into the drive-thru of a burger place. Those hazel eyes of hers are a bit unfocused and duller now than I've ever seen them before.

"What are you doing?" She asks in a small voice.

"You need to eat. I know you're feeling the aftereffects of that bite."

"I'm fine." The protest is strong willed as always but lacking her usual bite. I ignore her objection and order two burgers.

"Kind of presumptuous of you," she says as I hand her burger to her. "What if I'm a vegetarian?"

"I watched you inhale a plate of chicken alfredo last night at dinner," I point out. She snatches the wrapped burger out of my palm in response, shooting me a glare. Unwrapping the food, she looks at me. "Thank you," she mumbles reluctantly before taking a bite.

A few seconds later she breaks the chewing-filled silence. "What's a blood hunter?"

I stare out the windshield, forming my response.

"It's an old term to describe someone who hunts vampires. Mostly it's used for vampires who hunt their own kind."

I remember reading about the exact history of the term from the thick books my dad kept in his office. It's not a phrase thrown around very often.

Well, well, well. If it isn't the blood hunter himself.

Alina is dangerous with a weapon or in a fight, but it's her words that often wound the most.

"It especially applies to me, given that I'm human and vampire."

Juliette chews a bite of her burger in contemplation before asking, "How does that work? Being born a vampire?"

"Same as being born a human."

"Go on." She's abandoned her burger entirely, focusing her attention solely on me. My ears burn from the weight of her stare.

"You can be born or turned. We're a species, just like humans. Though half vampires are more like humans than vampires."

"What do you mean? Because you don't need to drink blood?" The dullness in Juliette's eyes is replaced by fascination, brighter thanks to the food and our conversation. I've quickly learned that knowledge thrills her more than any adrenaline rush could.

"That and our abilities aren't as powerful." I crumple the wrapper of my burger and toss it in the paper bag by her feet.

"Abilities?" Did she lean into me? She didn't seem this close to me a minute ago.

"Yeah. Enhanced speed, strength, hearing, that sort of thing." I check off each one with my fingers. "Mine are better than the average human, but I can't heal as fast as full vampires. That's given me the most trouble."

A fight with a few vampires I was asked to hunt down last year pops into my mind, the phantom pain of a knife slice making me absently rub my arm. It nudges Juliette's on the console separating us. We're mere inches away now, her lips slightly parted as she contemplates whatever question she will inevitably ask next.

"So you can smell things that I can't? Hear things better than I do?"

Those heightened senses allow me to smell her florally scent clearly, as if I stuck my nose straight in her shampoo bottle. If I strain, I can hear the rapid rhythm of her heartbeat.

"Yes," I reply roughly.

"What can you hear right now?" She whispers as if raising her voice might impede my abilities.

My eyes narrow in on her pulse point, Anthony's bite almost fully healed over by now, and she watches me closely.

Faintly, like I'm pressed against a door to her organs, I can hear her heartbeat get faster. Her smell wraps around me, her entire essence encasing me, until I'm drowning in all that is Juliette.

She's close.

Too close.

This can't happen.

"I should take you back home now." My words spill out, jumbled together on a flustered breath.

Juliette leans back in her seat but doesn't say anything further. Her breaths don't slow, and I find mild satisfaction in the fact that I'm not the only one affected by our proximity. I'm also a little wary because whatever just happened between us cannot happen again. We have a job to do. The people of Pine Falls shouldn't suffer because we're too distracted by each other to solve this case.

When we get to her house, she is in much better spirits. Better than she has been all night. We got off to a strange start with her friend joining us in the car and then everything that went down at the club. But now, her face is back to its usual pale shade instead of the sickly one it was before. The furrow between her brows has dissipated, and she doesn't even give me time to turn the car off completely before she opens her door and hops out. Chuckling under my breath I follow her up the path to her house.

Her family's neighborhood is nice—nicer than any place I've lived in a long while. It reminds me of the house I grew up in and the security of living in a small town like Bellevue. Pine Falls is much larger, but here in the suburban confines of Juliette's street, I can pretend I'm somewhere else. *Sometime* else.

The windows of the house are dim, the porch light the only one on. No one is home yet.

I've only been to her house when other people were around, even if they were off doing their own thing. Now that it's just us, I'm even more aware of her presence than when we were in my car.

She takes the time to turn on every single light downstairs, checking the shadowy corners of the rooms and behind curtains before moving on to the next one. I trail her in silence, content to watch her back while she clears the floor. And with the way her eyes track every shadow, that's exactly what she's doing.

The stairwell is still dim, causing Juliette to miss a step halfway up and stumble. My hand darts out automatically to steady her by the waist, her skin warm under the thin fabric of her dress. I resist the urge to rub my thumb across the silky material.

"Oops," she grins sheepishly. "Still a little shaky, I guess."

Our eyes meet in the diluted light. Even in the darkened stairwell her silhouette is clear, moonlight glinting off her eyes and teeth from an upper window. It feels like time has stopped, but I know it's only been a few seconds when I clear my throat and remove my hand.

"Juliette, I'm sorry. Again."

"Stop with the apologies, Alex. I make my own choices. It's not up to you to protect me."

If only it were that simple. She's right, but I should have known better than to bring her there. I didn't want to go in the first place, but I should've prepared her for what they might've wanted in exchange.

Something in the air shifts, or something has shifted between us. Whatever it is, Juliette straightens and continues up the rest of the stairs without looking back. She goes through the same routine on the upper floor—turning on all the lights and checking behind doors, in closets, and under beds. I wordlessly help her look for whatever assurance she's seeking.

Her room is as cluttered as it was yesterday. All the items and clothes and pictures tossed and hung at random tell a story. You can tell who Juliette is just by walking into her room—by glancing at the many trinkets on her dresser, the books on her shelves, and the sketches hung up behind her bed. I love it, but I'm also envious.

"Thumb drive?" Juliette sits at her desk, laptop open, holding her hand out in my direction. I dig it out of my pocket and place the drive in her palm. My fingertips linger for longer than necessary on her soft skin. If she notices or is affected by it as much as I seem to be, she doesn't show it.

The same footage we saw on the club's monitors appears on the laptop and she quickly finds the time we need. We look through all the footage from Serena Mitchell's last night at Sinner, from when the club opened to when it closed.

I watch Juliette carefully whenever her friend makes an appearance, but whatever she's feeling is locked down. The only time she reveals the slightest bit of emotion is when the man grabs Serena on the dance floor.

He only appears for those few seconds—not enough to make out his identity in the darkened club.

"Could it be Slade?" Juliette's gaze is intently set on the man's head, as if staring hard enough will make him face the camera.

I study the screen as well. The mystery man looks to be about the same height as Slade, and they have the same dark hair and affinity for fitted black suits.

Damn. I hate to admit, again, that Silas could be right.

Denying any involvement with Slade and Sinner until now was foolish. There might be actual proof tying him to one, maybe two victims, and I'm unsure how to feel. He is my cousin, after all. Family. He's the one who took me in and raised me after my parents disappeared. He's the one who knew I didn't want to be sent to the school in Bellevue where I would never fit in and abide by rules made to control me. For the longest time, I felt like I owed him for that, and it took me too long to realize Slade had just given me a new set of rules to follow instead—his own.

And now? Now I'm stuck following Silas' rules.

"Definitely looks like him," I agree at last.

"So, he lied to us." Juliette huffs and crosses her arms.

"He does that a lot," I concede. "He's very good at it."

She whirls around in her chair and pins me with a stare. "Alex," she begins. The way my name flows past her tongue makes my skin heat. "Why didn't you just tell me that your cousin owned the club?"

"It's complicated," I answer quickly. She doesn't seem to care about any complications; she just stares at me with one eyebrow raised expectantly, waiting for me to expand. I don't care that she doesn't care. Not right now. I don't want to delve into my past, I just want to solve this case. She doesn't need any reason to fear me or, worse, pity me. Sharing my past will only make it harder to cut ties when all this is over, and we don't need to get any more attached to each other than we already are.

"I should go," I say, and her face falls. "I'll talk to Slade again later this week. He may not be responsible for the killings, but he's probably lying about knowing your friend."

She nods and stands up, that damn green dress bunching around her thighs. My eyes probably linger longer than necessary. We stand there awkwardly before I break the tension between us and head for the door. She casts her gaze around the room, walking over to turn on her nightstand lamp—the one light in this house she's yet to switch on—in addition to the ceiling light.

"Do you feel safe here? I can stay if you want," I offer.

She's already shaking her head. "No, go home. My parents should be back soon. I'll be okay."

I'm not so sure about that, so I tell her, "If they'll be back soon then it's no problem for me to wait with you." What I don't say is that I can tell she doesn't want to be alone, especially after the night she's had.

"Okay, if you insist," she tries to joke but it sounds more genuine than anything.

"When will you see Slade again?" she asks after a couple minutes. I can see in her eyes that she wants to go with me to talk to him, but she refrains from saying so. Whether it's because she doesn't want to interfere with our "complicated" relationship or she's afraid to go back, I'm not sure. What I am sure of, though, is that even if she had voiced wanting to go, I would have refused.

Damn her for making me care. For making me care about something other than my need for answers. Damn her for looking at me and not seeing a monster. For seeing someone worthy of a partnership—maybe even of friendship.

And damn her for making *me* afraid. Afraid for her and afraid of the day she'll inevitably learn the truth about me. The day she'll see me the way everyone else does.

I don't know who I am, but being around her has made me see a sliver of who I could be. Someone that can be relied on for things other than cleaning up messes. Someone learning to care again. That's not something I want taken away just yet. Maybe not at all.

"I'm not sure. I should talk to my boss first." Being subjected to Silas' gloating is not something I'm looking forward to experiencing in the near future.

"Your boss. You've mentioned them before. Who are they?"

"He's a leader in the vampire community," I reply, not wanting to share too much information about him. Juliette never fails to be endlessly curious about my world. She's all but vibrating with questions, though she tries to be causal about it. "How many leaders are there?"

"One for every region and then those directly under them to manage the areas within those regions. Silas is the leader of the West Coast vampire community."

She seems satisfied with that answer and surprisingly doesn't bombard me with a million follow-up questions. Soon after, we hear her parents arrive.

"Alex! So good to see you again," Christy greets me with a hug when I come downstairs. Her family is too nice. The little voice in my head whispers that I don't deserve this. *I don't belong here.*

Juliette must sense my discomfort because she ushers me out the door, making excuses for why I have to leave all the while fielding questions from her parents about why she's all dressed up.

It isn't until I'm back in my car and halfway home that I realize my own parents were like hers. My mother was the kindest woman on the planet. She made everyone she met feel welcome. It's not just that I don't belong at the Jennings house—it's a vision of some alternate reality. A look at what my life could have been, had my parents not been taken from me.

I used to not dwell on that shit, but the past few years have had me examining my life with a whole new lens. And now, Juliette has gone and broken the entire fucking thing. I may be seeing who I could be, but the goals I once had are clouded. Solving this case and leaving Pine Falls doesn't seem so simple anymore. Everything is fractured, and nothing makes sense.

19

JULIETTE

NOTHING CAN PREPARE YOU for when your life completely changes. Sometimes it's gradual, like doing your job well enough that you eventually receive a promotion. Other times it's abrupt, like witnessing your best friend's murder or having your blood sucked by a creature you grew up believing was just a myth. And then having your blood sucked again, not even two months later.

Absently, I run my fingers over the now faded puncture marks on my neck. After Alex left, I shut myself in my room, feigning sleep when someone—probably my mom—cracked my door open to check on me.

I doubt that Meg will drop her concern for me and her inquiries about Alex. But I'm too exhausted to answer her questions; I have enough of my own going unanswered.

Was Slade Serena's secret boyfriend?

Why did Alex not tell me about his cousin?

Is he ashamed of his past? Alex being a part of this "Dead Boy's Club" at one point seems very likely.

After our visit to Sinner, the Dead Boy's Club and Slade are now at the top of my suspect list. I also wonder if one of them is capable of being my stalker. Anthony did seem particularly interested in me... or maybe he was just hungry.

Slade evokes equal parts fear and curiosity in me. Could it be that he killed Serena and—like Alex suggested—has now been trying to relive that kill with other women who resemble her? That still doesn't explain the multiple other random murders or my own attack.

The vampire I saw That Night seemed out of control. Crazed. In a frenzy, like Alex said occurs with new vampires. From what I saw of his cousin last night, Slade appears the furthest thing from out of control. But still, you never really know what goes on in people's minds.

Shaking my head in attempt to clear my thoughts of Slade and Sinner and crazed vampires, I focus on the soft beams of light from my lamp illuminating the darkest corners of my room. It looks the same as it always has, and I remember a night a couple of years ago at the end of my sophomore year of college. I still lived at home, and Serena was here with me most days as well. She never liked her father's mansion. She always said it was too quiet and still—not unlike my own room currently. The opposite of Serena in every way—bold and always on the move.

Thinking back to that night years ago, I had also struggled to fall asleep due to the thoughts crowding my head. Although my worries were much simpler and easier to solve back then. I was worried about Serena because I hadn't seen her all day. She couldn't come over after her classes were done because her father needed help with something. I was worried about my grade in my economics class. Worried that a guy—whose name I don't even remember—thought the text I sent him might be too awkward.

At around one a.m., I heard a creaking, then a knock. Serena had climbed up to my window and I rushed out of bed to help her inside. "What are you doing?" I hissed in a harsh whisper.

She gave me one of her catlike smiles and replied, "What does it look like I'm doing? Help me in."

I grabbed hold of her arm and hauled her over the window frame. She was in a tight black dress, and her dark hair was straightened down her back. In the dim light, I could make out her perfect face of makeup as well. Serena looked twenty-eight instead of eighteen. What was she doing with her father where she needed to dress up like that? *I thought.*

"Up for a sleepover?" She asked, peeling off her dress and rummaging through my drawers for some pajamas.

"Will your dad mind?"

Serena scoffed, "Fuck him. Besides, I'm not even supposed to be at home right now, so he won't notice." Her back was to me as she changed. Something was off with her. There was more venom than usual in her tone when she spoke of her father.

"Where are you supposed to be?" I perched on the edge of my bed, watching her closely.

She shrugged. "Nowhere I'll be missed."

I found that hard to believe. Serena wasn't someone who went unnoticed.

We climbed into my bed and laid side by side, staring at one another and whispering secrets into the dark like we always did. I told her about the cute guy in my history class, and she told me about the football player she kissed the day before.

We talked about nothing and everything. There wasn't much we didn't share. That night, though, Serena held back. Staring into her eyes I noticed they were red like she'd been crying, even though her makeup wasn't smudged. I knew her strange demeanor had something to do with her father, but we never talked about him so I didn't bring it up.

Now I lie in bed by myself staring at the wall where Serena should be.

"There's a new guy I like," I whisper to the dark.

I can practically hear her response in my head: *What are you going to do about it?*

"Probably nothing," I mumble into my pillow.

Coward. The ghost of her voice follows me into sleep.

It's surreal to me that barely a week ago I was struggling to trust that a vampire is responsible for the killings, especially now that I've been bitten again. Now I'm walking into a second vampire owned establishment in just as many days.

According to Alex, Crimson is a vampire gang notorious for not following directions. However, unlike the Dead Boy's Club, they aren't known for causing chaos. All they want is to live by their own rules regarding who they are and not follow the strict guidelines some guy in charge tries to implement. Alex even informed me that they have humans in their employ, which is how I found out that creepy guy from the Halloween party, Tyler, is a Crimson member.

I mentioned to Alex that Tyler knew Serena from some parties and that maybe it wouldn't hurt to ask him more questions, this time with a brooding vampire at my side. If the way Tyler behaved at the party is any indication, he's scared of Alex. Maybe scared enough to reveal something he might have held back from me at the party.

Alex and I enter a sleek gym I've passed a dozen times on my way to and from the restaurant. *All this time vampires were lurking so close, and I had no idea.*

The inside of the gym is about as empty as the restaurant these days. I think I even spot some dust on the row of treadmills. The only sound is the faint tapping of nails against a phone screen and the reality dating show playing on the TV in the corner of the lobby. I hear the clearly distraught star, Tori, lament about how Daniel decided to go on a date with Rebecca instead of her. It's all quite tragic.

"Is Tyler here?" Alex asks the receptionist.

She slowly looks up from her phone, short hair in effortless waves and makeup done to perfection, pointing vaguely to her right. Recognition jolts me from my assessment of the gym, stepping closer to the desk.

"I know you," I say and turn to Alex. "This is the girl who showed me that video of Serena." The girl—Marissa, I think her name was—scoots her chair back a couple inches, shrinking in on herself as Alex settles his gaze on her.

Is she a vampire too?

"Thanks for the lead," he says with a nod. The girl gives him a wary smile and points back to the main gym area. "Tyler's in there."

I'm torn between staying here and demanding more details about how she knew Serena, or going to find the person we came to see. Both people with the same connections knew Serena and knew she had a boyfriend. Is that a coincidence?

Tyler is the only one using the gym equipment, hoisting his upper body above the pull up bar. Sweat glistens on his forehead, and his face is beet red from exertion. He spots me first, his eyes lighting up, but the smirk forming on his face falters when he spots the tall shadow looming next to me.

"Tyler," Alex greets him stiffly, shoving his hands in the pocket of his hoodie.

The other man eases himself onto the floor and grabs a towel, making a show of wiping his face off and flexing his muscles before he addresses us. "Alex. What do you want?" Alex steps aside, allowing me to speak to Tyler.

"It's not Alex who wants something."

"Good to see you again, baby. It's too bad you're with Alex. I don't know how you can stand all of... *that*." He waves a hand at the man beside me.

"I'm not your *baby*," I say at the same time Alex bites out, "She's not your *baby*."

Ignoring him, I get to the point. "I wanted to ask you more about Serena Mitchell and her boyfriend."

Tyler's brows scrunch up and he stares at the ceiling, thinking, before snapping his fingers. "Serena! Right, that girl who was murd—"

"Did she ever mention her boyfriend's name?" I cut him off, getting a bit irritated. All Marissa said was she thought she heard Serena call him "K" once. Alex silently stands beside me, letting me lead this line of questioning.

"Look, you're a chick, so I thought you'd know this. Sometimes girls say they have a boyfriend just to get guys to back off. I don't mess with them if they do, even if they are lying. Some guys though, they don't care. So you gotta be careful." He taps the side of his head with a beefy finger.

"Thanks for the advice," I respond flatly.

At this point, I'm pretty sure Serena wasn't lying; although I definitely do not blame her if she was just trying to get this guy off her back. Am I not essentially doing the same thing? I'm pretending to be with Alex in front of Tyler. Well, not exactly pretending, but I can't control what Tyler assumes. And maybe I don't feel like correcting him.

"Like, if you had told me Alex was your boyfriend from the start, I never would've tried to hit you up. Understand how it works?"

The condescension in his tone is just enough to drown out the fluttering in my chest at "Alex" and "boyfriend" in the same sentence. Those strange feelings are overshadowed by my growing annoyance with this mansplaining frat bro. But at least he didn't call me "baby" this time.

"Did she say a name?" I ask again through gritted teeth, the same time Alex mutters, "You're such a dick."

Tyler whips the towel over his shoulder, apparently oblivious to Alex's comment. "Nah. All she said was," he clears his throat and continues in a high, inflected voice, "*Get the fuck away from me I have a boyfriend.*" He continues in his normal voice, "Then I said, 'You don't need to be so hostile. Does he have a name? Maybe I know him.' And she replied by smacking me in the face and walking off."

My lips twitch at the vision of Serena smacking this guy. I would very much like to do that right now. Judging by the tension radiating off Alex, I'd wager he'd like to do that, too.

"When was this?" I ask instead. Tyler smacks the towel against his palm while he thinks.

"Few years ago. Boss opened up a club on the south side, and she was at the opening."

So she was dating this mystery boyfriend for *at least* a few years? How much did she keep from me, exactly? And why? Could I not be trusted? I hate the heaviness in my heart at this information.

Tyler gives Alex a cutting glance. "Before your boys trashed it and drove us out."

Alex's glare could freeze even the hottest depths of hell. "A few years ago they weren't *my boys* anymore. I have you to thank for that, Tyler."

The two stare each other down and before I can declare that the testosterone in here is too suffocating and we should leave, Tyler speaks again, his tone irreverent once more. "Anyway, I started seeing her around a lot more after that. And you don't forget a pretty face like hers." For once, he seems solemn. Serena's effect on people was definitely not a silent one.

"Alex. What brings you back so soon?" An unfamiliar voice calls from an archway to the left of us. A man about the same height as Alex emerges, colorful tattoos spread out on his muscular arms, exposed by his tank top.

"Who's this?" The man asks, sizing me up. I do the same to him.

"This is Juliette. She had some questions for Tyler," Alex responds evenly.

"Silas is letting anyone help out on cases now?" The guy arches a brow dubiously.

"We're keeping it on the downlow," Alex says. "Juliette, this is Kai Nakamura. He's Crimson's leader."

I give him a small nod, not entirely sure how comfortable I feel in another vampire's presence so soon after last night. Especially another vampire with authority.

"They were just asking me some questions about that dead—" Tyler breaks off and shoots a nervous glance our way before looking back to Kai. "Her friend who... You know, the Knife Man," he splutters.

Kai purses his lips, folding his arms across his chest. "Right. Serena?"

I want to ask how they seem to know about her and our connection before remembering our attack was blasted all over the news for weeks. Honestly it's a miracle I'm not stopped on the street more often. If there were people on the streets to even stop me.

"You won't find what you're looking for here," Kai continues with a pointed look at Alex. "I know your boss probably wants to pin this on us, but we know nothing."

"I believed you the first time you said it. We're just trying to follow any lead we have," Alex replies firmly.

"We don't want to be mixed up in this, Alex. I think you should leave."

What looks like hurt flashes across Alex's face before he reins it in, twisting his mouth to the side. He and Kai stare at each other for a few tense seconds before breaking their gazes.

"Always a pleasure, Tyler," Alex drawls, jerking his head towards the lobby in a motion for me to follow him. "Sorry you didn't get the answers you were hoping for," he tells me, our arms brushing. The skin beneath my jacket buzzes with the small, innocent gesture. I won't forget the moments we shared the night before, especially in his car. He looked at me with such intent I could hardly breathe, let alone think straight.

In the lobby, the TV no longer plays the dating show from when we first walked in but the news.

"*The body was found near the water, in the warehouse district. Authorities have confirmed that the wounds the deceased sustained are consistent with previous victims of the Knife Man. If you have any information regarding these attacks...*" Footage of the docks across town flash across the screen. Rolling text on the bottom reads: *Pine Falls Knife Man Strikes Again*.

Alex stops at the desk, leaning against it to watch the news coverage. "When did they say the victim died?"

"I don't know. I just switched the channel," Marissa answers, her attention focused more on her phone than the TV or Alex.

"The warehouse district... That's close to Sinner," I whisper to him. Alex hums in agreement and heads for the door, holding it open for me.

Did this latest victim die before, during, or after our visit to Sinner? Or did they die because of our visit? The thoughts make me feel queasy, my stomach knotting from the confusion of it all.

Alex looks equally uncomfortable, his face scrunched in contemplation. Neither of us speak on the way back to his car, too caught up in questions and yet unable to voice a single one.

20

JULIETTE

The ice arena across town that the figure skaters use is freezing. It's nice in the summer—on the rare days it gets warm—but in the fall and winter it's hell. I'd rather endure the heat of actual hell than the blistering cold of an air-conditioned rink during late fall.

It's for Meg, I remind myself over and over, hugging my sweater-clad torso in the near empty stands. Since her scholarship is safe *for now*, Meg invited me, Josie, and Hayden to watch her skating practice. She's trying to include me, even if I've not been the most pleasant person to be around lately. A selfish part of me also hopes that accepting her invitation to watch her practice will ease her of my suspicious behavior for a while.

Three skaters, including Meg, are on the ice today. The winter showcase is in a few weeks, so their coach keeps shouting corrections at all three of them. Meg has complained numerous times about "just wanting to get through Halloween" before working on winter routines. But she sucks it up because she wants to go to the Olympics. I have no doubt that in a couple of years she'll be there.

Meg skates around elegantly, doing moves I would be way too afraid to do with blades strapped to my feet. She circles the ice, and my eyes follow, landing outside the rink near the doors to the entrance. The entrance where two familiar white-blond heads are making their way towards the stands, their matching all black outfits standing out in the icy arena. Alina and Anthony. If I never saw them again, it would be too soon. But my luck hasn't been the best lately.

Alina watches Meg with fascination, but Anthony keeps his focus on me. My pulse skyrockets at just the sight of the twins, remembering the other night when my blood was sucked. It still seems so surreal. I shove those memories aside for the more pressing concern of why they are here, and how they found me.

"Who are they?" Josie whispers in my ear from behind me as the twins so obviously head our way. I don't have time for an adequate explanation to give her before they're within earshot, climbing the steps, and straddling the bench in front of me. They both have the same smirk pasted on their faces, and Anthony seems to be bored with me already as he openly checks out either Hayden or Josie. Maybe both.

Good, I think. Maybe his lack of interest means he won't try and drink my blood again. Though I hope he isn't thinking he wants to try Hayden's or Josie's blood... The thought of that has me shifting ever so slightly in front of them.

"Hello again, Juliette," Alina says in that slightly accented voice. Her deep brown eyes contrast with her pale skin and hair. She's beautiful in a deadly way, and it's so at odds with her brother, who lounges on the bench. If I didn't know any better, I would think he was just a regular twenty something hanging out with his friends.

"What are you doing here?" I demand in an undertone, trying to keep Hayden and Josie from hearing.

Alina's smile widens and she leans in, "We need to talk about Alex."

"What about him?" I ask, firmer than I would have a couple of months ago, especially to someone as intimidating as Alina. But every day it seems I'm learning new things about myself and pushing myself to new limits.

I immediately feel defensive of Alex and whatever Alina has to say about him. They have a history. I'm strangely jealous of that, but I push down those nonsensical feelings.

"You shouldn't trust him," Anthony says with a piercing stare, suddenly serious. I haven't known him for long, but I doubt he adopts that tone often.

It's on the tip of my tongue to retort something back to him about the irony of what he just said. *Says the man who sucked my blood the other night with coercive consent at best.* If it weren't for Hayden and Josie sitting right behind me, I might have.

"Jules?" Hayden lays a hand on my shoulder. "Are you going to introduce us to your friends?"

Anthony's mouth lifts in a smile again. "Yes, *Jules*, aren't you going to introduce us?"

I exhale sharply through my nose and stand up, irritated. Some other spectators in the stands are gushing over the skaters, oblivious to the two predators among them.

"No, they were just leaving." I jerk my chin toward the exit and climb down the stands. After a couple seconds I hear two sets of footsteps on the metal benches echoing after me. Once we're in the safety of the lobby, away from the prying eyes and ears of my friends, I round on the twins.

"What the *hell* are you guys doing here?"

Alina looks at me, sizing me up. "You're a feisty one." She smirks when I glower at her and glances around the lobby, feigning adoration at the outdated interior.

"This is a public place, no? This practice is open to the public and we happen to be *big* figure skating fans."

I cross my arms over my chest and try to do my best impersonation of Meg whenever she's trying to win a fight. Or Alex when he wants answers—collected and unyielding. But Alina is intimidating as hell. The kind of girl who causes confusing feelings inside someone's head. Feelings that make it hard to remain firm *or* collected. "Answer the question."

She sighs dramatically and picks at her nails, perfectly painted, unlike her brother's. "We came to warn you away from Alex." Her near black eyes hold mine in a severe gaze. "Like my brother said, he can't be trusted."

"He screwed us all over," Anthony chimes in.

My brows furrow. "What are you talking about?"

I hate that they know things I don't, that I'm forced to ask them follow up questions to sate my curiosity. That Alex refuses to open up in any way with the questions I ask him.

"Your little boyfriend left the Dead Boy's Club a few years ago and spilled most of our secrets to his new boss," Alina explains. "And now he hunts us. His own friends. His own family." Her eyes glitter with malice and she practically spits out the last word.

Confirmation that Alex was in fact a member of the Dead Boy's Club doesn't stir panic like I thought it might. I know enough about him to know that he's shied away from sharing his past possibly out of shame or guilt. And if the display I was privy to at the club the other night is any indication to how the Dead Boy's Club operates, Alex may have taken part in many acts he now views as heinous.

"Well, thanks for the warning," I say tightly. "You can go now."

The twins shrug and saunter off to the doors. Alina glances back once. "Don't say we didn't warn you. Alex is only ever out for himself."

She pushes open the double doors, sunlight streaming in from the parking lot outside. Anthony lingers, and I almost leave him when he stops me. "I'm sorry... about the other night."

Again, that serious tone that sounds so foreign. I freeze, unsure how to react. I'm still not sure what is and isn't a joke to him.

"I shouldn't have done that. That's not how I usually am," he goes on. "It's no excuse, but I am sorry. And try not to let Alina get to you. I think she's scared. Her girlfriend, Naomi, is human." I don't have a chance to respond before he's pushing open the doors and following after his sister, leaving me in the lobby with nothing but confusion for company.

"Would you mind taking the trash out when you're done?" My mom calls from the restaurant kitchen to where I'm helping wipe down tables.

"Sure," I call back, my mind elsewhere as I complete the latest menial task assigned to me. I can't stop thinking of Alina's warning earlier that Alex is only ever out for himself. That I shouldn't trust him. Why warn me at all? I doubt it's because she cares about my wellbeing. Or maybe she does, and the tough, sadistic girl act is just that—an act. Maybe she really does want me to watch my back with him. The whole interaction has left me more confused than I usually am, and my fingers have probably rubbed a permanent dent in my forehead trying to parse together a semblance of understanding.

Tossing the rag I was using into a bucket, I head over to the kitchen entrance to collect the trash. The dinner shift was relatively better than prior days—a whopping ten guests compared to the usual six or so. Still, the money we made tonight is just a drop in the bucket of never ending bill payments.

The constant rain that plagues the area this time of year beats in a steady downpour as I push open the alley door. The earthy scent of weed and wet pavement hits my nose. Droplets of rain cling to the skin that isn't covered by my hoodie and jeans, a slight mist swirling in this stretch of space.

I make a disgusted noise as my fingers grip the wet, slimy dumpster lid, and I hastily throw the trash bag inside. The dull thud it makes when it lands on the bottom is drowned out by the rain and first claps of thunder promising a heavy storm tonight.

Turning around, I start to head back inside when something appears in my peripheral vision. A figure stands at the mouth of the alley, hidden from the streetlamps and almost completely cloaked in darkness. I stumble back out of shock, then fear. My heart pumps wildly in my chest as I stare into the depthless void of my stalker's hood.

It has to be him, *right*? I squeeze my eyes shut and rub my temples, wondering if he'll still be there when I open them again. Unsure if I'm hoping he will be or praying that he won't.

This is it, I think. Serena's killer has finally decided to strike. He's never been this close before. Now would be the perfect time—a defenseless girl in a dark alley with the rain and thunder to cover her screams, and wash away any evidence. Too bad I won't give him the opportunity.

"What do you want?" I shout down the alley, my voice echoing off the damp stones. It's nullified by the rain, so I take a brave step forward, then another.

He stands still, not a twitch of a muscle or a sign he's at all worried about my approach. I move to take another step, the dense drops splattering the alley and soaking my clothes, but I stop as my foot hits something solid.

The blood drains from my face, and I'm left feeling empty and cold and full of renewed horror as I look down.

No, no, no, no.

My shoe collided with another shoe.

A shoe that is attached to a foot, attached to a leg, attached to a still body, attached to a terrifyingly lifeless face.

A face I've seen before, with slight differences.

A face I see every time I close my eyes.

Lying before me is a dead body. Pale skin, dark hair, unseeing eyes. *Serena.*

No, not Serena. She just looks eerily like her.

The alley disappears and I'm back in my old living room, memories I try to keep at bay flooding me. Blood pools under my feet, caught beneath my nails and coating my skin. I close my eyes and rub my hands, but the image persists. I think I'm screaming, but I can't be sure.

I try to inhale, but it's as if my breath is caught in my throat, unwilling to move down into my lungs.

I'm fine. I'm fine. I'm fine, I chant over and over again in my head.

Who would do something like this? *Why* are they doing this?

And why the *fuck* do I have to see it again?

Weeks of separation from the crime has made me numb to it. Dull to the horrors that this killer has inflicted. Placing photos on my murder board and contemplating theories has made me forget. Not even being bitten again was as harsh of a reminder as the dead body at my feet. A reminder that whoever is doing this is sick. Cruel. *A monster*. And they need to be stopped.

Filled with a sense of urgency, I snap my head up and stagger away from the body just as the hooded man disappears through the mouth of the alley. Not giving myself any more time to think, I chase after him.

My sneakers slip on the soaked concrete, but pure adrenaline keeps me upright. Coming to a halt at the end of the alley where he stood, I pivot in the direction I saw him leave but see nothing. No one darting down the once busy street. He must have used that enhanced vampire speed Alex told me about.

Growling in frustration, I wipe my soaked hair off my face and think about next steps. I need to call Alex. I also need to tell someone about the dead body I found. The *second* murder victim I've encountered, I realize. Great. That won't be a good look for me.

Is the killer's goal to kill me or to put me in jail?

I step back into the alley, and my gaze snags on something white. A piece of paper sticks to the ground, nearly mush thanks to the rain. But I'm still able to discern the message inked on its surface.

You should have stayed away.

I back away from the note like it'll grow fangs and bite me. Fumbling for my phone, I rush to snap a photo before the rain completely washes the message away. But I'm too late. The paper finally crumbles from the force of the water, destroying the message along with it.

21

JULIETTE

THE POLICE, LIKE LAST time, were entirely unhelpful when they arrived. The alley and surrounding buildings swarm with cops and the forensics team, lights from the muted sirens shine off the brick and the pale skin of the body still on the ground. The rain stops but not before washing away all the evidence that could have been obtained.

You should have stayed away.

The running ink from the latest threat flashes around my mind, and my first thought goes to the twins and their surprise visit today. Their warning.

"Here." A uniformed officer practically shoves a cup of water in my hands. "Just a little while longer and we'll take you down to the station."

The cop's words are clipped and my irritation grows. *Take me down.* My mom rubs my shoulders in what I'm sure she thinks is a reassuring way while my dad busies himself by talking to another officer.

The cops want to take me to the police station for a "statement." But I'm not stupid—they're beginning to suspect me again. Maybe Laurence Mitchell was able to influence them after all, convincing them that I'm working with the Knife Man and that my coma was just a convenient alibi. Though I don't think the cops can arrest me because there isn't any evidence tying me to this crime. At least I *hope* they can't arrest me.

Even in my frantic state, I made sure not to touch the body, and my parents and the restaurant guests can all place me inside when the victim was dumped in our alley—according to a conversation I heard between the forensics team, it *was* dumped here. There are also no cameras out here, which is both a blessing and a curse. But still, I found the body. That's cause enough for the police to want to "take me down" for questioning.

They can't seriously think I'd be dumb enough to dump a body at my place of work, do they? My family's restaurant no less, where this could take our number of guests from a mere six to zero.

"Miss Jennings." A man dressed in a suit one size too large approaches me. I heard some of the other cops refer to him as Detective Michaels. I recognize his voice as the cop Laurence Mitchell was arguing with after I woke up from my coma.

"Do you need anything before we head out?" Detective Michaels asks.

Do I need anything? Is this his way of asking if I want a lawyer? What I really want is to call Alex and tell him what happened. To ask if he knows already that another body was found—*by me*. What I *need* is to not be suspected.

"No," I tell Michaels.

The police station is exactly how I pictured it would be. Stale coffee and sweat permeate the air broken up by the sounds of shuffling papers and ringing phones answered by droning voices. The fluorescent lights buzzing overhead make my head throb.

My parents were asked to wait in the reception area while the detectives "talked" with me. At this point, I'm not entirely confident they wouldn't suspect me—both the cops *and* my parents. Hell, even I'm starting to question my own sanity again. Someone has to be doing this on purpose. Implicating me, fucking with me.

Detective Michaels opens up a door leading to an interrogation room. They could have at least taken me to an office, made it less obvious somehow that I could be arrested in the coming days. The metal chair I'm forced to sit in is uncomfortably cold and stiff. There's another cop I've never seen before already seated opposite me.

For a brief moment I consider telling them about the figure I saw in the alley earlier—my potential stalker. I squash that idea because, again, what if he's not even real? Even though that note he left behind definitely was. *Or was it?* It vanished before I could even take a photo, the remnants of the paper whisked down the nearest storm drain.

"Miss Jennings," Michaels starts, settling himself in the chair next to the other detective. "You have to know how this looks. The first victim found at your home, by you. Another found at your family's restaurant, again by you."

I flinch at him calling Serena the first victim instead of her name, and completely disregarding the own injuries and near death I experienced.

"Two I've found, out of dozens," I add with the foolish hope he won't think I'm somehow responsible.

The other cop leans forward in his seat, a smug smile on his face. "Still an odd coincidence," he says.

"I've been thinking the same thing," I reply.

He considers me for a moment. "I think you liked the attention finding that girl and being attacked gave you."

"Excuse me?" I bristle at his assured tone—as if he knows anything about me.

"We've been keeping tabs on you, Juliette. Not doing so hot in school. Barely talking to your friends anymore. Hanging around with some guy with a record."

I don't even know where to start with this man, or all the things he just revealed. *They've been watching me?* Why does everyone want to watch me? I can't be *that* interesting.

"You think I *liked* watching my best friend get murdered? You think I liked almost dying? I was in a coma. I had a concussion. Of course I'm not doing well in school or wanting to talk to my friends." All of that is partly true. My concussion is a convenient excuse—one that I really shouldn't use anymore but can't seem to stop.

Michaels doesn't say anything, just lets the other guy talk. "See that's the thing. No matter which way we look at it, there's no way the killer would let you walk away from that. There was no forced entry into the house, so someone either let him in or he had a key." He must be consulting the Laurence Mitchell handbook of theories. "Are you working with someone? Is it that guy," he consults the file spread open before him. "Alex?"

Do I need a lawyer? I wasn't arrested, I can leave at any time. Right? My knowledge of police procedure only extends to what I've seen on TV and in movies.

"You know he's been arrested for assault before, don't you?" He continues and it takes monumental effort to keep my cool in front of them. Losing my temper would only further their suspicions of me.

"Alex has nothing to do with any of this," I say with a bite to my tone, trying not to let my shock show through my voice. *No, Detective Asshole, I did not know Alex was arrested for assault.*

The cop is relentless in his pursuit to make me doubt myself and my new partner-friend-person. "I bet if we looked hard enough you wouldn't have any alibis for the times the other victims were killed. Some of them sort of look like your friend, don't you think? Let me guess—you were in love with her, but she didn't want you."

Oh, *fuck* this guy. Of course, he would assume that a queer person would resort to aggression when their feelings weren't reciprocated. As if a straight man would *never* do that.

I take a deep, steadying breath. "I think you need a better theory, detective. That one's a bit dated. And offensive," I mutter with a scowl.

"That's enough, Detective Logan," Michaels finally breaks his silence.

The other cop, Logan, studies my face, a smug look on his own. I try to school mine into a neutral expression. I know I didn't kill that girl or the others, just like I didn't kill Serena. But his stare and his questions and the fact that I'm in an interrogation room still make me nervous. It's like when you see a cop pull up beside you at a stop light. Even if you've done nothing wrong, just the proximity of the police makes you wonder if you have.

"Are you going to arrest me?" I ask him, crossing my arms and feeling a bit weary.

"Did you kill Naomi Hart?" He asks me point blank.

Naomi? Where have I heard that name recently?

"No," I answer firmly, proud that my voice only shakes a little bit.

Logan cocks his head and considers me for a second. "Then no, I won't be arresting you. At least not tonight."

He and Michaels rise from their seats, and I hold in my breath of relief despite his not-so-subtle confirmation that I'm still a suspect. The door opens and another cop comes in, looking to Michaels, then Logan. No one says anything, and I take it as my cue to leave.

I walk out of there as fast as I can without looking suspicious, calling Alex as I rush down the hallway. He picks up on the first ring, and I breathe that sigh of relief I've been waiting to release.

"Juliette?" The deep, slightly raspy, timbre of his voice calms me. I feel a little lighter than I did just a minute ago. I don't have to do this alone. It's not the same as it has been.

My family and friends are supportive, but they treat me like I'm fragile glass teetering at the edge of a table, ready to fall and shatter at any moment. It's different with Alex. He respects me and my choices, and even though we haven't known each other long, I trust that he'll help me pick up the pieces when I inevitably break.

"Hey," I respond, relief palpable in my tone. "Something happened, and I need you."

22

ALEX

THE DINGY DINER WHERE Juliette and I had our first meeting is near empty, which makes it the perfect place to talk. She suggested we meet here for breakfast to discuss the prior evening's *events*. When she informed me she was calling from the police station, I was two seconds away from hopping in my car to meet her there. I could hardly sleep, thinking of all she's been through. All she's *still* going through.

My worry for her has steadily increased over the time we've worked together, short as it's been. Being threatened and finding another body is exactly the sort of thing I was hoping to shield her from by agreeing to work with her. If Silas finds out that the killer is now openly taunting a human... he won't like it one bit. Especially if he finds out that the human in question knows what the killer truly is and that we're working together.

He's already almost at his limit with me. He texted me multiple times last night asking where I'm at with Slade and the DBC. It's going to be literal torture for me to admit that he may be right about their involvement. But it didn't stop me from sending him information about a case on the East Coast about ten years prior—which he ignored.

Victims disappeared from their cars and later turned up drained of blood and beheaded. It's disturbing as fuck, but I remember it from when I was looking into what happened to my parents. Even now years later, it doesn't escape me that the time and circumstances are eerily similar to what happened to them. The only difference is that my parents were never found.

Juliette finishes recounting last night from seeing a mysterious figure, to discovering another body, to chasing after said mysterious figure. Honestly, it's a miracle my tongue didn't start bleeding from how hard I bit it when I heard about her encounter with the killer again. It's also a miracle that she's sitting in front of me right now having escaped the killer twice.

She ends her story in between sips of hot chocolate with extra whipped cream—she actually drank it this time, which feels like progress—telling me about the note she saw and how the police brought her in for questioning.

"Sounds like you had quite the day yesterday," I tease so I don't let my true feelings about the situation show and then add in a more serious and sympathetic tone, "I'm sorry."

Juliette waves my words away with her hand. "It wasn't your fault. Besides, that's not even all of it. Anthony and Alina paid me a visit."

Bewilderment and concern compete for space in my head. "They *what*?"

"Yeah, they showed up at the ice arena while I was there for Meg's figure skating practice. I don't know how they found me, but they warned me away from you," she speaks into her mug, using her spoon to scoop out the last of the whipped cream.

I sit with what she just said for a minute, imagining the twins telling Juliette to stay away from me. It's definitely odd that they told her to stay away and then that same day she sees a note saying basically the same thing. I'm sure she's put that together already, so I don't voice it aloud. She also doesn't seem too bothered by their visit, and she obviously didn't heed their advice if she's here with me. Still, that shadowy part of me that battles for prominence tells me that she is one step closer to finding out my past. Discovering who I truly am.

A monster.

"Can I get you anything else?" The waitress's question derails my dark train of thought. She's the same one who was here the other night. The diner is apparently just as short staffed as the rest of the city's businesses.

Juliette drains the last of her drink and slides her half-eaten plate of pancakes and eggs away. "Just the check, thanks."

"What do you mean, 'warned you away from me?'" I try to voice my question in a casual manner, but my temper gets the better of me and laces my tone with venom.

Juliette bites on her lower lip before answering, "They said you betrayed them. That you spilled their secrets to your boss, so you can't be trusted."

"It's not my choice to work for him." This time I try to temper my anger because it's not the girl across from me I'm upset with. I could easily give up all their secrets if there was a possibility of being set free for it, but I haven't and I won't. Because despite everything, Slade is still my family. I can't blame them for assuming that I would divulge their secrets to Silas, though.

Juliette nods in understanding even though I'm sure more questions are erupting inside her pretty head. I pull out my wallet before she can fish hers out of her bag and glance at the clock on the wall.

"Don't you have class?" I ask, changing the subject. The waitress drops the check on the table and Juliette waits until she leaves with our plates before telling me,

"There are more important things to be doing right now."

Deciding not to stick my nose in that particular piece of her business, I change the subject again. "I was thinking, all the victims have suspiciously lacked blood. The police hypothesize that the killer cleans their bodies and dumps them. Obviously, we know that's not the case. There's no blood in the bodies because he drains his victims."

"Right..." Juliette says slowly, trying to determine where I'm going with this.

"Serena was covered in blood," I say as delicately as I can. Even a vampire in a frenzy wouldn't leave such a mess behind. The way Juliette describes it, there was blood all over the place. "Maybe too much blood for one person."

"What are you saying?" Juliette's brows furrow, and I have to fist my hands under the table to resist the urge to smooth the line between them.

Looking around to make sure the few other diners can't hear us, I lean forward and explain, Juliette mirroring my movement. "Turning someone into a vampire is a very... *messy* process."

Juliette rears back, mouth parted and brows raised. "You think someone was trying to turn Serena into a vampire?" she asks in a hushed voice. I grimace and nod, remembering the few times I've witnessed the process.

It's unpleasant, to say the least. The first time I saw it done, I was eleven and Slade was fifteen. My father tried to turn my uncle's new human wife, and he forbade Slade and I from witnessing it. We were supposed to go to our neighbors, the Levitt's, house but we snuck back home. Slade and I heard the whole thing, taking turns peering through the cracked door of my father's study.

The turning wasn't successful. The woman who was briefly my aunt died. My uncle never forgave my father for that and soon followed his wife to the grave. Slade was forced to attend Bellevue Manor—the boarding school for vampires—after that, and I didn't see him again until I lost my own parents.

Funny how death can bring people together as much as it rips us apart.

The other two times I was unfortunate enough to witness a turning were when Slade made Anthony and Alina try it. Being half vampire I'm unable to turn anyone but my cousin still made me watch so I could *learn.* It was just as horrifying as I'd remembered. He brought in two human men he saw harassing a girl so when the turnings were unsuccessful none of us felt too guilty. That was what we wanted to do, deliver justice to those who committed wrongdoings. Somewhere along the way that mission became warped, and we became just as bad as the people we swore to hunt down.

I couldn't bring myself to witness all the other times the three of them turned people. Blood gets everywhere—from both the vampire who is doing the turning and the one being turned—and the screams and cries of pain as the human begins the transformation process are truly horrifying. Those noises will haunt me for the rest of my life.

We were the start of Slade's empire, formed of blood and screams in a ramshackle house outside of town.

Being half vampire has always had me feeling on the outs of the two worlds, but sometimes I'm thankful that I'll never fully experience the worst pains of either one.

"Who would want to do that?" Juliette muses under her breath, pulling me back to the present. My mind immediately goes to Serena's secret boyfriend who could potentially be a vampire. Who could potentially be Slade.

"Are you thinking what I'm thinking?" Her voice cuts through my thoughts and I should have known we'd veer in the same direction.

"Slade," I answer and she purses her lips, her hazel eyes steely. We'd already suspected him, but what a coincidence that after our little visit to him another body was found by Juliette and dumped at her place of work.

But if Slade was her secret boyfriend and he wanted to turn Serena for some reason, that doesn't explain the other murders. Slade isn't the type to go into a frenzy after a kill.

Juliette throws a few dollars onto the pile I already put on the table and shimmies out of her side of the booth.

"Okay, we need to go. We need to talk to Slade and get some answers. I know you said you would, but we should go together."

"Juliette." I maneuver myself out of the leather bench.

"I think you should talk to Alina as well. She seems to *like you*, like you," Juliette says, bitingly.

I almost laugh at that. Alina's never liked me—only tolerated me due to circumstance. She certainly doesn't *like me*, like me, though I'm usure why Juliette cares.

"Juliette," I say again, firmly this time.

She pauses, that blank look in her eyes replaced now with a fiery determination that makes my chest swell. I can sense her heartbeat quickening with every racing thought in her head.

"I will talk to Slade. *Alone*. He'll be more forthcoming if it's just me."

Her jaw flexes as she stares at me, silent. Despite the short time we've known each other, I can already identify when she's irritated. She can be pissed all she wants because *I* don't want what happened last time to happen again, and knowing Slade, there's a good chance it might.

He would hold whatever information he has over our heads until he gets what he wants, just like last time. He finds amusement in degradation, and it's better if Juliette isn't there to tempt his whims. Besides, despite our past, I know some piece of him still loves me—in his own way. Some piece of him still sees the scared fourteen-year-old kid he took in when he was still barely a kid himself.

Juliette opens her mouth to argue, but I hold up a hand to stop her. "He's my cousin, Juliette. I know him, and I know when he's lying. I also know when he sees something he likes, something he wants to play with. Go home and be with your family. I promise I'll call you as soon as I'm done with him."

She gives a reluctant nod and doesn't argue further even though her eyes are full of protest.

It's strange seeing Sinner during the day. Even after the countless afternoons I've spent here, the lack of thumping music and drunk people still throws me.

"Can I help you?" The bartender is wiping down the long counter when I walk in. I've never seen him before, but then again it's been a few years since I've been around and I didn't exactly look closely at the staff the other night. Slade keeps them loyal. In the years I lived with him, it was mostly the same people hanging around. If he brought in someone new, there's usually only two reasons: either he turned a lost soul looking for a place to belong or he's desperate enough to bring in an outsider for some reason.

"I'm looking for Slade. Is he around?" Before the bartender can reply, a familiar smooth, cold voice floats through the room.

"Well, you found him. What can I do for you, dear cousin?" Slade saunters down the last few steps of the staircase, wearing a deceptively charming smile. I hadn't heard him approach—a reminder of how scarily stealthy he can be at times. A skill he reserves for when he doesn't want other people to know he's there, when he's readying to strike.

The sleeves of his dress shirt are rolled up, showing off his one and only tattoo: a skull on his left forearm. A phantom chill skates up my own arm, right over the matching tattoo hidden beneath my sleeve.

I fist my hands in my pocket, trying to get them to stop shaking. My formative years were spent seeking his approval, his praise. Criticisms baked into praises were how he showed his love, and I ate up every crumb.

When he was teaching me how to shoot a gun, but I could never seem to aim it correctly. *Close, Alex. But if you want to be the best at something, you have to put in the work. Right now, you're mediocre. Do better.*

When I was learning mixed martial arts, thinking I could earn us some money by fighting. *You're almost there, but you should've been there weeks ago. I did not take us away from everything we knew so you could be a failure, Alex. Try harder.*

Those were the things Slade was so concerned with. A traditional life path was taken from him shortly before I fell into his custody, and he seemed determined to not give me a normal life. He'd rather me shoot guns and fight than have me attend high school and college. Rather me be around the sketchy people he collected than allow me to make my own friends.

I'm protecting you, he would always say. *The world is cruel. They'll take everything from you, so don't give them the means or reason to.*

Even now, I fear discussing with him what I came here for because I don't want to upset him. It was easier when Juliette was with me. She was an excuse to focus on something other than his full attention on me.

"We need to talk," I finally say. I eye the bartender, still wiping the already clean counter and trying to look like he's not listening. "Privately."

Slade's smile doesn't move an inch as he gestures up the stairs, towards his office. "Great work, Dominic. Although, I think you missed a spot there." He points to a part of the counter before ascending the steps, unaware of the way my body stiffens at his half praise to Dominic. Even the tone of his voice, the cadence he uses when delivering his criticism, is triggering enough for me to shy away from him. After all this time, I still don't know if he knows that he does it. If he knows how damaging his words were and still are to me and others.

Slade looks over his shoulder at me. "He's new. The regular girl has yet to show up for her shift, and no one can get a hold of her."

"Maybe she realized her boss was an asshole and decided to bail," I mutter under my breath.

His low chuckle indicates he heard me. Good. I don't care. Even though he's family, he should know what I think of him. Too many years I kept my thoughts about him to myself or was too afraid to think them in the first place. It's as much a reminder for me as it is for him. No matter how friendly he tries to come across or how many times he reminds me of our blood ties, he can't control me anymore. I won't let him.

Still, my heart is racing, and my clenched fists are starting to sweat. I should be lucky he didn't push me down the stairs for that comment and then tell me to make more of an effort with my insults.

As if he could read my mind, Slade slows on a step and turns to me. "You despise me so much, cousin. For the life of me I can't figure out why."

His smile is gone, and his true face shows instead. Critical assessment. Always searching for the unspoken words in someone's eyes or the twitch of their lips. I guess I have my answer—he really doesn't know how harmful he can be. Amazing how someone can be so observant of other people, yet entirely unaware of their own self.

"I never hurt you, and I never would." His tone is hard and firm, brokering no further comment on the matter as he resumes the path to his office.

No, he never did hurt me. At least not physically. Part of me has always wished he would, though. At times I wonder if a permanent, physical scar would be more validating than the emotional ones. Proof of the cruelty that he is ignorant to.

Alina passes us on the way down the hall, her usual aloofness wiped from her face in favor of worry. I almost don't recognize her without her smirk or confident gait. She nods to Slade but does a double take at the sight of me. Like a mask fitting perfectly over her features, the smirk returns.

"Well, well. Back for more?" She looks behind me, around the hall. "Where's your little friend?" There's a strain to her teasing voice. Something is definitely off with her.

That doesn't stop me from biting out, "She's not here."

Slade chuckles before he turns serious and addresses Alina. "Any news?" If he's curious about my *little friend*, he doesn't seem to care enough to ask after her himself.

Alina grips her phone in her hand, and her smirk disappears once more. She glances at me, then back at Slade.

"Later." With that, she stalks off back down the hall. I hope to catch her later, too. I have a bone to pick with her about her little visit to Juliette.

My curiosity sits at the tip of my tongue, begging to be voiced. It's rare that Alina loses her carefully crafted façade like that. Only a few times have I seen glimpses through her mask to the vulnerability that lies beneath. Whatever is going on here, it's clearly upsetting her.

Slade leads me to his open office door and the sound of it shutting behind us has unease settling in my stomach. I spent so much time trying to avoid him and this place, but twice in one week I'm here.

"You wanted to talk, so talk." Slade pours himself a drink from his bar cart despite the early hour. "And make it quick. I have matters to attend to. Places to be. You know how it is." He gives me a mirthless smile over the rim of his glass.

I clear my throat, hoping it will clear my thoughts as well. Slade offers me a glass of what looks like scotch, but I decline.

"I need you to be honest with me," I start. "Did you know a girl named Serena Mitchell?"

Slade's glass pauses on the way to his mouth. His profile is to me, so I can't read his expression well. His hesitation is answer enough, though. He's trying to craft a lie.

"Serena," he muses. "That's Juliette's friend, correct?" My unease twists and grows at Juliette's name coming out of his mouth. He certainly remembers her.

"Juliette didn't want to join you today? Shame. I liked her," he smirks. Now he's curious when he knows it will anger me. The urge to march over to him and clock him in the face is strong. If only to keep her name out of his mouth, saying it in that voice. A voice that preludes him using her to get to me.

"Stop evading the question."

The glass resumes its journey to Slade's lips as he turns to face me, and he takes a sip of the amber liquid. "I'm afraid I don't know what you're talking about, cousin."

"Answer the question, *cousin*. Did. You. Know. Her." My fists clench further in the pocket of my hoodie. They twitch with the need to be released from their spot, to grab him by the throat and not let go until he tells the truth. I spent too many years hanging on his lies and half-truths. I've run out of patience now.

Slade sighs a bit heavier than is probably necessary and sets his glass aside. "Yes, I knew her."

Before I can bombard him with another question or accuse him of what I am now more sure he is responsible of, he holds up a hand. If he didn't stop me with his hand, the look on his face would have done the trick. He looks... sorrowful. Mournful, even. I've only ever seen that look once—when he came to see me in the hospital after my parents disappeared.

The question slips out of me anyway, his answer more important than whatever it is he's feeling right now. "Did you kill her?"

His eyes snap up to mine. "No," he says quietly.

"Why should I believe you?" My voice is equally quiet, but harsh and demanding all the same.

Slade takes another sip of his drink. "Silas has gotten to you, I see. Turned you against me."

"Maybe. Or maybe I'm finally willing to see you for what you are—a fucking liar and manipulator."

He recoils like I've slapped him. "I've never lied to you." His voice is deep and low, his eyes boring into my own. He doesn't deny the manipulating part.

I give a harsh, humorless laugh. "You're doing it right now! Have you ever told the truth? Why can't you just be honest for once in your fucking life!"

"My reasons are my own."

I scoff, "Selfish reasons, I'm sure."

"I was honest, once. No one believed me," he seethes in a rare display of anger. I wince, knowing what he's referring to. The incident involving his high school girlfriend, Daisy, that got him kicked out of Bellevue and basically blacklisted in the vampire community.

"That's not an excuse."

Slade's grip on his glass tightens until his knuckles turn an unnatural white. "Everything I did, I did to protect you. To build a life for *us*."

"Yes, I know. The world is out to get me and all that shit. I don't want to hear it anymore."

"Because your life is so fantastic now," he says drolly.

"We're not here to talk about me." I ignore his barb and try to tamper my frustration down. "Just tell me you killed Serena Mitchell so I can be done with you."

My words are followed by a palpable silence in the room. Slade eases into his desk chair, calm and collected as he's always been. I wish he would rage at me. It would be better that way, I think.

He might have killed Serena, but do I really think he's responsible for the other murders? Is he truly capable of being a serial killer?

"As I've said, I didn't kill her. I knew her, though. I won't hide that fact anymore."

"How did you know her? Was she in your rotation of girls?" I sneer at him.

He sighs again, setting his glass down with a *thump*. "It's a long and complicated story. But you can tell Silas I'm not responsible. Get him off my back," he adds sharply.

I slowly walk to the chair opposite him and perch on its edge. "What are you talking about?"

Slade's condescending smile at my question reignites my irritation. "Oh, dear cousin. Someone is trying to frame me. Let me guess—Silas was the one to point you in my direction? Sure, you would have come to the possibility eventually, but he put the idea in your head."

I think back to that first meeting with Silas. The DBC were already on my radar. They always are with any kind of crime I have to investigate, but Silas has been ruthless about pursuing them as suspects.

"Maybe you are responsible," I accuse. "It wouldn't be the first time something's happened to a girl in your life."

As soon as the words are out of my mouth, I regret them. *Shit*. No matter how much I tell myself to hate Slade, there are still some topics best left alone. Daisy is one of them.

Slade stiffens at my remark and sits up straighter in his chair. His hands grip the edge of the desk and his amber eyes, hardened by his fury, burn right into me.

"Get out," he says in a barely constrained voice, a hint of that rage I wish he would just unleash evident in his tone. This is the one way to make Slade's cool demeanor snap.

Fuck. I'm usually better at thinking through my words before I speak them. In his presence, though, the need to make up for all those years where I kept my mouth shut overpowers all else. Now it's cost me answers. He was finally opening up, telling me some truths. His half-baked theory about Silas framing him is better than his silence or his dismissal.

"Slade…" I trail off, unsure of what I want to say next.

Do I apologize? Tell him I don't think he hurt Daisy like everyone said and I'm just a fucking idiot who apparently can't think before I speak anymore? He told me about her in confidence and I never doubted for a second he wasn't involved in his high school girlfriend's mysterious disappearance, even though everyone said he was.

"Out." The word is sharp as a knife and cuts just the same.

It feels like I have whiplash. One minute, I despise even being here, anxious as all hell to be out of my cousin's presence. The next, I'm wishing we could start over and racking my brain for anything to say that might make him allow me to stay. This constant confusion was a regular day for me growing up, and it's taken me until now to realize just how fucked up it was.

"If you come back here again looking to find answers, you will regret it."

Slade's parting words send a chill skating up my retreating back. He's never threatened me outright before. The worst part is that I know for once he's not lying.

23

JULIETTE

I drift into the dining room at the sound of my parents' hushed voices. They're gathered around the table, a bunch of papers spread out before them and using the mini ceramic pumpkin decorations as paperweights. They rifle through stacks with their heads bowed.

"Oh. Hi, honey," my mom says when she sees me lurking in the archway, a fake smile straining the edges of her mouth. "Did you need something?" I push off the wall and approach the table, ignoring her attempt at a polite dismissal.

The papers have varying content, but all of them have the same general messages. *Late payments. Insufficient funds. Loan request denied.*

"What's all this?" I ask, even though I have a pretty good idea what these papers mean. It's not a secret that the restaurant is struggling. And now that a dead body has been found in the alley—that the Knife Man was right outside the doors—no one will want to eat there anymore. I can't help but feel some guilt and responsibility for it all.

Dad shuffles some papers around, avoiding my gaze, but Mom sighs heavily and responds, "We're going to have to close the restaurant for the time being."

And there it is. What we've all been silently anticipating. These past few months have been like waiting for the other shoe to drop and, with her declaration, it finally has.

I have nothing to say besides, "Oh."

My mom begins explaining all the financial and legal issues that led to their decision, but I only half listen. My mind has drifted back to the killer and his seemingly personal vendetta against me. He had to have known that depositing the latest victim next to our restaurant would impact us like this. Is he upset that I survived his attack or that I'm investigating all of this? Assuming the killer and my stalker are two different people, the former has left me alone the last couple of months. Which tells me I must be getting close to finding out who is behind this.

I wonder what this means for us as a family. The killer isn't just affecting my life but the lives of those around me, too. No way will Hayden and I still be able to attend Pine Falls U. Will my parents have to sell the house? My eyes prickle at the thought before I get annoyed with myself.

So I'll tear up over us having to move but not Serena being dead?

In many ways this house is a friend to me, so I guess it's not that ridiculous to cry about losing it. It's one of the last familiar and comforting things in my life.

After some more explanations that I'm only half listening to because I'm stuck on the possibility of losing my childhood home, I bid my parents goodnight and trudge up to my room. The door to Meg and Josie's shared room is cracked, soft lo-fi music and hushed voices spilling out. They're studying. For a moment, I'm tempted to join them. To try and salvage my declining grades. Instead, I shuffle past and retreat into my silent, empty room like I have almost every night since the semester started.

Lately when I can't sleep, I've been dragging out my murder board attempting to piece together whatever it is I'm missing. It helps make my eyes grow tired enough that I pass out right there on the floor.

Tonight I'm not so lucky.

I've been staring at this damn thing for almost an hour, the many lights in my room making my vision go a bit blurry.

"Jules?" I hear just before my door opens. I'm not quick enough to cover the murder board, so I hastily shove it behind me, heart pounding.

"Your lights were on, I figured you were awake," Meg says as she steps into my room.

My lights are on whether I'm asleep or awake, but I guess you hadn't noticed, is what I want to say, but instead I reply with a hoarse, "Yeah?"

Meg looks around my messy room with a pinched expression. She keeps her own room spotless, even maintaining Josie's side of it.

"Remember the other night when I told you we could wait to talk? I think we should now."

Ugh. Her wanting to talk has been hanging over my head like the persistent storm clouds above Pine Falls. I don't want to talk about myself. I don't matter right now.

"I remember," I say flatly.

She folds her arms across her chest and peers around my body on the floor, furrowing her perfect brows. "What is that?"

"What's what?" I play dumb, hoping she's not referring to what I think she's referring to.

"That posterboard behind you." Meg steps forward and I leap to my feet, attempting to shove the board under my bed with my heel.

"It's nothing. Just a project for one of my classes."

"The same project you and Alex are working on?" she asks, disbelieving.

I fold my own arms and meet her intense stare. "Yes." Technically it's not a lie.

"Can I see it?"

"No," I snap, too quickly. Before I can get my bearings, Meg brushes past me and bends down to inspect the board.

She's silent for a long minute as she scans my work, and in those sixty seconds, I can hear every judgment, every question, and every worry.

"Juliette, what the fuck?" Meg demands harshly. "I know you've been struggling with Serena's death, but this is..."

"What? What is it, Meg?" My tone is angry, sharp, but it oddly feels good to have someone see my secret. To not have to hide it anymore.

"It's sick!" She shouts, tossing the board onto my bed as she stands. "This will not help you move on."

"Move on?" I scoff. "How can I move on? It's not as simple as it was for you. I'm not just going to go back to normal. I'm not going to go to parties every night and get drunk and forget that Serena ever existed!"

Meg stares me down, pity and hurt in her deep brown eyes. "I haven't forgotten about her," she says in a low, pained voice.

"Just leave me alone," I whisper, my voice cracking.

Meg looks at the board, then back at me before resolutely shaking her head. "No. You need help. We need to tell your parents about this, and you need to talk to someone."

"Meg, leave it alone."

She's still shaking her head, her mind made up. I'm trembling, my heart racing. Maybe I do need help, but shouldn't that be my choice? Right now, I need to escape. I need to focus solely on this investigation without worrying about getting caught, or inadvertently hurting someone, or another person close to me getting killed.

My own mind made up, I start packing a bag.

"What are you doing?" Meg demands, tracking my every move as she hovers by my bed. I don't answer her, not until I've hastily packed up everything I might need in a duffel bag.

"I'm leaving. I'm going to stay with Alex for a while. If you show anyone that board or tell anyone about this I swear to God, Meg, I'll never speak to you again."

That was too harsh. I know it was. But this is serious. I try to ignore the pain in my chest at the tears welling in her eyes at my words.

Before I can feel even more guilty or second guess what I'm doing, I race down the stairs and out the front door, texting Alex and asking for his address.

24

ALEX

THE SUIT I'M WEARING is stiff and uncomfortable. Silas sent it over so I would look "presentable" at his charity event tonight. I still have no idea why he even wants me there. Probably to parade me around and assure his constituents that he's got the "Knife Man" handled.

Or maybe he just wants me there to embarrass me. If that's the case, making me wear this stiff suit is one way to accomplish that.

I park my car down the street from The Grand Hotel, not trusting the valet with it. Silas has not so subtly mentioned to me before that I should get a different vehicle, and he would pay for it. As if I need to be in anymore debt with him than I already am. I wouldn't put it past him to have the valet "accidentally" wreck my car. If that means I have to run down the street in pouring rain to keep it safe, then so be it.

That car is also one of the first things I ever bought for myself when Slade and I started making money. It didn't cost much since it barely ran, and my cousin thought it was ridiculous. He swore it would break down within a week, but it's still here. One of the only aspects of my life I truly own.

"Can I help you?" The well-dressed man admitting guests into the ballroom questions me with clear disdain when I reach the massive open doors. He gives my slightly damp suit a quick once over and despite the expensive outfit his eyes linger on my tattooed hands and old sneakers (Silas' insistence to clothe me for tonight did not extend to shoes). There's a good line of people behind me, and the man seems eager to send me away and allow them in instead.

I stuff my hands in my trouser pockets. His eyes flick up to my own. "I should be on the list. Alex Osman."

The man swipes through his tablet, clearly thinking he's just humoring me until he stops and his eyes widen slightly. "Y-yes, of course. Mr. Osman, I see your name right here." He steps aside and waves his arm through the door. "Please, head on in and enjoy your evening."

Not likely, I think as I pass the threshold. My name is well-known around Silas' colleagues and employees. I'm known as the guy who will turn you in for the slightest infraction.

I swipe a glass of champagne off a waiter's tray the moment I enter the gilded ballroom, taking a sip and wishing it were something stronger.

The place looks different at night all decorated for the event. A banner that reads *Chamberlain Foundation Annual Charity Fundraiser for Underprivileged Youths* hangs proudly on one wall. I toss back the rest of my drink. Jeffers hangs out by one of the exits, acting as security, and I give him a nod which he returns. At least there's one person here who doesn't look down at me, or question why I'm here in the first place.

"They'll let anyone in here, it seems," a nasally drawl speaks to my left. In my periphery, I can just make out Oliver Chamberlain's profile: tanned skin and closely cropped black hair with a sneer splashed across his face. Where he lacks resemblance to his father, Silas, in appearance he makes up for with the same haughty attitude.

"Hello, Oliver," I say politely. I know better than to rise to his bait.

Oliver steps up to my side. "What are you even doing here?"

I shrug. "Your father invited me."

He looks like he wants to snap at me, but thinks better of it, instead choosing to inhale a sharp breath and reply calmly, "I don't know if you're aware, but this event is for people with money. You can't bid on these items with a pack of cigarettes." Oliver motions to the long table behind us laden with expensive items for the silent auction. Items that I would never be able to afford.

Instead of deigning to give him a response to his condescension, I pluck his champagne out of his hand and take a long drink, holding his gaze. "You're underage," I tell him calmly, and receive a scowl in return. He fidgets under my stare and eventually looks away.

Oliver and I are around the same height, but he's only eighteen. He might be tall, but he's still wiry and baby faced. His inexperience shows on his skin, while mine is etched into every scar, tattoo, and frown line.

"Alex, there you are." Silas strides over to us, breaking the tension between his son and me. "Oliver, Mr. Blake is having difficulty writing his bids down. Why don't you go help him?" He winks at his son, and Oliver scurries off to assist Mr. Blake—an old, obscenely wealthy vampire who can hardly read let alone write down bids for each item.

"Will Mr. Blake be a lucky winner tonight?" I ask, knowing exactly what Silas is up to.

Silas gives me his signature charming smile, "Perhaps." That smile disappears when he pulls me toward a deserted part of the room and levels me with a serious look. "Where are we in catching this killer? I've had many people asking me about it. They feel unsafe."

"I don't know why they would, unless they're human." Looking around, I note a few wealthy humans in the room, but none who would be complaining to Silas about the killer.

"He could target anyone next. You don't know how a killer's mind works." Silas pauses, and a slow, cruel grin spreads across his face. "Oh, wait... You do."

I immediately bristle at his comment, his way of reminding me of my place. Now I'm even more desperate to get out of here. So, I tell him what he wants to hear.

"I talked to Slade. You might be right about his involvement, but I think we should wait before we officially accuse him. I'd like to gather some more evidence first."

Silas scoffs. "What more do you need? Don't forget that he was kicked out of Bellevue for a similar crime."

"Daisy disappeared. She wasn't murdered," I amend.

Silas takes a sip of his drink, waving my correction away. Most vampires in our community are aware of Slade's time at Bellevue Manor—the boarding school most wealthy vampires or vampires from the East Coast send their children to. When Slade's girlfriend disappeared, they all laid the blame on my cousin. Even though he ran away, they still expelled him officially. He became my legal guardian shortly after and refused to send me there, despite my parents' intentions for me to attend.

"I have a plan," I continue, aiming to get this conversation back on track, even if I don't actually have a solid plan at the moment. There's a good chance Slade *is* responsible, but there's still a part of me that wants to protect him. Old habits die hard and all that.

Silas opens his mouth to speak, probably to throw more "concerns" my way about the progress of the investigation when we're interrupted.

"Excuse me, Mr. Chamberlain?" A well-dressed man with slicked back hair and satchel across his chest invades our shadowy corner. He looks familiar but with my mind occupied by keeping a civil conversation with Silas, I can't place him.

"Yes?" Silas hesitates.

"I'm here on behalf of Mr. Mitchell. He was unable to make it but sends his regards." The man reaches inside his bag, and I'm immediately at attention, thinking he's about to pull a gun on Silas. I'm confronted with the realization that I might not want to stop him if he did. Silas looks just as alarmed by the man's action, but we both settle down when he pulls out an envelope, not a weapon.

"Please accept this donation on Mr. Mitchell's behalf."

The man saying "Mr. Mitchell" a second time has me snapping my attention fully to him. Of course I recognize him. This is Laurence Mitchell's assistant. The one who tossed Juliette out into the rain that day. I have the sudden urge to punch him, but looking into his face, the way his gaze doesn't meet Silas' and how he shuffles around on his feet, reminds me that he's just a lackey. Same as me.

Laurence Mitchell is rich, that's just common knowledge in Pine Falls, but does his donation and affiliation with Silas mean he's a human? Or could he be a vampire? Surely Juliette would know if her best friend was the daughter of a vampire, right?

My "boss" doesn't acknowledge Laurence Mitchell's assistant. Just accepts the envelope and sends the man on his way.

"You need to sever any remaining influence your cousin has on you, Alex," Silas says in a low, warning voice and leaves me alone in the shadows. I barely have any time to collect myself after interacting with Silas when someone new approaches.

"Alex Volkov. Sorry, I heard you go by *Osman* now," an oily voice comes from my left. Scowling, I half turn to glance at Creed Ambrose. Ambrose is a councilmember from the Midwest, and he's paid enough visits to Silas over the last three years to know I go by Alex Osman—my mother's maiden name.

"I didn't know pets were allowed at this event," he sneers at me. I just roll my eyes and ignore him, and soon he moves on to more unsuspecting prey.

Creed Ambrose wants nothing more than to get out of the Midwest. Everyone who's even remotely involved in the politics of the Council knows his ambitions lie in the West. Some speculate it's because his son, Damien, lives somewhere around here, but I just think he'd rather take something away from Silas. Apparently they were rivals during their time at Bellevue together.

I'm left watching the event unfold from the outskirts. The wealthy attendees alternate between hobnobbing with one another to casting their bids for the extravagant items laid out on the table. Silas saunters around the room, ever the politician, while his son trails at his side.

"I couldn't be prouder of Oliver for putting together this fundraiser," Silas' voice carries across the room, and the younger vampire flushes from the praise. I roll my eyes. Oliver had as much to do with this event as I did in buying the suit I'm wearing.

My phone buzzes in my pocket, and I welcome the distraction. I should just leave, but I don't know how long Silas expects me to stay here. It's not like I can bid on anything or strike up friendly conversation with his guests. Even now, as I'm hiding in a shadowy part of the room, I'm receiving wary glances.

I take my phone out and see two messages waiting for me.

> **Juliette Jennings:** are u busy?

> **Juliette Jennings:** i found something

25

JULIETTE

A quick text to Alex and I had his address, followed by a few question marks as to why I need to know where he lives. The building is in a seedy neighborhood, and the creepy looking guy behind the lobby desk and broken elevator had me sprinting up the stairs to Alex's floor.

When I eventually worked up the courage to knock at his door, I realized he wasn't home. Something he did not mention in his text. I set up camp outside his front door, wondering where he could be and not caring what his neighbors might think. The duffel bag containing the few belongings I packed in my rush to get out of the house beside me. Sadly, I had to leave my murder board behind. Let my family see it and think I'm deranged, or that it's just a product of my brain injury. At this point, if it doesn't concern the investigation, then I don't care.

Before I decided to come to Alex's apartment, I went to the library to sulk a little bit. He was rightfully confused as to why I wanted his address, and I worried I would be burdening him with my presence. Maybe I'm overstepping, asking if I can stay with him. There's only one way to find out, and I'll need to wait until he gets home to get that answer.

In an attempt to counteract the nervousness pooling in my gut, I pulled out my laptop and the flash drive containing the security footage from Sinner, deciding to rewatch what was on it while I waited.

My closer inspection of the footage had me discovering something potentially major. My blood chilled as I stared at the screen, confused by yet another *coincidence*. I texted Alex right away. Wherever he was, he needed to see what I found.

Now I'm not so patiently sitting outside his door waiting for him to get back, my laptop resting across my legs. My fingers tap a nervous rhythm on my knees and the flickering fluorescents in the hallway are giving me a headache.

My patience wearing thin, I reach back into my bag, grabbing my phone to text Alex again. However, when I reach for it, my fingers brush against an unfamiliar piece of paper. At first I think it's the flier advertising Laurence Mitchell's stupid lecture from the other night, but it's the wrong texture. It's thick and folded, almost like a card, and when I go to pull it out, the scent of blood envelops me.

I yelp and toss it on the floor like it's burned me. Frantically I glance around the hall as if the person who put it there is somewhere near. With shaky hands, I pick it up again. My stomach roils at the message and what it was written with, for on the paper five words inked in blood stare up at me:

Walk away or you're next.

This message is more obvious with its threat than the others. Where did it even come from? I've been alone in this hallway for hours. The only other place I've been besides home was... *the library*. Someone must have stuck it in my bag when I wasn't looking. *Dammit!* The killer was probably right next to me, but I was too busy wallowing at the fact that my friends and family are overly concerned about me to even notice.

Footsteps sound, then the stairwell door screeches as it opens. Alex steps through, and my breath gets trapped in my lungs.

If I thought Alex looked good in a black hoodie, he's absolutely devastating in a suit.

His grey eyes find me—sitting on the dirty floor in front of his apartment—widening a fraction. He takes in my appearance, the note in my hand, and the duffel bag next to me.

"Juliette." My stupid heart flutters at the way he says my name, concern apparent in his tone. "What's going on?" He looks tired, tension radiating from the stiff set of his shoulders.

I tear my gaze away from him and shove the note back into my bag, hoping he didn't see too much of it. I'll show him later. Right now we have more important things to discuss. I shoulder the bag and stand, brandishing my laptop at him.

"You gonna open the door or what? I have something to show you."

The tension I sensed from him eases a little, the corner of his lips twitching as he digs around his suit pocket for his keys.

"Sorry to keep you waiting," he says without a hint of apology in his tone.

He hesitates with his key over the lock. Is he nervous to let me inside? I grew up with Hayden, it would take a lot to faze me.

Alex's inner turmoil must cease because he puts the key in the lock and twists it, shoving open the door. He holds it open for me to walk through and tugs my bag off my shoulder, slinging it over his own instead. I stride into the small space with a mumbled thanks and heated cheeks.

His little studio apartment isn't what I expected. It's not messy, but it isn't necessarily pristine, either. The furniture and decorations are sparse, but what does occupy the space is so... *Alex*. A hoodie thrown over a leather armchair. A bare bookcase with just a few titles, but based on the cracked spines, I know Alex must have read them at least a dozen times each. The bed is made, but it's rumpled slightly. I can picture him lounging on it like he did at my house, fully letting his guard down and finding comfort. I feel like I could be safe here, but I don't know if that's because of the space itself, or the man who lives in it.

Alex turns on the lights and shuts the door. "It's not much," he mutters not quite meeting my gaze.

I'm already shaking my head, my eyes drifting to a framed photo on the tiny dining room table. The single chair next to it makes my heart ache.

"Why are you all dressed up?" I ask, trying and failing to ignore the overwhelming scent of him—clean and spicy.

"Some charity thing my boss made me go to."

"Vampires have charities?"

He scoffs and sets my bag down at the table. "They call it charity. I call it an excuse to flaunt how much money they have."

"So, no different than most human charities," I snort. "At least you look good." The words are out of my mouth before I have time to stop them.

A smirk plays on Alex's lips, "You think I look good?"

My face flames, and I rush to add, "I mean, objectively. Who doesn't look good in a suit?"

It's not my best lie. My stomach certainly wasn't doing acrobatics at Detective Michaels in his ill-fitting suit. I try to play it off, but my stammering betrays how I really feel.

"*Objectively*, of course. But I think the many people who stared daggers at me tonight would have to disagree." He takes a step towards me.

I try to swallow as he takes another step, and another, but my mouth is completely dry. The lights are dim in his apartment and cast half of his features in shadow. His eyes gleam in the dark, making them appear silver instead of grey. With him prowling towards me the way he is, I'm faced with the reality that I am, in fact, *very* attracted to Alex.

It's more than that, though. I'm not just attracted to his looks but who he *is*. Alex is casually considerate and has a hidden sense of humor that I've come to enjoy pulling out of him.

"Are you sure they were glaring at you?" I all but whisper.

He gives me a strange look before replying, "Yes." He matches my tone, his whisper a quiet rumble. "Especially the women." Is he teasing me? Where is the brooding man I've come to know? Not only does the suit showcase his defined build, but it's apparently bringing out his playful side as well.

"I think they might have been attracted to you, idiot." My insult was meant to regain some control over this situation, but my breathy voice belies it. He chuckles softly.

Alex steps even closer to me. Close enough that I can smell the faint trace of alcohol on his breath when he speaks next: "And how does a woman look at someone they find attractive?" At my silence he lowers his voice even further, a cocky grin lighting up his features. "Should I get a mirror so you can see for yourself?"

My eyes widen, and I shove him away as he laughs. It's like all the tension in the room snaps. The lights seem brighter, our voices seem louder, and the distance between us feels miles longer than it was a second before.

"You're insufferable. What's gotten into you tonight?" Alex just shrugs his shoulders in response. "And here I thought you were a humble gentleman."

"I'm many things, Juliette, but a gentleman isn't one of them." His stare burns into me, and I force myself to look away. I can't tell if he's still teasing or if he really thinks that about himself.

"I think you sell yourself short," I tell him. "You're a lot better than most guys I've met, without even trying."

Alex is quiet for a few moments, and I take the opportunity to set up my laptop. "You really mean that?" he asks, all the playful flirtation gone.

"I do," I say softly, not trusting myself to look at him. I know if I do, I'll be sucked into those eyes again, and this night could take a turn I'm not prepared for. We have a job to do—there's no time for distractions.

Alex must come to the same conclusion because he says, "You said you found something?" Clearing my throat, I find the file on my laptop. I try to ignore the rush of adrenaline that hits me when Alex grabs the top of my chair, leaning over me to look at the screen and giving me another whiff of his spicily clean scent.

We both watch Sinner from two months ago opening up for the evening. Slade strides in, barely acknowledging any of his employees before disappearing upstairs. The twins arrive next—Alina making a beeline for the bar while Anthony chats with the DJ. Finally, the bartender comes into view.

Naomi Hart. The latest victim and the one the killer made sure I found. That's why her name sounded familiar to me when I was at the police station. She was the bartender on shift the night Alex and I went to Sinner, and who Anthony mentioned was Alina's girlfriend.

Fuck. Alina scares me, but I can't help empathizing with her. Especially now, knowing what she's just lost.

Naomi reaches the bar and leans over to give a chaste but sweet kiss on the lips to a seated Alina. They talk for a few minutes in hushed voices, small smiles peeking out of the curtains of their hair, before Alina is called away by her brother. Then Naomi goes about her night, working her shift.

"Shit... she was the bartender." Alex runs his hands through his hair, a gesture I've now come to realize is synonymous with his nerves. I know we're thinking the same thing.

"Another connection to Slade," I say.

Alex straightens, the warmth from his closeness abandoning me, and he sheds his suit jacket. The dark ink covering his forearms shows through the white of his dress shirt. It's the most I've seen of his skin, and I long to push those sleeves up to examine his tattoos more closely.

"Slade's not an idiot. He wouldn't kill his own damn bartender."

"Do you think someone is setting Slade up?" The same way they are trying to scare and traumatize me, apparently.

Alex blows out a breath and gnaws on his bottom lip, my gaze snagging on the movement. What does that lip feel like, I wonder? What would it feel like to press my own against his...

Enough, Juliette! Calm down. Be professional.

"It's possible," Alex says at last. "My boss seems keen on pinning him with these murders."

"Would your boss do something like this?" I say quietly.

I don't know the first thing about his mysterious vampire boss, but the little I know of Slade is that he doesn't seem dumb enough to allow so much evidence to trace back to him.

Alex doesn't respond, just fixes his stare at a distant point out the grimy window. He abruptly changes the subject to what I dreaded discussing. "You were holding a note when I arrived. What was it?" Those grey eyes meet mine imploringly.

Sighing, I reach back into my duffel and pull out the note for him to read. Alex's lips purse as he scans those five words. "I agree."

"Sorry?"

"I agree with the note." He slaps the paper against his palm, jaw clenching. "I think you should walk away."

I shove my chair back to face him. He's got a good six inches on me, but I don't back away. "Are you serious?"

"Deadly."

"Nice choice of words, asshole."

"Shit's getting dangerous, Juliette."

"You think I don't know that?" My voice raises as I continue, "That's the exact reason why I have to keep investigating. I have to find out who is doing this." For Serena, I don't add. For all those other innocent people... Maybe even for me.

Alex stares at me for what feels like an eternity before he holds the note out. "You asked me to respect your choices, and I will." I go to grab the note back but he pulls it away at the last second. "But don't think for a second I won't be watching your back twenty-four-seven."

He lets me take the note, and I turn back to my bag to hide my flushed cheeks. Why does this man make me blush over the littlest things? Even when he's being an overbearing asshole. We're just working together, for crying out loud.

"Well, that's what partners do, don't they? Protect each other."

"Not partners," he corrects.

I roll my eyes. "Right. Two people working together for mutual benefit. My bad." He hums his agreement. "Oh, by the way, can I stay here for the foreseeable future?" I add attempting nonchalance.

"I figured that was your plan, what with the duffel bag and all." He nudges my shoulder with his and stalks over to the fridge. "Yes, you can stay here. But we switch on and off with the couch."

"Just until we find the killer," I assure him.

He pauses his perusal of the fridge to cast me a look over his shoulder and reassures me, "We're going to catch them."

"I know we will. What's our next move?"

Alex shuts the refrigerator door. "First, we order pizza. Then we come up with a plan."

While Alex pulls his phone out, my eyes catch on the photo on the table again. I carefully pick it up, studying it. A boy with dark hair and grey eyes beams up at the camera, held up by a man and a woman—his parents, I presume. My own lips twitch up as I stare down at the smiling family. The man looks like Alex and Slade, with only slight differences. His eyes are sharp but kind. They don't hold the tiredness or contemplation I so often see on Alex, nor the cunning cruelty I saw from Slade. The woman is stunning: brown hair and skin, soft features. She smiles in adoration at her son instead of the camera.

I'm so lost in the photo, this happy moment captured forever, that I don't hear Alex come up behind me until he's tugging the frame out of my hands. He looks at it for a few seconds, lost in the image like I was, before placing it back on the table.

"Your parents?" I ask, even though I already know the answer. It's doubtlessly them, Alex is a perfect combination of the two. He nods, eyes still glued on the photo.

"What happened to them?" I whisper. I'm reminded of the research I did on him back when we first met. That news article about him being orphaned at fourteen.

The air around us is still, and I wonder if he'll answer me. He seems completely absorbed in that moment in time—the same way I sometimes get stuck in my memories of Serena.

"I don't know," he whispers back. Even though he's standing right next to me, he feels a million miles away. There's pain in his eyes—a shadow that wasn't there before. I curse myself for bringing it up, for opening the door to his obvious hurt.

Tentatively, I reach out and touch his arm. It's nothing, a soft touch he might not even register, but after a few moments, I realize it's not just for him. It's for me too. I want to comfort him, but I also need the reminder. The reminder that he is real—this is real—and I'm not alone. *We're* not alone. There's someone else who understands our particular brand of grief and pain.

"Sometimes I feel like I'm the only one who cares what happened to Serena," I say into the quiet. "Like everyone else moved on, and I'm the only one keeping her memory alive. It's exhausting," I admit with a sigh.

Alex doesn't speak for a long while, content to relive the happy moment from the photo. But when he does, the sorrow laced with his words spears me in the chest.

"We were in a car crash. When I came to, my parents were gone. They never found their bodies. I've been trying to find answers ever since then." He places the photo back on the table. "I know how you feel. Everyone else gave up, convinced they're dead. Most of the time it feels like I'm the only one who remembers them, that my scars are the only reminder the accident even happened at all. Maybe it's foolish to think they're still out there somewhere, but that hope has kept me going on the darkest of days."

I squeeze his arm, bringing his gaze back to mine. "It's not foolish to have hope. And if it is, then we can be fools together." I try my best to believe in what I'm saying. If not for my own sake, then for his.

Alex's gaze is intent on mine, full of longing and understanding. He clears his throat, smoothing a hand over his dress shirt. "I need to get out of this."

"Yes, you do. Keep it on any longer and I'll start to forget what a bad boy you really are," I joke, the tension and sadness in the room lifting. Alex rolls his eyes, muttering, "Can't a guy just have tattoos and like wearing hoodies without being labeled a *bad boy*."

Rifling through my duffel bag, I realize I forgot to pack pajamas. I decide it's fine to just sleep in my jeans and hoodie, but Alex refuses to let me.

He comes out of the bathroom in sweats and a long-sleeved tee, spotting me reclined on the couch nibbling on a slice of pizza that was just delivered. "Here," he says, moving over to a small dresser by the bed and pulling out a stack of clothes. "You can change into these."

I take the pile from him and head into the bathroom, inspecting the plain grey t-shirt and sweatpants he's given me. The shirt hits my mid thighs, and I have to roll the band of the sweatpants over a few times to keep them from falling down.

Secretly, I love it.

I'm drowning in his scent as much as the fabric. Spicy and slightly earthy, like he doused himself in good cologne (not the cheap kind Hayden uses) and then stood in the rain. In the privacy of his small bathroom, I shamelessly stuff my nose into the fabric of his shirt and take a deep breath. These clothes smell like Alex. They smell like safety.

Alex is leaning against the kitchen counter on his phone when I emerge from the bathroom. He gives me a cursory glance and then resumes tapping on the screen. "You can go to bed if you want."

I am tired, but my mind is still buzzing with energy. My senses are dialed up to eleven just by standing in his space, surrounded by all things *Alex*. The bed does look cozy, though, and I'm sure his sheets smell just as good as his clothes do. God, I feel like such a creep.

There's a gun safe next to the bed that I hadn't noticed before. I almost trip when I see it. I mistook it for a nightstand, but there's a digital lock with a keypad smack in the center of it. I've never really been around guns before, and I'm sure that's what's in there even though I've never actually seen Alex carrying one.

"I feel bad taking your bed," I say, deciding to ignore the concealed weapons for now.

Alex shrugs, still focused on his phone. "Don't be. The couch is pretty comfortable, so I don't mind. Besides," he looks up from his phone, "we're switching on and off, remember?"

"Right." Satisfied that I'm not being too intrusive of his space, I sink down in his bed. It's a bit lumpy and squeaks when I roll over, but the blankets are soft and it smells just like I imagined it would.

This night has filled me with a wide range of emotions. For so long I've only been dealing with a few. The addition of more complex and confusing feelings is an unwelcome development. If I'm being honest, it frightens me. And as someone who has felt true fear in the form of a killer vampire, my *feelings* should not elicit the same terror.

I close my eyes, hoping sleep will take me before my memories pull me back to unpleasant times. Alex shuffles around a bit and then the lights shut off, drowning me in darkness in an unfamiliar place. My pulse picks up speed, and I fist the sheets, trying to let the panic subside by counting to ten, and then doing it again.

"Juliette?" Alex's voice cuts through the dark. "Are you okay?" Right. His vampire senses are probably alerting him to my haywire heartbeat.

Confronting my embarrassment, I squeak out, "C-can you turn the lights back on?" Flashes of glowing eyes and blood-soaked fangs keep me from being ashamed of the tremble in my voice.

More rustling, then a light clicks on next to me—Alex standing right there. "Juliette," he murmurs my name and I let out a sigh of relief at the wash of light and the familiar person beside me. "Hey, it's okay," he continues, pulling my hands from their death grip on the sheets.

"I'm sorry," I get out between deep inhales. "You can turn it off if it bothers you." *Please don't.*

Alex studies the panic I'm sure is etched across my face. "It won't bother me. I should've realized."

As if acting on instinct, he brushes a strand of hair off my face. My breath catches at the feel of his warm skin against my own. His fingers still, like he just realized what they're doing. He goes to pull them away, but my hand darts up to grasp his wrist, keeping his touch on me. Grounding me.

Seconds pass by in silence, our gazes locked on one another, before he gently removes my grip on his wrist. "Goodnight," he says in a low, gravelly voice.

Tentatively, as if he's worried I might shove him away, he leans down and presses a soft kiss to my temple.

I lay there as he retreats back to the couch, body flushed and confused. Rolling onto my back, I continue my calming breaths. The phantom touch of Alex's fingers and lips follow me into sleep.

26

JULIETTE

My morning was just as equally strange and exciting as last night. For starters, when I went to use the bathroom after waking up I found Alex—shirtless and brushing his teeth. I let out an embarrassing shriek of surprise at the sight of him, probably messing up my only chance to see the rest of his tattoos. Alex just chuckled through his toothpaste at me.

The second strange yet wonderful thing was watching Alex cook breakfast. It was a simple scrambled eggs and fruit meal, but he dug up a packet of hot chocolate and served it to me with extra whipped cream—he remembered exactly how I like it. This man is both frustrating and amazing. He truly doesn't realize how kind and considerate he can be, and that infuriates me. Whether he believes it or not, he's a true gentleman.

The third thing made more butterflies erupt in my stomach than when I saw him half naked. When I came out of the bathroom after breakfast, Alex handed me a pile of clothes. My clothes. That he freshly washed, dried, and folded, while I slept the morning away.

I gave him the brief story on why I wanted to stay with him, how my friends and family are too concerned for my well-being and why that is such a problem. It's not really a problem, but I'm aware of the path of self-destruction I'm on. I don't need to hear their pleas to get me off it.

Alex and I are similar in that regard. We're both willing to do whatever it takes, even if it means putting ourselves in danger. I feel safer when I'm with him, though. Especially after our interactions last night.

Thoughts of last night filter into my head. He hasn't brought up the... *intimate* moments between us, and I'm sure as hell not going to be the first one to discuss it. Twice he invaded my space, and I all but welcomed it, hoping for more to happen between us. This "partnership" is slowly heading off the rails and onto a new track of unprofessionalism.

Maybe that wouldn't be such a bad thing. Except who am I to think I deserve any sort of happiness right now? How could I when Serena isn't here to share it with me?

Besides, who knows if Alex and I will keep in touch after we solve this case. There hasn't been much thought on my part about what comes after. Right now, I'm focused on my dead best friend and vengeance. Two extremely healthy hyper fixations for the average college student.

With my new word for the day being *professionalism*—yes I'm aware of the irony given that I'm currently staying in my partner's apartment, wishing I could have seen more of his half naked body—I focus on the task at hand.

Currently I'm staring at a gorgeous view of the ocean, grey and roiling like Alex's eyes, with heavy clouds overhead. It's a lookout spot he knew of. He said he comes here to think. More flutters erupted in my chest at Alex taking me to his secret spot. Silently, I tell those butterflies to pipe down because, again, we have more important topics to be focusing on.

A pack of cigarettes sits on the dashboard and, feeling adventurous, I tentatively ask, "Can I have a cigarette?"

Alex gives me a questioning look, one of those dark brows arched in my direction. "You smoke?"

"Yeah, all the time." I have never smoked a cigarette in my life. But something about Alex brings out a different side of me. A side that wants to try new things.

He shrugs and pulls one out of the pack for me, putting it in his mouth first to light it. Our fingers brush as he hands it over, reminding me of his comforting touch last night. The fleeting thought that this cigarette was just in his mouth—a mouth that was on my forehead not twelve hours earlier—causes a pleasant warmth to cascade through my body. This is certainly not the no-nonsense attitude I was hoping to achieve today. We're off to a *great* start.

I bring the cigarette to my own lips and inhale. What I don't expect is the pain. The tobacco scratches my throat on its way to my lungs, and I immediately cough it up, causing a disrupted cloud of smoke to filter between us.

Alex's low chuckle pulls me back to myself. "Smoke all the time, huh?"

"Shut up," I mumble and hand the cigarette back. He pops it back in his mouth and inhales expertly, aiming the smoke out the crack in the window.

"How can you even smoke that," I accuse more than ask.

He's silent for so long I don't think he'll answer. *Shit*. There's still so much about Alex I don't know. Did I just offend him? Maybe smoking is to him what sketching once was to me: a comfort. Although his is not the healthiest outlet, it could still be important to him.

"I smoke because..." He trails off and runs a hand through his hair. "It's hard to explain."

Shifting in my seat, I turn to face him. "Try me."

He avoids my stare and just when I think he won't respond he says, "I smoke because it makes me feel like shit." The words come out in a rush, and Alex avoids my eyes. I'm a bit taken aback by his statement.

"You... want to feel like shit?" I ask carefully. He nods. "Why?" I add in a gentler tone.

"What I said last night about not being a gentleman? I meant it. I've done things in my life that I'm not proud of, and sometimes it feels like I was able to walk away with nothing more than a slap on the wrist." The police mentioned Alex had a record that day they brought me to the station, but he's never mentioned it himself.

"Smoking makes me feel like crap, but I don't mind," he continues, picking at a tear in his jeans. "It's barely a punishment, but it's one I deserve all the same."

My heart sinks in my chest at his words. I was right, he thinks so little of himself.

"Alex, I don't believe that." I reach a tentative hand forward, but he shies away, avoiding my gaze.

"You don't know me," he says, voice hard.

"Okay. I didn't know you *then*, but I do know you *now*. And the guy I know is caring and thoughtful, and I don't believe he would do anything that might intentionally hurt someone else." My tone is even, but just as resolute as his was.

"You don't mean that," he mumbles to the window, tossing the cigarette outside.

"I do. I know what it's like to feel guilty, to be your own worst enemy. No demons hurt quite like your own."

Alex finally looks at me and, for once, his expression is open. He's not brooding like he usually is or looking at me with some type of amusement. He looks... vulnerable.

"I wish I met you sooner," he says under his breath, as if he didn't mean for me to hear. The vulnerability in his eyes is replaced by an unguarded heat as his gaze locks on me. Time seems to stop.

Similar to last night, everything fades except for Alex. All I can see is his stern but beautiful face. All I smell is the scent of him—rain and spice. And all I can feel is my heart, suddenly beating rapidly in my chest, rivaling the waves crashing on the nearby shore. I feel myself leaning towards him, and I swear he meets me halfway. Our mouths are mere inches from each other, and I want nothing more in this moment than to bridge the gap and feel his lips meet mine.

But that's not the plan. Kissing Alex won't further this case.

"What about Anthony?" I blurt. A weak attempt at shifting the sudden tense mood in the car.

Alex looks like I just dumped a bucket of ice water on him. "What about him?"

"Could he be the killer?" He definitely has the creep factor down. Though, his apology the other day was certainly unexpected.

"You said the vampire you saw that night had dark hair."

"The lights were off. Besides, it looks like he dyes his hair anyway. It could've been darker two months ago."

Alex rubs his jaw. "You're right. That's not his natural color. It's Alina's, and as long as I've known him, he's dyed it to match her."

"He loves her."

"Of course he loves her, they're twins." Alex throws a confused look my way.

"I'm just trying to determine what *kind* of love he has for her."

"Jesus, Juliette. They're not the fucking Lannister's."

I can't help the small laugh that bursts out of me. "Just making sure! Someone who would do... *that* with their twin would definitely be down to murder people, too."

"And you're basing this assumption off *Game of Thrones*."

"Maybe." I shrug.

"One of the victims was Alina's girlfriend. He wouldn't do that to her," Alex points out.

"What about to frame Slade?"

"Anthony would never frame Slade. He owes him too much."

"That could be the reason he wants to frame him. Get rid of Slade, erase the debts."

"No offense to Anthony, but he's not smart enough for that. He's too rash. Framing someone takes a lot of planning and patience, both of which Anthony lacks." He's right. Anthony is not a likely suspect. If my memory is correct, the vague silhouette of the vampire I saw that night was tall—much taller than me. Anthony only has a few inches on me, and I really don't see him callously killing a bunch of people. In some ways, he reminds me of Hayden.

It just seems too easy for the killer to be Slade. Everything has conveniently been pointing to him. There's no particular reason for me to believe he's committing these murders, other than the fact that I just don't think he is. It's the same way I don't believe Alex could be the killer. Not everything is that simple, especially with this case.

"Okay, so Anthony isn't the killer, even though framing someone to erase a debt does seem like a viable motive," I say with resolution. Alex snorts, fingering his pack of cigarettes. "What's so funny?" I question, even though there's not a trace of humor in his eyes.

"Debts are a good motivator. I should know," he murmurs.

I bite my lip, wondering if I should bring this next topic up. Alex has made similar comments before and has mentioned his overbearing boss a few times.

"So... you have debts, Mr. Osman?" I aim for a casual tone but don't execute it well.

He sighs heavily, pocketing his pack of cigarettes before staring out at the dreary afternoon sky. "I do. That slap on the wrist I mentioned? It's more complicated than it seems."

"What happened?" When a few beats go by, I worry he won't answer—that he won't indulge my newest line of questioning.

I add, "You can tell me anything, Alex. I'll never judge you." I parrot one of the first things he texted me. A throwaway message from the night of the frat party, but one I still remember.

"When I was with Slade, I did a lot of things I'm not proud of. One night, he sent me to beat up some of Crimson's guys near one of their gyms. Tyler was one of them," he gives me a knowing look. That explains the hostility between the two and why Tyler always looks so afraid of Alex.

"Anyway, I did my job well, like I always do. Tyler was sent to the hospital, and I was arrested."

"Slade bailed you out?" I inquire.

Alex shakes his head. "No. Anytime any of us are arrested, the Head of Council is notified. *He* bailed me out." So Alex's current boss, Silas, was the one to collect him. "Then he found out just how much bad shit I've done and gave me an ultimatum."

I'm on the edge of my seat, utterly captivated by Alex's willingness to share a piece of his story with me. Even with the sordid history, I'm not afraid of him. I can see in his eyes that he's waiting for that moment when I will be, and in my expression, I try to convey that will never happen.

"Silas told me I could spend the rest of my days locked in his underground prison as punishment for my crimes, or I could work for him in *cleaning up the city*." Alex fumbles around for the pack of cigarettes before pulling another one out and lighting it up. I don't miss the way his hands shake as he does so.

"So now you work for him," I say. He nods around a puff of smoke. "For how long?"

"Until he deems me worthy of absolution." He takes a long drag in contemplation. "It doesn't even matter. I do the same shit I used to, just under a new boss. They all think their way is the right way and are completely unaware of how many people they hurt."

The car is silent for long moments, the roiling sea below the cliff the only noise. Then Alex confesses, "I knew what I was doing with Slade was bad. The guilt ate at me constantly. But I didn't know what to do. He was my only connection in this world. If I left, I would have been alone. No money, no place to live. He took me in when I was just a kid, but he also ruined me for anyone else, and he took away any shot at a normal life. In many ways, I'm glad Silas picked me up."

"I'm sorry, Alex. I hate Slade even more now. And your boss."

Alex snorts again, this time with a bit of humor. "Silas isn't all that bad. He could've thrown me in jail, no questions asked. At least he gave me a choice."

"He didn't give you a choice, Alex. He gave you an *illusion* of one. We all deserve a second chance, but not like this. Not if you're doing the same shit, like you said, just under a new controlling boss." He nods like he's had this conversation with himself many times.

"Sometimes I wonder what my parents would think of me. Of what I do." He stares intently at his left wrist, the cigarette burning and forgotten in his other hand. "I tried giving up once. I told myself they were dead and I should just join them. That the universe was telling me I was never meant to be here without them."

"Alex—" I'm horrified at the idea that, had things gone differently, he might not be sitting here with me.

"I know. It's bad. But I snapped out of it pretty quickly. If my parents and I were all dead, then the last piece of their memory would die with me."

"That's how I feel about Serena. Except there are plenty of people left alive to remember her." Bitterness invades my mouth and I recall our conversation last night, how sometimes it feels like I'm the only one who even cares she died.

"Can we switch to less depressing topics please?" Alex breathes out with a forced chuckle. With one last puff, he puts out the cigarette and tosses it outside.

I lean back in my seat, watching him closely. "Like murder?" I joke.

"Yes," he looks at me with a glint of humor in his eyes, feigning a sigh of relief.

"Actually, I have a question."

Alex rolls his eyes half-heartedly. "Of course you do."

I bite my cheek to keep from grinning. "How do you kill a vampire?"

Alex's eyes widen before he sputters, "What?"

I shrug. "Could be useful for when we catch this guy."

"I know how to kill a vampire—don't worry."

"Yeah, but if you're not there for some reason…"

Alex shifts in his seat to face me. "Okay, there are two ways to kill a full vampire. The fast way and the slow way."

"Fast way? Like a stake through the heart?"

He mutters something like, "Jesus, the things you believe from movies," and shakes his head. "No. You have to cut off the head. But a bullet through the brain will also do the trick."

"Wow. Okay, noted. And the slow way?"

Alex grimaces. "Drain them of blood. They won't die, but they'll weaken significantly and eventually waste away to nothing."

"What about half vampires?"

"Planning on murdering me, Juliette?" He arches a brow. I make a motion with my hands that tells him to get on with the explanation. "Half vampires are just like humans in a lot of ways, as I've explained before." He gives me a pointed look. "There's no special way to kill us. We die like any other human."

I sit with this new knowledge for a minute, wondering if the killer is a full or half vampire. "Have you ever used your fangs?"

"Once or twice. I don't like blood that much, and it's not like I really need it." He considers before adding,

"I used to drink it out of politeness at family gatherings when I was young, and there were the few occasions Slade practically forced it down my throat." Everything I've learned about Slade just makes me detest the vampire even more.

"Your dad was a vampire, wasn't he? Did you ever see him... feeding on anyone?"

Alex rests his head on the seat, lost in thought and probably memories, too.

"My dad never drank from people in front of me or my mother. I think he and my uncle used to buy blood from somewhere, but I don't really remember. I've seen plenty of DBC members feed before, though." He shudders and bile rises up my throat leaving a sour taste in my mouth. I understand his distaste seeing as I've been an unwilling participant to vampires feeding. Twice.

Again, comfortable silence accompanies us in the car. Alex sits there, probably ruminating in his past, while I drift towards notions of the future. It's a very real possibility that this will be one of the last times we're together like this in his car, so I try to savor the moment.

But will he really let me go so easily, knowing all that I do about the vampire community? And about him? I can't help but think there's something more between us, that something has shifted in the past couple of days.

We're no longer just partners—even though he refuses to call us that—or a tentative friendship. We might be on the path to something more.

Do I deserve that? Do I deserve to feel these things and have thoughts and hopes for the future? I want to so badly—just like I want to stop being burdened by my guilt. Yet I can't shake the feeling away.

Much like the waves on the shore below, my guilt and grief rescind for a time and then they come crashing back. Predictable and powerful.

27

ALEX

Juliette's soft snores fill my otherwise empty apartment. It's weird having someone else here. She's the first person I've ever brought here. After spending some more time at the lookout point, we went to dinner at Sal's Diner—which is slowly turning into our unofficial spot. That's another weird thing I'm not used to—sharing a place with someone like that.

When we came back to my apartment last night, Juliette looked so exhausted, and I know she had been dodging calls and texts from her family all day. I let her take the bed again and swore it wasn't out of pity... even though it sort of was.

I'm rolling a cigarette around in my fingers, wondering if I even want to smoke it, when the bed creaks. I hear the rustle of sheets as Juliette stirs awake. It's after eight in the morning. I'm not sure if she has class, but I don't want to wake her. She also alluded to the fact that she's stopped attending classes altogether. She just looks so peaceful, and I know she needs the rest. Seeing her in *my* clothes, wrapped up in *my* sheets, in *my* apartment does something strange to my chest that isn't entirely unpleasant. My apartment is starting to smell like her, too—lilac and vanilla. I don't hate it.

"Good morning," she says groggily, noticing my stare. God, I hope I didn't look like a total creep just then. I smush the cigarette back into the pack and sit up a little straighter in my chair.

It's silent again in this stupid, lonely apartment as she rouses. My eyes drift to the photo of my parents on the table. Beside it are the clothes she wore yesterday. When I couldn't sleep—preferring to watch the steady rise and fall of her breaths—I washed her clothes for her. Again. She only brought one extra set of clothes and no pajamas. At least her rush to get away from her family gave me something to do while my insomnia plagued me.

"Your clothes are there if you want to change." I point them out to her. Part of me doesn't really want her to change. I shouldn't like the way my shirt falls on her thighs and my sweats hang loosely off her hips. Clearing my throat, I abruptly look away.

Juliette stares at her neatly folded clothes before crossing the room and picking up her sweatshirt. "You washed my clothes again?"

A grunt of affirmation is my only response. I can't read her expression, and thankfully she disappears into the bathroom to change before I ruminate too long on it. Deciding not to read into the situation further, I start making breakfast.

I've never really been a breakfast guy but based on the way Juliette dug into the eggs I made yesterday morning, I'll gladly prepare it again. Growing up, my mom always made sure I left the house with something in my stomach, but living with Slade for a good portion of my life ruined that habit.

Most days, I wouldn't even roll out of bed until noon having spent my nights fighting, keeping an eye on things in the club, or the million other things my cousin made me do. Sometimes just the smell of breakfast food makes me sick due to the many mornings I spent nursing a hangover while Anthony devoured eggs and pancakes.

Juliette shuffles out of the bathroom just as I take the pan off the burner. A small note of satisfaction blooms in my chest when I note she kept my shirt on, knotted up so it fits her better. A sliver of her pale skin shows between the hem of the tied shirt and her jeans. Who knew that tantalizingly soft piece of skin could look so inviting.

While she eats, I sip my coffee, content to watch her scarf down her eggs like she's never eaten in her life.

It's kind of cute, the way she looks like an angry kitten guarding her kill.

"What?" She questions me with a glare around a mouthful of eggs.

I shrug, my lips twitching up. "Nothing."

"Mhmm," she hums as she makes a dent in the whipped cream of her hot chocolate. I was lucky to find the box of packets in the cabinet yesterday. Apparently I had gotten it for myself at some point, but never drank any.

"So…" Juliette starts with a coy smile forming on her lips. "Halloween is tomorrow. What are you dressing up as?"

I give her a flat look. "I don't indulge in Halloween."

"So serious," she teases, then continues in a poor imitation of me, "I'm Alex Osman and I don't indulge in Halloween." I just roll my eyes and try to hide my traitorous twitching lips again with my hand. Juliette goes back to her drink.

She lifts her mouth away from her mug, sporting a whipped cream mustache. Without thinking, I reach across the table and wipe it off her top lip. She stills, as does my thumb just centimeters away from her mouth.

"You had a little something there," I mumble and hastily pull my arm back. The sudden urge to lick my thumb clean overwhelms me, but I settle for swiping it on my jeans. She nods and slows her eating, not saying anything.

Intent on avoiding what I just did altogether, I head towards the sink to deposit my mug.

I know her family and friends are hovering around her, waiting for her to break so they can clean up the mess, but Juliette is not fragile—she's probably one of the strongest people I've ever met.

People often confuse strength with power. They think it's usually loud and flashy. But Juliette's is a quiet strength. She knows what she wants and goes for it, but she will ask for help when she needs it. She doesn't want her friend's or family's help, but she wants mine. And that makes me feel something I haven't felt in a long while—worthy. Even if I don't think I deserve to feel that.

My phone pings, snapping me out of my strange reverie. It's an email with the autopsy report for Naomi Hart.

I open up the attachment—sent by one of Silas' tech guys who has been hacking into police and medical examiner's reports for the case—and scroll through. All these reports are usually the same, which is why I don't bother to do more than skim. Some words stick out to me, though, and I go back to the beginning to read through more carefully.

"What is it?" Juliette asks. "You've got that look on your face." She adopts a low voice and elaborates, "The 'I'm Alex Osman and I will figure out whatever it is you're hiding' face." I barely hear her mocking me again, too focused on reading through the report, noticeably different than the last ones.

"Naomi Hart wasn't drained of her blood like the other victims," I finally inform her once I'm done scanning. "And her throat was slit."

Juliette rises from the table with her dishes, placing them next to mine in the sink before looking over my shoulder at the phone clutched in my hand. Her warmth seeps into my back. "Really?"

"Yeah. No puncture wounds like..." I hesitate, watching her rub the scar on her neck out of the corner of my eye. "Like the others," I finish.

She bites her lip and leans against the counter. "Her blood wasn't drained?" I shake my head. "Then it's not the Knife Man? Why would they make sure I found the body and leave a creepy note?"

"The notes might not be coming from the Knife Man," I add. My phone is clenched tightly in my hand, mostly out of rage that someone has been sending her threatening notes in the first place.

Her brow scrunches in confusion. "Why would someone who isn't the Knife Man be threatening me?"

"To keep you away from the case, most likely."

"Could they be working for the Knife Man?"

I shrug. "It's possible."

Although, the more I think about it, the less I believe that theory. I only know of one vampire who makes it his mission to keep humans in the dark about our world—Silas. Would Silas really murder an innocent just to prove a point, though? Before the thought even fully forms, I know my answer. He would, or he would have someone do it for him. Especially if that innocent worked for Slade. Everyone is guilty by association when it comes to my cousin.

Another thought enters my mind: would he kill someone to try and frame Slade? To arrest him once and for all for a reason that wouldn't spark a war in our community?

No. He may hate my cousin and long to see him rot in his underground prison, but he wouldn't risk the exposure. The way Silas has been acting about the murders hasn't been out of worry for humans, but fear that our secret will be revealed.

"We should go back to Laurence Mitchell's," Juliette pipes up. "Maybe you can convince him to let me look through Serena's stuff."

I pocket my phone and face her fully. "With my 'I'm Alex Osman and I will figure out whatever it is you're hiding' face?" To my delight, that gets a chuckle out of Juliette before she quiets again.

"Exactly."

"When we go inside, let me do the talking," I say as we climb up Laurence Mitchell's front steps. I can't tell which house I hate more, this one or Silas' concrete rectangular monstrosity.

Juliette halts beside me and gives me an affronted look. "Why you?"

I barely bite back a smirk. "You remember what happened last time you came here, don't you?" She smacks me on the arm and continues ahead of me, huffing something about rude men under her breath.

Juliette pounds on the door with her fist and I wait a pace behind. I never did get around to talking to Laurence Mitchell about his daughter, but then again, that was just a formality. I can glean all I need to know from Juliette. She probably knows more about Serena than Serena's father does, anyway.

An older woman in a maid uniform answers the door, warily looking between us. When her gaze lands on Juliette, she hastily goes to shut the door. Juliette stops it from closing with her shoe. "Hello again, Joann. Is Laurence home?" She asks in a saccharine, sweet tone.

"I'm under orders not to allow you inside again," the woman replies tartly.

"What about me?" I ask, stepping up to Juliette's side.

Joann surveys me, her face barely fitting through the gap she's left in the door. Her gaze is pointed as she asks, "And you are...?"

I pull out one of my cards—I make sure it's the one meant for humans this time—from my pocket and hold it in front of her.

"I'm a private investigator. I've been meaning to talk with Laurence Mitchell." The maid jerks her head in Juliette's direction, the younger girl openly scowling at the older woman.

"Why is *she* here then?"

"*She* is—" I start until I'm interrupted by Juliette.

"*She* was Laurence Mitchell's daughter's best friend and wants to find the person who killed her." Juliette gives the woman a false, syrupy sweet smile. "Surely your boss wants the same thing?"

Joann looks between us again, contemplating, and decides to finally open the door wide enough to let us both through. "I won't be reprimanded for your actions again," she scolds, pointing a finger at Juliette. "If he asks how you came inside, leave me out of it." Then, her voice softens, "Serena was a sweet girl. I hope you find who killed her." With that, she marches off, and I follow Juliette through the massive foyer to the back of the house.

Juliette doesn't bother knocking when we come to a stop in front of a pair of doors; she just lets herself right in. Laurence Mitchell sits at his desk, mild surprise flickering through his gaze as we barge into his office unannounced.

"Miss Jennings," he says in an almost bored tone, barely deigning to give us a glance. "What are you doing back here? You obviously didn't understand my message when you left here last time. Should I call Caleb and have him deliver it again?"

I've only seen this man from afar, or gracing the covers of news articles and magazines. He reminds me of Silas and Slade—a powerful man who knows he can get whatever he wants through intimidation and fear, all while keeping a cool façade.

"Give me Serena's things and we'll leave," Juliette says, ignoring his words completely. Apparently she doesn't want to take my suggestion that I do all the talking seriously.

"Who is this 'we?'" he asks, his cool blue eyes skipping over to me. "Who have you brought with you this time?"

"Alex Osman." I step towards the desk, which he still reclines behind, and drop a card onto the surface. This time I make sure to pull out the one meant for vampires. There's a theory I want to test after seeing his assistant at the charity event the other night. Mitchell picks it up without taking his eyes off me and gives it the barest of glances.

"Interesting," he murmurs, spending a second or two analyzing the back of the card. My own gaze skips above his head to the framed photos and accolades on his wall. One photo has me doing a double take before returning my focus to the man at the desk.

Mitchell holds my card in one hand, not backing down from my stare. He spent extra time on the back of my card because he can *read it*.

The photo of him in front of Bellevue Manor as a young man, standing with a group of his peers just further proves that to me. I recognize a younger Silas in the photo—hair slicked back and towering over everyone else even as a teen.

Another young man looks like Creed Ambrose, his appearance fresh in my mind from our run in at the event the other night.

The fourth person in the photo has my heart stalling in my chest. I know the moment Juliette sees it because she lets out a sharp breath, barely audible. The fourth student in the photo, in this group with three of the most power-hungry vampires I know of, is my uncle. Slade is a spitting image of him, which is why Juliette reacted the way she did.

I haven't seen a photo of my Uncle Ivan in years. Slade refused to keep any, stating that his father "took the coward's way out of life so why should he be mourned?" While I don't necessarily agree with Slade's reasonings for essentially erasing any trace of his father, I can understand his anger.

I don't know what to do with the revelation that not only is Laurence Mitchell most likely a vampire, but he appeared to be friends with my uncle. And Silas. Which means my boss knew what Mitchell was and chose not to inform me.

"Give us her stuff and we'll leave," Juliette repeats, breaking the tension in the air, oblivious to what just transpired. But Mitchell knows I know.

Finally, he looks away from me, tossing my card back on his desk. "I don't have it."

It's Juliette's turn to clench her fists now, but before she can say anything, Mitchell thumbs through some papers on his desk, producing his own business card.

"You gave me a card. Now it's my turn." He hands it over to me.

Law Offices of Thomas and Smelter, the card reads, followed by a phone number.

"Familiarize yourself with that number, because the next time you show up at my home unannounced, you'll be hearing from them."

Juliette begins to protest more, but I give her a firm shake of my head. I'm not sure if I believe that Laurence Mitchell doesn't have his daughter's stuff, but I have more pressing issues concerning this man to consider at the moment.

Is he really a vampire? Why else would he have a photo of himself at Bellevue? More importantly, if he is a vampire, that would mean his late daughter was one, too. Why wouldn't Silas mention this?

I cast a sidelong glance at Juliette as we trudge out of the house. Her best friend might have been a vampire, and she has no idea.

28

JULIETTE

Maybe I'm a fool for thinking Laurence Mitchell would hand over Serena's things—especially after how well my first visit here went, but where else would her diary be? I truly believe that in finding it I might also find some answers.

Alex has been acting weird ever since we left the Mitchell house. He's been broodier than usual, not meeting my eye, and lost in thought with his gaze fixed firmly on the road ahead as we drive back to his apartment. We're stopped at an intersection near the campus when I suddenly have an idea. An admittedly stupid idea that will definitely bring back lots of traumatic memories for me, but it's the only one I have at the moment.

"Turn right," I direct him. He gives me a curious look but follows my directive. "At the next light turn left and then right again."

He doesn't respond, just steers the car in the direction I tell him to. No questions asked.

"Juliette, what are we—" He begins, but stops when we pull up to a house that's been vacant the past two months. Flimsy bits of police tape flutter in the misty wind.

"Just trust me." He studies me for a long moment before shutting his eyes in exasperation. "Fine," he relents.

Walking up the path to the front door, I'm instantly transported back to That Night. Everything looks basically the same, give or take some overgrown weeds in the yard and general emptiness of the place.

Fear overtakes me as I reach for the door handle and push it open. I'm surprised to find that it's unlocked, just like That Night. When I step inside, I expect to see Serena having the blood sucked out of her. I can still smell the tang of it and hear the phantom beats of my heart racing.

Wait, no. My heart *is* racing—in the here and now.

The house is completely empty except for the gigantic bloodstain on the living room floor. I guess they couldn't get it out after all. Serena isn't here, nor the vampire who attacked us both, but her ghost lingers in every corner.

I'm staring at that blood stain—now a dark brown color—when a hand lands on my shoulder. I jump, expecting that vampire to be here right now, wanting to attack me again. To finish me off this time. But it's not.

It's Alex. I was lost to my memories, almost forgetting he's here with me.

He's here. Alex is here. I'm safe.

I'm fine.

I'm fine.

I'm fine.

Two months ago, I would have never imagined I would feel safe with a vampire. Now, there's no one else I'd rather have by my side.

"You good?" His deep rasp of a voice permeates throughout the silent house. I swallow past the fear still trying to take root in my body and nod.

"Yeah. Are you?" I ask, remembering his odd behavior on the way here.

Alex doesn't respond right away. He shoves his hands in his pockets and slowly paces the room. "I think Laurence Mitchell is a vampire," he says without preamble. My eyes practically fall out of their sockets I open them so wide.

"*What*?" Could Laurence Mitchell be the killer, then? I've never liked him, and there was no love lost between him and Serena, but could he kill his own daughter?

Alex explains the photo I saw when I was first in Laurence Mitchell's office, how it was taken at the vampire boarding school—Bellevue Manor. How Laurence looked at the back of Alex's card, the letters that can only be revealed by water and heat, or a vampires enhanced sight, and seemed to be able to read it.

"Humans don't go to Bellevue," he repeats from his recounting. "Only vampires and half vampires are allowed to attend, so that photo proves to me—"

"That he's a vampire," I finish for him, breathless. He nods grimly with the confirmation. "So Serena..."

He rubs the back of his neck, clearly avoiding looking at the blood stain in the middle of the room. "Was likely one, too."

"She was drained of all her blood," my voice comes out small and hoarse.

Alex is here. I'm safe. I swallow past the fear climbing up my throat, along with the memories threatening to drown me.

"You said one way to kill a vampire was to drain them of blood."

Alex doesn't say anything about the blood being too much to only have belonged to Serena. He doesn't say that the killer probably wanted to turn her, which of course didn't work if she was already a vampire. I know all of this already, and as much as I've been torturing myself lately, I don't want to relive any of it right now.

Wordlessly I turn for the stairs, trying to push the blood stain and Serena's lifelessness from my mind. I came here for a reason, and hopefully I'll find something in the hidden pockets of her old room.

Upstairs, four doors remain propped open, as if the occupants might be returning at any moment. The house is still. Old floorboards creak under our feet as we tread on them. I don't glance into my old room, or Meg's or Josie's. Serena's is at the end of the hall, beckoning me closer, its door like the open maw of some great beast luring me in before devouring me whole.

I let it lure me and step inside.

There's nothing left here. It's just how I found it after her funeral all those weeks ago. Not even a forgotten push pin or piece of tape adorns the walls.

Pacing the length of her room, I check in the corners of her closet and think of any place she might hide something. Alex watches me with a concerned look on his face from the doorway. I ignore him and instead smack every inch of the walls, jiggle the doors, and stomp on the floor hoping for a secret to reveal itself.

One finally does.

In the corner of her room next to the window, a floorboard creaks a bit louder than the rest. When I press heavily on it, I can see it lifting slightly on the edges. My heart just about stops when I come to the realization something could be hidden under there.

Dropping to my hands and knees, I pry at the plank, my fingers shaking and affecting my grip. Without a word Alex kneels next to me and halts my hand with his own, effortlessly pulling the loose piece up. I try to convey gratitude in my eyes. In his own, I see understanding and patience.

Underneath the floor is a dusty crevice with a single item tucked away inside. I pluck it up gingerly, cradling this last piece of Serena in my hands as if it might be the key to solving everything. It very well could be.

"It's her diary," I breathe out. I recognize the green leather cover and gold foiled *Diary* on the front. How many times did I see Serena scribbling in this over the past year? Slamming it shut when someone walked into the room. I knew it was hidden somewhere. And here it is, in my hands.

Is it violating or wrong to read a dead person's thoughts? I'm hesitant to before remembering there could be information here that could help our case. Serena would want that. She might have even hid it in here knowing I would find it one day.

Without sparing another thought, I crack the leather cover and begin to read.

29

SERENA

I HATE HIM.

Who does he think he is, telling me I have to marry some guy I've never even met?! I hate all of them. All the men in my life. Well, almost all of them. I've only ever been a pawn in their stupid power games.

But I have a plan to get back at him. To embarrass him. To make him feel even an ounce of the hatred I feel every single day. Because that's the worst part of all of this—he doesn't truly hate me. He wants what's best for me, but he's too much of a controlling asshole to see that I'm suffocating under the weight of his thumb.

When Mom died, he at least acted like the doting father for a little while. He bought me dresses and dolls and let me eat dessert before dinner. That kind of loving father shit. When we moved here to Pine Falls, I thought it would be a fresh start. That he wouldn't be Mr. Mitchell, rich and powerful businessman. I thought he would just be Serena's Dad.

I couldn't have been more wrong.

I shouldn't have been surprised when he arranged that stupid meeting tonight. I didn't want to go to dinner with him, but I was curious enough. I thought maybe he was trying to repair what little relationship we had left.

Wrong again.

Instead, some guy I have never seen before sits down next to me, and my dad tells me we're getting married.

Fuck that!

He wants to arrange my marriage as some sort of antiquated business strategy. And to "protect me." Something about how it isn't safe for people like me in our world. Half vampires, he means. This guy he wants me to marry will "protect me."

"I knew his father, Serena. Trust me on this." Fuck that. So what you knew his father. That was like thirty years ago. Ugh writing this down isn't nearly as satisfying as saying it to his face would be.

He doesn't know I'm already with someone, someone who I love more than I'll ever love my dad or this random guy he wants me to marry. Luckily I have until I graduate to figure out how to get out of this.

I don't know what to do. I snuck into Juliette's room, but I didn't tell her anything. I know she could tell something was wrong, but how do I tell my best friend that my dad is a vampire? That I'm a half vampire? This secret has been weighing on me ever since I met her.

I keep replaying that fight my dad and I had the night of the Homecoming dance years ago. Juliette and her mom showed up at the end of it. They never asked me what we were fighting about, though I secretly hoped they would. I wanted to tell them that my dad wanted to send me away to a school for vampire children. Looking back, I probably could've told them. They might not have believed that part, but they would have at least seen my pain. I still don't know why he chose not to send me.

I wish I could tell Juliette everything. I wish I could tell her about K and this entire situation I've now found myself in. But my father is right about one thing, our world isn't safe. It's why Juliette was never allowed over when we were growing up.

It doesn't matter now. What matters is how I'm going to get out of this marriage.

I figured it out.

Finally, after stewing in my anger for a year, I've found out how to get back at him. It came in the form of a suit-clad man trying his best to imitate my father.

He came by this afternoon, delivering some mail that was at my father's house. He's his new assistant, apparently. I laid on the charm, giving him the sultry persona I've used so often. Just like I wanted, he completely bought it. He was absolutely enamored—I could tell by the way he lingered by the door. He kept coming up with things to say, and I let him, indulging in his poor attempts at conversation.

I will make him fall so deeply in love with me that he will deny me nothing. He will do anything for me, as long as it pleases me. God, I sound like a CW villain.

I can think of no better way to stick it to my father than through his assistant. I'll have access to everything. *I'll know exactly what my father is up to at all times. Who he's dealing with. Where he's going. Even when we lived in the same house, I never had the opportunity to see what exactly he does for a living. I didn't care at the time, but now I do. I want to see him fail. I want him to wonder where his documents are and why no one will want to associate with him.*

If his business crumbles, then so does this ridiculous marriage contract. No one will want to do business with a man who can barely get a grip on their own company.

I'm ecstatic and smiling like a maniac as I write this. I shared my plan with K, and he's just as excited. He was very impressed when I laid it all out, and he doesn't mind that I'll have to flirt and pretend to fall in love with someone else. He hates my father and my future husband just as much as I do—though I barely know the latter. It will take time and lots of patience. Rome wasn't built in a day. And it won't be destroyed that easily, either.

I went to Sinner tonight. I needed to talk to my future husband. But that was a big mistake because Caleb fucking followed me there!

He dragged me home and then left, so now I'm stuck here and it's barely ten o'clock. It gives me more time to work on my plan, though. It's not going as well as I hoped it would. Caleb is more loyal to my father than I thought. Apparently my father saved his life or something. Turned him mere weeks before I met him. I don't know. Caleb rambles on about nothing all the time, and it takes everything in me to pretend like I give a shit about what he says. It's cruel, but he's just a means to an end for me. I have to stay detached.

I'm worried that Juliette will start to suspect something. Can she hear me on the phone at night with K and Caleb? I can't tell her I'm seeing someone without telling her why, though. She's too curious for her own good. I really want to tell her, but it's not safe. The vampire world is not safe.

But she's strong. Stronger than she gives herself credit for. Maybe I'll tell her soon. I'll

30

JULIETTE

I THINK I'M IN shock. Not only does the diary confirm that Serena was a half vampire, but she was also involved in an arranged marriage, did in fact have a secret boyfriend, was seducing her father's assistant for information, and was intending to use that information to destroy her father.

Alex hasn't said anything, either. We both sit cross-legged on Serena's floor, her diary a weighted presence between us. There are pages upon pages of her detailing her attempts at retrieving files from her father's office, her sordid affairs with her mystery boyfriend K, her interactions with her fiancé, and duping Caleb into thinking she was falling in love with him.

"This is very... informative," Alex finally says.

"It was Caleb we saw pull her off the dance floor." Alex nods in agreement. Serena also revealed that Caleb is a vampire. I guess in hindsight it makes sense. I did think he was surprisingly strong for someone of his size.

"Then he took her home. It looks like something cut her off in the final entry. Maybe after he left that's when the killer showed up," Alex finishes my thought. I shiver at the thought of Serena home alone, placing her diary back in its hiding spot intending to return to it. Answering the front door, not knowing whoever is on the other side is going to kill her.

"I think the arranged marriage was with Slade," Alex adds. He fiddles with a tear in his jeans, staring at the open pages of the diary. "Shady businessman. She went to talk to him at Sinner. His attitude towards this whole thing—not wanting to be involved."

I'm not that surprised that someone like Slade would be involved in a marriage contract. Especially if it was to align himself with a powerful figure such as Laurence Mitchell. "Should we confront him again?" I really would rather not.

"*I* will. Even though I've pissed him off, I think he'd tell me the truth if I wore him down enough."

He wants to pay Slade a visit by himself, *again*. After what Alex has told me about their past I don't trust the two to be around each other. I sigh but don't say anything. One of the reasons Alex agreed to partner with me was to keep me safe, but what about *his* safety?

Well, if he wants to meet with vampires who may or may not have been involved with Serena...

"I'll meet with Kai, then," I say decisively.

"I'm sorry?" He looks at me, a cute little furrow in his brow. I almost laugh at the fact that anything about this man could be described as 'cute.'

"I think someone in Crimson was her secret boyfriend. I mean, why else keep it secret? If Serena's dad was getting into business with the Dead Boy's Club, then she would keep a relationship with their rivals a secret. And I don't think Kai is someone her dad would approve of. Don't you agree?" Alex stares at me for a good thirty seconds before slowly nodding his head, catching on to my line of thought. "I mean, she did refer to him by the letter 'K,'" I add to further convince him.

"That's a good theory, but I don't think you should meet with Kai alone. He doesn't want to be involved in this anymore than Slade."

"Another reason he was probably Serena's secret boyfriend," I point out, my voice going up an octave at the end. "He wouldn't want anyone to know now because he never came out and said he was seeing her when she died. It would make him look suspicious."

"Another reason he could have killed her," Alex says, mimicking me.

I give him a flat look. "C'mon, Alex. You know Kai. Do you really think he could kill a bunch of innocent people?"

"I don't know what to think anymore, Juliette," he replies, frustration evident in his tone. "I need to talk to my boss. And Slade. We can meet with Kai when I'm done."

"This is my investigation too, remember? And I want to talk to Kai. I can find someone else to back me up if you refuse." We stand at the same time, Alex rubbing his eyes. If he doesn't want me to speak to Kai alone, then I'll find someone just as dangerous to bring with me.

"Juliette—" he starts, and I'm loathe to admit I've become familiar with his exasperated tone.

"No," I say sharply. "You go have fun with your boss and Slade. I'm going to talk to Kai. What happened to respecting my choices?"

Alex glowers down at me, arms crossed against his chest. I rise to my full height in a lame attempt to assert some control. He unfolds his arms at my fierce expression, his own softening. "Is it such a crime to be worried about you? You've basically dropped out of school, not to mention pushed away your friends and family. Now you want to march into the territories of vampires who have asked us to stay away." I swear I see a flash of pain in his eyes as he speaks.

I take a step back, furious.

"Not you, too." I furrow my brow, my throat tightening uncomfortably. "Why can't everyone just leave me alone! I don't need your pity, or your worry. I'm fine."

The look Alex gives me is one of shock and disbelief at my harsh words.

"I'm fine," I repeat, a bit more forcefully. He continues to stand there, completely still and staring at me with such a sympathetic expression I want nothing more than to wipe it off his face.

"I'm fine!" I shout, stepping up to him. My palms land on his chest, hard. He barely moves. I do it again. And again.

And again.

"I'm fine!" I continue to shout, pounding on his chest. He finally sways, grunting, but it doesn't satisfy me like I thought it would.

"I'm fine. I'm fine. I'm fine." My mouth lets loose the familiar chant, my fists against his body the beat. I keep saying it over and over, unable to stop even when my vision fully blurs with tears and my shouts become incoherent through the force of my sobs. I continue to say my mantra as if it will save me, even while I crumple to the floor, my knees saved from a collision with the hardwood only by Alex catching me.

Two months of pent-up emotion finally spills over in the form of tears and babbling. We sit until the sun dips past the horizon, the blue light of dusk painting the floor through the window. Alex cocoons me in his arms while I sob, trying to convince myself the words I keep repeating are true. But I know they aren't.

After saying the same thing for so long, I no longer believe it. I can't be sure if I ever did. No one says they're fine unless they mean the opposite. It's taken me a whole two months to finally admit that I'm *not* fine, instead of ignoring any other emotion besides guilt and anger and fear. Truth be told, I don't know if I ever will be fine. But here—safely sheltered in Alex's arms—I feel like I could be. One day.

With one last sniffle, my eyes sufficiently dried out, I pry myself out of his grip. We don't speak on the way out of the house and back to the car, Serena's diary tucked safely in my jacket, and for that I'm grateful.

I may have finally broken down and shed those tears I tried so hard to repress, but that doesn't mean I'm ready to fully acknowledge it.

Silence follows us back to the apartment, but it's not pressing or tense. It's almost comforting. I bask in it, a bliss numbness overtaking me. It's like I'm experiencing an anesthetized form of the intense emotions I just let loose. I cried it all out of my system, for now.

Thankfully, I fall asleep almost immediately. Alex let me have the bed again, and I would have argued if not for the irresistible siren call of sleep. For the first time in a long time, I don't dream of vampires, dead bodies, or blood. Even after returning to the scene of the crime, for once I am able to purge myself of those memories, at least for this one night.

31

ALEX

I leave Juliette at the dining table pouring over a digitalized version of her murder board that she's created on her laptop. Silas has been messaging me nonstop since yesterday asking for updates, and oh do I have some for him.

"See you later?" I call to Juliette from my position halfway out the front door. She lifts a hand in farewell. I'm tempted to stride over and kiss her forehead like I did before.

It pained me to see her break down like she did last night. The weight of seeing her like that hurt. She's not fine, despite her repeating it while pounding my chest with her small fists. And she knows she's not fine but doesn't seem in a rush to do anything about it. At least not yet.

I can understand.

It's taken me ten years to accept the fact that my parents might not be alive. I'm still holding onto a sliver of hope, but deluding myself into thinking they survived a head-on collision definitely stunted my grieving process. I want to find answers more than anything, but that drive can cause people like me and Juliette to push everything else to the side.

So, yeah. I want to kiss her and remind both of us where she is right now, and that even though I'm leaving, I'm not going anywhere.

The drive to Silas' compound is made quicker by my urgency to get there and to leave as soon as possible. Hopefully Oliver has fucked back off to Bellevue already.

I pass a school, the kids filing into classrooms all dressed in their costumes. Growing up, we didn't really celebrate the holiday, but when Slade and I moved to Pine Falls, we started to. It was the one time a year my cousin and his friends could truly be themselves in public and no one would bat an eye. Naturally, Silas doesn't approve of the day.

As I told Juliette, I couldn't care less about Halloween. Why contribute and participate in a day where our kind is villainized and misconceptions are spread like wildfire? To prove my point, a kid in a Dracula costume hurries inside with makeup paling his complexion and sinking his eyes, fake blood painted around his mouth. Sure, we have out outliers like this 'Knife Man,' but as a whole, the vampire community is no less dangerous than the human one.

Luck is on my side as I roll up to the gate at Silas' place. Jeffers is manning the security booth and leans out the window with his arms hanging over the sill.

"What's up man? Caught the killer yet?" He gives me a half smile, amusement dancing in his dark eyes. I'm sure Silas has complained about my lack of progress enough for everyone to know about my supposed incompetency.

Rolling my eyes, I huff a laugh and bump his extended fist with my own. Thank God there's at least one person who works for Silas that isn't a complete douchebag. "Almost. Maybe I'd make more progress if Silas got off my back every once in a while." Jeffers snorts, and we exchange friendly goodbyes as he opens the gate.

Silas is in his study, as usual. "Enter," his lilting voice calls from behind the heavy door.

It seems like Oliver did return to Bellevue leaving me to face Silas alone in his study. He gives me a cursory glance when I walk in before returning to some papers at his desk. He's so similar to Laurence Mitchell in mannerisms and in their shared cold, authoritative aura. It makes me blurt out my first update before he has a chance to speak: "Did you know Laurence Mitchell is a vampire?"

Silas places his papers down and leans back in his chair, fingers steepled beneath his chin. He regards me for a long, painful moment. "Yes," his replies simply.

I startle. "You knew he was a vampire this whole time and didn't think to inform me?"

My "boss" shrugs a shoulder, his steely eyes at odds with the casual movement. "I didn't think it relevant." My mouth hangs open at this confession.

"Why the *fuck* not?

Silas' gaze sharpens as he venomously spits, "Watch your tone and remember your place."

"You didn't think it was important for me to know that his daughter, the first victim, was a half vampire?" I narrow my eyes not buying his bullshit.

"Serena being half vampire had nothing to do with her murder, as evidenced by the following deaths."

"But she might have known her killer personally," I point out, frustrated. If Serena and her father ran in influential vampire circles, the suspect list could narrow exponentially.

"Is Laurence Mitchell's assistant a vampire, too?" Based on Serena's diary, I'm pretty sure he is, but it'd be nice to have some confirmation.

Silas pats his perfectly coiffed blond hair, too distracted by the trees outside the windows to focus his full attention on me. "He works for the man. Put that investigator hat on and figure it out for yourself."

Lowering his hand, he deigns to look at me once more. "What else," he says impatiently. "Anything new with the witnesses? Any new leads?"

I wonder if he would be able to provide information on Juliette's potential stalker, even though he doesn't seem in a particularly giving mood today.

"One of the witnesses mentioned something about a stalker," I say carefully. "She claims to have seen a man watching her and disappearing quickly."

Silas returns to his papers. "Oh. That." He scans a page before glancing at me. "Juliette Jennings?"

Shocked that he seems to know exactly what I'm talking about, I simply nod in confirmation. He waves a hand like the situation doesn't warrant further explanation.

"I had Jeffers keep an eye on her. Just in case the killer decided to finish her off."

Anger boils through my veins in betrayal and at his casualness about the situation. Juliette questioned her mind—is still questioning it—and doubted if the hooded man she was seeing was even real. He is, apparently. And he was sent by Silas. And he's *Jeffers*. He's not here on an ultimatum like me—he chose this life. He chose to scare Juliette under the guise of "keeping an eye" on her. The one guy I could tolerate in this place turned out to be no better than the rest of them.

"And the notes?" I venture carefully, clenching my teeth and *watching my tone*.

Silas is annoyingly silent for several seconds before responding with a pointed look, "Humans have no business interfering in our affairs. You know this."

He levels me with a look like it's my fault Juliette was sent multiple letters containing threats. In a way, it sort of is. The notes started shortly after we met. I knew Silas would disapprove of a human being involved in the case, but to stoop to threatening letters and sending men to watch her in order to scare her away? It's disgusting.

He's no better than Slade, I realize. It's a thought that's been on my mind, and this latest revelation confirms it. Slade and Silas are the same type of callous, just donning different masks.

Swallowing heavily, I prepare to ask him a final question. His answer will either solidify his position as completely awful or create more doubts in my head.

"What about Naomi Hart. Did you kill her to scare Juliette? Or to get at Slade?"

Silas purses his lips, abandoning his papers again. A flash of anger enters his expression. "You assume I had something to do with it?"

"Naomi Hart's murder came with a note and a stalker."

Silas leans back in his chair, exhaling. "Yes, I killed her." He scoffs, "Well, *I* didn't but I had someone do it. That girl, *Juliette*, should have walked away sooner."

I don't like the way he sneers Juliette's name. Not one bit. He eyes me suspiciously, like he's working out how I came to the conclusion that he's responsible for the latest murder.

"I'm not as dumb as you think," I tell him in a low voice. "The autopsy report may have helped me a bit, too." Silas straightens at that, fury evident on his face.

"You weren't supposed to get that report."

"You're no better than Slade," I accuse as I raise my voice. Fuck *remembering my place*. "You'd kill an innocent person just because they work for him? Were you trying to frame my cousin as well as scare Juliette away?"

Silas stands, and it takes everything in me not to shrink away from his full height. He's taller than anyone I've ever met, and even when I was first brought to him I've never seen him so angry.

"You dare compare me to him? That *filth*?" he spits in disgust.

"You're a hypocrite," I seethe. "I won't work for you anymore. Not like this."

Silas laughs, harsh and cruel. "You'd break our deal knowing what your only other option is?"

Before I can respond or even think about the consequences of what I've already said, Silas is bellowing for a couple of his favored guards, Stephan and Devin. The two beefy guys who brought me to Silas that first time a few years ago enter the room. They block the doorway—the only exit—with their muscled bodies, folding their arms across their wide chests and awaiting further orders.

"Take our friend here down to a cell." Silas is all too happy to give that order.

As Stephan reaches for me, I clumsily dodge his grip and whirl back to Silas in a panic. "Who will solve this case if I'm down there?" *What will happen to Juliette?*

"I'm sure we can figure it out. Your cousin will be joining you down there in no time." He gives a flash of his fangs before turning back to his desk. I pointlessly resist Stephan as he pulls me away from Silas and down the hall, Devin at our backs.

Slade is going to be framed and arrested for these murders, that much I'm sure of. I don't know what Silas has fabricated to back up his claims or why he hasn't done so sooner. Maybe it was because I was around. Even with our troubled history, I still chose to defend my cousin and deflect any negative conversations about him any chance I could.

When we get to the foyer, Devin produces what looks like a pillowcase from a side closet and pulls it over my head. Then the two guards frog march me out the door. Honestly it's all a bit much. I think they like to pretend they're in a low budget action movie whenever Silas calls on them to do something other than stand around his office.

The crunch of gravel beneath our feet is replaced by the loamy forest floor. I can feel the presence of the towering pines and firs and wonder where exactly the entrance to the infamous prison is. Obviously they don't want me to know, not with the pillowcase over my head. It smells faintly of lavender, and I hate it. It's nothing like the pleasant vanilla and lilac smell I've grown accustomed to in my apartment.

I don't bother resisting anymore. The guards are much larger than me and seem intent on getting me to the prison with zero fuss. If I fought back, it would only make this worse. They could beat me up, knock me unconscious. I wouldn't be able to heal as fast as them. I know these two drink blood on the regular. I'd be no match for their heightened abilities.

The walk takes about ten minutes before I hear the beep of a mechanical lock and the hinges of a door swinging open. All I can think about is Juliette and the case. But, if I'm honest, mostly Juliette.

Will she think I abandoned her? She wouldn't know the first place to look, I can't remember if I told her about the prison.

Maybe I did, during one of our conversations. I've never opened up to another person the way I did to her—even if it was only a fraction. Will she think I'm dead? In a decade, will she be feeling like I do about my parents now? Will she be furtively searching for someone who might not even exist anymore?

Thoughts race in and out of my mind against my will as I'm led down what I think is a narrow metal staircase. It's deathly quiet beneath the earth until another door opens. Then the banging starts.

The deafening sound of muffled bellows and hammering fists meeting metal assault me from all sides. I gather that we are walking down a corridor, the noises not stopping until I'm shoved forward, my palms scratching against hard concrete. I'm barely able to right myself before I hear a slam, the cacophony of sounds ceasing.

Thankfully, my wrists aren't bound, so I tear the pillowcase off my head. I'm met with darkness.

A cell, beneath the earth. Completely dark.

I'm alone—in the worst way possible.

32

JULIETTE

Alex still hasn't texted me back, and quite frankly, it's pissing me off.

When he left earlier today, I was too absorbed in completely suppressing my emotions to say a proper goodbye. If I knew he would be MIA for hours, I would've tried harder.

After the distraction of creating my murder board on my computer from memory, I allowed myself to think more on the fact that I'm not fine. I don't know what to do with that information yet. I'll just ignore it like I have everything else the past few months. It's just another thing to think about after this case is solved.

I'm really hitting all the destinations on my journey to rock bottom.

Neglect hobbies and education: check.

Fall out with friends and family: check.

Repress any and all emotions except the ones currently keeping me afloat: check.

I can't believe I let myself fall apart in front of Alex. But also I *can* believe it. Whether he likes it or not, we've become friends. I've felt closer to him than anyone else in a long while. Even Serena.

I meant what I told Alex yesterday—I need to speak to Kai. And since he originally didn't want me to go and now he's nowhere to be found, I will have to resort to another escort. I'm not completely neglecting my well-being by walking into vampire territory by myself. At least, I'm not there *yet*.

"Yes?" the feminine voice on the other line purrs. I shift in my seat, trying to remember the lines I rehearsed in my head before calling her.

"Hello, Alina. Will you do me a favor?" She hums at my question, and I can just imagine her lounging somewhere with a smirk on her beautifully cunning face, examining her nails. Or poking at her fangs. Or whatever obscenely attractive, dangerous vampire women do.

"Juliette. Isn't this a pleasant surprise. Happy Halloween," she trills. "What is this favor?"

She doesn't question how I got her number—stole it from Alex's phone while he was sleeping, seriously though he needs a better passcode than one-two-three-four considering his line of work— so perhaps she's already guessed or just doesn't care.

"Happy Halloween," I mutter, forgetting everything I planned on saying. I clear my throat and muster my courage, remembering the purpose of this phone call. "Will you accompany me to speak with the leader of Crimson?"

A long silence follows my question, then a high laugh sounds. "You're bold asking that of me. Don't you know that man hates my guts?"

I don't bother telling her I already guessed that. I'm sure lots of people fear, despise, and love her in equal measure.

"I was hoping you wouldn't care."

Another laugh. "You hoped correctly. As if *Kai* could intimidate *me*," she says with enough arrogance that would make me second guess her if I hadn't met her before.

"Cool. So I'll meet you at the downtown gym in an hour?"

"No need. I'll pick you up."

Alina arrives outside Alex's building precisely one hour after we get off the phone and I text her the address. A sleek, sporty motorcycle idles on the curb as she lounges against it. How does she make *lounging* look sexy?

"Nice ride," I say, if only to avoid looking at her directly.

She pats the front of it affectionately and cuts her gaze to mine. "Don't just stand there, get on." Her head tilts delicately towards the bike.

Instinctively, I back up a step—my mom's warnings while I was growing up ringing through my head: *Don't ever get on a motorcycle, those things are death traps.*

"You don't have a car?" I squeak out.

Alina levels me with a look that's almost... disappointed? "*Non fare la bambina*," she tuts, whatever that means.

When I stare at her blankly she exclaims, "Don't be a baby! Come on, let's go."

She grabs a helmet from a compartment at the rear and practically throws it at me before sliding her own over her head. *At least it's not raining*, I think as I put the helmet on. I hope my mom never finds out about this, but I take solace in the fact that this is the least of my offenses lately.

Before I've even fully settled on the seat behind her, Alina revs the engine and we fly down the street. My arms wrap around the vampire's waist, and she apparently takes that as a signal to go faster.

While speeding down slick pavement in a machine that shouldn't stay upright is terrifying, it's also... exhilarating. I've never felt anything like this. I've never felt so *free*.

Alina takes the turns so sharply I'm sure we're going to topple over onto the pavement. But she maneuvers the bike expertly, and soon my fear dissolves into contentment.

By the time we get downtown, I'm almost smiling.

"So? How was your first ride on a motorcycle?" Alina asks with a wink over her shoulder after parking down the street from the gym. I take my helmet off and run a hand through my surely frizzy hair.

"That was... wow," I respond, breathless.

She chuckles, but it's not a threatening sound like it normally is. Alina sounds... pleased. There's a sparkle in her dark eyes, and it makes me wonder if she feels as free as I did whenever she rides her bike.

The Crimson gym is just as deserted as the last time I was here. Now even the receptionist is missing, but I'm sort of glad she's not here. It's weird to be confronted with people Serena knew and hung out with that I had no idea about. Which is one reason why I don't want to linger too long talking with Kai.

Speaking of, the muscular, tattooed vampire stalks through to the lobby with an irritated air about him.

If he's coming to confront us before we've even made it all the way inside, he definitely saw us through some security cameras.

"What the fuck are you doing here, Alina?" He slows his approach, and Alina gives him one of her signature feline smirks in response.

I step between the two. "I asked her to come with me as an escort. Nothing more. I want to talk to you."

Kai scoffs. "An *escort*? She's far more dangerous than me or any of my men. You would have been safe here without her." Sincerity, and a bit of hurt, lace his hard tone.

"Thank you," Alina purrs, sidling up beside me. Kai glares at her and I once again step in front of her to get his attention.

"Serena Mitchell. Did you know her? Not just from the news and parties... but did you really know her?" I cut right to the chase, fearful he will kick us out again. Alina could probably take him, but I'm not really in the mood to witness a vampire fight.

Kai sets his jaw, and through gritted teeth, replies, "I already told you *and* Alex that I don't want to be involved in this. Please go."

"You were her boyfriend, weren't you? She referred to you by your first initial, 'K.'" I meet his eyes, doing my best to let him know that I don't condemn him—or her—for this secret, as much as it hurts that I was kept in the dark. I just want answers.

Sighing, Kai takes up a spot against the wall, a far off look in his eyes. "Yes. We were together for about three years." Alina gives a low whistle, and I shoot her a glare the same time Kai does. She shrugs and plops into the vacated receptionist seat.

"Why didn't either of you say anything?" I plead. "Why wouldn't Serena tell me?"

"Serena had her reasons. She worried about me, about what her father might do. He didn't approve because Serena was also engaged," he nods to Alina, "to her boss."

"Slade."

Kai waves his hand. "Yeah. Some business arrangement between him and Serena's father. She worried that if people knew about us, Slade or the DBC might try something."

I take my own seat on a bench across from where Kai stands. I'd guessed at what he's revealing, but to have it confirmed is something else entirely.

Arranged marriages, secret boyfriends, vampires, murder... What has my life turned into?

"Did you kill her?" Alina asks bluntly, booted feet propped up on the reception desk.

"*No*," Kai straightens up and levels a furious look at the other vampire. He then looks to me. "I've been trying to find out who killed her, same as you. I even sent you in their direction hoping it would lead you somewhere." He jerks his chin at Alina.

"The girl with the video—your receptionist. You told her to show it to me?"

He nods. "Marissa, yeah. She's my cousin. We'd been working with that video for weeks, and I figured showing it to you wouldn't hurt. She was allowed into Sinner as long as she was with Serena."

"Not anymore," Alina says under her breath.

"You think the DBC has something to do with this?" I ignore Alina's scoff at the insinuation.

"I think that Alex will figure out who is killing innocent people in this city. I don't know you well, but if Alex trusts you, then so do I."

My chest warms at his words and at his assumption that Alex and I have a mutual, trusting partnership. It's the first time I've thought about it, but we do. I trust him, even if he is ignoring my messages. A couple more hours of that and I might start to get worried. The true test of friendship.

"But like I said, I don't want to be involved. Silas has eyes on all of us, and I just know he'll look for any excuse to pin this on one of us," Kai continues.

Alina mutters something in Italian that sounds a lot like "bastard." At least we can all agree on one thing. I haven't met Alex's "boss," but from what he's shared, I dislike the vampire already.

"I trust that you didn't kill Serena, Kai. But if you hear anything useful, will you just tell us straight up, next time?" I stand from my seat and motion for Alina to join me by the doors.

Kai nods and backs up to fill the doorway to the main part of the gym. "Yeah. I should've done that from the start. I was worried about myself and my guys. It's not safe for anyone out there these days."

I give him a look that I hope conveys my understanding and turn to walk through the door Alina is holding open.

"Hey, Juliette," Kai calls. When I look back at him, he hesitantly tells me, "I'm sorry. About what happened to you. And Serena. Neither of you deserved that."

A strange prickling sensation fills my throat and behind my eyes. *Oh, God. Am I going to cry again because someone feels* sorry *for me?*

It's nothing I haven't heard before, but it feels different this time. Most people just gawk or whisper when I'm around; or they recognize me from the news reports. To hear someone say that I didn't deserve to be attacked, not just that Serena didn't deserve to die, makes all those complicated emotions I've been stuffing down feel validated.

"Thanks," I barely choke out.

"She talked about you all the time. I hate that these are the circumstances that caused us to meet." His voice is thick, like he's trying to keep his own emotions at bay. I just nod and turn to leave again, afraid of losing it.

Alina and I silently walk back to her bike, but when I stop beside it, she continues on and motions for me to follow: "Come on, it's a beautiful day let's keep walking."

It's freezing cold and overcast, but any day it's not raining in Pine Falls can be considered beautiful, I guess. I fall into step beside her, stuffing my hands in the pockets of the hoodie I may or may not have taken out of Alex's closet. After staying with him for a few days, I can confirm that he has multiple and not just one that he wears every day.

"Grief is so complicated," Alina says. I stare at her sidelong, wondering where she's going with this and why she brought it up in the first place. "When I lost my parents, I had to keep it together for my brothers sake. Even though we are twins, he's so *young*." She taps her forehead, "In here."

She kicks a pebble with the toe of her boot, and when we reach it again, I punt it down the sidewalk. We continue taking turns kicking the pebble all the way down the street.

"When I lost Naomi, no one was there to hold me together. Anthony tries, but it's not the same." She stops and pins me with a questioning look. "Who is holding *you* together?"

I open my mouth and then abruptly close it. What is she getting at? "Why are you telling me this?" I'm certainly not holding myself together, and if I am, I'm doing a terrible job. So who *is* holding me together? Are my parents? Meg? Alex? It feels rude to burden them with my problems.

"What I'm trying to tell you, Juliette, is that you need someone there to hold you together for when you eventually fall apart." She gives a dainty shrug. "Humans are like cars—or motorcycles. If you don't check them regularly, all sorts of problems can arise."

"You're being weirdly kind," I narrow my eyes and deflect.

She gives me a smile that is all teeth with a peek of fang. "I can be nice."

"Who is holding you together if Anthony isn't doing a good job?"

I get a small huff of laughter in response, but then, "Even if he's doing a bad job he's still there. He still loves me. That's enough, for now."

My mind goes to my family and friends. They've been trying this entire time to help me, and all I've done is push them away.

"We're alike, you and I," Alina continues, and when I open my mouth to object, she raises a perfectly manicured hand at me. "Stubborn, though I prefer determined. Smart. Brave." She checks each adjective off with her fingers, and my face flushes with each word.

"I'm not brave. There are lots of things that scare me." *Like you*, I don't add.

Alina rolls her eyes. "You know, they say bravery isn't being fearless. It's being afraid of something and doing it anyway." We've made it back to her bike, and she gestures to it in support of her argument.

Should I take it as a compliment, that Alina thinks we're alike? Or should I be worried? I don't see myself as brave, but if Alina does, then maybe I can borrow some of her bravery. She seems to have plenty, and I could definitely use some.

"Because we're so alike, I know you'll find Naomi's killer and get justice for her, same as you will for Serena." Alina's tone and expression have suddenly turned serious. Determined. Trusting. All I can do is nod and accept the helmet she offers me.

The engine rumbles to life beneath our legs. "Back to Alex's?" Alina asks.

"No, actually. Can you take me home?"

No one is home when Alina drops me off. Where they all are, I have no idea. But I'm glad for the solitude. I'm here for my murder board and to solve this case once and for all.

The board is no longer on the floor where I left it when I fled the house the other night. Someone has propped it against the end of my bed, the back face-out just waiting for me to come home and be questioned about it.

I can picture my mom perching on the edge of my bed as she gently turns the board around. *Juliette, do you want to explain this? No one is going to judge you, honey. We just need help understanding.*

Settling onto the floor, I pull the board down and stare at it for a few minutes already seeing things I forgot to add to my computerized version. The article about Alex's accident, for instance. I rip it off because it should have never been on there in the first place.

Red string provides a visual guide for the few connections I was able to find between victims—Sinner being the main one. My gaze snags on the section I made for the second victim, Milly Johnson.

A post it note is stuck to the board and on it is a hastily written scribble about where she worked, *Law Offices of Thomas and Smelter. Where have I seen that name recently?*

Eyes widening, I realize where. The business card Laurence Michell gave to Alex if we wanted to bother him again.

It's like my mind bursts, and information I've discarded or deemed inconsequential fills every crevice.

The second murder victim worked for Laurence Mitchell's lawyers.

The dean's assistant was killed the night of Laurence Mitchell's guest lecture.

Serena likely knew her killer, if she did indeed let him inside the house.

Her father had reason to kill her.

Laurence Mitchell is a vampire.

Laurence Mitchell tried to pin Serena's murder on me.

The evidence isn't concrete, nor is it particularly overwhelming, but it's something. He's been under our noses this entire time—always there but dismissed as just another entitled rich guy.

I have to tell Alex. I have to do *something*.

Fear twists in my gut, but I stand up and grab my bag to head back out. I think of what Alina said earlier, how bravery isn't being fearless: it's being afraid of something and doing it anyway.

The past few months I've tried to be brave. If not for myself, then for Serena. I can be brave—*truly* brave—tonight because I'm petrified. Petrified of confronting a possible killer and solving this case once and for all. If I do solve it, what comes after?

But my fear is not going to stop me from finishing this. For getting justice for my friend. For the other victims. And for myself.

33

JULIETTE

WHAT AM I DOING. What am I doing.
What am I doing!

Those four words play on repeat in my mind all the way to Alex's place. My body carries me on autopilot as my brain malfunctions. No sane person would go to someone's apartment and steal a gun with the sole intention of confronting a vampire serial killer. But I never claimed to be a rational person when it comes to this case.

Alex gave me a key, so it's not like I'm *really* breaking in. Also, in my defense, I've tried to get ahold of him all day and have been met with radio silence.

It is stupid to do what I plan to do without someone knowing about it, so I sent Alina a text and promptly shut my phone off. With her, I could expect either a demand she come with me or threats to stop me and do it herself. I have to be the one to do this—to confront the possible killer and finally put this case to bed.

The passcode to Alex's safe is easy to guess. It's the date he was in that accident and his parents disappeared: October fifteenth, making the code one-zero-one-five. I remember it from that news article about him. At least it's not one-two-three-four like his phone.

I'm not expecting the large array of guns Alex has stored in this little safe, but I don't have time to examine each piece like I want to. I take a random pistol and make sure the safety is on before sticking it in the waistband of my jeans. My knowledge of guns is limited to the shows I've watched with Hayden over the years. This could go very badly for me, but my thoughts are occupied elsewhere to be too concerned for my own safety.

Laurence Mitchell killed Serena. He attacked me, then proceeded to drain dozens of people of their blood. At least that's the theory I'm running with right now and am ninety percent sure is correct.

The connection was easy to find once I knew where to look. The business card for his lawyers that he gave Alex is the same firm Milly Johnson worked at. Even if he claimed to love his daughter, it's not hard for me to believe he would kill her if he found out she was trying to sabotage his business and the marriage contract with Slade. The dean's assistant was killed the night of his lecture at the college, so that one is easy to connect him, too.

Alex did say the killer is likely in a frenzy and Laurence Mitchell is too composed for that. I don't let the thought deteriorate my assertion that Laurence Mitchell is the killer, though. In my gut I know going to his house is the right move. A stupid move, but right.

There are lots of ties of the killings to Slade and the DBC as well, but after closer examination, those ties seem forced. It's not wild to assume that someone actually was trying to frame the other vampire, and who better than the man he was supposed to go into business with?

The walk to the bus stop, the ride on the bus, sneaking through the fence, and the trek to Laurence Mitchell's house is a blur of fear, anger, and determination. Serena's words from her diary and Alina's words from earlier today keep flashing in my head:

But she's strong. Stronger than she gives herself credit for.

We're alike, you and I. Stubborn. Smart. Brave.

Those words are what keep me going as I pass house after house, giant Halloween decorations looming over me and casting eerie shadows on the sidewalk. It's too late now for trick or treaters, but remnants of candy wrappers and costume glitter decorate the streets as well as carved pumpkins and skeleton statues.

I pass the house with the motion-activated witch, and it begins to cackle, making me jump. What I thought was mildly entertaining in the rainy afternoon last week is frightening in the dark.

The house at the end of the street has no decorations or lights on, making it far creepier than any of scarily decorated homes in the rest of the neighborhood. I hesitate at the end of the driveway, wondering if I should go to the front door or not.

What's the point? I think. There's a gun nestled between my spine and my pants. Breaking in through a back window will be the least of my wrong doings tonight.

Luckily for me, a window on the side of the house is open just a crack. It's low to the ground, so I assume it leads to the basement. One good thing about this ostentatious house is that it's situated further from the rest on the street. I stick to the shadows, but I'm not too worried about a neighbor seeing me and calling the cops.

I slide the window open, and it's just barely big enough for me to fit my body through. Before I can let fear or common sense talk me out of it, I lower myself into the darkness of the house.

I've been attacked by a vampire in my own home. Been bitten by one in exchange for information. Have shared close proximity with another for the last few days.

Confronting a possible vampire serial killer is nothing. At least, that's what I'm telling myself.

One good thing about heightened levels of anxiety is the sharpness it brings to my senses. My ears prick with every little sound as I attempt to traverse the pitch-black room. After another step, my forehead collides with what feels like a chain swinging from the wall. Reaching up, I find it with my fingers and tug.

Soft light filters through the room from a bulb directly above me... illuminating a pair of icy blue eyes inches from my own.

34

ALEX

Drip. Drip. Drip.

Water drips from somewhere, the repetitive noise echoing in my skull. There's not much I can do in my new eight by eight concrete home besides sit and be hounded by all the thoughts waging a war in my mind.

I've already exhausted all possible means of escape. This place is sealed up tight—not a crack in the smooth flooring or walls. I'm huddled across from the steel door, willing it to open. It's too cramped in here for me to stretch out much, so I have my knees pulled against my chest, contemplating next moves.

Logically, I know it's futile to plan an escape. No one leaves Silas' prison without his say so. They took my phone, and even if I still had it, I doubt there would be service this far underground.

I hope Juliette is okay.

It's the only thing I can do, trapped here in this cell, thinking about her and my past and all the mistakes I've made that have led me to this moment. But was it a mistake, defecting from Silas? He turned out to be no better than Slade. And I don't think Slade would kill an innocent person the way Silas did.

Panic grips me as I wonder what he'll do with Juliette. Will he kill her next? God knows she won't stop investigating even if I'm gone.

Then, for the millionth time in the hours I've been trapped down here, I start thinking of how stupid I am. Stupid for thinking I could have any kind of future with her given the life I lead. Stupid to imagine us together outside of the case. Asking her on a real date, kissing her, laughing and smiling without anything holding us back.

Stupid to think I could trust anyone in this world, Jeffers' betrayal hitting me hard. Was it even betrayal? He was just doing his job.

A different sound joins the dripping water, tearing me from my self-pity. Scratching and clicking...

Before I can dwell on the new noises too long they stop, and my cell door swings open.

"Poor baby, all locked up." *Alina.* I bolt to my feet, peering into the gloom beyond the metal door. "You want to stay there forever? I knew you were a masochist," she clucks her tongue.

Cautiously I start forward, only partially sure this isn't some sort of trick Silas is playing on me.

"Alina?" I whisper, and finally she shows her face.

She's holding a set of keys in one hand, waving them back and forth. "Let's go," she angles her head down the hall, urging me to follow.

The other vampire moves like a cat, barely making a sound on the cement floor. No bangs or shouts greet us, and I'm sure it's because they can't hear her even if they were fed blood regularly to keep their senses sharpened.

"What about the others?" I question as we take the stairs two at a time.

Alina snorts. "You want them out on the streets?"

"I thought you and Slade might want to free some of your men."

"If they are stupid enough to get caught, they don't have a place with us." She glances at me. Right. I was one of those people stupid enough to get caught. But I was looking for a way out of the DBC long before that.

We escape into the night, the smell of damp pine trees pressing in around us, and I'm too curious about how and why she broke me out to feel any sort of relief just yet. It feels like any minute now someone will catch us and I'll be dragged back into the cell I barely spent six hours in. Or this will all turn out to be a panic induced hallucination. Then I'll wake up and all ideas of an escape will have just been part of a hopeful dream.

After ten minutes of trekking through the underbrush of the forest and no explanations from Alina yet, I ask, "How did you know I was down there?"

"Juliette mentioned to me that she couldn't get ahold of you. Then she said you went to see Silas. I put two and two together. Besides, she needs you. I did not sign up to be a little human's babysitter."

My brow furrows at that. "What are you talking about?"

Alina turns and places a finger on her lips in answer, shushing me. "I'll tell you when we're clear of his territory. Someone will discover the broken cameras and guards I killed soon enough, so let's not waste time chit chatting."

She whirls back around and I follow, trying to keep up with her silent yet brutal pace. How she can stalk through the forest so quietly and quickly is impressive, and I'm reminded of the days where watching her work like this was an everyday occurrence.

After twenty minutes of hiking, we reach a creek. Light from the moon reflects off the thin streams of water careening between stones, and Alina whistles twice after checking the surrounding area.

Branches shuffle and twigs crack as across the creek a figure steps out of the darkness. "Is it done?" A smooth voice asks.

Alina waves an impatient hand in my direction. "Obviously."

Slade steps forward, the moonlight bathing him. I don't spare him a second glance, even though I'm more confused now why he joined Alina on this breakout mission. I whirl around to her and demand, "Tell me what you meant about Juliette needing me."

She digs around in her pocket before producing a cell phone, my phone I realize as she hands it to me. I try to turn it on but a black screen is all that it shows, my reflection boring into it.

"Your human has done something stupid," Alina sighs.

"Tell me." My words come out as a growl.

Alina motions me across the creek, towards Slade. Once we're clear of it she begins to explain: "Juliette went to confront Laurence Mitchell. She thinks he's the killer. Her text to me said that someone should know where she went, since she couldn't get ahold of you."

Guilt stabs me for not being there for her, for not sticking things out with Silas until this case was solved.

"She's there right now?" My voice is shaky and panicked, and I hasten my steps. Alina grabs my arm in a firm grip, yanking me to a stop.

"You're making too much noise," she hisses. "I have it handled. You'll get to her before the night is up." Her gaze drifts to the moon high in the night sky.

As we walk on, Alina takes point and forces me to be in close proximity to my cousin. She charts a path that makes the least noise possible through the heavy woods, and we dutifully follow, though I'm not as silent as the other two vampires.

Laurence Mitchell is the killer? I try to distract myself with thoughts of the case but all it does is make me think about Juliette. If he is the killer and she went to confront him, she could be dead. She could be having the blood drained out of her right this second. She—

"Alex," a low voice comes from my right, a hand resting softly on my shoulder. "She'll be fine. There's nothing you can do about it right now, anyway." *Story of my fucking life.*

"It'd help if we could get out of these damn woods faster," I grumble, frustrated that Slade could sense my anxiety so easily.

Slade *tsks*. "And bring Silas' men down on us? There are cameras everywhere. Trust Alina—she knows what she's doing."

It's hard to trust someone you've seen brutally attack others before, but she did get me out of the prison and seems to be concerned about Juliette's wellbeing.

Well, concerned in the only way Alina knows how to be, which is mildly at best.

Still, I can't help but remind myself that she lost someone too. Her girlfriend, Naomi. Should I tell her what Silas revealed? That he had her killed to scare Juliette and hopefully provide more false evidence that Slade is the killer? I doubt that would do any good right now, so I keep it to myself. When this is all over, I'll tell her. She deserves to know.

"You did know Serena Mitchell," I accuse Slade, if only for something to distract me.

Slade sighs. "Yes. I never lied about that," he points out. For Slade, that means he eventually told the truth about it. "I knew her father, he went to Bellevue with mine. It was strictly business for us to merge families. Laurence wanted a hand in every pot and still does. He figured aligning himself with the richest of Silas' adversaries wouldn't hurt."

"Silas was okay with that?"

"He didn't know," Slade shrugs. "The engagement was kept quiet—not even the twins knew. We were to marry when Serena was finished with school, and then I'm sure Laurence would have spun some story to Silas."

A few beats of silence pass as I study my cousin sidelong. "Did you want to marry her?"

"It would've been good for business. Laurence Mitchell is a wealthy and powerful vampire." His words sound rehearsed, flat and depthless.

"What about Daisy?" I question carefully.

Slade is silent for many long moments. Moments in which I'm sure he'll just pretend he didn't hear my question.

He ultimately responds with a simple, "Daisy is gone."

"You've never tried to look for her?"

The look he gives me is enough to squash any further questions on the topic. "Marrying Serena Mitchell would have been good for business and would have helped my people. End of story."

"Good for your people, huh?" I can't help the bitterness that seeps through my tone.

Slade straightens his cuffs—seriously why is he wearing a three piece suit for a trek in the woods? "I admit that I wasn't the best guardian for you, Alex. I failed not only you but your parents as well."

"I agree," I mutter.

"I know you do, Alexi," he says my full name with longing and what I think might be regret. I try not to let it affect me too much. "You had many opportunities to turn on us, to turn on me. You never did, though."

A twig cracks under my boot and Alina shoots me a glare. I meet it full force and then address Slade. "I was forced to hunt your people."

"That is the extent of your sins, cousin. Any moment you could have told Silas all that we get up to, and I could have finally been hauled down to his little prison. But you never did."

"Don't read into it. I just wanted to put all that behind me. It wasn't some sort of forgiveness on my part."

Slade says nothing, and I wonder if I should tell him how torn I've been all these years. How a piece of me died each time he told me to hurt someone, or steal something, or deal something dangerous. I craved his approval and what we used to have—a family. Now I know better. Any hope of being a normal family died when my parents and Daisy went missing. When both our lives were irrevocably altered.

As if the universe wants to spare me from any awkward, heartfelt conversations, a break in the woods appears, revealing a deserted forest road with three vehicles parked along it.

"How did you get my car?" I ask Alina and she tosses me the keys from atop one of the tires.

"I have my ways," she responds with a cryptic wink.

Slade lingers at the driver's side door of his black BMW, nodding toward my car. "You better go, cousin."

I pull the door open but before I get in, I turn back to him. "Silas will pin these murders on you. He'll find a way." Slade's grim face etches itself in my mind as I turn the key and the ignition roars to life.

Why did I tell him that? To warn him? To scare him? To let him have some preparation before Silas and his men storm Sinner or Slade's home?

Shaking my head, I push the thoughts away. *None of that matters right now.*

That's the thought that spurs me down the road and in the direction of Laurence Mitchell's neighborhood. That's the thought that distracts me from wondering if tonight will be the last time I'll ever see my cousin again.

35

JULIETTE

"It's you!" I gasp, placing a hand over my racing heart. "You scared me."

"You're the one who broke in," Laurence's assistant says flatly. It's the first time I've heard him speak a full sentence.

The light only illuminates part of his features, and he's completely expressionless. This is the man Serena pretended to fall in love with. The one she used. The one who loved her back for real.

Does he know that she played him? Does he still love her? Does he know Laurence is the killer? Maybe he'd be willing to help me. He works closely with the man, surely he knows *something* is up with him?

"What are you doing here?" Caleb asks. We're only about a foot apart, and he doesn't seem in any hurry to create more distance between us. He moved so silently and was obviously able to make his way through the dark. I didn't realize it before, but now I know that he has to be a vampire.

"I'm here to see Laurence. Will you take me to him?" I should tell him my suspicions. He will probably call the cops if I pull a gun on his boss without including him in my plan.

Caleb nods once, slowly, and turns on his heel for a set of stairs directly behind him. "You could've knocked," he calls from ahead.

"He's the Knife Man, you know," I say in a hushed voice. My declaration is enough for him to halt halfway up the stairs.

"Is that what you think?" he responds, voice low, his back still to me.

Before I can even open my mouth to reply, he spins around and grabs me much like the day he threw me out of the house.

"What are you doing?" I shout in surprise as he carries me up the rest of the stairs and practically drags me down a hallway. We pass the massive foyer and Caleb shoves open a set of doors to the right of the front door, revealing a luxurious, but very dark, living room.

And also revealing a gagged and bound Laurence Mitchell tied to a chair in the center of the room.

"What the fuck!" I cry.

Caleb pushes me to the floor as soon as we clear the threshold. That's when he sees the gun tucked into my pants and yanks it away from me. The stupid gun was supposed to be my idea of protection, and I forgot about it the moment I actually needed it.

Laurence squirms in his chair, muffled shouting coming from behind the duct tape over his mouth. And then it hits me.

I've connected a lot of the victims and circumstances of their deaths to Laurence Mitchell. But recently I have rarely seen the man without his assistant by his side. Whatever can be connected to Laurence can be connected to Caleb as well.

I stand quickly, not wanting to turn my back to either vampire.

"*You're* the killer," I whisper, my words barely audible above the sound of my pounding heart.

Caleb prowls toward me and I retreat further back. Suddenly I'm no longer here, but *then*. That Night. I can see it now, this room just as dark as that one was. The features that were hidden so well in the shadows now scream at me with a familiarity that I hadn't noticed before.

It's him. It's really him. He's the one I saw over Serena's body. The one who attacked me. The one who has a starring role in my nightmares. My stalker. The one sending me notes. The one who I think is finally going to finish me off.

I was prepared to face Laurence Mitchell and accept him as the reason for all my problems. I expected to find him in his office like always. I would pull the gun and make him confess. And then... and then what? I would shoot him? I don't know what I would have done, but the prospect of facing him like that wasn't anywhere near as terrifying as facing Caleb like this.

More muffled shouts from Laurence, and my back hits the wall. Just like That Night. Caleb comes closer. I close my eyes but open them quickly. I won't give him the satisfaction of seeing me afraid.

"Why?" My question fills the minute space between us.

I have to know before I die. I have to know his reasoning for all of it. Why my best friend had to die.

Caleb smiles, but it's sad and small. He almost looks... remorseful. "It's a long story," he says, and his tone mirrors the quietness of my own. The softness of it completely at odds with the gun he's now holding against my ribs.

I swallow audibly. "Please tell me." Laurence continues his violent thrashing and shouting, but the sounds of his struggling dull when Caleb opens his mouth and begins to speak.

Serena – That Night

The knocking at the front door persists and I sigh, shutting my diary and tucking it back in its hiding place beneath my floorboards. I stand and stretch, taking my time as I smooth down the dress I haven't changed out of. He always comes back for more. It's good to keep him waiting sometimes.

I don't bother with shoes. The wood floor is cold on my feet, but I relish the chill. Caleb continues to pound on the front door, and I slow my steps further. He knows I'm upset with him.

Kai's cousin, Marissa, invited me out to Sinner tonight, and even though it's owned by my fiancé, I haven't been there too often. Not that Slade would even see me. He hardly acknowledges me. It's better that way, I guess. Especially with Kai. I'm surrounded by men who think they have any right to me, but Kai's the one I truly want. Free drinks from Sinner don't hurt, though.

"What do you want Caleb?" I ask when I open the front door. I don't bother hiding the annoyance in my voice. I'll break things off with him soon. It's not like he's been very helpful in my mission to destroy my father.

He's useless to me now, but unfortunately I was a little too good in convincing him. The poor guy has actually fallen for me.

"Serena," he says, breathless. He pushes past me and into the living room. Rolling my eyes, I shut the door and turn to find him pacing in front of the couch. I'm still pissed at him for dragging me out of Sinner, so I don't bother giving into his dramatics and asking what's wrong.

"Let's run away together," he finally says, stopping his pacing to look at me.

I laugh in surprise, and at the audacity of that statement. "What the fuck are you talking about?"

"Let's go. Run away. We can be together, far from here. You don't have to be engaged to that criminal anymore and we can both be away from your father."

"Caleb... no." Is he insane? God, I made him fall *too* in love with me. I have to break it off now.

"I love you Serena, and I know you feel the same." This is actual torture. I might die of embarrassment for him, but I have to do what must be done.

"Caleb, stop." I hold up a hand before he does anything more extreme, like get down on one knee. "I don't love you. I'm sorry to say this, but I used you to try and get information on my father's business. Also, I'm seeing someone else so this," I motion between us, "will never happen."

He stares at me, mouth open and brows furrowed, for what feels like an eternity. Then he lets out an awkward chuckle. "That's not funny, Serena."

"I'm not joking, Caleb. And if you tell my father, he won't believe you. Or worse, he'll question your loyalty." My gaze trails to the clock on the wall that Josie found at a yard sale a couple months ago. It's still early for me—I could try and hit up another club. Or I could wait for Juliette to come home and convince her to watch a scary movie with me. Either way, I need to wrap this conversation up and get Caleb out of my house.

My gaze jerks back to his when suddenly he's right in front of me. "What are you—"

I'm cut off by his hands wrapping around my throat. I claw and kick and struggle as best I can to get away from him. I never pegged him as the violent type or I would have never approached the conversation the way I did.

Fuck. I think he might want to kill me.

Half vampires can have the same enhanced abilities as full ones, but only if they drink blood regularly. Something I have never taken an interest in. Watching my dad down goblets of blood twice a week should have normalized it, but all it did was remind me how different we were.

Caleb's fingers squeeze harder and my vision starts to blacken around the edges. My movements are weak and slow, my breath trapped before it can reach my lungs.

"You bitch!" Caleb screams at me. "I should have listened to your father. You're a manipulator, just like he said." A tear slips from my eye, and I taste its saltiness rolling onto my lip. I'm going to die, and the last thing I'll hear is confirmation that my father really does hate me.

I close my eyes to block Caleb's icy blue ones. They resemble my father's too much, and he's not the last person I want to think of before I die.

Instead, I think of Juliette. My best friend. The closest thing I'll ever have to a sister.

I think of her laugh, her soft smile, the way she rolls her eyes whenever her cousin says something stupid. I have hope that she'll make Caleb pay for what he's done. That's enough to bring me peace as the darkness washes over me and I leave this world forever.

I think of Juliette. And I think of how quick my death will be.

Just like that, I'm gone.

Caleb

"Serena?" I shake her body but it's limp. Lifeless.

Oh god, what have I done?

I drop her body onto the floor and shove my hands into my hair, resuming my pacing from before but now for an entirely different reason.

Lately, I've been lost to my rash emotions, but I thought I had a handle on it. I don't know what's wrong with me. I talked to Laurence about it asking if it has something to do with the change, but he told me not to worry.

Only now I've killed his daughter, and I'm pretty damn worried.

I sink to my knees beside Serena's body, her pale skin even whiter in death.

Wait a minute. She's dead, but so was I. Her father brought me back from the brink. He saved my life.

I can do the same.

Cradling her body close to mine, I push her silky hair back to expose her neck. I've never done this before and haven't even seen it done. But I have vague recollections of the night it was done to me.

First, I bite my wrist, letting the blood that flows from it drip into her mouth. Then I sink my teeth into her own flesh.

I'm not prepared for the taste. I thought blood would be metallic and unpleasant, but this is... wonderful. It's sweet and completely aromatic, totally at odds with the girl it belongs to.

I drink from her, knowing I should stop and feed more of my blood into her mouth, but I can't.

Laurence has never allowed me blood, and I can see why. It's addicting.

Before I know it, I've made a mess of myself and her and the floor around us. I'm frantic with my drinking, not caring if the blood gets everywhere in the process.

Why have I never done this before?

A scream breaks me from my trance. Another girl, I think one of Serena's friends, stands a little ways away. Convenient timing, too, because I am nowhere near satiated. This craving is like nothing I've ever felt before.

My limbs feel lighter, stronger, and faster as I move towards her. My vision is sharp, and my hearing keen even in the dark with this new girl screaming. This is the best feeling in the world. Why would Laurence hide this from me?

The girl screams again, but I shove her into the wall, my nails pressing into her skin as I hold her still. My sharper hearing makes her shrill screams grate on my every nerve, her frantic pulse annoyingly thunderous.

Her blood is tangier than Serena's was. For the first time since the change, a sense of completeness fills me. It's like I've been missing a piece of myself this whole time, and through their blood, I've been able to find it.

Why didn't Laurence tell me about this?

A car revs from somewhere outside, and I come to my senses.

Again I think, *what have I done?* Especially as I stare at this semi-conscious girl covered in her own blood. Not to mention the dead one behind me. That experiment failed terribly. Vaguely I'm hit with the thought that I just killed someone—and maybe her friend too. I killed someone who I thought I loved. Who I thought loved me.

Panicked by my own lack of restraint, I toss the girl away—too roughly on account of my newfound strength—and go back to grab Serena. Maybe cleaning her up and burying her will be enough to appease the guilt creeping up on me.

I didn't mean to kill her... *I don't know what's wrong with me!*

She was cruel in those last moments, but she didn't deserve to die for it.

I'm a monster.

Using my new speed and strength, I swing Serena's limp body into my arms and dart out through the back door, not stopping until I find a creek a few miles away.

Carefully, tenderly, I clean the blood off her body. I remove her dress. I find a field of flowers nearby and set her in it. It's beautiful, just like her.

"I'm sorry," I whisper over her dead body.

But the apology does nothing to quench my newfound thirst, and I'm already parched again.

36

JULIETTE

"Don't you understand?" Caleb's voice is pained, his face so close to mine as he recounts the story of how this all started.

He waves the gun in Laurence's direction, the older man still futilely shouting and struggling against his bonds. "He did this to me! I didn't mean to, and now I can't stop." His voice breaks and a pang goes through my chest. I shouldn't feel sorry for him, but I do.

"Laurence found me on the side of the road." Caleb takes a step back and my breaths come a little easier. "I was in a hit and run while riding my bike a few miles from here. Laurence stopped and turned me. He knew I would be loyal to him for saving my life. And I am—*was*."

The sympathy for this killer returns. Caleb didn't ask for this life. Hell, it doesn't sound like he was even shown how to live as a vampire.

I hate Laurence even more because he created this.

All the deaths, all the senseless murders, can be traced back to him after all.

"You should've just let me die," Caleb says in a choked whisper aimed in Laurence's direction. Then he looks back to me and the apologetic look on his face has my heart pumping in overtime. "I tried to fight it. I did. But I didn't know how. I didn't know what to do." He sounds on the verge of tears and something that feels a lot like pity lashes through my chest at his broken voice.

"I wish you hadn't come here," he continues, hardening his tone. "When I found out you survived, I was glad. You were one less person who died because of this. Because of me. But now I *have* to kill you." He jerks the gun at Laurence. "Then I have to kill him."

My breath shudders out of me and tears prick my eyes. He's right—I shouldn't have come here. All that awaits me is death. I got my answers, but they'll be useless when I'm gone. My only hope is that Alex is able to put the pieces together and avenge me like I tried so hard to do for Serena.

"What will you do?" I whisper.

Caleb positions the gun back at my ribs. "I'll leave Pine Falls like Serena and I should've done all those weeks ago."

"So you can wreak havoc in a new city?"

"If I stay here, I'll die!" Caleb shouts at me. "That guy, Silas, he'll eventually figure it out and send his blood hunter after me."

The mention of Alex has my chest clenching. I'll never see him again. I don't know what to do or how to get out of this. Fear has gripped me, and I'm worried it won't let go. I'm not brave—Alina was wrong.

Caleb presses the gun further into my skin, and I squeeze my eyes shut, refusing to cry. And then his hand wraps around my throat.

My eyes pop open to find Caleb with a determined look on his face, his hand wrapping tighter around my throat. I claw at his fingers, but it's no use. A wave of helplessness washes over me—even stronger than before. I've wondered all this time how Serena felt before she died. What she thought. Now I'm about to meet my end by her killer, too.

His fingers tighten around my throat until my vision blackens and there's no way I can suck in a breath. I wonder if this is exactly how Serena died. For a second I'm transported into another place, another time. Seeing her last moments and not mine.

At least I can be grateful that I'll die this way, instead of being drained of blood. These are the things that run through my mind at death's door.

Pity, sorrow, regret. These also run through my mind.

I'll never see my parents again. Do they know that I love them? That I want their restaurant to succeed despite the financial burden on their shoulders?

I'll never hear another one of Hayden's awful jokes. In the past couple of months, how many of them did I refuse to laugh at out of misplaced guilt and stubbornness?

I'll never see one of Josie's smiles. When was the last time I was responsible for one?

I'll never be subject to one of Meg's interrogations. Right now it doesn't sound so bad. I wish I could tell her everything. I wish I *had* told her everything.

And Alex.

Oh, Alex.

We've only just begun our story—our relationship. Friendship, partnership... whatever we are.

Ours paths never would have crossed if not for the vampire currently closing off my airway.

My past selfishness makes an appearance in my thoughts as well. I feel selfish for dwelling on such things when I've received extra time that I now feel I misused. Time that all the other victims were robbed of. If, by some miracle, I make it out of this, I vow to use my time wisely.

My ears start to ring, and my thoughts drift back to Serena. Did she think of me before she died? Maybe I'll see her soon, wherever I end up, and the soul aching guilt and fear I've felt since her death will finally go away. We'll be together, and it will be okay because if I couldn't even stop my own murder, then I'm absolved from being unable to prevent Serena's. I can move on from this life and into the next with the knowledge that I tried. I tried to find the killer—the monster who took so many innocent lives—and I did.

Maybe Alex will find my body, but maybe I don't want him to. I'd rather it be him than my parents, or Josie or Meg or Hayden. I know what it's like to stumble upon a loved one when they've been drained of life. Alex can handle it. He will funnel his rage and sadness into finding my killer, just like I did for Serena.

Just when my vision darkens completely, my body limp and weightless, a miracle happens.

A miracle in the form of Laurence fucking Mitchell.

I'm thrown to the floor, my head bouncing off the wood with an audible smack. Stars burst in my vision, and when I pry my eyes open, the dim room is suddenly too bright. I can make out the shapes of Caleb and Laurence fighting not far from me. The ties Laurence was contained in are loose around the chair. He must've gotten out somehow while Caleb was choking the life out of me.

The two men grapple for control, and in their struggle, the gun Caleb pried away from me skitters across the floor in my direction.

This is my chance.

I could end this right now.

Even though I can barely move and my head hurts so bad I feel it might explode, I *refuse* to die here like this.

Rising onto my knees, I crawl towards the gun laying in the middle of the room. Laurence and Caleb are shouting at each other, but through the ringing in my ears and pain in my head, I can't make out a single word.

My fingers graze the cool metal of the pistol, and I pull it towards me by the barrel. Somehow, in my dazed state, I'm able to flick the safety off and aim. It seems heavier than it did before, but I don't let that deter me.

The two men keep moving around, so it's hard to focus on my target. They're so engrossed in their argument that they're completely oblivious to the fact that I'm pointing a loaded weapon in their direction. Caleb gets Laurence under him and pins his body to the floor.

This is my chance. He's still, his back to me, speaking in a low, venomous voice to his boss.

I don't think about it any further. I aim the gun at his head—where his brain should be, remembering

Alex telling me the most successful ways to kill a vampire—and I pull the trigger.

I don't expect it, but I'm knocked flat onto my back again with the force of the shot.

The sound the gun emits when triggered is also unexpected. I knew guns were loud, but right next to your face without ear protection in a confined space makes it near deafening.

None of that matters to me, though. All I can hope is that my shot hit true. I don't have the energy or the strength to sit back up and check that the bullet reached its target. All I'm capable of in this moment is lying on my back, staring at the paneled ceiling.

My hands feel sticky. I move them around a little and realize the two men must have seriously hurt each other for this much blood to be on the floor. Again, I pay no mind to the fact that I'm lying in a pool of blood.

All I can do is close my eyes, and let the familiar darkness take me.

37

JULIETTE

"LITTLE HUMAN?" A VOICE speaks from somewhere far away. An icy grip encircles my wrist, and a mouth finds my pulse point. That jolts me back to my senses enough to activate my fight or flight.

All I see is pale skin and dark roots of someone's hair. Caleb. *He didn't die?* The hand reaches for me again and, on instinct, I bite down on the smooth skin.

"Ow!" the person says with incredulity then swears in what I think is Italian. "You bit me! That's *my* thing, sweetheart."

My eyes finally adjust enough to see Anthony on his haunches beside me, cradling his hand and sucking on the bite mark I left behind like an animal licking its wounds.

Not going to lie, seeing him inflicted with my bite instead of the other way around feels pretty damn good.

Unfortunately, I don't get to bask in that feeling for long. Blackness creeps back into the sides of my vision, and I have the sudden urge to vomit, pass out, and cry all at once.

Anthony snaps his fingers in my face, uncaring about his minor flesh wound now. "No, little human—don't pass out again." I sway, and he catches me around the shoulders. "My sister told me to come here and help you. If you die, both she and Alex will kill me."

I groan as the pounding in my head reaches a new crescendo and, against all my instincts, collapse into the vampire's arms.

Flashing lights stir me. Vague images of blood, gloved hands, and muffled voices reach me. From my hooded gaze, I see Caleb's dead body—*oh my God I* killed *him*—rolled off of Laurence. Hands grab at the other man, and then me.

Where did Anthony go? Or did I dream that entire interaction up?

My body is placed on something cushioned, but my mind is still processing everything that happened this evening. The paneling on the ceiling moves which tells me I'm either concussed—*again*—or someone is moving me.

Finally I realize it's a stretcher. I'm on a stretcher, and an EMT is staring down at me with concern. "Can you hear me, miss?" She glances ahead and then back down at me. "Can you tell me your name?" I don't respond—there's no energy left for me to even speak my name.

I discovered Serena's killer, the person responsible for so many deaths.

I was attacked.

I killed someone.

Caleb would have killed me, would have killed Laurence, but it still hurts me to think I was capable of doing something like that. Am I no better than him? He acted out of fear and guilt and shame, is that not the same as what I did?

No, I'm quick to reassure myself. *You acted in self-defense.*

Still, a part of me feels horribly for what Caleb went through. I could see in his eyes how ashamed he was of who he became. It's a look I've seen too often in someone else. The one person I want to talk to more than anything right now. To have by my side.

"Alex," I manage to whimper. Hoping someone, anyone, will understand what I want.

The EMT of course, has no idea of the thoughts running through my head. "Your name is Alex?" Her voice is so hopeful at the possibility I'm able to recall my name that I almost feel bad when I shake my head no.

"Alex. Please," I beg, hoping she'll understand, but the confused furrow of her brow relays that she has no idea who Alex is.

As if me saying his name summoned him, a voice breaks through the remnants of buzzing in my ears. "*Juliette!* Let me through," he roars. His deep voice is a balm to my soul, to my injuries. I try to sit up and reassure myself that he's actually here. That he came for *me*.

But gloved hands keep my body pressed firmly into the stretcher. "Don't move," the EMT warns. "You have a concussion; it's best to lie still."

What felt like cotton stuffed into my ears slowly fades, revealing hurried chatter and worried exclamations. The lights from the ambulances and police cars are bright—too bright for my damaged brain to take at the moment. I close my eyes against their assaulting glare, but warm hands on my face have me opening them again.

Alex. He's here. I'm *safe*.

There's still a slight chance that Alex is a figment of my concussed imagination, but based on the impatient look the EMT gives him, I have faith that his presence is real.

"Juliette," his voice comes out breathless and his grey eyes are tainted with worry. "For fuck's sake, I thought you were dead."

He doesn't berate me for coming here alone, nor does he admonish me for stealing one of his guns. Instead, he surprises me by pressing his lips to my own.

When his fingers graze my skin, when he pulls me into his body, when our lips touch, I know deep in my heart that this is real. I could never conjure up the feeling of his warmth against mine, not in any way that feels like this. Maybe I'm still questioning my sanity when it comes to certain things—entering the home of a vampire I highly suspected was a serial killer being one instance—but now I know as he holds me and our lips gently press together that this is *real*. The doubts, guilt, fear, anger, pain, and sadness I have carried for so long, settle, if only for a moment, but it's a moment I never want to end.

He pulls back, much to my disappointment, but keeps his hands in place on my cheeks. His eyes rove over my features, assessing me.

"I'm okay," I croak out, even though I feel anything but. I just want that concern in his brow to go away. Reaching up with a hand that is sluggishly slow, a rub the spot right above his nose in between his eyebrows with my thumb.

He relaxes under my touch, and his eyes soften slightly. I take it as a win for now. Ever since I met this man, he has been overly preoccupied with my safety. I don't think my actions tonight will make that go away anytime soon. If anything, they'll make him even more hyperaware.

"Sir, we really need to load her up and get her to the hospital."

The EMT stares at Alex with obvious impatience and he smoothly steps away to allow them to roll me to the waiting ambulance. He doesn't stray far, though, taking up a position near my head with one hand resting on my shoulder.

The ride to the hospital along with the subsequent evaluations and scans by different doctors are a blur, but Alex stays firmly by my side through it all. He asks questions, he rubs my hand with his thumb, and he gives me reassuring looks. Maybe it's the drugs they've given me or just his presence, but for once, it feels nice to relax and let someone else take the reins.

At some point, I must lose consciousness again because the next thing I know, I'm waking up to find Alex watching me carefully from a chair next to my hospital bed.

"Again?" I croak, glaring at the multiple wires and machines in and around my body.

"You have another concussion, damage to your windpipe, and a sprained wrist," Alex informs me. "Can't take you anywhere," he tries to joke, but it just makes me reflect on how stupid I was to go there alone.

"Alex," I start, my voice raspy and throat sore.

He places a hand over my mouth and scoots his chair closer to the bed. "Don't." Leaning down, he smooths my hair back from my face, a tenderness to his expression. "You caught the killer, Juliette. You did what you set out to do."

"I killed him."

"You did. You're a lucky shot, too."

"Where were you?" I ask, if only to get the horrible images from tonight out of my head.

Alex inhales deeply then proceeds to tell me how his day went. How he confronted Silas—who apparently was sending people to stalk and threaten me and killed Naomi Hart—and told him he was done working for him. Alex tells me of his short stint in the infamous vampire prison before Alina broke him out and sent him to Laurence Mitchell's house, informing him of what I was up to. She also had Anthony come help me and call 911 before he disappeared.

"Of course Alina knows how to break someone out of an impenetrable vampire prison," I remark, and Alex snorts in agreement. "Does she know about Silas killing Naomi Hart?" I add somberly.

"No," Alex says, sucking his teeth. "I didn't tell her."

"You should. She deserves to get vengeance for her girlfriend." Alex fiddles with the ID bracelet around my non bandaged wrist. "Also, your boss sucks," I spit out. I'm so angry at the vampire leader, and my rage only intensifies knowing there's not much I can do in retaliation.

"Not my boss anymore. But he does suck," he agrees.

"Will they come after you? Since you escaped?" New fear and worry floods me. We may have stopped a vampire serial killer, but the dangers of the vampire world still surround us.

Alex gives my hand a gentle squeeze. "Don't worry about that. I'll figure something out."

"What about Slade? Is he in the clear?"

"Silas so desperately wants to pin something on Slade. He operates outside of the Council's rules but has never openly disobeyed them. Or, at least, he's been successful in hiding what he does. I think Naomi Hart was killed because she could be tied to Slade."

We sit in silence for a few minutes, the steady whirs and beeps of the machines in the room filling the gaps.

"Caleb loved Serena. I think we were right in thinking that he picked some victims because they looked like her." I recount what Caleb told me in those terrifying minutes before I thought I was going to die. His past with Serena, and how he killed her. His instant regret and the thirst he was never able to control.

"I think he felt bad," I surmise. "I think because he couldn't save her, deep down he tried to save girls who looked like her. To reenact it and hope for a different outcome, but his thirst overpowered any hope of that."

"Caleb should've known you can't bring any vampire, even a half one, back to life like that," Alex replies. But Caleb *didn't* know. No one bothered to show him how to live his new life, they just took advantage of him.

In a way, Caleb was a victim too.

Another victim to a powerful man who thought he was entitled to another person's choice and freedom.

"What?" Alex murmurs when he notices me staring at him for too long.

I reach up and trace his cheekbone. "I was thinking about how much I want this thing between you and Silas to stop. I hope he lets you go and you can live your life free of him. Slade too."

Alex captures my roving finger in two of his own. "I hope so too." He presses a kiss to my skin, and butterflies erupt in my stomach, along with a warmth.

I want to ask if he'll kiss me for real again when he places my hand back on the bed and stands. "I'm going to see what they have for food."

"Hey, wait." He stops with a hand on the door, looking back at me. "Where are my parents?" I ask tentatively.

His eyes widen as if he's mentally chastising himself for not mentioning them before. "Something came up with the restaurant. They were here when you were out earlier but promised to be back as soon as possible."

Biting my lip, I trace the pattern of the scratchy hospital blanket and nod. "Do you want me to stay?" He hesitates before leaving.

"No, I'm getting hungry anyway so good timing." I shoo him away with my hand, and he rewards me with a half-smile.

Not two minutes after Alex leaves, a knock sounds on the door and is pushed open. Immediately I straighten up in bed, glaring at the newcomer. "What do you want?"

Laurence Mitchell raises his arms—well, one arm since the other is in a sling—in a show of surrender. "I just want to talk."

"Are you here to thank me?" I question bitterly.

"You could say that, yes." In all the years I've seen Laurence Mitchell around, he has never looked as disheveled and stricken as he does now.

I pretend to examine my chipped and dirty nails. "I'm waiting."

"Thank you."

He proceeds to tell me how he discovered Caleb was the killer after the late vampire began acting strangely. "Some things weren't adding up, and when I looked at the locations of the murders and the victims…" So he came to the same conclusions I did.

"I confronted him," Laurence continues, a faraway look in his eyes like he's reliving the memory. "He tied me up and was wondering what to do with me when he sensed you in the house." And from there I know what happened next. "It's all my fault." His admission almost makes me black out again I'm so shocked.

I lift my gaze to meet his only to find him frowning at the polished tile floor. "It is. And you'll have to live with that."

Sighing, he inches towards the bed and takes the seat Alex vacated. I don't like him so close to me but laid up in bed there's not much I can do about it besides yell at him to get away. Since he's opening up a little, I refrain from doing so.

"You wanted to send her to Bellevue but then didn't. Why?" I change the subject.

He casts his gaze to the window. "I thought it would be safe for her there. But then I heard about a student going missing and I remembered all the... unsettling events of the school's history."

"Unsettling?" As if a school for vampire children isn't already *unsettling*.

"Yes. Mostly disappearances. The students who disappeared have never been found. And it's almost always half vampire children that go missing. Some say the school is cursed." He shifts his stare to his fingernails. "Even if it is just a ghost story the students like to tell, I didn't feel comfortable sending Serena there."

"It seems like you picked and chose when to care for her."

He sighs but it's not because of impatience or irritation, he just sounds tired. "There comes a time in life when you think you could have it all. And even when you do have it all, you always want *more*."

"That's not a common trait, Mr. Mitchell. You *did* have it all. And you fucked it up. Serena should have been enough—she was enough for me."

"And now that she's gone you have nothing?" he asks seriously.

"No." I swallow to keep the tears at bay. "I have the memory of her. And I have more people who shine as brightly as she did. I feel sorry for you—that you had that once and destroyed it. That you'll probably never find that again."

My chest warms knowing that when I leave this hospital, I'll have people on my side to help me. Just like last time, sure, but this time I'm willing to accept that help.

"You're right," he sighs again, this time dejectedly.

"I don't know what you came in here looking for, but I can't give it to you."

"I suppose I was looking for who my daughter was. I thought perhaps you carried some of her with you."

"And did you find what you were looking for?"

"I did." He rises from the chair. "I loved my daughter, Miss Jennings. Or I tried to, at least. And when I realized how horrible I was, it was too late. At that point, I just wanted answers, hoping that would be enough to make up for how I treated her." A pained smile lifts his lips.

"You were doing your own investigating?" I ask.

He nods. "Yes. It's why I began to notice things about Caleb in the first place." Without any further comments or a goodbye, he exits the room and I'm left with even more conflicting emotions and thoughts.

Every murder can be traced back to Laurence Mitchell because he's the one who turned Caleb. He turned him and didn't properly assimilate him to life as a vampire. He bears a major burden with all those deaths, and I can tell he's feeling that guilt.

The man who just left my hospital room was not one I recognize. The cold, put together businessman has now been replaced with a guilt ridden, emotionally confused one. Do I believe he loved Serena? I can't be sure. Maybe in his own, warped way.

I do believe that he will never be the same, and maybe that's a good thing. It's just a shame that it took his daughter being murdered for him to reach this point.

"Trick or treat!" a voice bellows from outside my room, pulling me from my rumination on the enigma that is Laurence Mitchell. A sharp *shushing* follows the shout as my cousin is admonished by one of the nurses for making too much noise.

"Halloween was yesterday, idiot," Meg grumbles as she, Josie, and Hayden pile through the door and into my room. My lips twitch upwards at the sight of them alive and well.

Hayden ambles over to the bed, concealing something behind his back. With a hum of suspense, he brandishes what looks to be a bouquet made of candy bars.

"Thanks?" I grab it and examine the contents. "Did you make this?" The structure is quite impressive, with a variety of full-sized candy bars held up on wooden dowels to create stems and bite sized candies acting as petals.

My cousin beams at me. "Yep. Took me all night."

"It took him an hour with lots of swearing, a hot glue gun, and some assistance," Josie amends. "When we found out we couldn't visit you until this morning, we couldn't sleep and needed something to occupy our time."

"And with the lack of trick or treaters this year, Aunt Christy hardly made a dent in the bags of candy she bought," Hayden shrugs. Laurence Mitchell's swanky gated neighborhood still had plenty of trick or treaters, if the litter of candy wrappers I found on my trek to his house was any indication.

My friends settle in the one chair and around my cramped hospital bed, laughing and talking. They don't avoid what happened, but they also know there's no urgent need to discuss it yet. That I might not *want* to discuss it just yet.

Now I notice little things that I didn't before, when I was lost in my grief and anger.

The way Josie's smile has a sadness to it.

The way Hayden jokes around more often than he used to, as if he's trying to raise everyone's spirits just in case someone needs a laugh.

The way Meg's gaze lingers on the empty space where Serena should be.

We're all grieving, in our own ways. Just because they decided to try and continue living without Serena doesn't mean they forgot her completely.

In fact, I think it's the opposite. I think they miss her as much as I do and are continuing on for her. Watching them act normally is different now. It's the first time in recent memory I don't feel on the outside looking in. A weight has been lifted off my chest now that I finally got justice for Serena like I set out to do and that I know I was never alone in my grief.

Embarrassingly, I start to cry. For months I repressed the instinct, but lately it feels like I want to cry all the time. Or maybe I *need* to cry. I do have two months of pent-up emotions to deal with.

They all stop their chattering at once to look at me, my name echoing around the room before I'm enclosed in the world's tightest group hug.

Soothing tones invade our cocoon, murmurs of:

"Don't cry."

"It's okay."

"We're here for you."

"Are you alright?"

Light invades the warm darkness of our hug as they pull away, studying me with concern. "I'm fine," I sniffle, and I think I actually mean it this time. "I just love you guys. And I'm sorry."

Their voices once again meld into one consoling amalgamation.

"Are you sure?"

"Don't be sorry."

"We love you too."

These words bring me comfort and regret. This is how it could have been all this time, if only I was willing to accept it.

I forced myself not to feel anything for so long. I thought it made me braver, stronger, and somehow more capable. I told myself I wasn't allowed to feel because Serena isn't here to feel anything anymore, so why should I? I was wrong—so wrong. And it feels right to finally give myself permission to do what I should have done all these weeks.

I can't heal without acknowledging that I'm broken. And maybe I knew all along that I was, but I sure as hell didn't want to do anything about it.

Now I'm ready.

If I can survive being attacked by a vampire—*twice*—and losing my best friend, then I can do almost anything. That I'm sure of.

My friends don't stay long after that, mostly because a nurse came in and told us we were being too disruptive. Hayden charmed her into letting them stay another ten minutes which Meg decided to use to interrogate me: "So you caught the killer. Was your creepy board any help?"

I snort and inform her that yes, actually—it helped a lot.

At Hayden and Josie's lack of shocked faces, Meg tells me, "I told them after you left. Your parents know, too. We also know that Alex isn't a student at Pine Falls U, but nice try there."

"Is he a detective?" Josie asks.

"He's an investigator... Sort of," I amend.

Meg arches a brow. "How is someone 'sort of' an investigator?"

"Exactly!" I fling my hand in her direction, finally feeling validated, but my friends look more confused than anything.

Eventually our ten minutes expire, but they cram in enough questions about my adventures with Alex like staying at his place, going to a dangerous nightclub, and confronting Laurence Mitchell. I leave out all the vampire stuff, though. But based on the way Meg lingers by the door with a curious look, saying she "took a few things off the murder board before the others saw," has me wondering if she may know more than I'd like her to...

There's no reason for the others to be aware of it. Most of the time, I wish *I* was still ignorant to the vampire world, but then I remember that it led me to Alex. And he alone is worth it.

As if his ears were tingling, the half vampire of the hour quietly enters the hospital room after my friends leave—such a juxtaposition to their chaos—and sets a paper bag on the bed between us.

"Did you get lost on your way to the cafeteria?" I joke.

He rolls his eyes, and it's such a familiar gesture it causes warmth to spread through my body.

"I saw you were with your friends and thought I'd give you some privacy."

"They know about you," I say, accepting the sandwich he brought me. "Not the vampire stuff but the investigator stuff." Well, Meg might know about the vampire stuff but I keep that to myself.

Alex takes a bite of his sandwich before replying. "So do they approve?"

"Hard to tell with them. Meg could act like she hates you but actually loves you. Hayden is pretty transparent. But Josie... She may be all smiles and flowery perfumed hugs but sometimes she can be a real bitch." He chokes on his bite of turkey and wheat and I snicker.

"Noted." He wipes his mouth with a napkin. "So, about that kiss we shared."

"Go on..." I encourage, hoping it'll lead to another one.

"I'm sorry. You were barely lucid, and it wasn't right. I got caught up in the moment."

My lips fall into a frown. "It was just a heat of the moment thing?"

"Well, no. I've wanted to do that for a while but—"

"Alex Osman, are you flustered?" His cheeks redden in answer. I've never seen this man look so unraveled before and sickly I love that I'm the cause. "Don't worry about the kiss. Sure, I was recently concussed, but I liked it."

His relief is visible, which is why I'm surprised when he says, "I don't think we should do it again, though."

"Oh..."

"It's not that I didn't also like it, I just..." Alex runs his hands through his hair looking for the right words. "My life is a mess, and I need to sort some things out before I can pursue anyone. Romantically." Now *my* cheeks are flushing.

Waving a hand over myself—with the myriad of wires and bruises on my body—I say, "You're looking at the poster child for a messy life."

I understand where he's coming from. I'm disappointed we aren't immediately going to further our relationship, but neither of us is in the best place for that. Besides, he didn't say nothing would ever happen again, just nothing right now.

I can live with that.

38

ALEX

IN THE PAST WHEN I've completed an assignment, I dreaded what Slade—and later Silas—would have me do next. But now, as I coast down the forest roads that will lead me to my former boss's compound, an air of possibility surrounds me.

Juliette deserves all the credit for solving this particular case, and there's the looming threat of what Silas will do to me since I broke out of his prison, but the air of possibility remains. For once I'm not thinking of how to get out of Pine Falls, but how to stay.

The guards at the gate let me onto the property without a second glance, solidifying the nagging thought that Silas expected me to come back to him. I park in my usual place and am greeted with the sight of Devin and Stephan waiting for me outside the front door. At least Jeffers isn't here. I might really do something I'll regret if I see the vampire responsible for stalking Juliette.

"I don't need an escort," I bite out. They ignore me and flank my sides as I step into the house.

Silas has his head bent over his desk but straightens up when I walk into his study. "Alex. I didn't think you'd be back so soon." *Sure.*

"We need to talk."

"We certainly do. Congratulations, by the way. You solved the case." His smile is anything but congenial.

"I didn't do shit. I was locked up here while two more people were almost murdered."

My heart pounds at the reminder of how close Juliette came to leaving this world. I don't want to think about what I would have done if she was killed.

Silas tilts his head at me, scrutinizing my face. "They survived without you." Those words are like a punch to the gut. Sure, Juliette doesn't need me to protect her like I originally thought, but she still seems to want me around.

"I'd like to make a new deal," I offer.

"Oh?" The humor evident in his tone only makes my ire for him grow. This is a vampire who killed an innocent and had another stalked and threatened for his own means. He should be grateful I'm not looking for retribution. Not yet, at least.

"I won't tell the other council members that you had Naomi Hart killed and Juliette stalked, and in return, you let me live in peace."

Silas barks a laugh. "You think they would care about some *bartender* who worked for your cousin—a known criminal?"

"Creed Ambrose would. He wants your job, right? No vampire with ambition wants to be placed in the Midwest to rot. And," I add, "wouldn't it be a shame if people found out you're choosing to look the other way at Laurence Mitchell turning a vampire without the Council's permission? A vampire who went into a full-fledged frenzy because he wasn't properly assimilated? Not a good luck for the vampire in charge of the Vampire and Human Assimilation Society." Silas stiffens at my words, and a spark of satisfaction goes through me.

"Counteroffer," he proposes through gritted teeth. "Assuming Councilman Ambrose would even believe you, you have no proof that I had that girl stalked and the other killed. But, I am willing to entertain the idea that you do."

"Get to the point. What's your offer?"

"Give me Slade Volkov."

"What—"

"Convince your cousin to turn himself over to me to atone for his crimes, and I will leave you and that human girl you've taken up with alone."

Damn. This *should* be an easy decision, but things are never simple when it comes to Slade.

"I'll talk to him, but there's no guarantee he'll agree."

Slade's words from last night filter into my thoughts: his admittance that he failed me. Perhaps that part of him will offer himself up to Silas, for me.

"Good luck, Alex," Silas says with a cold, conniving smile. "If you fail to give me Slade, I will have to take you back instead."

The entire drive back to the city, I play out different scenarios about how my next conversation will go. I pass the store with all the televisions playing the news—the one I saw a couple of weeks ago on my way to meet Juliette for the first time. Now, instead of reports of another murder from the Knife Man, the newscasters are declaring that the killer has finally been caught.

I'm not sure what story Silas has spun regarding Laurence Mitchell's assistant being the murderer, but I don't care.

As long as Juliette and I stay out of it.

The haunted, anxious energy that was emanating in the city for months is still there, but it's faint. A hopeful resurgence of normalcy has sprung up between the skyscrapers and sidewalks. People are still wary, sure, but I've seen more people out and about on my drive to Slade's penthouse than I have in the past two months.

Digging through my wallet, I find the old elevator access key that Slade gave me years ago. His apartment is on the top floor kept private from all the others. Something stopped me from throwing out this key in the past few years. Probably because I hoped to break into his apartment at one point, but now I'm content to use it to just talk to him.

Weekend afternoons are when Slade relaxes at home for a while, before heading to Sinner to cater to the night crowd. That's what I find him doing as I step off the elevator into the ambiently lit black marble foyer. It's a far cry from the rundown house we started in ten years ago.

"Alina?" Slade calls from the living room. A beat passes. Then, in resigned exhaustion, "Alex."

His heightened smell informs him of my presence, and I'm glad for it. This way, I don't need to announce myself. I can just walk in and start talking.

"We need to talk," I say simply, entering the massive living room and watching the clouds drift by the floor to ceiling windows.

"You've been free almost twenty-four hours and Silas hasn't dragged you back to that hole in the ground," Slade remarks, gesturing to the black leather armchair across from him.

I sink into the chair. "That's actually what I wanted to talk to you about."

"He's letting you go? I must say, cousin, I have a hard time believing that."

"No. He wants you in exchange for my freedom."

"I see." My cousin lets his gaze drift out the window, staring into the misty city below as he thinks over what I've said.

We sit in silence for long minutes, until he asks out of nowhere, "Why did you change your last name?"

The question takes me by surprise, disarming me. "I didn't want any ties to you," I admit quietly.

Slade purses his lips in disapproval. "You shame your father in spiting me."

It hurts because it's true. And it's made worse by the fact that I was so focused on how Slade has failed me to remember those who didn't.

My parents.

"I recognize my wrongdoings when it comes to you, Alex. But you can't blame me for all your problems." He shifts in his seat. "Let me rephrase—*please* don't blame me for all your problems."

I stare at him, lips trained to respond but not knowing how.

My problems are vast, and I could probably make a therapist cry with all the darkness in my head. The demon on my shoulder never quits, and it tells me how much of a monster I am any chance it gets. It tells me I don't deserve someone like Juliette while simultaneously reassuring me that someone else made me this way.

Maybe that's a little true. Maybe I let someone else shape who I am, but deep down, I'm still that lonely fourteen-year-old kid—confused and grieving for parents he's not completely sure are dead. I fear I will never know peace, or find the strength to confront my many issues, until I get closure on that front.

"I accept," Slade says resolutely. He stands abruptly, and I rush up to join him.

"Wait... What?"

"I accept the terms Silas has laid out," Slade reiterates. His amber eyes soften as he looks down at me, placing a hand on my shoulder.

"I recognize that look in your eye," he says with a sad smile. "You're thinking about your parents?"

I nod.

"Go to Bellevue, Alex. If answers are to be found anywhere, you'll find them there. I should have never taken you so far from all you knew," he adds regretfully.

Slade lets go of my shoulder and gracefully strides out of the room. "I have some things to put in order before I go. Good luck in Bellevue."

"Wait," I jog after him. "Why'd you agree?"

My cousin stops and turns to me with a look I can't quite decipher.

"I'm only doing what I should have done years ago. Looking out for you."

Without another word or a chance for me to respond, he disappears down the hall.

I let myself out of the penthouse and shoot off a text while I'm at it.

> **Me:** Silas Chamberlain killed Naomi.

A reply comes through instantly.

> **Alina Russo:** Bastard. Someone ought to do something about him.

> **Me:** Someone really should.

If anyone is capable of taking care of shit, it's Alina. Silas is a fool if he thought he'd get out of this without a scratch.

And a fool for thinking I would just let it go.

39

JULIETTE

Happiness is the sound of cutlery clinking; it's the buzz of chatter. At least, for my family it is because it means the restaurant's average amount of diners is no longer six.

We're almost at capacity and have a waitlist that extends through the rest of the night. The people of Pine Falls are apparently ready to move on with their lives now that the killer has been caught.

To be fair, most of the patrons are here for me. My parents called up everyone they could think of and told them to get to the restaurant for a free meal and to celebrate my (second) return from the hospital.

This time there is much more fanfare. I returned from my first stint in the ICU shrouded in anger, guilt, and repressed sadness. The streets weren't safe, and people were scared. But tonight, people are ready to celebrate.

Thanks to some anonymous benefactor, all the restaurant's overdue bills—as well as my racked-up hospital bill—were taken care of. It's how we're able to give eighty percent of the people in here free dinner. I have a feeling I know who the anonymous benefactor may be... Someone trying to clean up a mess and make up for all the hurt they've caused. Maybe it's not too late for him to redeem himself, after all.

I try to keep my bitterness at bay when I notice most of the attendees of this impromptu party didn't help support the restaurant one bit these past couple of months but are lined up for free helpings of Mom's fettucine now.

That's why I have Meg.

"Seriously," she groans. "The Stewarts are some of the richest people here and they're going back for seconds? Your parents should charge for that. Can't believe they didn't come in one time in the last two months but are here now to take advantage of the free food."

Hayden pops a cocktail olive in his mouth from the open jar behind the bar. "Agreed. Bunch of mooches."

"Hayden!" My mom snaps from door to the kitchen. "No snacking, clear the tables." My cousin gives a mock salute to my mom and saunters around the counter.

"Have fun," Meg smirks.

"Can't believe I'm the only one who has to work tonight," he grumbles. "It's a *party*!"

"Sorry." I tap the side of my head. "Injured brain."

"Juliette," my mom calls, and I swivel on my stool towards where she's beckoning me into the kitchen. Leaving the murmuring dining floor behind, I follow her into the bustling kitchen and down the hall that leads to her and my dad's shared office.

"I have a gift for you," Mom announces, moving behind the desk.

"A gift?"

"Mhmm." She pulls a drawer open, bringing out a small box. "I saw it in a store when I went to pick you up from the hospital." I take the box from her and lift the lid.

A gold necklace with a small golden butterfly charm lay inside.

"Wow," I breathe. It's simple yet beautiful and elegant.

"Here, let me put it on." Mom takes the box back and lifts the necklace out, sweeping my hair aside to clasp it. "There." She touches the charm and steps back.

"Butterflies represent hope and transformation, or at least that's what the little card it came with claims," she laughs. I finger the charm, liking it even more now.

"Thank you," I say as tears spring to my eyes.

Mom pulls me into a hug and I let the tears fall. Tears of sadness, regret, guilt, anger, hope, happiness, love... I feel it all. And I don't hate myself for it.

"The day my sister died was the hardest day of my life," Mom speaks into my hair. "No one warns you about the regret when someone dies. 'What was the last thing I said to her?' 'Was it nice?' 'Did she know I loved her?' 'Did she love me?' 'What if I could have somehow stopped that semi from ramming into their car?'"

We pull apart, taking seats in the chairs by the desk.

"Even now, ten years later, I have days where all I can do is analyze the last moments of my sister's life and our time together. And what I last said to her." A tear rolls down her cheek and she swipes at it with her hand. "And grief! I hate that word—grief. It's such a small word to encompass all the big feelings we have when someone leaves us."

"I'm sorry," I squeeze her hand. My parents rarely talk about Hayden's parents.

Mom waves my apology away.

"Don't be sorry," she points to my necklace. "Just have hope. Hope that it will get better, and that the grief won't swallow you whole. And if it does," she adds, "then you're lucky you have so many people to pull you out of it."

"What was she like?" I was only eleven when my aunt and uncle died, and they lived on the East Coast so we rarely saw them.

Mom stares up at the ceiling, lost in her memory. "Exactly like Hayden, if you can believe it." We both laugh. "She was always trying to make everyone else happy. That's why she moved to Bellevue—Hayden's father was from there."

"Bellevue?" I sit up straighter in my chair.

"Yes, in Vermont. We never went there to visit," she twists her mouth to the side. "We picked Hayden up in Burlington. I'm sure Bellevue was just as gorgeous."

"Christy!" Dad's voice travels down the hall to us. "Need some help, here."

"Coming!" She shouts back and stands, patting my cheek.

Bellevue, huh?

40

Juliette
Two Weeks Later

Fear is a constant presence in everyone's life, but the duration of its stay depends on a variety of factors. I've known true, bone chilling fear, so why is a man I've come to trust causing my heart to beat so erratically?

He arrived in the form of two unexpected knocks at the front door. My mom answered it and was ecstatic to see him again. I haven't seen or spoken to Alex in almost two weeks. Even though we kissed and formed a mutual bond required to successfully hunt down a serial killer, it seemed like we weren't meant to be together beyond the investigation.

Until he showed up at our door.

Until he walked inside.

Until his eyes softened when I came down the stairs to greet him.

Until he sat across from me in the living room.

Before his arrival I was in my room sketching. I've been doing it a lot more now after my new therapist suggested it might help. And it has. Now whenever I have a nightmare—thankfully those are no longer a nightly occurrence, but they still happen every once in a while—or get lost in a painful memory, I pull out my pad and start to draw whatever is haunting me. Get it out of my system.

I used to think you could only make art if you found inspiration in life, but now I know that's simply not true. Art is everywhere, not just in living things. There's a haunting beauty to a portrait of a dead girl and terrifying truths in sketches of fangs and blood.

My therapist told me that when I was done with my sketches, I could either destroy them or keep them. It didn't matter what I did with them. The only thing that mattered was I was now the one in control.

The sketch I was working on before Alex arrived, though, is one I'll definitely be keeping. It may or may not be a rendering of a certain broody half vampire now sitting across from me. But his nose is hard to get right—I'll have to redo that.

"Juliette?" Alex says my name in a tone that implies he's probably said it once or twice already.

I snap out of my intense study of his nose. "What?"

"How have you been?" he chuckles.

"Oh. Good days and bad days, well mostly neutral days and the occasional horrible day."

"I'm sorry," he says it like a question.

"Don't be. It's okay, really." I offer a tentative smile.

Grief is a process, I hear my therapist remind me in the back of my mind.

My first step in that process was saying goodbye to Serena and accepting that she was truly gone. To accomplish that, my friends and I had a good old-fashioned bonfire, with my murder board acting as the sacrificial accelerant. We tossed the posterboard shrouded with papers and photos and red string into the flames like one would toss a small child into the deep end of the pool—mercilessly and with a hint of amusement.

Hayden popped the cork on a bottle of expensive champagne he swiped from the restaurant, spraying us each in turn before passing it around. The alcohol along with the smoke from the fire gave me a headache, but for once I didn't care. Not as we laughed and shared our favorite memories of Serena, dancing to the music coming out of Josie's phone.

It was messy and tearful, but I'm sure Serena would have far preferred our version of farewell over the stuffy funeral her father threw.

Now I'm in the process of accepting. Accepting that Serena is gone but she lives on in everyone she ever loved.

Accepting that my life will still go on, even if hers won't. Accepting that that's okay.

These past two weeks have been filled with uncertainty. Going back to my classes after facing a vampire serial killer and being attacked—again—was severely underwhelming. My time with Alex opened my mind to new possibilities for the future. Possibilities I've been too afraid to act on.

You would think that after all I've been through I wouldn't be scared of the small things anymore, but I am.

How do I tell my parents I'd rather solve crimes than study marketing?

How do I explain that ever since I've stuck my toe into the vampire world, I want to fully jump in?

They suggested I take a leave of absence, and maybe I will. Especially with what Alex came here to ask: "Are you up for a trip?"

A trip? With Alex? *Alone?*

"For... a case? I thought you weren't working for Silas anymore."

He better not be. That vampire caused too much harm and withheld too much information for his own gain.

"It's not for Silas," Alex assures me. "I have to go to Bellevue, in Vermont. If there's anywhere that might have answers about my parents' disappearance, it's there." He rubs the back of his neck.

"Besides, Silas is... no longer with us."

My mouth drops open. "*What*? Like he's dead?"

Alex nods grimly.

"Did you kill him?" I ask in an undertone, not condemning him but curious.

"Not me. Let's just say he got what was coming to him, in the form of a fierce but pissed off white haired vampire." We share a smirk.

"So... why do you want me to come to Bellevue with you?" I get back to the topic at hand.

Alex shrugs, but there's an intense look in his grey eyes. "You're my partner." The way he says it makes it sound so obvious, so inherent.

"I thought we were just two people working together for mutual benefit," I speak around the lump in my throat.

God, I hate that I cry over everything now.

My *partner* twists his lips to the side and squints in mock contemplation. "Well, since this case is solely for *my* benefit, it makes more sense to call you my partner. Or assistant. Whichever you prefer."

I roll my eyes at him and stick my hand out. "Partners."

His warm hand grasps mine. "Partners."

"We could revert back to the old reliable 'two people working together for mutual benefit' because I have reason to go to Bellevue, too."

He raises a brow at me. "Do you, now?"

I lean into him, and he meets me halfway. Then, I whisper the suspicion I've kept to myself for the past two weeks.

Epilogue

The party was in full swing downstairs, but the boy remained in his room. He checked and rechecked his outfit in the mirror: dress shirt, trousers, vest, solid navy-blue tie, and grey blazer.

The manor grounds outside his window were damp with a fine layer of snow, the night air full of mist and possibility. The fog obscured his favorite tree, the one fifty yards to the left of the courtyard. Still, the boy took a moment to try to view it through the mist. He had been at Bellevue for most of his adolescence. This place was a second home to him, yet it was still so foreign.

Closing his eyes, he pictured his tree—his safe space.

The space no one could sneer or taunt or insult him. Despite his best efforts, the noise of the party below intruded on his moment of peace.

The Winter Ball was what all the students at Bellevue Manor looked forward to at the start of each new year. It signified the end of the fall semester and the start of winter break before the other kids went back to their lavish homes and he had the place to himself.

The boy had never gone to the ball before, but this was his last year. So he figured he should experience it at least once before leaving this place for good.

A knock at the door suddenly broke his gaze from the window. He nervously fidgeted with his tie. The boy was supposed to go to the ball with the girl he's secretly eyed for years, and recently, he found the courage to confess his feelings to. He was admittedly a little surprised when she agreed to attend the dance with him—he always thought she viewed herself as better than him. Most everyone here did.

The boy opened his door, but it was not who he thought would be standing on the other side.

A slam of wood into plaster. A tie nervously touched a thousand times now unraveled. A shattered mirror. An open window. A lonely tree.

The party was in full swing, but the boy would not attend.

Acknowledgements

There are so many people to thank for making this book possible.

Hope—Your friendship and help are invaluable. This book would not be what it is today without your edits and advice. I don't know what I would have done without you. Not only are you wonderful to collaborate with, but your friendship means so much to me.

To my beta readers, friends, and street team—Your support and enthusiasm means more than you will ever know. I truly could not have done this without the excitement and encouragement you continue to show me. Ke, Vaidehi, Teresa, Diana, Reagan, Una, Taye, Kat, Madhu, Ky, Brytt, Cece, Mara, Thiffa, and so many more: You are all amazing. And to Cait, thank you for the advice and letting me freak out in your DM's.

To my wonderful cover designer, Alex—Thank you so much for bringing my vision to life. You took so much stress off of me and I couldn't be happier with the end result.

To my brother—Thank you for being so excited for me and telling everyone that I wrote a book (even if I didn't particularly want you to lol). I'm so lucky to have a sibling and best friend all-in-one.

To my dad—You definitely indoctrinated me to your obsession with vampires. I promise I will eventually read Anne Rice's *The Vampire Chronicles*.

Larissa and Hallie—Your excitement also spurred me on and I'm forever thankful to have two amazing life-long friends such as yourselves. Hallie, thank you for reading early drafts of my other works in progress and encouraging me to keep going.

To my mom—Not everyone is fortunate enough to have supportive parents. Thank you for encouraging me to try new things and being proud every step of the way.

And lastly I would like to thank myself. Or, my *past* self. Thank you past me for finding the courage and motivation to *finish* something. No matter what ends up happening, I'll be thankful for that.

About the Author

C.M. Kennedy is a writer of all things fantasy, romance, and paranormal. When she's not writing about imperfect heroes and ridiculously attractive vampires, you can find her reading, playing any form of video game, working on a puzzle, baking, or hanging out with her cats. You can follow her on Instagram and TikTok @cmkennedyauthor